best lesbian love stories 2005

best lesbian love stories
2005

edited by angela brown

alyson books
los angeles

© 2005 BY ALYSON PUBLICATIONS. ALL RIGHTS RESERVED.

MANUFACTURED IN THE UNITED STATES OF AMERICA.

THIS TRADE PAPERBACK ORIGINAL IS PUBLISHED BY ALYSON PUBLICATIONS,
P.O. BOX 4371, LOS ANGELES, CALIFORNIA 90078-4371.
DISTRIBUTION IN THE UNITED KINGDOM BY TURNAROUND PUBLISHER SERVICES LTD.,
UNIT 3, OLYMPIA TRADING ESTATE, COBURG ROAD, WOOD GREEN,
LONDON N22 6TZ ENGLAND.

FIRST EDITION: JANUARY 2005

05 06 07 08 09 a 10 9 8 7 6 5 4 3 2 1

ISBN 1-55583-882-0

LIBRARY OF CONGRESS CATALOGING-IN-PUBLICATION DATA
    BEST LESBIAN LOVE STORIES 2005 / EDITED BY ANGELA BROWN.— 1ST ED.
        ISBN 1-55583-882-0
        1. LESBIANS—FICTION. 2. LOVE STORIES, AMERICAN. 3. BROWN, ANGELA, 1970–
    PS648.L47B467 2005
    813'.085089206643—DC22   2004057407

CREDITS
COVER PHOTOGRAPHY BY BRAND X PICTURES.
COVER DESIGN BY MATT SAMS.

for L.R.

Contents

Introduction

It's interesting that around the time I started to become involved with a very wonderful woman I was working on an anthology that deals quite a bit with the dynamics of lesbian relationships. I'd gone through a long dry spell—dating incessantly but never finding anyone I really connected with. Then *bam!* I found a sweet, smart, sassy partner in crime. Like a fool, I thought it would be the answer to all my problems. But then I discovered that being in a relationship doesn't necessarily make things easier—in many ways it makes life more complicated, especially since I'm a bit of a hermit. I realized I'd have to let someone into my cave, examine my drawings, help me light fires. But all that came—and continues to come!— with a tremendous amount of joy, wonder, and love. Even curmudgeonly hermits like myself need a little fondness every once and a while!

Many of the writers in this anthology explore the ins and outs of lesbian relationships, but all from different angles. Judith Frank's "Gravel," for example, examines how a serious illness can both tear a couple apart and bring them together to create a foundation that is sturdier than ever. In Mary

Vermillion's "The Accident," a woman struggles to live an open life with her closeted partner in a gossipy small town. Carol Guess's exquisite "Parting Agents" shows us a woman who's been around the block a few times but suddenly realizes what it means to make a commitment. In "Featherless Ducks," Anne Seale's sneaky protagonist gets her comeuppance (or does she?) when she attempts to juggle her partner *and* her secretary with hilarious consequences.

In this book, the third volume in the Best Lesbian Love Stories series, you'll find stories that will inspire you, entertain you, make you think hard, and, of course, make you laugh out loud. They say laughter is the best medicine. Well, this book is sure to give you your recommended daily allowance of that very necessary medicine—an elixir to combat (or at least lighten) the ever-present dyke drama in lesbian relationships!

All kidding aside, I'd like to thank the very talented writers who have helped to make this book a beautiful, moving, tender collection. I couldn't have done it without you.

—Angela Brown

Writing My Love
Claire McNab

Diana K. Broswell is on the phone when I'm shown into her office, so I have time to admire my editor while she's concentrated on something else. She gives me a quick grin and waves me to a seat. The tawny tones of her voice contrast nicely with her blond hair. I contemplate her with pleasure, thinking of how I've spent hours at my computer getting her description just right, as if she were a major character in one of my novels—which, in a way, she is.

This woman is incandescent! She's not traditionally beautiful, but her face is full of humor and intelligence. To-die-for cheekbones. Shoulder-length golden hair. Her eyes blue-gray, her mouth frankly tempting. She has a luscious figure—high-breasted, flat-stomached, long-legged. Dynamite!

Diana K. Broswell, senior editor at Crimson Loon Press, and the woman I secretly adore, puts down the phone. "Vonny!" she says. She's always pleased to see me, but I suspect that's mainly because of my healthy sales figures.

My name is Vonny Smith, but I'm better known by my pen

name, Veronica Vanderveer, author of best-selling romance novels. My last book, *Torrid Hearts*, not only won numerous awards but also garnered some of the best reviews of my career. My favorite quote, which, slightly edited, will be featured on the cover of my next romance, came from a normally acerbic critic. She was moved to say: "Adverbs and exclamations proliferate and clichés abound in Vandeveer's *Torrid Hearts*, but scorching sexual encounters ignite the pages in a conflagration of desire."

A conflagration of desire is what I feel for Diana K. Broswell. It's a stressful situation: I'm in love with her, but she doesn't love me. Yet.

I've never told Diana how I feel. Why not? Because I've a fair idea that if I did spill the beans, she'd stare at me, bemused. Or even worse—amused. Then she'd say something soothing. Diana wouldn't want to alienate Veronica Vanderveer, best-selling author, so she'd deal kindly with lovesick Vonny Smith's unrequited passion.

Apart from the fact that I don't take rejection well at the best of times, Diana is far too important to me to risk undermining our present friendly relationship with a declaration of love likely to go down like a lead balloon.

Diana picks up the phone again and asks Rose to bring in the folder with the cover art for my latest novel. Rose appears almost immediately. She's only been at Crimson Loon Press a few weeks and is one of those constantly up people who chirp a lot. "Hi!" she says to me. "I just loved *Torrid Hearts*!"

"Thank you."

Is it my imagination, or do Rose's fingers brush against Diana's hand when passing over the folder? I feel my eyes narrow. My task will be difficult enough without competition like this young woman. I frown, forced to concede she's quite attractive, if you can cope with her supercheerful attitude.

Rose leaves. Diana smiles at me. She flips open the folder.

"Here's our artist's idea for the cover of *Drumbeat of Desire*," she says, leaning over her desk to hand it to me. "Your name will be larger than the title, and there'll be a photo of you on the back cover."

If you've read any of my books, you know what I look like. Okay, I admit it: The image has been retouched, but only slightly. In truth, I'm not bad looking, if you like the intense dark-haired sort with a strong jawline.

I inspect the cover art. It depicts two impossibly beautiful women gazing longingly at each other beneath palm trees on a yellow tropical beach edged by aquamarine water. One woman wears a brief swimsuit, the other tailored shorts and a tight top.

"Sorry," I say, "it won't do."

Diana is immediately concerned. "There's a problem?"

She hasn't seen a manuscript yet, just a brief outline of the story. With my sales record, Crimson Loon will give me a book contract on the strength of a short description. At this point I'm supposed to be well-advanced in the manuscript for *Drumbeat*, but I'm seriously behind schedule, having been too busy planning my strategy to win Diana's love.

"I've made some changes to the plot we discussed," I announce.

"Oh? Anything major?" Diana raises her elegant eyebrows. I forgot to include them in her description. They curve beguilingly.

"Well, for one thing," I tell her, "I'm changing the main character's name from Gloria to Dee."

I'm thinking, as I say this, of the subliminal effect on Diana when she reads love scenes featuring a character with her initial.

"Dee?" Diana could hardly be less impressed. "I thought we'd agreed Gloria was a perfect name for a swimsuit model."

"She's not a model anymore. I've made her a professional woman."

Diana's eyebrows rise a touch higher. "Just what sort of profession would she be following on a remote tropical island?"

"That's changed too. I'm setting the book here, in Los Angeles. Dee's an editor with a lifestyle magazine."

Now Diana's winged eyebrows have settled into a puzzled V. "And Gloria's—I mean Dee's love interest? Is Marilyn still running an ecotourism business in partnership with Ashleigh, the oversexed other woman?"

" 'Fraid not. It's a catering firm now. And Marilyn's had a name change. She's Velda." I think of Rose and add, "And Ashleigh, the other woman, is now Roxy."

"I see," says Diana, but of course she doesn't see how my strategy is spelled out in the initials—a D falling for a V. I can only hope Diana's subconscious mind is receptive.

"This doesn't sound anything like the book we signed a contract for," says Diana, now unambiguously frowning. "Publicity's gearing up for a tropical island."

"Sorry," I say, contrite. "I wouldn't make these changes if they weren't absolutely necessary for the vision I have of *Drumbeat*."

Diana represses a sigh. Or perhaps it's a snarl. I hate to cause her angst, but I remind myself it's for a good cause—our future happiness together.

"You're not changing the title," she announces in a don't-argue tone. "*Drumbeat of Desire* is already in the catalog."

"I wouldn't dream of it," I say. To placate her, I add, "There'll be lots of hot sex."

"You do that so well," Diana concedes. "Our readers can't get enough of you."

I acknowledge this truth with a modest nod. I've been good for Crimson Loon's bottom line, and Crimson Loon, in turn, has been very good for me.

You'd think, since I write romance, I'd have some luck in

the heart department. In truth, my fictional characters have a great deal more success in love than I've ever achieved. Sure, over the years I've had romantic flings, and twice something rather more substantial, but I've never really experienced the tumultuous, all-consuming emotions about which I write so confidently. At least not until now.

Once I realized Diana was the Love of My Life, I sat around for ages waiting for her to notice my romantic potential. Didn't happen. So now I've been forced to take a more active role. I'm going to woo her through my writing. I'll pursue her, entice her, court her in the pages of my current manuscript. My hope is that I'll be able to sneak in under her defenses and she'll slide into love with me before she's aware what's happening. In short, she'll realize that for her, Vonny is the One.

You'll be wondering if Diana K. Broswell is available, or if I'm planning to break up a happy twosome. Until a few weeks ago, I had no idea about Diana's life outside the office, try though I might to turn our professional conversations toward more personal subjects.

Fortunately, Diana and I share a dental hygienist, Bonnie Flint. Bonnie has very large white teeth and a tendency to dish the dirt.

Last month, just as Bonnie was poised to plunge her instruments into my mouth and scrape away merrily, I said, "Bonnie, you know everything." She didn't contradict me. Supercasual, I went on, "I was just talking to Diana Broswell the other day…"

"Ah, Diana!" Bonnie's tone was warmly approving. "She assures me Crimson Loon Press could be interested in publishing my international dental thriller."

"You've written a thriller? A *dental* thriller?"

Bonnie frowned at my astonishment. "Why is that a surprise? Dental hygienists can lead exciting lives."

"I'm sure your novel has great promise, or Diana wouldn't

be interested," I said hastily. As Bonnie readied her instruments anew, I asked, "How well do you know the real Diana? To me she's a bit of a mystery woman."

That turned on the gossip spigot. Bonnie, hacking away at deposits of dental plaque on my back molars, gave me the lowdown on Diana K. Broswell, starting with where she was born—Omaha, Nebraska—and moving on to the reason she became an editor—"She's got a passion for the written word. A positive passion!"

Then the news I'd been obliquely fishing for: Diana had ended a ten-year relationship, apparently amicably, sometime last year.

"Gaa?" I said.

With a dental technician's ability to interpret communications from an instrument-crammed mouth, Bonnie responded, "Nothing serious since. Diana's just playing the field. Why? You interested?"

"Gaa," I said, shaking my head to indicate my entire lack of any interest whatsoever.

Bonnie gave an irritated cluck. "Hold still, Vonny. You barely avoided a serious gum laceration."

After my teeth were polished and my gums were given an A rating, Bonnie fixed me with her interrogator's stare. "What about you, Vonny? In a relationship at the moment? After all, you do need to research all those hot scenes you write."

With the thought that any day now Diana could be in the same chair having *her* teeth cleaned while Bonnie gossiped about *me*, I hastened to describe my present single contentment, adding in a throwaway line that I wouldn't be averse to becoming half of a couple at some vague point in the future. "If the One comes along," I said, visualizing Diana in my arms, "The Right One."

"There is no right one," muttered Bonnie. "You think there is, but you're wrong in every instance."

Bonnie is mostly straight and has been married three times. I met her current husband a while ago, when he came in for a freebie teeth cleaning. He's a short-order cook who smokes strong-smelling cigars. I'm guessing this may contribute to Bonnie's present bleak view of Mr. or Ms. Right.

Four weeks later, here I am sitting in my editor's office, ready to put my plan into operation. "Diana," I say, "I'm beginning to feel I could do with your special help on this book."

She spreads her hands. "Well, of course, Vonny. That's what an editor's for. What do you want to discuss?"

"Actually I was thinking of e-mailing different key scenes to you as I write them. You know how I value your feedback."

She doesn't look particularly taken with this concept. "Normally I'd prefer to wait for the complete manuscript," she says.

"I need help with *Drumbeat*. A lot of help." I play my trump card. "I really don't want to miss my deadline."

The thought of a missed deadline—a missed Veronica Vanderveer deadline—clearly disturbs Diana. "I'll do anything necessary," she says.

I smile, quite genuinely delighted. "You're the best," I announce, meaning it more than she knows.

The moment I get home I rush to my computer and start tapping away. This is how I always work, the words just flowing out of me, page after page, gushing in a white-hot creative flood. Revision will be needed, but the heart, the soul of my writing will already be in place.

Velda had not built her awesome catering empire by chance. She herself personally tried every new dish in her state-of-the-art kitchen. Now, with a cry of horror, Velda realized her kava soufflé had fallen completely flat! Never before had this happened! In her kitchen she was queen, and the ingredients of every dish merely obedient servants to her steely will.

"Why?" she cried, gazing despondently at the ruin of her creation.

Deep, deep down Velda knew the answer, but she was not yet ready to confront the barely tamped passion that simmered inside her. She wasn't obsessed with Dee! It was impossible! She wasn't enchanted by Dee's face, her body, her melodic voice.

Velda knew if she were to admit she was now ruled by passion, food preparation, her area of true excellence, would become a distant second best!

Now for Diana's alter ego, Dee...

Meanwhile, miles away, Dee, her blond tresses in disarray, sank her white teeth into her full, voluptuous lower lip. How could she be feeling this rising passion for Velda? Certainly she admired her professional colleague, especially after she'd received her industry's highest honor—the Golden Spatula of Excellence—but what she felt now was far more than admiration! Her loins burned with a rapacious heat that knew no assuaging!

Her defenses had been breached two days ago, when Velda, sitting across the desk from her, had laughed. Velda's customary intense expression had vanished, as if the sun had come out on a dark day. She had laughed, tossed her dark hair, and Dee had admired the clean line of her jaw. And at that moment something had snapped in Dee's heart!

I write on, my fingers a blur upon the keyboard. Then, without reading it over, I attach the file to an e-mail with the subject line "Key Scenes for Your Feedback" and send it off to Diana K. Broswell.

Surely at a subconscious level Diana will recognize herself in Dee, and me in Velda. Could it be plainer? Both Dee and Diana are editors. I frown. To be closer to real life, perhaps I should have made Velda a writer, not a caterer. I have no illusions about my abilities in the food area. My cooking might sustain life, but gourmet it ain't. My frown lifts when I recall that Diana has no idea whether I can cook or not. Still, it wouldn't hurt to have Velda exhibit writing skills like me. I'll put that in as soon as Diana gives me feedback on the pages I've sent.

I hang around, waiting. Diana doesn't respond. I check my e-mails every few minutes, but no luck. Finally, just as I'm resigned to the fact Diana has other business to attend to and might not yet have even read my pages, the phone rings.

"Vonny, I've spent some time on the material you e-mailed."

"Yes?" I say, listening keenly to see if her manner toward me has changed. I can't detect anything different.

"What I don't find is sufficient motivation for this relationship."

"No?"

My bewilderment must be obvious, as she adds, "I'm sure it's there in your head, Vonny. It's just not on the page. Your readers won't understand why these two women are so attracted to each other."

"Raw animal passion?"

Diana chuckles. "Our readers can always do with more of that. But before you toss Velda and Dee into bed together I'm suggesting we understand more of what motivates them to fall for each other."

I feel flat, let down. "Okay," I say.

"And don't forget the complication. Something must stand in the way of their love."

Claire McNab

"I'm well aware of the romance genre's requirements," I snap. "There's Roxy, the other woman, remember?"

I can't ruffle Diana. "Forgive me, Vonny. Of course you understand the structure of a romance novel."

"Anything else?" I ask, rather coldly.

"Exclamations," she says. "You use too many." She pauses, then goes on, "And there are a lot of rhetorical questions..."

These are complaints Diana's made about my writing before. I make my usual vague noises about rationing myself to only a few of each per chapter. Hey, I might not be the world's best stylist, but my novels *sell*!

After the call ends, I wander around my apartment, bleakly brooding. Clearly no seed has yet been planted in Diana's subconscious. I brighten as I consider the challenge ahead of me. Motivation to love? I can write about that from firsthand experience. I mean, who wouldn't love Diana? She's totally adorable.

Early the next morning, after a tumultuous night of fragmented dreams, I sit at my computer, eager to explain what motivates Velda and Dee to fall in love.

From childhood, Velda had always had a sixth sense about people. When she met Dee for the first time, Velda knew with uncanny certainty that blond, svelte Dee was decreed by fate to mean much to her!

Now, several years later, their business lives were intertwined. Velda was well on the way to becoming the catering guru in American society. Perfect Panache, the lifestyle magazine Dee edited, was a huge success, due in no small way to the fact that Velda was a natural writer and her "Cater Your Way to Success" column was a must-read for every aware woman!

But Velda knew herself to be lonely—an isolation forced upon her by her preeminent position. Whom could she trust to love her for herself and not her power and money? Then one day, chatting with Dee in Dee's sumptuous corner office, Velda's heart unexpectedly went zing! She realized, with a shock of life-shaking proportions, that she was falling head over heels for Dee!

I lean back in my chair to consider what I've written. I nix a couple of exclamation marks, reflecting that what I've put down is largely true. Although I'm totally devoid of psychic ability, I have, like Velda, known Dee/Diana for several years. Then, one wonderful day, while sitting in her office—which by the way is not sumptuous but rather utilitarian—my heart had gone zing!

Depressingly, so far Diana's heart is apparently zing-proof. I aim to do something about that.

Previously, Dee had taken Velda for granted—indeed, had taken her considerable skills and talents for granted! Had forgotten she was a living, breathing woman with wants and desires!

Velda was an asset to Perfect Panache, *her catering advice eagerly consumed by readers. Dee and Velda met regularly to discuss topics for future articles or to plan functions for which Velda's company would cater. Lately Dee had come to particularly look forward to their meetings. She found herself turning their conversations in more personal directions. Her interest in Velda grew. Here was an intensely attractive woman who combined comely features with a sterling character. Why had she no one important in her life? Why did she go home—like Dee—to a luxurious yet lonely apartment each night?*

Wait! Did Velda go home alone every night? Unheralded, a worm of jealousy twisted in Dee's mind!

I'm pleased with that last thought. Maybe, at some level, Diana will come to realize that Veronica Vanderveer/Vonny

Smith will not be available forever, and this will impel her to strike while the iron is hot.

I e-mail the new material to Diana, admitting to myself that I'm a little concerned. What if Diana doesn't get it? What if she doesn't realize I am Velda and she is Dee? A love scene between Velda and Dee should do the trick. Who among us hasn't fantasized about being one of the two aroused, panting people? Not that Diana would actually pant. Panting doesn't suit her. Perhaps I'll have her breathless with longing. Or gasping, maybe. Breathing heavily?

I really enjoy writing love scenes. To fill in the time until Diana calls, I start...

"Coffee?" asked Dee, closing the front door of her opulent apartment behind Velda. "We can sit in the kitchen and work on the menu for the conference."

Her heart thudding madly, Velda followed Diana's lissome form down the hall and into the kitchen. Diana turned, her expression unreadable. Leaning against the kitchen sink, Diana said, "You're flushed." She herself was breathing as though there were not enough air in the room.

I'm shocked to see my fingers have typed "Diana" instead of "Dee." Memo to self: Don't blow it!

Her heart thudding, Velda followed Dee's lissome form down the hall and into the kitchen. Dee turned, her expression unreadable. Leaning against the kitchen sink, she said, "You're flushed." She herself was breathing as though there were not enough air in the room.

Velda's eyes widened. Dee didn't suffer from asthma, so could this be reciprocal desire? Heat raced through Velda and blew away the last vestiges of reserve. "Dee!" she cried, pressing her feverish body against Dee's. "I must speak my love!"

No, that would never do. Diana/Dee would have to be won by stealth, not the full-frontal approach.

Heat raced through Velda, but her face remained cool. "Dee," she said, hoping desperately the quaver of desire in her voice was not noticeable, "Perfect Panache will be hosting the Posies for the Print Model of the Decade in just a few weeks. We really must discuss menus."

Dee frowned, wondering why disappointment throbbed in her veins. She hadn't expected Velda to share the disconcerting passion that bubbled in her blood, but she had hoped for something more than this businesslike approach. "The menus," she repeated, her voice dull. "The menus."

I scowl at the monitor. That hasn't got them into bed together, where they belong. Not that a bed is strictly necessary. Unbridled passion on a countertop is okay. Or perhaps in front of a roaring fire on a priceless Oriental rug? Then there's always the vertical to consider...

"Don't move!" Velda commanded, desire surging within her like a tide of molten longing. Roughly, she pushed Dee against the sink. "I must have you here!"

Her kisses poured in burning multitudes on Dee's face, her neck, her heaving bosom. Dee groaned, a matching fire speeding madly through her veins. "Don't stop!"

The phone rings. Distracted, I snatch it up. "Hello?"

"The motivation's working for Dee and Velda," says Diana, "but where's Roxy?"

Damn it! Roxy—the "other woman" in my plot outline for *Drumbeat of Desire*. My eyes automatically narrow when I think of Rose, Diana's assistant. Surely Diana wouldn't fall for someone so nauseatingly upbeat. Suddenly I'm jolted by a horrible thought. Bonnie the dental hygienist did say Diana was out playing the field. Maybe she's met someone she really fancies! Maybe there *is* a Roxy in the equation!

"You seeing anyone at the moment?" I ask Diana before I realize what I'm saying.

"Pardon me?" She sounds surprised.

I gasp, horrified at what I've done, then say quickly, "I said, you'll be seeing Roxy at any moment."

"Oka-a-ay," she says, drawing the word out as though she's a bit amused by the turn the conversation's taken.

I put down the receiver, my cheeks burning. Then inspiration strikes! Maybe I can use this gaffe creatively.

Velda handed Dee the copy for her next catering column. "Are you seeing anyone at the moment?" she inquired.

Dee looked surprised. "I thought you knew...Roxy and I are dating."

Hiding her furiously seething jealousy beneath a warm smile, Velda said, "Wonderful! You can use Roxy to test my catering column's latest quiz. It shows how food preferences indicate if your lover is the One for you."

Dee's brow creased. "I don't understand."

Seizing the chance to be close to Dee's slim perfection, Velda leaned over to point to the pages she'd just handed to her. She inhaled Dee's perfume, recognizing the heady scent of Moonlight Concerto. Momentarily dizzy, Velda braced herself against Dee's desk. As her head cleared, she said, "It's very complex, but I've made it simplicity itself in my column. A reader notes food preferences in carefully chosen areas for herself and for her lover, then tallies the score. The results reveal with stunning accuracy the likelihood of true love with this particular lover!"

Velda smiled enchantingly. "Why not fill in Roxy's food preferences and yours just to see how it works?"

"I'd rather not." Dee's face was stern.

Little did Velda know, but last night Dee's heart had been shaken with doubt. Was Roxy the One for Dee? Or was this just another empty affair? Was this a Chinese food romance— momentarily fulfilling but ultimately leaving Dee hungry for true love? Was this just another wasted night on the highway of loneliness?

I rather like that last phrase: *highway of loneliness.* I stop smiling when I think it's *me* stranded on that highway, unless Diana comes to her senses and realizes I'm the One.

Okay, now to bring Roxy into the story. As she's the "other woman" she has to be attractive, but I can give her fatal personality flaws. Unfaithful and shallow is the way to go. A vision of Rose comes into my head. Gritting my teeth, I write Roxy/Rose into my manuscript.

"Dee," she whispered in a throaty growl. "Come here."

"I'm busy," said Dee, her eyes on the work she'd just taken from her Gucci briefcase.

"Too busy for this?" Roxy slid her hand under Dee's silk shirt, cupping the suddenly eager nipple with her searching fingers.

I sigh. This is harder than I expected. I remove "suddenly eager." No way am I happy to have any part of Diana responding to Rose. I grit my teeth again. "Be brave," I admonish myself.

With great effort, I write a generic love scene. Roxy pants, groans, and generally makes an entire production of it. Dee is more moderate, although I do allow her one shout of exultation. After all, I reason, she's a woman with normal carnal desires, and her body would respond to Roxy's sexual skills.

After I e-mail these new scenes to Diana, I'm suddenly

submerged in the deepest depression. This isn't going to work. Diana doesn't see that I love her passionately.

It's my day for gritting my teeth. Hand on the helm, don't turn back, all that sort of thing. I go back to my writing. I produce the scene where Velda surprises Dee and Roxy together. That's painful to write, and I find tears running down my cheeks as Velda, her heart broken, gathers the tatters of her dignity about her and sweeps out, leaving Dee calling, "Velda, come back!" after her.

I continue writing. No one interrupts me, as I've told all my friends I'm in big trouble with a looming deadline and cannot be disturbed. Late in the day the phone rings. Hoping it's Diana, I rush to answer it. "Rose here!" the woman chirps vivaciously. "Diana asked me to call. She's printed out your pages and taken them to her dental appointment this afternoon. She'll get back to you tomorrow."

"Diana has a toothache?" I ask, immediately concerned.

"Checkup only. And cleaning." Rose sounds sickeningly cheerful, as though dental matters are something to be enjoyed.

After Rose hangs up, I fling myself into the nearest chair, my heart sinking like a stone. Cleaning means dental hygienist, and dental hygienist means Bonnie Flint. At this very moment, Bonnie could be gossiping about me! I console myself with the thought that she's more likely to be gossiping about Gwyneth Paltrow or Ellen DeGeneres.

The next day, when Diana calls, I question her about her teeth. "They're fine."

"And Bonnie?"

"Bonnie's fine too. Why do you ask?"

"No particular reason," I say. "Did she mention me?"

"As a matter of fact, she did. She spoke highly of the care you take of your mouth." She sounds amused.

"That's nice." There's an unfortunate silence. I fill it by saying, "I spoke to Rose yesterday."

"Hmm?"

"She's awfully perky, isn't she?"

Diana laughs. "You could say that."

We discuss the scenes I've sent her. Her suggestions, as always, are mostly helpful. We don't, however, see eye to eye about Roxy. Diana wants Dee to be more emotionally involved with Roxy. I don't. After some argument, we agree to a compromise. Dee will fall for Roxy, and only at the last will she see what a shallow, unworthy creature she is.

And so we fall into a pattern: I write, then e-mail. Diana edits and calls or e-mails me back. There's a certain pleasing rhythm to my days, but Diana is showing no sign that she's tumbled to the fact that she is Dee and I am Velda. Or that Rose is Roxy.

At last, as the end of the book nears, I have to admit defeat. My strategy looks so good on paper, but in practice it's a total failure.

All my days now are gray around the edges. It's an effort to keep writing *Drumbeat of Desire,* knowing Diana's pulse will never pound for me. One morning I wake with a new resolve. The final pages will have a dose of cruel reality. *Drumbeat* will have a bittersweet ending. Velda will tell Dee her love, and Dee will say, "I'm sorry, I don't feel that way about you, Velda. It grieves me to say it, but you're not the One."

I throw my heart and soul into this renunciation scene. I sob my way through the last lines. Velda has lost Dee forever, but, agony though the parting is, Velda is now a better woman for loving her. I include that wonderful thought: "It is better to have loved and lost than never to have loved at all."

I try to recall who said that first—maybe Nora Roberts? Note to self: check quote. Nora can be touchy about plagiarism.

With heavy heart and stuffy nose, I send the e-mail attachment to the woman who doesn't love me. Later I look morosely at the phone as it rings, then pick it up just before the answering machine can cut in. "Hello?"

"About *Drumbeat of Desire*," says Diana, "I don't like your final scene. I think Vonny and Diana should end up together."

I haven't enough spirit to argue. "Okay," I say. "I'll rewrite."

I put down the receiver with a sigh. Of course it's good editorial advice. Naturally my audience would want a happy ending, so of course Velda and Dee should end up together.

Then my heart takes a gigantic leap. I hear Diana's voice as though she's in the room. Vonny and Diana. *Vonny* and *Diana!*

I snatch up the phone and punch in her direct line. "Diana?"

"Yes?"

"You said...you made the connection..."

"I did."

"Do you mean...that I'm..." I can't say the words.

Diana's chuckle is tender. "Oh, yes, Vonny," she says. "You're most definitely the One."

Lesbians in
Poughkeepsie

Judith Nichols

Maria waited for the animated women to tumble out of the bedroom.

Al, the woman across the table from Maria, had asked twice, "What's wrong?" Nothing was wrong. Maria liked to smoke marijuana, but skipping this particular pot opportunity didn't bother her one bit. Abstaining seemed like the only civil thing to do. Maria longed for a larger, less isolated life that included people and domesticated animals—fat curly terriers or blue-eyed huskies. Once she even thought about bringing home a lime-green parrot. But love seemed to necessitate chaos and certain grief, and because of this Maria spent her adult life alone.

Al had announced to the oddly connected dinner companions that the smoke from cannabis would leave her choking for breath. Maria couldn't imagine leaving wheezy Al in the dining room by herself, and clearly no one else planned to stay behind with her. Maria pulled her chair up closer to the table and asked Al variations on questions she might use during office hours to draw out an awkward student. Maria imagined she looked curvy and fully present as she leaned back to listen to Al talk. The tips of Maria's fingers pressed the sides of the table from time to time as if she were testing her own distance from the concrete world.

Maria took down details while trying to be open to what she heard. Al had a heart-shaped face and a mullet haircut peppered gray at the temples. She was evasive about naming the place of her origin or discussing her daily work, but Al could talk at length about subjects including toxins in marijuana, PCBs in the Hudson, and the hazardous substances contained in the wax on fruit. "Within you," Al said, "cells may be dividing in deadly ways because of the toxins on an apple skin you ate yesterday."

Al is a cow, Maria thought, and then she admonished herself for thinking it. *Dull, didactic, unstriking:* These words would have provided more precise diction to describe Al. Al had glasses made for a retarded person and needed to floss her oversize front teeth.

The thing was, a word like *cow* couldn't even begin to catch all the ways in which Maria found a person like Al appalling. Al was the reason Maria spent her life alone. Isolation came as a result of the existence of women like Al. No, that wasn't true. This statement would be a good example of an unkind and inaccurate hyperbole. Maria was constantly running up against inadequacies in the language of observation as she used it.

Al would have tested her beliefs about sex and companionship to their breaking point, Maria thought, realizing she was starting to exhaust herself while doing nothing but sitting there pretending to listen. Maria's head was cocked in pain. She accepted the fact that she was lonely beyond description.

She could hear the women in the bedroom giggling and coughing. One woman yelled something that ended with a hard crack on the floor. Maria jumped.

In the early mornings, when Maria couldn't sleep, there was a delicious indulgence she enjoyed while fancying herself as infinitely open to the world. The touch of any hand might be a comfort, as would the skin of any belly, the breath from any mouth. Maria liked to imagine that she was, in a word, a slut. This word, this fantasy, could keep her expectant and aroused with a kind of unspecific desire until dawn began to tumble through the dirty windows of her apartment.

The room where Al and Maria waited for the return of their dinner companions seemed smaller than it had when all the lesbians had been sitting around the table eating and drinking together. At the very moment when Al started illuminating possible ramifications of cyanide in Coke cans on subways, while picking at the debris between her two front teeth, Maria heard the creak of the bedroom door, smelled a waft of sweet smoke, and saw a woman's head poke through.

It was Annabella who came out of the bedroom first. Beaming with a sense of her own gracefulness, she moved fluidly with long limbs and loose hands toward the flickering dining room table. Maria knew this walk well by now. She had met Annabella about sixteen months earlier and had, for a time, been enamored of that very walk. Annabella had night-time animal eyes and a low hairline that made her appear rather masculine or mischievous. Her olive skin suggested an exotic religious heritage, but Annabella had grown up in Macon, Georgia. A completely secular single mother, she seemed to outgrow the lives she created for herself before she even finished imagining them.

"I'll kill you dead if you tell anyone about this," is what Annabella said as she plopped down smelling of pot next to Maria at the dining room table. She had taken charge and introduced herself to the table full of lesbians that evening. "Hi. My name's Annabella. I'm an avid heterosexual with aesthetic appreciation for women," she'd said, staring around, expectant. Maria heard the woman next to her expire like a balloon letting out air as it flies out of the mouth and into a wall.

Annabella said "I'll kill you dead" again in a stage whisper and threw her arms backward as if they were weighted and burdensome. Every gesture she made seemed suspended and in need of response.

Maria was attending this dinner party of local lesbians, some of whom she had never met before, as part of her New Year's resolution to break her cycle of isolation and live in the present.

"I will kill you dead if you fuckin' tell," Annabella said again, this time without any attempt at whispering. By now it would be fair to say Maria wished Annabella had not come with her to the party. She tried to remember how she had gotten Annabella invited.

Maria raised her eyebrows and waited for the words that certainly sat right on the tip of Annabella's pink tongue.

Annabella stared toward Maria, incredulous, then reached out gently to take hold of Maria's chin. Maria had the face of the Mona Lisa, or some other placid woman. She had lips that concealed readable expression, a lush set of eyebrows, and sensuous skin. There was nothing not to like in Maria's face. This might have been what Annabella was thinking as she held her chin in her hand and assessed Maria as if she might paint her portrait.

"You really believe you're way beyond reproach, now, don't you?" is what Annabella hissed to Maria.

Annabella called Maria "the virgin," and this title was something Maria usually embraced with good will. For some reason not fully articulated, Maria found Annabella entertaining. "Are most lesbians virgins?" Annabella had once asked.

Maria rubbed her own chin and concentrated on the knot forming between her shoulder blades and the bottom of her exposed neck. Like a ball of rubber bands, her muscles coiled until her shoulder started to lift and rise toward the peeling ceiling, where colorful, pendulous balloons with pink or brown Magic Marker nipples floated on suspended lengths of yarn. In the dining room with the Salvation Army furniture and the distorted stained-glass goddesses, the floating breasts were the only signs of hope.

Outside the window, a siren screamed through the street and an infant wailed in the apartment next door. On top of all that noise, a large aircraft dragged its belly across the night sky with a labored sound that shook the crumbling block, making the brownstones in the building, where the women sat with half-full wineglasses and dirty dishes, shift and press into themselves. The conversations around the room froze.

"Jesus Christ, it sounds like the world is finally ending," shouted one of the hosts, the one who had run for treasurer of Poughkeepsie. She pulled another plump joint from her flannel breast pocket and bounced it lightly as a paper bird in front of everyone's eyes.

In her mind, Maria made a list of the women around the table as a way of relaxing herself. There was Annabella, of course, who was in rare form, as usual; Astrid, the horse trainer from Millbrook; an Israeli graduate student from the city whose name Maria could not pronounce; Amy, an African-American administrator; Alisa-Ann, a chef from the Culinary Institute with a Greek accent; Andrea, the very verbal kick-boxing mother; two unemployed artists, the hosts, one of whom was the candidate for treasurer; and Al.

The latter had shown her disapproval of smoking marijuana the first time by rolling her eyes and announcing her propensity for choking, but this latest time she threw her hands flat down on the table with a thump, clattering the wineglasses and making the candles flicker.

"Smoking again? Not in here, you don't," said Al.

"Oh, grand," said Annabella with a laugh that sounded like a bark. "A conscientious objection from righteous field!" Then Annabella lifted her wineglass in the approximate direction of Al and Maria felt an echo of ghostly vibrations, jet engines in her stomach.

"A softball allusion?" said Al to Annabella, leaning across the table, as if taking in Annabella's face and upper body. "Do you play yourself?" Al was waving her hand toward Annabella as if she wanted to slap her lightly, a fly on a lampshade.

Annabella touched her temple with her wineglass.

"Oh, too bad," said Al. "A little headache? Whenever I find someone with a gift for sparring, it always turns out they're too drunk to give me a go." Al smiled toward Annabella in such a way that her nose seemed to droop over her thin lips and protruding jaw, accentuating all her enduring qualities. There was a pause that stretched out over the table like a length of flammable silk.

"So, what do you do?" Al asked Annabella, as if trying to scoop the conversation up and give it legs.

Examining her cuticles, then picking up crumbs on her thumb, Annabella said, "I buy art with other people's money for the college, for Vassar. I'm trained as a curator."

"No, no, I mean what do you do for your headaches?" said Al.

Annabella's flashing black eyes darkened. Maria noticed that Annabella was settling into a posture that people who talk with their hands often hold when they are thinking. She had become perfectly, frighteningly still.

Annabella stared up at Al as if she had just noticed her for the first time. "Oh my goddess," she said, enunciating each word. "Who is that gifted pain in the ass?"

Al balled up her sturdy fist and shot her middle finger up and across the table in a kind of salute. Al and Annabella stared at each other for what seemed a full minute before they both started laughing. The whole table shifted in a way that was close to a collective twitch, and someone got up to find another bottle of wine. Maria heard the woman next to her quietly finish her point regarding the benefits of coffee enemas given twice daily.

{}

Annabella would have seemed, at first, to be a gold mine for stories. In corners before faculty lectures, in the dining hall with students nearby, and in the common hallways where colleagues walked hurriedly, Annabella blurted, free-associated, and summarized with a sense of urgency and recklessness, but the stories never really added up to much. It was as if Annabella had a pressure to talk, a fitful need to undress her own life from start to present every time she and Maria met.

Maria had been delighted to find someone so outrageous at the college's late-August opening-year cocktail party. The air was humid, and the festive tent outside the college president's house swarmed with the perfumed sweat of exposed nerves.

"Will you take me home with you sometime?" Annabella said as Maria gathered her resolve to flee the reception.

Maria laughed.

"Really, will you? Tonight? Teach me everything you know?"

It took Maria another minute to realize Annabella was mostly kidding. But the proposition hung, and Maria felt strange for having thought about it as a possibility. Fact was, Maria had begun to wonder about her own sanity as she imagined undressing Annabella and watching her recline onto a wide velvet bed with white cotton sheets escaping from the top and edges.

{ }

At the dinner party, the lesbians were getting restless. Astrid, Amy, and Alicia-Ann, the chubby lesbians, were trying to boil the water in the pitcher by holding their hands together over the lip in giddy communion. Andrea, the kick-boxer, and one of the hosts were yelling at each other in agreement about *Legally Blonde*'s representation of sexism in the workplace.

"How do you two know each other?" Environmentally sensitive Al was trying to engage Annabella once again.

"Who two?" asked Annabella, her pencil-thin eyebrows arched.

"You and that one who doesn't smoke pot. You and Maria," said Al. "Are you lovers?"

At this, Annabella invoked what must have been hiding inside her all along. Someplace, out of her depths, came the loudest howl Maria had ever heard. "Hell, no," said Annabella. "You think Maria would take me when she could have any one of you lovelies?"

{ }

Maria watched across the table as Andrea regaled anyone who would listen to her autobiography of a single-mother-kick-boxer-bodybuilder. Andrea had the kind of smooth skin and distinctive facial features that made a person want to look closer and more critically. Andrea talked out of one side of her mouth as if her face were slightly paralyzed. She was an astonishingly foul-mouthed woman with perfectly straight teeth. She had grown up in Pine Plains and gotten pregnant at the age of sixteen. She told how she had reached a point in her thirties where fat would not stay in her system. "Any fat cell that thinks of clinging to my ass gets burnt up faster than people from the eighty-first floor. Fizz, pop," Andrea said.

For a minute, it looked as if this analogy might be enough to stall Andrea's storytelling. The room hushed and fell. Someone groaned. Andrea held up her hand like a traffic cop toward the one who objected. Then she looked straight at Maria.

"You have kids?" she asked Maria.

Maria said she didn't.

"Maria can't tell a kid from a goat," yelled Annabella, who liked to brag about her own qualifications as a completely lousy mother. Annabella called herself an anti-nurturer or, alternatively, a non-mom. Annabella laughed out loud. Most of the lesbians across the table from Maria looked at Annabella with stony faces and cool eyes.

"I thought you seemed like you might be alone. Are you single then?" Andrea the kick-boxer asked Maria.

Feeling her mouth twitch the way it did when she felt she was being examined, Maria nodded yes.

"I have two girls and they are killing me," Andrea said. "They try breaking my heart about six times a day. You think about relaxing sometimes, getting a movie, going to bed early, but how can you do it when they're out there and the sky is falling on their heads? Picking up STDs and driving too fast with skinny boys sounds mild compared to what's coming. You're lucky you don't have to think about it. I mean, you're really lucky you don't have anyone."

"That's so sweet," said Annabella, pouring herself more wine and throwing her arm up over the back of Maria's chair.

"The other bad thing about kids is the breast-feeding and the saggy tits," Andrea said. "My girls are fifteen and seventeen and they've pretty near sucked me dry. I thought the tits might come back, but once they're gone, they're gone. You can build all the muscle you want, but the breasts, hell, they just hang there."

Someone blurted, "No way. You have a gorgeous body, Andrea."

Andrea nodded along and said, "That, ladies, is almost true." Suddenly she was standing up. "I think you need a drink," she said to Maria. As Andrea moved closer with the wine bottle, Maria felt Annabella nudge her repeatedly with her stocking foot under the table.

"Turn up the music!" Andrea said sternly to the woman sitting closest to the stereo, from which something new agey was floating, quietly as dust, into the room.

Someone, maybe the Greek, said, "Andrea, dance for us. Come on. You have great moves and great tits, baby," and at this Andrea set the bottle down and said, "Look, show me a little respect, would you?" Everyone started laughing at that.

Button by button, Andrea undid her shirt. First she showed Maria how building muscle had defined her arms and shoulders, how it had cleaved her chest neatly in half, which could mean great things if you wanted to wear scooped tops or V-necks or muscle shirts. Andrea flexed and turned this way and that, and the whole table cheered. Someone threw a five-dollar bill at her feet. Reaching behind herself, Andrea undid her bra and shook herself so that her breasts hung free. Standing there, she shone as if her skin had been licked all over in honey and sunlight. She leaned toward Maria and smoothed her cheek and neck with her fingertips. Maria took a sip from her glass and looked at the table while the lesbians whistled and cheered.

Then the room sort of hushed so that the music played unfettered. Andrea reached down, modestly holding her breasts in one hand, picked up her clothes, and put the money on the table. She hunched and hurried into her bra and looked flushed as she sat down, still buttoning up.

Annabella yelled, "Come on, girl! You earned that cash!" Her voice rose louder when Andrea ignored her. "What's wrong with you?" Annabella said. "Didn't your mama teach you it's a dog-eat-dog world?" She crumpled the bill into a tight little ball and flicked it at Andrea. One of the hosts leaned toward Annabella and said quietly, "That's enough, you. Now, stop it."

{ }

Maria wasn't surprised to see Annabella becoming obnoxious while drunk. The first time she had seen her drunk was a couple weeks after meeting her. Annabella had called her in tears later that evening saying she couldn't bear to watch another minute of the news. "There is no news, only history now," she said, as if it was somehow profound, something worth writing down.

Annabella's dramatic ways on the phone made Maria want to hang up and go back to grading papers. An hour later, despite her better judgment, Maria found herself at Annabella's campus-owned apartment.

A tour of her small apartment ended up focusing on gifts from wealthy lovers, mainly New York art collectors who had come through Annabella's life and left again, never to return. The two women slipped quietly past the door where Annabella's son was sleeping. There were cashmere throws draped over chairs in the hallway and sofas with silk batik, a bronze sculpture of an eyeball, photographs of chess players and a series of drawings of noses, a two-thousand dollar vacuum cleaner tipped over next to the blinking but silent television, a string of pearls on the mantle, and finally, ending in the bedroom, a black velvet duvet covering a king-size bed.

Annabella confided, as she pointed out a photo of herself next to her very pretty younger sister, that she had thought of herself as manly until recently meeting so many strong lesbians up in the north. As Annabella ran her hands along the plush bed and stared up at a drawing of a nude woman who had sprouted a tail, she asked a question Maria could not make out.

"Do you think I'm terribly masculine?" she said.

Annabella had lit some strange-smelling candle on the table next to the bed. This smell combined with the twang of Indian music made Maria slow to speak.

"Well, do you find me even slightly attractive?" asked Annabella, spitting the words out as if they were distasteful.

It was exactly then, as she stared up at Maria asking this question, that her son, a child of about eight with protruding ears, popped into the room in his blue Superman pajamas.

"Mom," he said, climbing into her lap and reaching up to hold her chin as if it were a door knocker, "I'm hungry."

"He's supposed to be asleep," Annabella whispered, as if this very quiet voice might be suggestive enough to return the boy to his blankets.

Annabella stiffened and sighed, then gently tucked the boy's long hair behind his ears. She looked out the window.

"He won't take a bath," she said to Maria. "And then I keep trying to get him in the shower with me, but he's stronger than I am." She looked as if she might cry again.

"I'm so hungry, Mom," the boy said, pushing harder into her lap and throwing his head out to the side where she could not reach his hair. His feet had flown up on the bed and it was surprising how long he looked, all draped out like a man. Maria could hardly believe the boy was only eight. Annabella dropped her hands onto the bed heavily.

"Go see what's on TV," she said in a louder voice. The boy just looked up at her and put his thumb into his mouth. "Go see what's on television before I kill myself," she said.

The boy did not budge but looked off at the wall, distracted. Without speaking, Annabella stood up, rolling the boy off her lap. He landed with a soft thud on the floor. Lying there, he looked completely collapsible except for the sly smile that cracked his otherwise unreadable face.

{ }

The party lesbians started transforming into the sleepy lesbians, and Maria imagined how she would finally be able to make a break out the door and head back to her car. There she could blast music and drive down the wind-blown blocks, where garbage cans clattered forth and a grocery cart full of empties rumbled by with an old man pushing it, his trench coat floating behind him like smoke. There was the problem of Annabella, who would expect a ride home. Maria could already see the final moment when Annabella would spin out of the car in her sweeping camel overcoat, exclaiming how horny she was. "I'm horny," she would call up to the streetlights with her mouth open wide. She might have to phone that new man in the psychology department, she would say, bending back into view in the car window so that her face loomed white as the rocky moon. "I'll hump the pillow while he talks to me about the weather." Maria could imagine the way Annabella would look as she moved away, graceful as a queen, laughing toward her lit door.

"You really need to stretch out more," Andrea said to Maria, startling her from her thoughts. She had come over from across the table in a kind of bodybuilder's squat. Her body seemed close even though the table divided them. And then Andrea, muscular, foul-mouthed Andrea, went on some more about being sorry for acting so crazy, for acting like such a *puta*. "I'm just nuts with the wine sometimes," she said. "Forgive me."

"Don't let Maria snow you," Annabella said to Andrea, calling out to her like she thought Andrea might be deaf. "Maria can be a little whore too." Annabella winked and grabbed Maria's thigh. "Goodbye and good luck, my love," she said as she stood up, moving away with a flourish.

Andrea came over and took the free chair next to Maria.

31

"Please listen for a minute," Andrea said. Maria was way beyond the point of trying to resist conversation. She was too tired to object, even though she had decided, somewhere in the middle of Andrea's floor show, to give up her resolution of trying to embrace humanity.

"Looking at you from down the table I can tell you must spend way too much time thinking," Andrea said sort of stiffly, as if she thought Maria might be angry, or worse, in a hurry. "After a while," she said, "all that thinking can really build up in your neck. It sucks. Pretty soon, all the parts of your body begin to revolt. Trust me. I know about this kind of thing."

It was true that every time Maria tried to bend or turn she felt the cords and muscles connecting her head to her body tighten and coil into a resistant column of soreness. She felt like a tangled puppet in the classroom. When she put her car into reverse, she often imagined she heard people's bones being crushed under her wheels.

Then, without asking, Andrea reached up and pinched the skin at the nape of Maria's neck. When she couldn't get a good angle, she stood up and moved behind Maria, brushing her hair out of the way. After a couple minutes, she began to produce fierce leverage and heat by pressing her thumbs along the cords that were pulling. Pain and crackling of muscles and tendons being moved past each other made Maria close her eyes. Inside herself, Maria heard a scratchy sound, like stiff fabric being softened into something smooth.

"You'll feel bruised tomorrow. When you wake up, you should really call me," Andrea said. "You probably won't, but you really should."

Maria thought about the pile of papers she needed to grade. Some of them would be interesting. Maybe two of them would find their brilliance before concluding. She would stand up to look through the window from time to time and see ice-cov-

ered trees and bundled-up students moving along the sidewalks. She might think about some woman she had loved
briefly, a skirt pulled up in passion, or a kiss delivered while
straddling distinct lives. Then, Sunday night would descend
and she would eventually fall asleep on the couch, feeling a sky
above her with no stars and bareness below it. Maria imagined
weeks full of nights like this one spreading out, falling slowly
over each other, snow-still, graceful, moving steadily away
from some center inside of her. Maria thought about Andrea,
and how when she pushed her phone number toward her on a
paper napkin it looked possible that she might just pull it back
and stuff it in her pocket. This, more than anything, made
Maria feel hopeful.

The Unripened Heart
Stefanie K. Dunning

Green. It was buoyant and clinging around us. Night was iridescent. It stuck to us like silver glitter and became condensation on our brown skin. We sparkled as we made our way through the heavy, close bouquets that weighed down the branches of dogwoods and brushed us nonchalantly as we strained to see the walk-worn trail beneath our feet. It was no use; night covered the ground. We cut a new path through the woods with a cacophony of sharp breaking and crackling.

Perhaps it was because it was eighty-nine degrees at nine P.M. that the night felt magical, but this was a typical Atlanta July night. Perhaps it was because we had just stolen a box full of goods—we didn't know what—off the loading dock at the overpriced health food co-op and we imagined ourselves being pursued by a well-manicured blond man in a hemp shirt. As we tromped through the thick, dark woods I wondered when we'd stop and pry open the box to see what booty awaited us. As I thought greedily about it, guilt spread through me. How did I become a thief so easily—I, who had always worked so hard and so proudly for everything I had?

It had been Nia's idea; she had communicated to me soundlessly that we should take the box. We'd been scavenging in the Dumpster of recycled magazines behind the co-op when Nia saw the box. I'd been flipping through a year-old *Glamour* magazine, looking for images I could use in a collage, when she nudged me. She yanked her head toward the box then peered at me. We both looked around us at the same time, checking the parking lot for cars, for people. I had never stolen a thing in my life. And Nia was the kind of person who'd drink water at dinner so she could be sure and leave a tip for the waiter. But she was known to switch course unexpectedly, for no reason, just for the fun of it. Something in me vibrated like a persistently strummed string. I sprinted for the box as an orange light exploded inside my eyelids.

As I felt my chest expand with the mouthfuls of air I gulped in, I heard Nia's sandals slap the asphalt just behind my left ear. She was laughing lowly under her breath; it took us two minutes to cross the huge parking lot, another fifteen seconds for her to grab the box, and another two minutes as we turned back and recrossed the parking lot ("Don't look back!" "I'm not, don't *you* look back!" we panted between breaths). We raced up the hill behind the Dumpster and headed for the woods fifteen yards ahead. I felt giddy as we stopped for a minute to catch our breath and to see if we were being pursued. The sun had just fallen below the horizon; it was hard to tell if someone was chasing us in the silky darkness that seemed to have pooled up in the parking lot behind the co-op. We plunged into the woods.

Nia's thick-soled sandals fell evenly on twigs and branches as she made her way through the woods. Did she know where she was going? We were headed in the general direction of the MARTA subway station, but it was so dark in the woods that not even the moon, which was half full, penetrated the thick canopy of the trees' full cover. I thought about what it would mean to turn around and go back through the parking lot so we could catch the bus on the street, near the comforting glow of the tattoo parlor's neon sign.

"Nia," I whispered, "I don't know if I feel right about stealing this box. Should we go back?"

"Are you crazy?"

"No…"

She sighed. "If you want to take it back, go ahead. I'll wait here."

That was as good as her refusing. We walked silently for a few more minutes.

"Nia," I whispered again.

"Yes?" she answered, almost in a yell this time.

"When are we going to stop?"

"When we get out of the woods."

"When will that be?"

"I have no idea." I thought I heard some panic in her voice. "Just keep walking. The woods have to end eventually. We'll probably bump into some houses soon."

I saw the hazy orange of sodium lights up ahead. I was about to mention this when Nia did.

"Okay," I said. "Let's head for those lights."

So we kept going; the more we walked, the farther the lights seemed to get, and the trees seemed thicker. We kept crackling along and we lapsed again into silence.

We had walked through these woods this morning and they had seemed beautiful—and brief. The sun had been high and bright at ten A.M., and the air still had an edge of crispness because it wasn't hot yet. It was a fresh, open morning whose cool caress suggested possibility. In the deepest part of the woods, some pink and ivory dogwood blossoms remained despite the July heat, for it was cooler in the heavily shaded thick part of the wood. It had been amazing to walk into what felt like an oasis of spring, with the cooler air, the buds decorating the trees with the faint scent of their perfume. We had paused and silently fingered the low hanging flowers, smelled the gentle scent on our fingertips, and marveled how the same flower could produce a different scent on our hands.

"Yours smells kind of musky," Nia had said as she held my fingertips close to her nose.

"And yours smells kind of fruity," I told her. We walked on in silence, turning the experience over and over again as we repeatedly touched blossoms and extended our hands for the other to smell.

I had watched Nia's legs—long and very brown from the summer sun—slice easily through the woods before me. Now I wished I could see her form, but I only saw the outline of her almost bald head in front of me: The moonlight—which was feeble but gave off a slight glow—made a small portion of her face visible; as she turned her head to look to her left, I saw her eyebrows were knit together as she moved confidently through the tangle, which was totally inexplicable since she had no idea where she was going. I wondered if the trees were laughing at us.

Walking through the woods, I suddenly felt tucked away from life, beneath a pocket of trees, with Nia's muscular legs cutting through the night and the thick green. For once I wasn't working or doing schoolwork. I had finished; we had both graduated, and now summer stretched around us before graduate school would shape and cleave our lives in the fall. So we had woken up around eight o'clock, and Nia had made pancakes with raisins. I felt happy and whole as sunlight streamed into our tiny apartment and as a thick ribbon of smoke rose from the *nag champa* I had lit when I woke up. We were listening to Roy Ayers—"My life, my life, my life in the sunshine"—as it vibrated off the walls while Nia made pancakes.

Stefanie K. Dunning

I'd been lying on our futon couch with my eyes closed, listening and smelling, when Nia put the plate of pancakes on my
stomach.

"I want to do something new and off the beaten path
today," she said as she picked up an unlubricated pancake and
began eating it with her fingers. "Like just go to Little Five
Points and hang out. Maybe we can find that poet guy,
Morpheus, and listen to him."

"What's new about that? We've done that at least twice," I said.

"Well, I said new *and* off the beaten path. That's off the
beaten path. We can find some other new thing to do."

I nodded and let the plate of food rise and fall as I breathed.
I had no other plans and little money; so going to Little Five
Points to do free yoga on the grass and listen to homeless poets
scream sounded good to me. What new thing we would do, I
didn't know. Maybe get a tattoo? Another piercing?

"Why aren't you eating?" Nia said when she finished her
pancakes.

I continued to lie there, letting myself feel how free I was.

"Let me feed you," she said. She picked up a pancake and
tore it into pieces. She put them in my mouth. I kept my eyes
closed and spat out the raisins.

"You don't like raisins?"

"Nope," I said.

"Hmph."

We both laughed. When I opened my eyes, she was bent
over me. Her eyes flashed golden from the sun, which shone
through a window to her left. Three freckles formed an imperfect triangle beneath her right eye. I reached up and touched
each point in the constellation. Her hair was beginning to
grow out a little, and her breath was milky, dewy against my
cheek. I ran my hand over her rough head as I had hundreds,
maybe thousands, of times. We had been close, but we'd never
crossed into each other's country.

38

"Let me give you a bath," she said.

I blinked up at her and said nothing. She stared at me. Finally I said, "Do I stink?"

"You know what I mean."

I did. But I was surprised because Nia had had boyfriends and only boyfriends, though she didn't have one now. I was thinking, as she looked down at me, daring me to take this challenge, that everywhere I'd just put my hands I could also rest my lips. I wondered who this alien was, peering down at me from her world, suspended in a shaft of light that was beginning to widen and intensify.

"Is this your new thing for the day?" I asked, more sarcastically than I wanted to.

She waved me away with an outstretched hand and walked toward the bathroom.

I tripped over a thick root poking through the surface of the ground but didn't fall. Nia stopped in front of me and found me quickly; her hands grasped my shoulders.

"Are you okay?"

I nodded, and though she probably couldn't see it in the dark, she understood me.

"Let's rest."

"Okay," I said. We stood near each other panting, listening.

"I wonder," she said after a moment, "if this is how they felt. Those slaves who escaped."

"Or died trying," I added.

"I mean, here we are, in the middle of the night, running through the woods feeling like someone is on our tail. It's spooky. And it's so dark out here."

"Well, I'm sure they felt a lot more afraid than we do."

"Imagine it...running from a plantation—maybe some slaves even ran over the very space we're in now, were going in the very direction we're going now...walked these very same steps."

"I doubt it," I said flatly.

"Why?"

"Because we're headed south."

"Whatever. You know what I mean. Think about creeping through the night but also having to move quickly, knowing that either freedom or death would be your reward or your punishment." She paused, thinking. "I would've done it. I wonder what the journey was like. What kind of conversations they had. What kinds of things they did in the woods that maybe they couldn't do on the plantation."

"Like what?"

"I don't know...but it must have felt...weird...and wonderful to suddenly realize there was nobody to watch you, to punish you, to discipline you, to keep you from doing what you want to do. To know you could begin to be yourself as soon as you took that first step into the nighttime wilderness, to know you could be free for the first time and no longer a slave..." I made out her smile through the darkness. "Wouldn't it be weird if we were stuck in some kind of time loop?"

"Huh?"

"I mean," Nia began, and I heard her slide her back down the trunk of the tree to sit, "what if we did get caught back there, at the co-op, and maybe we got shot by the owner and we're dead now, but we don't realize it."

"Listen, woman, this is not what I want to hear. I want to get out of the woods and to the MARTA station."

She laughed, loudly. The sound of her laughing, vibrating richly like a brass gong against the trees, scared me.

"Think about it. Can you prove to me right now that we're alive?"

I didn't say anything. She was grabbing hold of an idea and following it someplace I didn't want to go.

"What if this is purgatory? Just think—we'd be ending our lives as thieves."

"Well, what are we supposed to do about it now?" My guilt came back and itched up my spine.

"I don't know. Maybe go back, take the stuff back?"

"Now?" I almost screamed, feeling panicky. Then I remembered where we were and lowered my voice again to a whisper. "But we're not dead. Nor are we going to die in a minute."

"You don't know that." Then she laughed again, rich and moist, into the night.

I sighed, unnerved again by her inexplicable ease.

"Let's just sit here and be quiet for a minute," she said. "Then we can go toward the lights."

I sat next to Nia and rested my head against the tree. I listened to her thinking in the dark. She was sitting on our box of stolen goods and was a head above me as a result. I felt like a kid, sitting next to my big sister, foolish for not having played the game. Lacking in creativity for not having imagined we had crossed into some supernatural moment.

I closed my eyes and thought back to the morning, to the shower. Nia and I had seen each other naked a million times. Before moving into our apartment we'd been roommates on campus. Going to an all-girl college meant that people were less rigid about maintaining physical boundaries. It wasn't an unusual sight to see two women, platonic friends, holding hands or walking with their arms around each other. It wasn't unusual for roommates, to save time in the morning, to shower together. Nia and I had done this more than once in the dorm, as had many other girls, and we had even done it occasionally since we'd moved in together. But this time, when she *asked* me to bathe with her, or rather, when she asked to *wash* me, was different.

There is a way to look without looking, and I realized I'd never seen her body before. I'd never really focused on her skin, dappled with fragments of rainbow from the uneven light of the large crystal prism she'd put up over the window in the bathroom. She stood in front of me, waiting. I turned on the water, stepped into the shower, and wondered what was going through her mind. As steam filled the bathroom I felt like I'd faint. The contradictions that zoomed through my head, the questions I needed answered, made me dizzy. I wanted to turn around and ask her exactly what she was doing—but there she was, standing so close her nipples brushed against my back. My mouth, which had been open to ask a question, closed now.

I froze.

"Hand me the soap," Nia said, calmly.

I started to reach for the soap but realized this would require me to bend over and she was standing so close. While I was thinking about how to get the soap and maintain our girls-in-the-locker-room decorum, Nia pushed me out of the way and grabbed it. I was waiting for her to laugh, to break the tension that had arisen between us like tight skin on over-boiled milk.

"Want me to wash your back?" she asked innocently.

I nodded. She turned me around and lathered my back.

"After I wash you," she said, "you'd better wash me."

Usually I was very aggressive when I desired someone. Wasn't it just last week that I'd seduced a woman twice my age, who was also my former professor? Taking Dr. Smith to bed was easier than peeling an orange. Despite her hardness and her attempts to retain a friendly yet professional air with me, I'd broken through her barrier as if it were as fragile as the shell of a soft-boiled egg. And she had been just as wet and salty as a half-cooked yolk.

But Nia was in the "friend" category. And there was too much unsaid to make the switch. I told myself I should turn around and kiss her, seduce her, take her to bed, and stop shivering like a virgin. But something held me still under the rush of the water and the gentle scrubbing of her fingers on my back.

Nia finished my back and went on to my legs; as she got down on her knees she said, "You have a perfect body." She washed me like she was watering her shrine, slowly and quietly. I didn't think I could wash her as calmly; I didn't know what I'd do when my turn came. And I was wondering whether she would wash *everything* when she started washing everything.

"Let's go," Nia said and stood up. "You carry the box for a while."

She handed it to me. I put it on my head, which was wrapped with African cloth. "Okay," I said quietly.

I sighed; I was impatient to get out of the woods. I saw myself on the train—which would be well lit and efficient and far away from mosquitoes, which were beginning to feast on us. I wondered what was in the box and wished we had a flashlight so we could figure out if lugging it two miles through the woods was worth it. It could be anything from boxes of tofu to natural tampons; it could be brown rice or whole-wheat flour. It wasn't heavy enough to be oil or juice. As I considered what could be inside I realized how stupid it was for us to steal it. We weren't *that* poor. But we were feeling adventurous.

"Nee," I said.

"Yeah?"

"What do you think is in this box, matey?"

"Pirate's gold?"

We laughed.

"Diamonds, maybe?"

"Only if they're made from soy," I said.

"Girl, I wouldn't be surprised. It's amazing the things they can make with soy."

"Or maybe—"

"Stop," Nia said as I bumped into her.

"What?"

"I heard something."

"What?"

"Like someone else is here."

I said nothing. She lowered her voice to a whisper. "Let's just get real low and listen."

I whispered my agreement. We crouched and listened. After a moment, I heard it too. Someone else was crackling through the woods just as loudly as we had been. A range of dangerous looking men and animals clicked through my brain like a slide show. After a few minutes it was clear it was a human being, not an animal. The footfalls were even, and the rhythm suggested two legs, not four. We heard a male cursing under his breath and then a ringing, alarm-like noise, and then the walking stopped. I was frantic as I imagined he had some kind of device to find unarmed women in the woods. We heard a click, then saw a small light that indicated he was much closer to us than we'd thought. It was a cell phone; he had taken it from its holder and opened it, illuminating its screen.

"Shit," he said into the phone. "About time, boy. I've been walking around Five Points for three hours looking for you!" He paused. "I'm coming!" He hung up, and the light went out. He put the cell phone back and started walking faster.

About ten minutes later we heard him break into a run in the distance as he cleared the woods. That meant we too were almost out of the woods. When he was clearly gone and the only sound was a thick wind nudging the sleepy tree branches, we relaxed. I realized then that Nia and I had been holding hands.

"We're almost out," I said in a low voice.

"Yeah."

We waited, hesitated. We didn't move, and we kept our hands together, though now all of my attention was there, in the space between my flesh and hers.

I had noticed this morning that Nia's fingers were long and thin, her short nails neat though she only trimmed them with her teeth. She had washed me gently, erotically, but she hadn't tried to make love to me. When she was done, she had handed me the soap and the sponge. I felt anger well up inside me. I took these instruments and waited, stared at her. I wanted to ask her what she wanted from me, what she wanted me to do—but that didn't feel right. My body was like a drum on the outside—my skin felt tight—but inside everything was liquid and moving.

I looked at her body for the answer, but I couldn't interpret the data. Finally she said, slowly and out of time, as if she were reading the wrong lines in a play, "Go ahead. We don't have all day."

I reached out and put my hand on her shoulder; she looked at me, I looked at her. It was as if we were both suspended in that moment, in a watery cocoon. But I worried about what would emerge from this placenta; who would we be to each other when we broke the flimsy barrier of the shower curtain? I took the soap in my hand and lathered the sponge. I washed her chest; her breasts hung like yellow pears from a brown tree. I wanted to taste them and let the water and even the soap (which smelled like raspberries) trickle into my mouth like sticky sap. If she gave even one sign, one clear indication that she wanted something more, I'd stop my trembling and act. But she stood still, and she was unbelievably calm.

As we sat holding hands under the tree, blanketed by the darkness, I wondered if she was thinking about it too. It seemed clear now what she had wanted from me this morning, but I'd been unbelieving. I'd been afraid because I'd walked this road before with straight girls and discovered it was a dead end. So I had finished washing her, as she had washed me, and built an amazing dam within myself to stop the flow.

When I was done she said, "See? Was that so hard?"

I got out of the shower, ripping the curtain down as I went.

My body was wet and raw as I glared at her. The narrow aperture was closed. Nia stood shocked and naked in the bathtub. I walked away loudly; I was half afraid that in my haste I'd slip and fall on the slick, hardwood floor. When I was dressed, she came after me with a towel wrapped around her.

"I'm sorry," I said before she could. "I overreacted."

"No," she said. "I was…wrong to put you in that position."

I nodded. "Forget about it."

"I'll never forget it," she said meaningfully, then sat very close to me, like she was going to do something. I got up quickly.

"Let's get ready to go," I said, and went to the kitchen to wash the dishes.

I saw her go to her chest of drawers and pull clothes out. I turned my back and washed the two plates, the bowl she had used to mix the batter, one big wooden spoon, a spatula, and the skillet she had used to cook the pancakes. I put the box of raisins back in the cabinet along with the flour, sugar, baking soda, and salt. I threw away the now-empty carton of eggs and put the skim milk in the refrigerator. By the time I finished, she was standing in the living room in jean cutoffs, a white T-shirt, and thick-soled sandals. She wore a cloth anklet and a silver ankh necklace. A knapsack was slung diagonally over her shoulder.

She stood waiting for me. "Can I get a hug?" she asked, eager to mend the tear between us.

I wanted to remain angry, but I let it go. I hugged her and it felt like it used to.

I was about to ask what the hell had gotten into her when she shouted that the bus was coming down the hill and if we ran we'd make it. So we pulled the door closed behind us and checked to make sure the lock caught, and then we raced for the bus.

Now it was so quiet in the woods I couldn't even hear her breathing. I couldn't hear my own breath; it had become so slow and soft. But I could feel her hand against mine, our palms sweating against each other. It was still hot out, and a trickle of sweat ran down my back.

Before I had time to think about it, I asked her, "What was up with that shower thing today?"

She didn't move or answer. I waited in the silence, her hand hot and wet and unmoving in mine. We hadn't loosened our grip though the man had been gone for a while. How long had we been sitting under the tree now? How long had we been in the woods that couldn't have been more than two miles wide or long in any direction? Had we been walking in a circle all night? Would we miss the last train?

Would Nia ever speak into that darkness and answer my question? I wondered how much time had passed before she spoke.

"You freaked out," she finally said. "And over something we've done dozens of times."

Red ink bloomed on the screen of my eyelids, and I had to open my eyes to see if someone had shone a flashlight in my face, but no, all was perfect, velvet darkness.

"I mean, I don't know why that was so hard for you."

I shook away her hand. Again, without thinking, I spoke. "Listen. You know why it was hard. Why are you fucking with me?"

I felt her move beside me, but I couldn't see where she had gone. I felt coolness where her body had left an empty space next to mine. The silence was filled with the boom of my knocking heart.

"Nia?" I called into the night, but my voice died as it hit the bark of the trees. The woods now seemed thicker than ever as they absorbed the sound of my voice.

"I'm right here," she said, standing suddenly in front of me.

I stood up, knowing she was near because I felt her breath on my lips. We were almost the same height, give or take a quarter of an inch. She put her hand on my shoulder, and then I felt the fleshy crush of her lips on mine. With her other hand she pulled me closer, and our bodies touched completely except for a separation at our knees. I placed both my hands on her head and felt the tiny, silky hairs stand up on her neck as I caressed her ears. I put my lips below her right eye, where I knew a pyramid of stars shone. I knew her body now as if it had been etched in my mind with a fiery pen. I let my hands travel and felt my usual deftness return. My tongue had just tasted the silver of the ball in her belly button, and I pulled off her shorts. I was shocked to see she wasn't wearing panties.

"You little hussy," I said. "You planned this all along."

I felt Nia smiling in her fingertips, playing with my hair. Her legs shook a little as I rubbed between them with my flat palm. My hand came away wet and smelled sweet. She seemed to stop breathing as I kissed her and tasted her. She stopped me and, taking my head wrap off, she made a blanket for us to lie on. When I touched her again, she was breathing and moving under me, like waves, like a rush of hot air. At first timidly, then unafraid, she touched me like she knew me, and I felt myself falling, the world spinning like when I was waking from a dream. My usual poise and control began to slip from me. I let myself crash into her. Now the silence, which had retreated or gone unnoticed as we panted and moaned, crowded around us, and I rested my head on her breasts, which were full and dancing to the beat of her heart beneath my ear.

After a while she said, "Let's open the box."

"But we can't see."

"So?"

We laughed together, two low keys in the night. In the darkness we groped for the box, which I'd been sitting on. We worked to rip it open.

"Ready?" she asked, her voice taut with excitement.

"Yes," I said breathlessly.

We put our hands inside the box and began to feel the objects inside. Nia giggled as she pulled something out and ripped open a package. I felt her groping for my face and then she put something in my mouth.

A tart fruitiness burst on my tongue. We laughed. I sucked and heard her do the same. As we sucked, she rummaged through the box.

"There's other stuff too," she said. "But I don't know what it is."

I felt around and found packages of things I couldn't identify.

"We could stay here all night and just discover what's in the box," she suggested.

"Mmhmm," I said, my mouth full of fruity wetness.

We moved the box from between us and lay down, our calves on a bed of scratchy pine needles. Looking up, we found a good sized opening in the trees above us. Because of the moon's ascent it seemed like the sky was moving. We watched as the moon climbed, and when it was almost directly overhead I turned and looked at her. She was just visible as a skimpy finger of moon wiggled itself through the forest. I traced the thin line of her silhouette with my finger and then my palm.

"I don't want to leave the woods now," I told her. "I'm worried the night won't last long enough."

I saw her face open into a smile. She turned toward me and her face disappeared except for the thin line of her ear, her shoulder, her hip, and her foot.

"Yes," she said as we played thumb war, "I was kind of scared at first, but now it seems so peaceful and sweet."

"We should spend the night here," I said, listening to the crickets around us.

"Okay. But do you think we'll sleep?"

"I seriously doubt it," I said, and winked at her.

"What do you think those runaway slaves did to pass the time when they slept?"

"I have no idea. Looked for constellations in the sky? Talked about what they would do when they were free? Or…"

"Or what?" she said, waiting.

"Or maybe they didn't talk. Maybe they just disappeared into the darkness. Became one of the trees for the night."

"Hmm," Nia sang. "Interesting."

Her hand was cool in mine, the smell of the dogwood blossom growing stronger as the night cooled and slid into morning.

We waited for dawn with open eyes.

"Are you excited to see what is in the box?" I asked her as black night began to fade to deep purple and then to lapis blue.

She touched my face. "No. I already know what's in the box."

I smiled. "Should we take it back?"

We watched as purple turned to blue. *It's amazing,* I thought, *how fast the sun rises.*

"Do you really want to take it back?" She looked at me, and now I could see her quite clearly. "I mean, we should decide before we get out of the woods."

I looked around; I saw now that we were only about a quarter of a mile away from the edge of the woods. Had it really taken that long to walk less than two miles? We also had been very close to the path all along. We had only deviated slightly.

I was about to answer when an animal swaggered a few feet in front of us. It was a large gray speckled fox with an orange butterfly sitting on its back. I blinked hard as it made its way past and looked at Nia to see if she had seen it too.

"I saw it," she said. "Do you think the butterfly fell, you know, is dead or dying?"

I shrugged, slightly unsettled by the sight.

"That's so weird," she said and stood up. She wiped her shorts and legs. I looked again at the fox, now disappearing through the trees. She looked at me, smiling, waiting for my confirmation.

"Yes," I said. "It is weird."

We both strained our eyes in the direction the fox and butterfly had gone.

"Let's not take the box back," I said, looking down at it. Nia had closed it back up at some point.

"Good. We can go home and make some new discoveries then." She bent to pick up my head cloth. She shook it out and folded it. My dreadlocks fell around my shoulders.

"I don't know why you don't wear your hair down more," she said, brushing a dread behind my ear. "You look so pretty with your hair out."

The sun was rising and beams of light slanted through the trees, illuminating the woods. She leaned toward me and kissed me.

"Your face is golden where I kissed you," she said. "From the sun."

Then she turned and ran the rest of the way out of the woods. I heard her laughing as she raced through the clearing. She was a golden blur against the moist green around us.

When she got to the edge of woods, she yelled, "Free at last!" and let out an undulating call. The sun was now halfway up and bathing the world in golden pink and lavender hues. I heard a train rattle in the distance. Stretching my legs, I prepared myself to run after her.

Parting Agents
Carol Guess

Eleanor the sculptress worked with iron, concrete, and fiberglass, huge projects that took up space in the sky. She blew glass apples and hung them from barbed-wire trees. Her gestures were also art. She wore steel-toed boots, paint-stained jeans, and lipstick. Her hair was gray and her eyes were gray and the hook on her left arm was shiny silver. She lived in West Seattle in a bungalow off Fauntleroy. She said putting toothpaste on her toothbrush was difficult but tying shoelaces was worse. She seemed so restless. I felt small next to her. Later she told me she was afraid of me too.

Back then I lived in Ballard near the Nordic Heritage Museum. The neighborhood was haunted by sea widows and girls whose Santa Lucia candles had set their yellow hair on fire. It was July, the one month in Seattle when the rains stay away and the sun can stain you. It had been a year since Clea had dumped me for Jane and then dumped Jane for one of her students.

Eleanor saw visions and patterns and made saints' shrouds

and set things on fire. She had an arm of flesh, an arm of teeth. Ghosts and her guard up.

The first time she called the number I'd scrawled on a matchbook she said to meet her on Pike at a busy street corner. When I pulled up she was smoking on the curb, looking through a gallery window. Inside hung giant mosaics: pink girls made of tiny tiles flying through the air on rope swings, rainbow roller skates laced tight up their calves. "The early '80s are interesting now," she said.

First auto repair shops, then urban gardens. Roses. Small plots of carrots and peas. Lilacs, lilacs, lilacs, lilacs. Light spilled from a doorway. A man ground a cigarette into ash and took a long last swig of coffee. We approached a shadowy stretch of shut-down shops. In red on a white concrete block wall: PARTS AND SERVICES. She pushed me up against the blocks, touched her cheek to my cheek. I kissed her too fast and she slowed me down with her lips. "I thought so." "Fabulous." We could do this. A group of men approached us. Her hook at my back was a feather, a knife. "First thing you do is single out the alpha male. If you take him down, the rest just run." The men passed quietly. Fags. One smiled. We walked back to my car, her truck. She'd made something for me. Cool to the touch. A sheet of metal with a blue wrench attached, the welding mark a lipstick pucker. In raised letters: CLOSE ME CAREFULLY.

"It should say 'open,' " I said.

She closed my mouth with her mouth to explain.

A few days later Eleanor drove from West Seattle to Ballard at three A.M. just to touch me. All the long twenty minutes to my door she talked on her cell phone, reporting what went on at every turn: "We're doing one lane here on I-5. God, there's always an accident. This time it's a trailer sliced open. Now some guy in a Jeep thinks someone's going to let him into the carpool lane. I just passed him. I always get what I want and I always do what I say I will. By the way, I'm in love with your voice."

We were still talking on the phone as she pulled up to the curb. It was awkward to hang up, our first moment of sadness. In my arms she said we were trouble together, not safe like girls I'd had before. "A gun is meant to be fired," she said. "A fast car is meant to be driven fast." Lipstick and pearls and dirt underneath her nails. Her face was pale. Thick silver hair. She was impossibly lovely, a fierce and subtle beauty. We had the kind of sex I'd imagined I could have if I ever let someone go too deep. I was in too deep. "You're in deep, babe. Say it," she told me. I spoke into her hair. I spoke in whispers everywhere.

Nearly every day she recounted a different story about her missing arm. In some parallel world all her stories were true.

She had a way of holding the metal tip of her hook, cradling it with her right hand. She had a way of worrying it. The arm part was nicked. Scarred, scabbed fiberglass. She held the pincers of her hook together with thick rubber bands used to castrate sheep. When she fucked me with her right hand it was as if she used two. This was the first time I'd slept with the same girl twice since Clea. A breakthrough, Jane called it when I phoned to tell her. I listened for jealousy, but there wasn't any.

{}

Eleanor's studio was unmarked and unlisted because her art was unsolicited. She placed her pieces around the city herself. She never asked permission for this—or anything. Her apartment was filled with art and the detritus of art: colored pencils, scraps of newspaper and wood, little bits of metal, feathers, and shotgun shells. Her art extended to her body, green leaves and red blooms inked to the bone on the arm that ended early. The tattoo was unfinished because of the pain, but someday, she said, she'd find the nerve to bear it.

On our fifth night together she took me to a strip club. As we drove downtown I told her about stripping in Manhattan, how it had given me power I'd kept to this day. She told me about working phone sex lines and shooting heroin in San Francisco. We passed the boxcar elevators and a longshoremen's bar.

"That's where I go when I want to fuck with longshoremen," she said. "Did I mention that I came up with the idea for my next piece? Train tracks turning into water. I'll show you sketches when we get back home."

The club had a suburban vibe, like a smiley face or a minivan. We walked in on a girl dancing to "Little Red Corvette" in a red, white, and blue bikini top.

"I give her a D on athletic ability," I said.

Eleanor nudged me. "Watch this one."

A thin girl with long muscles in her legs and arms was climbing the silver pole. At the top she slid down slowly and flipped backwards, then climbed again, this time hanging from the top by one leg. When it was over she ignored the dollar bills folded over the glass partition.

"You've seen her before, then," I said.

"Here and there."

"How here and how there?"

"I bought a dance from her about a year ago," Eleanor told me. "I could tell she liked girls. A couple weeks later I was standing in line at the corner market. Didn't recognize her in clothes. She gave me a big grin and invited me back to her place for lunch. She wouldn't let me touch her. She never asked my name and I never asked hers."

A short blond in a nurse's uniform came up behind us. Eleanor touched my arm and gestured toward a booth. We sat down next to each other while the nurse crouched in front of my girl.

"Are you two together?"

"We're very together," Eleanor said.

"Would you like to hold hands?"

Eleanor gave her forty dollars and the girl gave her a lap dance while I watched. A metallic taste rose in my mouth. Limbs everywhere, jumbled, a star over Seattle. Eleanor moaned and watched me watch her. After the dance the nurse sat beside us but looked only at Eleanor and said she liked girls.

When we got home we kissed on her sofa. Eleanor dragged me onto the floor and climbed on top of me backwards. That night in bed we talked about Patti Smith, the last noticeable earthquake, and ghosts.

"Are you afraid?" I asked her.

"Throw in the towel, babe. It's already happening."

She was right. Something bigger than the two of us had taken over. I woke with one foot tangled in the bra she'd bought in Paris.

I could not remember Clea's face.

When I climbed out of bed Eleanor had already left for her studio. There was a note on the kitchen table:

Off to the studio. Snoop if you'd like. See you tonight.
P.S. The guns in the closet are loaded.

{}

Eleanor was a ghost accident. I could see what she caused but not how she'd caused it. We'd go to the co-op or art supply store and men would hit on her from my point in our painting. They'd move the perspective and she'd move it back again, but the in-between was all about power. The first time she tied me to a chair was the first time Jehovah's Witnesses visited my house. I listened from the bedroom as she answered the door. Sure enough, they were transfixed by her passion as she spoke of His bondage and His lock on her heart.

Some weeks later, Eleanor woke with a rash flushed red across her wrist.

"You'll see a bird today," she said. "I hope it isn't dead. Might be."

That morning a bird flew into my windshield, leaving a thumbprint of blood and a twisted feather.

"When my wrist flares up something dies and something is reborn. I came up with another project today. I'm going to cast a woman's face and hands."

She told me about parting agents, the slick skin of cheesecloth soaked in plaster. She told me about concrete mixed with white sand to cast a pale shadow inside the sculpture. The woman's hands would be underwater, water made of silk and wire. I imagined Eleanor's hand molding mine, my stillness as she slicked me, my face emerging from its shell casing, flushed with a peculiar kind of success.

She came to my house with a trunk full of tools, her voice distracted. She set up shop in my garage and for an hour we worked side by side. It took us a while to hear the knock at my door.

My next-door neighbor, Laurel, filled the vestibule, her short legs like bruises beneath her belly. She was pregnant with her seventh child. Her six kids stood single-file behind her. Eleanor came into the hallway and lit up like a motion sensor.

"Pleased to meet you. I'm Eleanor."

"Sorry. Eleanor, this is Laurel. Laurel, this is Eleanor."

"Come in," Eleanor said.

"I can't, but thank you. I just stopped by with a loaf of bread."

Eleanor watched through the window as Laurel walked home. "Who's that and what's with the kiddie parade?"

I explained what I knew.

"She's beautiful. Her face is unique—that square jaw, those cheekbones. That's her, Portia. She'll be my model. I'm going to cast your friendly neighborhood mom in a piece that's all about pain and desire."

{}

Most of Eleanor's recent art was about her ex-wife. She'd been in something long, beautiful, and dazzling that snapped shut like a fan. She rarely talked about her ex, but I'd seen pictures, so I knew what I was up against. They'd lived together on Capitol Hill in a huge bungalow they'd restored together. The only memories she shared with me were about the house. Her ex had added a sunroom onto the back, a room made of windows salvaged from demos. For weeks the garden was strewn with glass and panes framing grass and late-summer flowers.

One afternoon Eleanor picked me up in her rickety truck. I'd packed a picnic of mango, bread, cheese, and chocolate. She wanted me to see her studio: two tables in a corner of the Puget Sound Sheet Metal shop. Her friend Raz let her use the space for free, "Or sort of. We go to clubs together and I give him advice on how to get girls." The sheet metal shop was near the steel factory, two squat, dilapidated buildings under the West Seattle Bridge. To get into the shop yard, Eleanor had to pull the truck onto a narrow median then run across traffic to unlock the gate. Once the truck was parked inside we sat in the bed and ate our picnic as we watched the sun muck around with the cranes on Harbor Island.

A fuzzy feral cat ambled out from under a pyramid of gutters and peered at us with cat-specific emotion.

"Portia, I have this funny feeling I'll run into the little blond stripper again," Eleanor told me. "The nurse who danced and said she liked girls."

"I remember which one."

"Bet I run into her."

"Will you sleep with her?"

"I don't know what I'll do."

"Whatever you want. I guess we're different. I don't want to sleep with anyone else."

"You have a crush."

"Get out. On who?"

"It's obvious. I don't need to say it. You know—Mrs. Neighbor Lady." She jumped off the truck. "C'mon. Let's go poke around inside."

Eleanor's corner of the shop was always shifting. First Raz had her near the defunct fire extinguishers, then he'd moved her across the yard, into the building with the sheet metal machines. An old camper missing its wheels and most of its kitchenette was parked beside a hole in the corrugated metal walls. Eleanor stored her stuff inside: a welding hood, a jacket, and right-handed gloves.

"Have a lefty." She handed me a discarded glove. "Someday I'll find a right-arm amputee and we'll set up a trade. Hey, wanna learn how to weld?"

I put her hood over my head. "Love to."

"That's it, babe. Safety first."

The narrow window inside the hood didn't seem to let in any light at all. When we left the shop the Seattle sky looked positively Floridian.

Eleanor drove the truck across traffic onto the median, then ran across the street to lock up the gate. I pointed out a bunch of white boys in baggy jeans prying open the back of a van.

"Don't stare, babe. They'll think we're cops."

"Or longshoremen's wives."

"That'll put the fear of God into them. Have you ever been to Alki Beach?"

"Never."

"C'mon, little first timer." She maneuvered the truck past a skinny girl with a stroller. As we approached the train tracks we heard a sharp whistle. The light at the intersection flashed blood-red. Eleanor sped up and revved the truck over the tracks in front of the oncoming train.

"Eleanor?"

"Babe?"

"Do you feed the cat?"

"Mostly not. Keeps the rats and mice down."

"Does Raz make art like you do?"

"I'd say so. He wouldn't call it that. He'd call it work. But his stuff is high-end. You get a roof or flashings from Raz—you've got art, babe. He knows how to do what needs doing well." She took a cigarette from her jacket pocket and lit it while she turned the wheel with her hook. "Then there's the pony cart he's making for the dominatrix. Shit like that. That stuff's mostly for barter, if you know what I mean."

We were driving the curve of Alki Beach.

"Portia?"

"Yes?"

"That train was close."

"I know."

"Did you see how close?"

"My hands were over my eyes."

"I won't sleep with the nurse."

"I know that."

She swerved into the parking lot of a fish-and-chips stand. We stumbled out onto the sand. With our legs tangled in sea grass she grabbed the back of my neck and kissed me.

"There's a ghost in Luna Park, a woman who died for love. She threw herself off a Ferris wheel because she'd been jilted by her faithless lover."

"Every carnival should have a ghost."

"Every beach should have a faithless lover."

"Faithful."

"Which one are you again?"

We watched the Seattle skyline become stars on blue paper. She put both arms around me and I felt from her left arm the small green leaves and I felt from her right arm stern muscle and I could touch flesh and steel at the same time, which was, in another language, a metaphor for love.

I wanted to thank someone or something. Clea? The West Seattle Bridge? Parts and Services? Thank someone because I'd found her, somehow, on Fauntleroy Avenue, beyond the little white gate, past the low-slung arch of white flowers, through sky-blue mesh, past blue fish, in a chamber of French music and images of her death and into her arms and blood-red spread bed.

In the morning we tipped sand from our shoes.

{}

Because when she touched me I became a drawbridge.

Because I saw the bleak broken heart of her depression.

Because she wanted to take me to Spain and sleep in a tiny room above a bakery.

She undressed me with one hand. She wrestled me to holy ground. We watched each other as it all shook down.

"Teach me how to use a gun," I said.

"Teach me why you want to use one."

At night she slept with her small arm tucked neatly under a pillow. She rarely let me see it, the only thing she seemed to want to keep from me, an unsent letter. I wanted to slit open the pillow with the silver knife she used to pare envelopes, revealing the writing beneath: the writing on the wall.

"This is falling."

"Have you ever—"

"Never."

We hadn't said "I love you."

"I'll say it first."

"Let's never say it."

At night we put on music and danced for each other. When I got shy she put her hand and her hook on my shoulders and looked me fiercely in the eyes.

"You're hot," she said. "Own it."

I got down on my knees.

She said, "I sent you a letter, but the ghost of Luna Park intercepted it and set it adrift in a bottle at Alki Beach. The letter I wrote you was beautiful. It missed you by inches, a gun so dangerous one glance at the closet could set it off."

I said, "A poem begins in the mouth."

The Burlington Northern connected our lives, Ballard to West Seattle. We shook when we heard the whistle, thinking of our close call, thinking of the house one of us had left behind that night to sleep curled and curved over her girl's dreamy body. In the dim, in the steel, in the blight of urban decay beneath the West Seattle bridge, we fucked in her studio among the giant machines we both respected. We fucked carefully, knowing to flip the wrong switch might bring down the house. Pinup girls smiled at us from every post. The sun rose through shattered windows, and feral cats found morning meals.

"If this is happening to us, it means it can happen."

"I see stuff, Portia."

"Yes, and it scares me."

"Roll over."

I flipped onto my stomach.

"Close your eyes."

It was dark in her bedroom. She never lit candles or left a light on in the kitchen. She took darkness straight, as she took everything else. Her fingers on my back were busy making letters.

"What's this one?"
"I"
"Good girl. And this?"
"A."
She wrote "M" and "F."
She wrote "I am falling" and left the rest for me to guess.

{}

Clea called.

She called from Phoenix, where she was spending the summer with her student. They were "together" she said. "A couple," she added. I told her I was happy for her and to be gentle with the girl because she was so young. I was very well-behaved. I didn't say a word about extra credit or staying after school, and I didn't say a word about Eleanor because I didn't trust Clea not to meddle. I didn't say that forty-eight and twenty-three don't work too well together, and I didn't say I'd slept with Jane and that the two of us had compared notes about Clea's prowess. I just said "Peachy" and hung up and burned things: letters she'd written and a book she'd given me. I burned incense and smoked some of the pot I'd hoarded. I burned a chair and coughed up smoke.

I became obsessed with whether I should tell Eleanor that Clea had called, whether not telling her was lying, whether telling her would create trouble.

Eleanor woke me, knocking on my door at six A.M.

"How was it to talk to Clea?"

When I asked Eleanor how she knew, she said she'd felt it as a scratch in her throat.

"She's fucking the infant. They're a couple, she says."

"People fall in love. Whatever. Why does it matter who she's with? You and I have something fantastic. Let her have what she needs and move on."

"Can't you join me in my righteous ex-girlfriend rage?"

"You want rage? Let's get my gun and go."

We drove out of the city, past Shoreline, past Everett. We drove all the way to Bellingham, a tourist trap and also the heroin center of the Pacific Northwest, where I'd once taken photographs at an abandoned concrete factory. In the dust, among boxcars and tires and rusty metal. Eleanor fired the gun at spray paint cans wrapped in alcohol-soaked rags and we ran away from the fireball, toward Seattle: toward the Ballard Bridge, Lake Union, the Fremont Troll, and men trolling in Volunteer Park. We ran toward the Panama Hotel, past the dogs barking in the shelter along Interbay, past the Belltown P-patch and the Hammering Man. We ran so far and so fast there were no maps to take us back again.

Danger.

Danger.

I'd never felt such faith.

Nights later I wanted to touch her and thought she wanted me to until I lay on top of her and she stopped my hand. "Hold me." Her voice was so low I almost didn't hear. "Just hold me. Both your arms around me." I tried to touch all of her, but she was hiding. Her hook watched like an eye from beside the bed.

{}

Eleanor's favorite bar was under the highway in a building full of artists' live-in studios. Recently one of the most talented of the bunch had been evicted when her studio was targeted as the location for a French restaurant. "The people who eat in this place are going to spend more on one night's dinner than these artists spend on a month's rent," Eleanor told me. The woman who'd been evicted had moved to a loft in Tacoma. There was a vibe in the air at this time around Tacoma. Seattle was closed, but Tacoma was open. Portland was also open, but could be closed soon—who knew? "This row of studios is called Death Row," Eleanor said.

The door and storefront of the Anvil were trellises, iron ironed into flowers. Glass doors stood five feet behind the iron gates. Inside several dogs slopped water from a dish on the concrete floor and the pool table stood waiting. Night traffic passed so close we felt it through cues on green felt. Eleanor was more beautiful than reckless, but she was both, her cue balanced between her hand and her hook. The dude who took her on at pool was sorry later.

"Did you see the expression on his face when I beat him?"

"Or when he realized we were together."

"I don't think he did."

"You said 'girlfriend.'"

"That wouldn't mean to him what it means to us."

Halfway home I tailgated a slow driver, then honked as I passed him.

"Now you've seen my road rage," I said. "Do you hate me? I don't have many bad habits."

"I do."

"Like what?"

"I'm a sadist."

"Give me an example."

"I could bury someone alive in a box," Eleanor said. "I'll never hurt you, Portia. But you'll see the sadistic side of me someday and you'll be afraid." She finished off her beer and ordered another. Back home she drank on the stoop while I smoked, wondering if this meant I was a smoker again.

"Sometimes I just go cold, Portia. You won't like it. It'll scare you."

"I love you."

Eleanor wobbled up the stairs. "That's the biggest mistake you'll ever make."

A few nights later Eleanor went out drinking with the girls from the forge. She came home at two A.M. and kissed me everywhere, leaving lipstick marks it would take sand to erase. "Back in the day I would've slept at the forge or gone home with Lydia Harding," she said. "Lydia Harding! She is so fucking hot! She was flirting with me like crazy, but you're a homing device. By the way, Portia, Raz wants to watch."

"Only if I can watch you and Laurel."

"That's happening soon."

"I mean when you cast her," I said.

And so we gathered in my garage. Laurel worried her hands in her lap but otherwise sat still. I smoked, and Eleanor drank rum in her soda while she laid out the materials: water, plaster, newspaper, cheesecloth. Laurel had on a long blue skirt with yellow flowers and a matching shirt that ballooned in the front. I had the sinking feeling she didn't understand she was about to get naked.

Eleanor approached Laurel with a handful of cheesecloth bound like a bouquet. She smoothed the cloth over Laurel's belly, over her shirt, covering the blue sky, covering the yellow sun. Laurel closed her eyes as if alone for the first time since her eldest child was born.

When Eleanor had covered Laurel's belly—thick fabric bunched under cheesecloth, an unrecognizable shape—she squatted in front of Laurel's chair.

"This isn't going to work. With the fabric beneath it, I mean. It's too lumpy for the shape to make sense. What should we do?"

Genius.

I left the garage quietly. I'll admit I put my ear to the door, but if they made noise it wasn't meant for me to hear. The scene in my garage was nothing like what happened later with Raz, which didn't mean much to me one way or another. It didn't mean much to Eleanor, either, which surprised her.

"I'm losing my edge."

"We're edgy together."

"I could find the nurse, you know."

"I know."

"This is terrible."

"What?"

"What I've done."

My stomach contracted. She'd slept with someone or shot someone. Or both.

"Just say it."

"I've fallen in love. It terrifies me. A few months ago I would've taken that stripper home and enjoyed her body. Now I'm so into you that I can't. It's awful."

"I'm sorry."

"Don't be. I love you. I'm drunk as hell."

Raz had sat in a chair in the corner. Having someone watch in real life was different from what I'd imagined in fantasy. It made everything less charged, not more. I got ticklish. He kept a respectful distance, his hand in his pants, which we told him not to take off. When it was over there was a long, awkward pause while Eleanor and I realized we were going to have to kick him out so we could fall asleep.

"Let's have a smoke," I said finally, crawling out of bed. I grabbed Raz with one hand and my robe with the other. We sat together on Eleanor's back porch and rolled cigarettes, talking about the Middle East and why we wished we lived in Canada.

After he drove off, Eleanor joined me. She rolled a cigarette with one hand and lit a match off a matchbook by folding the tip to touch the black strip and striking. I didn't always remember that everything she did she did with one hand. At the same time that I forgot this I also forgot that her hook was metal and not flesh. When she used it to pick up hot pans or hammer nails I winced, feeling it.

"I'm shy," she said. "This is totally new."

"Have you ever done that before?"

"No, but I've done weirder stuff. I'm shy because of you, Portia, because when I touch you it's about love and I feel like everyone can see that. And you see through me. It scares me. I don't like it."

"What can I say? I mean, I'm good at seeing. Like, one of my ex-girlfriends used to say this thing about her dog but also…"

Eleanor covered my mouth with her hand. Then she straddled me and undid her buttons. She tied her shirt over my eyes and pressed me back against the pillows. She rocked against me until I was really ready then pushed my blindness between her legs. We fucked and slept then woke at three A.M. and fucked again, facing each other, our hands sloppy. She asked me for things in a whisper, and all I could think about was making it perfect for her. We fell back asleep until seven, when she climbed out of bed and put on her robe.

That afternoon I got a letter from Clea, an envelope with nothing in it. At first I thought it was a mistake, but then I decided it meant something. It reminded me of the story of Eleanor's tattoo. I'd asked her once how she'd picked the design.

"I felt it under the surface of my skin. I knew the sleeve would be about flowers and birds and vines, but I couldn't see it. The artist brought out the design with ink."

Clea was sending me a cryptic message. It bubbled under my skin but refused to break through. Something had happened or was about to happen. Soon the design would emerge, startlingly bright.

Captain Clarrie

Cheyenne Blue

Clarrie and Joybelle are driving to California from Texas, chugging across the dusty moonscape of New Mexico in a Buick that has seen better days. They're heading for Pasadena, to the annual Trekfest Star Trek convention. On the parcel shelf there's a ridged rubber Klingon forehead that can be attached with epoxy, a wild wig of matted black hair, and a bat'leth—a fierce looking weapon, although this one is made of cardboard. It complements Joybelle's Klingon warrior costume.

Clarrie's costume is more restrained. She has a Starfleet uniform—black, with the red shoulders signifying command—neatly pressed in her sports bag. There's also a shoulder-length wig of fox-red hair, which, Joybelle likes to lovingly tell her, makes her look exactly like Captain Kathryn Janeway—as much as any fat black dyke can look like a petite Anglo-American redhead, anyway. Clarrie doesn't like her costume much; the Starfleet jumpsuit makes her ass appear huge, and the red wig looks plain weird with her dark skin. She only wears it for Joybelle, who has a crush on the actor who plays Captain Janeway.

Joybelle loves *Star Trek*, and attending the convention is her idea. In her spare time at work, whenever Manny's Stop 'n' Shop is quiet, she balances a pad on the cash register and writes purple fan fiction involving Captain Janeway getting it on in sweaty lesbian clinches with her Klingon archenemy. Joybelle reads her stories aloud to Clarrie sometimes, but Clarrie has to fight the urge to laugh. Still, she goes along willingly with the role-playing games and throws herself into the captain's role with great enthusiasm. Indeed, memories of Joybelle the Klingon forcing Captain Clarrie to eat her out have often dampened her panties and sent her scurrying to the restroom at work for a quick fingering.

Right now they're a day out from Dallas and looking for a motel for the night. The sunset bleeds into the long expanses of I-40, the burning summer heat becoming almost tolerable, and Clarrie's Triple-A map shows a town coming up called Santa Rosa.

"We could keep going to Albuquerque," says Joybelle.

She never likes to stop; the hypnotic rhythms of turning wheels and wind noise through the passenger window that won't fully close make her want to keep moving. She says it helps her write, and Clarrie wonders how, if that is the case, Joybelle can write at all in the stagnancy of Manny's Stop 'n' Shop.

"Sure," Clarrie agrees amicably and cranks the aging Buick up a notch so that they might reach Albuquerque before it's totally dark. Maybe there'll be a cheap motel next to a cozy dyke bar, one that serves burgers that aren't overcooked, one where she can dance with her lover to some tunes from the jukebox. Right. And maybe the *Star Trek* universe is real, and the universe of Dallas is the alternate. Perhaps then her misogynistic cheapskate boss—the only attorney in town who would hire her as a paralegal—could be vaporized in a flash of phaser fire.

Joybelle's looking at the map—never a good sign. She's the only person Clarrie knows who drives from Main Street to their house on Creosote Avenue—a distance of maybe half a mile—via the back blocks and Wal-Mart parking lot, a "short-cut" that takes three times as long.

Joybelle's finger stabs at the map. "If we go this way," her finger traces a wavering path over the grubby paper, following an imaginary line Clarrie can't see, "we'll be in Albuquerque sooner."

"No way." Clarrie releases a hand from the wheel to squeeze Joybelle's thigh. "Babe, your shortcuts need a brown-bag lunch. The freeway is straight."

"All the more reason to take the bent way!" Joybelle wheezes laughter at her old joke and lights up another ciga-rette. "Besides, Roswell's just to the south. Who knows what we'll see?"

Clarrie rolls her eyes. "Yeah, right. And maybe the Enterprise will land in a cow paddock and you and Captain Janeway can go off to live in steamy dyke bliss."

"*Voyager*. Janeway's ship is *Voyager*." Joybelle tuts in annoyance at Clarrie's ignorance.

"Whatever. But no little green men are gonna come out of the sky and dissect you. Don't you want to get to Albuquerque ear-lier?" Her fingers curl over Joybelle's thigh, creeping higher under the cotton shorts.

Joybelle shifts stickily, peeling her legs from the vinyl seat, and props one foot on the dash to allow Clarrie better access. "Sure. And find a big bed with you in it. But in the mean-time…" She lets the words trail off hopefully and pulls off her panties.

Clarrie takes the hint and dips her fingers inside, tickling the furred lips, feathering her lover's clit. One hand on the wheel, two eyes on the highway, and two fingers in heaven.

Joybelle comes with a sigh, takes her foot off the dash, sits up, and opens her eyes. "There! Quick! Turn!"

How the hell does she do that? wonders Clarrie in exasperation as she swerves for the indicated exit so abruptly that the Klingon forehead bounces off the dashboard to disappear among the McDonald's wrappers on the floor. Every time, Joybelle manages to spot the exit at the last second. She resigns herself to taking the shortcut and hopes they'll make Albuquerque before the bars close.

The road is graded dirt and the Buick bounces wildly over the washboardy surface. Clarrie decelerates; they can't afford car repairs. "You're sure this is it?"

Joybelle refolds the map and squints at it. "Yeah," she says definitively. "This is it. It's not far."

Clarrie cranks open the window to let the cool desert air play over her skin. She slows down as the road deteriorates, but not slow enough, and the car bottoms out over a creek wash. To her left the fall of the landscape draws the eye to the distant hills. *Mexico?* she wonders. Surely she can't see that far. The evening reeks of solitude, and Clarrie, who has never been this deep into the desert before, shivers. She leans forward, concentrating on the road, straining to see in the looming darkness.

Joybelle's leaning forward too—she's peering upward through the windshield to see the stars come out. "It's beautiful," she breathes.

With each bouncing mile Clarrie grows more and more worried. If she looks behind, she can see the ribbon of freeway lights getting farther away, but ahead she can see nothing. Simply the expanse of grass and sage—no buildings, no Motel 6. Her stomach rumbles, reminding her of that burger. She'll have blue cheese on it, she thinks, and screw the diet.

Joybelle turns to her with shining eyes. "It's just like *The X-Files*," she says. "You know, the episode where Mulder gets abducted by the alien craft and they carve his chest open with a chainsaw."

"Great," says Clarrie shortly. Joybelle's words increase her sense of unease. *How can anyone really want to be here?* she thinks, and slows the car. "Let's go back to the freeway. This isn't going anywhere."

"Just a little bit more," wheedles Joybelle. "I'm sure we'll get back to the freeway soon, and it's so beautiful."

They crest a slight rise, the freeway no longer visible behind them. Clarrie has never felt so alone, even with Joybelle next to her. Something small and reptilian scurries across the road in front of the headlights and she gasps, nerves strung tighter than fencing wire. The car swerves, tilts alarmingly, then rights itself. Clarrie's pulse thunders in staccato beat and she's close to crying. This out-of-control feeling is not like her; she's the practical one, the resilient one, the one who pays the electric bill and makes sure there's gas in the car. Joybelle's the artistic one, the dreamer who comes home with Girl Scout cookies neither of them will eat, simply because the kid looked at her so hopefully. But Joybelle's comfortable out here in this nothingness, leaning forward to peer at the sky, elbows on her knees, dark curly hair falling to her shoulders.

"Please," says Clarrie, and the catch in her voice startles her. "Please, can we go back to the freeway?"

Joybelle turns, surprise in her face, but she softens when she sees Clarrie's expression. She reaches out and touches Clarrie's cheek. "Of course, hon. I'm sorry. It's just so wide and beautiful out here. I'm looking for UFOs."

Clarrie's heart lurches again. "Please don't say that," she says quickly.

She has Joybelle's full attention now, dragged away from the alien landscape. "But you don't believe in that stuff," Joybelle says. "You mock me when I sigh over *Star Trek,* laugh when I ask if you think *The X-Files* is fact, not fiction."

"You only watch *Star Trek* to drool over that captain," Clarrie says through dry lips. Panic comes in waves and her thoughts whirl. What if they can't turn? What if the car runs out of gas or gets stuck? What if they have to spend the night out here?

"Oh, yeah, her too," says Joybelle, "but really I watch it for the dreaming of 'what if?' You know, what if we could travel to the stars?" She sighs softly, and the rushing wind from the open window swallows it up. "And we're living a 'what if?' now, on this cow track in New Mexico." She turns her face to the window again and her voice deepens. "Look at all those stars. Surely somewhere in the universe there's an alien dyke looking out a car window on a cow track saying, 'I bet there's life out there.' "

"Just as long as she stays out there and doesn't pay us a visit," says Clarrie.

It's fully dark now, and Clarrie slows, stops. The dirt road is narrow; turning will be difficult. With the engine idling, the emptiness is accentuated. She hears insect noise, the rustle of something out in the sage. It's a coyote, she tells herself firmly. Just a scavenger.

Joybelle looks out the side window. "Don't get too close to the edge," she says. "The ground looks soft. I'll direct." Clarrie puts the car in park and Joybelle jumps out.

Joybelle's spatial skills are as bad as her map reading. It's why the Buick has so many dings, but this time Clarrie has no choice. Slowly she turns the wheel to full lock, edging forward across the track. Joybelle urges her on with confident sweeps of her hand. Clarrie creeps forward a little more, then stops, fumbling for reverse. It takes her three tries before the gear grinds into place. It's as if this landscape has sucked her strength, her ability.

Back and forth she edges, each time a bit closer around. She dares not follow the full sweeps of Joybelle's signs; they'll probably get stuck. It's the fifth reverse when Clarrie's foot slips off the clutch and the car lurches backward, a great kangaroo bound that leaves the car's back wheels in the soft sand. Clarrie throws the gear into first and floors it, but the wheels spin hopelessly.

"Stop! Stop!" Joybelle, waving her arms around, comes over and bangs on the roof. "You're digging her in deeper." She folds her arms, legs astride the track marks, and assesses the situation. The moon lifts graciously over the rise, gilding her with silver.

Clarrie leans her head against the steering wheel and waits.

Joybelle strides over to Clarrie's window. "We've got three options as I see it," she says. "We can wait to be rescued, which will probably be tomorrow. We can try and dig ourselves out. Or we call Triple-A."

Of course. Clarrie digs in the glove box for her cell phone and flips it on. "No service," she sighs. Defeated, she lays her head back down on the steering wheel.

"Two options then."

Joybelle's enjoying this, Clarrie realizes. *Finally, she's living an adventure, and it's giving her a confidence she's never had. Maybe the radiation from all those atomic bombs exploded in New Mexico is sapping my strength and channeling it via a Vulcan mindmeld to Joybelle.* The thought makes her laugh helplessly. *I must really be losing it,* she muses.

Joybelle regards Clarrie steadily. "Looks like we dig," she says. "Or you'll be a puddle of nerves by morning. Besides, I'm hungry." She opens the trunk and rummages around. "What we need is some cloth. We dig the back wheels out, put the cloth underneath for traction, and you drive slowly out."

Clarrie raises her head and stares at Joybelle in bewilderment. "How do you know that?"

Joybelle shrugs. "I just do. Maybe Mulder did it on *The X-Files.*"

Right. The last reminder she needs. She remembers Mulder's screams as aliens hacked into his chest.

Clothing is strewn inside the trunk as Joybelle rummages. "Looks like it's gotta be these." She holds up the Klingon battle dress and the Starfleet captain's uniform with the extra-large ass. "Everything else is too skimpy. Just try not to tear them, okay?" She throws them down and bends to scoop the loose sand with her hands. Her face peers up through a tangled mass of hair. "You gonna help me?" she demands. "Or are you nailed to the seat?"

Reluctantly, Clarrie leaves her faint sanctuary and goes to help dig. Outside, the air smells stronger—there's a sharp tang of sagebrush—and the night noises seem louder. Every minute or so she scans the horizon for low-flying orange lights.

They're working the Starfleet uniform under the second wheel when they see a flash of light. Clarrie freezes, but her heart leaps so hard she thinks it'll fly through her chest and splatter onto the side of the car. Come to think of it, didn't that happen in *The X-Files* too?

Joybelle pauses as well. "Dig faster," she says in a trembly voice, so different from the assertive Amazon of a minute before.

The lights glide closer. If there's engine noise, the wind is whipping it away from them. Joybelle shivers, but she reaches into the back of the car and pulls something out.

The lights glide to a stop beside them. With relief, Clarrie makes out the outline of a white dual-cab pickup. The driver cuts the engine and rolls down his window. "Need a hand, ladies?"

Clarrie opens her mouth to thank the stranger, but Joybelle beats her to it. "Thanks, but we're fine. Sweetie, get in and start her up. Drive out nice and slow."

Clarrie notices the rancher's trembling hands, his gaping mouth, but she's too eager for that blue-cheese burger she's sure is waiting for her in Albuquerque to wonder why. Starting the engine, she obeys Joybelle's directions, and the Buick noses out of the soft sand onto the graded dirt again.

Joybelle darts back and rescues their costumes, shaking the

sand out of each one. The metal studs on the Klingon battle-dress glint in the pickup's headlights. She throws them in the backseat and, with a wave to the slack-jawed rancher, slides into the passenger seat, propping her feet on the dash. "Just drive, hon," she says.

Clarrie rushes to obey, and the car grinds its way back toward the freeway.

For long minutes neither of them speaks. Clarrie is bemused and somewhat ashamed. She is the practical one; she should have dug them out, dealt with the rancher. Instead she was paralyzed by memories of TV shows. But Joybelle... Ah, her lover had come into her own, strong and determined. Clarrie remembers how the muscles in her arms stood out in the moonlight as she dug.

She turns to Joybelle. "Wonder what made that rancher turn so pale?" she asks. "One minute he wanted to help us little women, the next he was pastier than an unbaked tortilla."

Joybelle turns toward her, and the moonlight shines on the ridges of her hastily applied Klingon forehead. "Who knows?" she smiles. "And who cares?"

Clarrie reaches back with one hand, finds the despised red wig, and puts it on haphazardly over her braids. She taps an imaginary communicator pin on her chest. "Captain Janeway to Klingon Warrior Joybel'eth. Report to my quarters immediately for some heavy duty. And bring a toothbrush."

Joybelle's hand steals over her thigh, tracing the line where her shorts end. "Yes, ma'am!"

Third Date

Yvonne Zipter

Reggie looks at the one sister, sitting off to the side. In another setting, she might be mistaken for a Goth girl, light on the makeup. She has been sedated, Reggie has been told, and sits very straight, swaying ever so slightly as if she were a palm tree caught in a gentle breeze. Reggie wonders if it's safe to let her sit there alone like that, worries the momentum will gather until suddenly she topples over.

The other sister is in a tight-fitting, low-cut black dress under a square-cut shorty jacket with elbow-length sleeves. On her head sits a black pillbox hat with a shoulder-length black veil speckled with black velvet dots. Reggie wonders idly where she has seen this hat before, then thinks perhaps it was on Jackie Kennedy at JFK's funeral some twenty-five years prior. The woman in the pillbox hat is wailing in an ostentatious fashion and flailing at a man in a black suit whom Reggie thinks she remembers is her husband.

She looks for Angela, sister to the aforementioned sisters and Reggie's reason for being here. Reggie finds her in a huddle of weepers, which acts as a sort of choral backdrop to the whole event—with occasional soloists, it appears, as one of the women lets out a piercing cry and would slump to the floor if it weren't for the arms on either side of her holding her up. Wakes were never like this in Ixonia. Reggie asks herself, not for the first time, if it was a good idea to come here.

But then she remembers why she did. The phone call came toward the end of Reggie's third date with Angela—which is to say, first thing in the morning: After a long, long, *long* illness, Angela's grandmother had died. Furthermore, Reggie remembers calculating later that the grandmother's last shudder of breath—for they hear all of the details later that morning at Angela's mother's house—came at approximately the same time as a particularly intimate moment in the date.

After all that, Reggie feels she is part of all this somehow, and it is only right that she come to the wake. And although three dates does not represent much of anything by most people's standards, for lesbians it is tantamount to a commitment, so of course she's here, standing off to the side, feeling the wrinkles in her panty hose begin to gather in coils around her ankles, which she forces herself not to confirm visually lest she draw attention to herself.

Even though she *is* wearing panty hose, things feel pretty airy to her under the large floral-print skirt she's wearing; she wishes now she had opted for her usual attire of pants. She feels chilly, even with her pink angora sweater. She sneaks a peek at her ankles after all, and the nylons are looking rather elephantine, just as she suspected. This really draws attention, she thinks, to her Birkenstocks, which, though not appropriate, she concedes are still better than the Adidas, her next-best viable option. It is when she looks back up, past the humongous pink and yellow flowers of her skirt, that she realizes she is the only one here not wearing traditional black. She slumps against the wall.

"Regina!" Angela's fierce and watery whisper startles her, but before she can react in any way she finds herself in the vice grip of Angela's mournful hug. With her arms pinned to her side, Regina awkwardly pats at Angela's kidney region or thereabouts while Angela sobs loudly in her ear.

Regina E. Schnackenberg, she thinks, *you're not in Wisconsin anymore.*

Reggie came to New York a scant six months ago to become a writer, finding nothing among the cornfields and cows of Ixonia, Wisconsin, worthy of her self-assessed extraordinary talent. Her parents seemed surprised when—a year before Reggie was due to graduate from the university at Platteville—she announced that she intended to leave those hallowed halls where once her high school teacher and some other boys—students at the time—made a cow climb to the third floor of the elevatorless ag building as a prank: Cows are notoriously incapable of going *down* stairs. Reggie doesn't remember how they got the cow out.

That her parents seemed surprised is surprising to Reggie. After all, when you name a girl in a German Protestant town "Regina," shouldn't you expect the unexpected? It was her mother who came up with the name. An avid fan of royalty, Eleanor Schnackenberg kept a rather hefty scrapbook of clippings of anything pertaining to royal families, England's in particular. The scrapbook had a special appendix for Princess Grace of Monaco, showing that it was possible for anyone to achieve royal status, and another appendix for King Edward and Wallis Warfield Simpson, showing that things don't always go as planned. The appendixes were both now yellow and crumbling, though Reggie's mother still thumbed through them, one or the other, depending on her mood, with some regularity. Reggie's father, Otto Schnackenberg, who might have objected to the name Regina, was too busy repairing shoes, singing in a barber shop quartet, and racing slot cars on the special course set up in the basement to notice much about names.

Here at the present moment in Brooklyn, Reggie manages to slither free from the clamp of the grieving Angela's arms.

"Angie, honey, let's sit down, okay?" she suggests, leading the red-nosed Angela to a nearby chair while surreptitiously checking her own ribs for fractures. Angela blows her nose loudly. They make their way to the vinyl-padded folding chairs, which let out a rather indecorous sound when they sit down. Reggie feels an impulse to laugh, but seeing Angela's drippy face makes her think better of it.

The only wake Reggie had been to in Ixonia was when Mr. Berger had been in some sort of freak hay-baling accident just outside of town. There was crying, of course, but it was very quiet, discreet. Reggie had seen worse at a screening of *Love Story* in nearby Oconomowoc when she was in high school.

With Angela shudder-sobbing next to her, Reggie hears a murmur ripple through the room and notices an elderly woman with heavy black shoes and a wooden cane hobbling down the aisle toward the coffin at the front of the room. Reggie's eyes are not the only ones on the old woman, and she watches to try to determine why. A long dramatic silence ensues while the woman walks and walks—and walks—down the thirty-foot aisle. About ten paces from the coffin, the old woman throws down her cane and runs, catapulting herself onto the body in the coffin.

"Angela! Angela!" she shrieks. "How could you do this to me?"

Reggie looks quickly to her date, who is weeping afresh, then back again at the coffin, confused, until she realizes the grandmother's name must also be Angela.

Two men hurry to the old woman, who is shouting laments at the body while clinging fiercely to it, and try to pull her off. She is apparently less frail than she first appeared. Reggie notices, off to the side, a young fellow of about twenty in a houndstooth jacket with suede patches at the elbows—the sedated sister's boyfriend, Eddie or Freddie, Regina thinks she remembers—holding on to the end of the coffin.

"Hey," he is saying in a loud stage whisper. "Hey, somebody help me! The casket's slipping off these things." And indeed, with four bodies now variously positioned over, on, and in the coffin, it is beginning to slide backward off the tastefully draped horses on which it rests.

At last they wrest the old woman from the body and lead her to a chair. Her hands cover her face. Her knees buckle suddenly, and it looks like she's about to faint, but the two men hold her firmly by the elbows.

Sympathetic murmurs surface behind Reggie, and then whispers.

"Her sistah," one woman says knowingly, with a pronounced Brooklyn accent.

"Ohhh!" replies the listener, in a steady upward ascent of understanding.

"They were close," the first woman confides, as if this explains it all. "The Pasquinelli sistahs," she adds, despite the fact that Angela the Elder had married Frankie Colletti more than fifty years ago and the sister, Rosa, had been married to Myron Friedman for forty-eight years.

"Ahhh!" says the second woman, satisfied.

Eddie or Freddie is slumped against the wall tugging at his collar and wiping his face with a hanky, having been rescued from casket-catching duty by two funeral parlor employees. Reggie wonders if *he* will faint, and there is no one to hold his suede-covered elbows.

Then Reggie spots the cane still lying in the aisle, just a foot or two away. She picks it up, thinking she'll give it to Rosa, but then realizes she hasn't got the nerve to enter the knot of Pasquinellis, Collettis, and Friedmans. She turns to Angela the

Younger to give her the cane, but she's no longer there. She's holding the sedated sister's head to her bosom while both women shriek and cry and gesticulate. At the front of the room a tight circle has formed around Rosa, who keeps trying to make a break again for Angela the Elder. The din in the cavernous room—at least twice as large and high as the homey little funeral parlors back in Ixonia—is overwhelming.

Reggie feels a sudden need for air. She leans the cane against a chair and makes her way to the back of the room. Before walking out the door, she turns for a moment and surveys the chaos. She shakes her head in disbelief. *What,* she wonders, *will the fourth date bring?*

Pigeon Hill

Leslie Anne Leasure

Sara taught me to hold my breath when the dust blew down across Pigeon Hill. "The air is poison," she said. "The water is worse." She measured *worse* in millionths per liter. Sara wore her hair short, bangs back, clipped with pink plastic barrettes.

She told me each ounce of the dirt on Pigeon Hill was like evil fairy dust—loaded with cancer, mysterious illnesses, and lowered property values.

For years a company had been dumping something called polychlorinated biphenyls into the landfills and washing chemicals into the sewer system. I didn't know anything about it.

On Pigeon Hill, the 7-Eleven accepts food stamps and the playground behind the Housing Authority is called Rape Park. The Pentecostal church on the corner has revivals every other weekend, and Lucy Deckard hasn't taken her Christmas lights down since her boy died in December '63.

I had startled Sara as I came out of the trees behind the trailer park, and she dropped her beaker. It was the summer of

'89, or just about. I had two weeks left of my senior year.

"Damn it." She knelt and picked up the glass with gloved hands. "Sorry. You scared me."

I was just as surprised to find her there. I was taking the short-cut home from school. Sara worked for a student environmental group at the university, testing pollution levels in the dirt.

I knelt to help her. "Can I give you a hand?"

She caught my wrist. "You'd better not. This is like touching Chernobyl."

Her hand, gloved, on my skin. A small scar under her eye, a birthmark on her throat, blond hair dark with sweat. The tender crook between forearm and bicep. I wondered if I paused noticeably before moving my hand back. (Don't look up from your locker in gym class. Don't hug a second too long. Don't want.)

Sara said the EPA was washing its hands in blood. "And women? The miscarriage rate is thirty percent higher out here."

"Really?" I knew my father couldn't sell our house or even get a loan to fix it up because the value had dropped. He looked at the peeling asphalt siding with a kind of helpless rage.

"I'm Sara," she said, and really looked at me for the first time. She had an expression I couldn't identify, and I figured it was because I was so tall. I was five-eleven and growing.

"Tara," I said.

"We rhyme," she laughed. "Sara, Tara."

I stood there, watching her wrap the beaker's remains in paper. The late-afternoon sun washed the poisoned ground with dappled sepia.

Back in 1908, there were three men who lived on a hill in Indiana. One, named Glasgow, lived near the bottom of the hill. He raised rabbits and pigeons. Another, named Wade, lived near the top of the hill. His house nestled in a grove of flowering locust. The third man, Ross, worked at the mill near Glasgow.

The railroad ran past the base of the hill, and the trains stopped at the mill for grain. Ross, along with others, shoveled the grain into the cars. Spilled grain washed into the creek. Glasgow's pigeons ate the grain, drank the water, and flew up to roost in the locust grove.

Wade and Ross laughed together, and Wade said, "If the pigeons get any worse up here, people will call it Pigeon Hill."

And so they did.

My grandmother, Verna, made her coffee with instant crystals and hot tap water. We lived in her house on Lemon Lane, near the crest of Pigeon Hill. My father was a truck driver for the RCA plant and was gone for a week at a time. When I was ten and my sister Courtney was six, my mother got so wasted she locked us out of our house in the middle of winter. Social Services came, and Courtney and I spent a week in foster care until my father got home from California. Mom had been in and out of halfway houses and rehabs since then. Sometimes she'd call in the middle of the night and apologize for being a terrible mother, but when she did you could always hear the distinct sounds of a bar in the background. I loved her, even then.

The day I met Sara my house never looked so small. The wallpaper was stained with Verna's cigarettes, and the pictures of me and Courtney looked like a whole other life.

I could hear the police scanner in the living room. In the mornings, it was the police scanner, followed by the soaps, then back to the scanner for afternoon rush hour. Verna took the obituaries with coffee and dry toast.

Courtney sat at the kitchen table flipping through a *Cosmo*. I dumped my backpack on the floor and pulled a pop from the refrigerator.

"Dad call?" I asked Courtney. Dad would call around rush hour to check in. He'd been doing that for years.

"Not yet." She held the magazine out to show me two prom dresses. "What do you think is better, the low neckline or the lace?"

"Ugh, neither." I wasn't planning on going to my senior prom, but Courtney, a freshman, had been asked by a guy in my class. She already had a dress too. "Do they all have to look so...puffy?"

She slapped the magazine down on the table. "I don't know why I'm even asking you."

This was our ongoing argument. "What, just because I think it's stupid to spend enough money to buy a car on a dress, a haircut, and fifty-two tanning sessions?"

"It's your *senior* prom," she said as if that were point, set, match.

"There isn't anyone I want to go with, anyway," I said, knowing that wasn't entirely true.

A month earlier I had looked up *lesbian* in the dictionary, even though I already knew the meaning. The printed definition, *female homosexual,* didn't help me. I wanted to see the word to make sure I really existed. If there were a word for it, I wouldn't be the only one and the way I felt about girls wouldn't be some kind gross perversion.

I had this dream. There was this woman, and we were playing Frisbee on a beach by the ocean, laughing and chasing each other around the sand. And then we kissed, and her lips tasted like strawberry lip gloss. And I woke up and thought, *I'm gay.*

Up until then the thought was in my mind, but it was sort of translucent. I sensed the outline of it, like a ghost or something you can see out of the corner of your eye but that disappears when you turn to look at it directly.

I wanted to see Sara again. I thought about her all through school the next day. I laughed at myself, thinking I had only talked to her for fifteen minutes while she took her dirt samples. "We rhyme," she'd said. I could hear the sound of her laughing. After school I took the same route home but didn't see her. Not that day, and not for a few days after that. I wondered if she was some kind of apparition, like the dream, sans lip gloss. I even spent part of a Saturday wandering around the college campus, hoping I might run into her, but I didn't. If I had known her last name, I would've tried to call her. At night I constructed elaborate scenarios in which I rescued her from everything from psychopaths to dragons, and I imagined playing an amazing saxophone solo under her dorm-room window even though I'd never picked up an instrument in my life.

I finally saw Sara, just about when I'd given up hope, at the creek near the railroad tracks. She coaxed water into plastic bottles and labeled each one with a black marker. "Why is it called Pigeon Hill?" she asked me.

The mill was long since gone, as was Glasgow, but I told her the story as she panned for PCBs in the stream.

"A few years ago the newspaper said it was because so many pigeons roosted in the dead tree over there," I told her. "But they were just guessing."

She glanced up at the tree, squinted, and cocked her head to the side. She always looked up and to the left when she was thinking about something. "Locust tree," she said, naming it and shaking her head. "They're really sensitive to toxins."

Sara took off her gloves and sat next to me. On each of her fingers were silver rings with different stones. Her hands were long and bony. *She's irresistible when political*, I thought. I felt guilty for not paying attention.

"I didn't think it was so bad," I said, twining long grass around my thumb. "I mean, they wouldn't let people live in a place that was actually dangerous, right?"

"Yeah, sure," she rolled onto her side and leaned her head

on her hand. "The chemicals from the capacitor plant were poured down the drain. They ended up at the treatment plant, which sold the sewage as 'organic' sludge to farmers. Loaded with this stuff, all over the place. Free fill. The corporations are very concerned. According to their press releases."

We were less than a foot apart, lying on the ground and facing each other. Her pack rested at her back, and we heard the traffic from the road and the PA system from the lumberyard behind us. I wanted to tell her that I'd looked for her, and that I'd missed her, but then I thought she'd probably think I was weird.

I picked a dandelion and flicked the flower at her. "Mama had a baby and its head popped off," I hummed.

"That's weird, isn't it?" She picked up the flower and peered at it. "I mean, where does that little song come from anyway?"

I shrugged. "I don't know. It's just one of those things you pick up."

"Yeah, but I grew up in Pennsylvania and we said it too. I mean, it's not the kind of thing you see in a book or anything." She rolled the flower head in her cupped hand like dice. "Did you ever wonder why those things are so violent? I mean, what about that lullaby, 'The cradle will fall, and down will come baby, cradle and all…'?"

"You think too much." I laughed and thumbed another dandelion at her.

She slapped it away, reached over with the first one, and held it under my chin. "Mmm, do you like butter?"

I felt the petals at my throat as she softly rolled the dandelion along my jawline and down. "That's not a buttercup," I told her.

"I know." Then she said, "I was hoping we'd run into each other again."

"Really?" Rush. Saxophones. Dragons. I tried to breathe normally. "Why?"

She rolled onto her back, put her hands behind her head, and drew her knees up like she was about to do sit-ups. "Well. There's this party up on the hill, and I thought maybe you'd like to go with me or something."

I wondered about the "or something."

"Sure," I said. "That would be great."

On Pigeon Hill, Elias Grumman keeps watch for all of the schoolkids in the morning. Ostensibly he's only waiting for his granddaughter to get on the bus, but the mothers know he's there every morning, sipping a cherry slush. In winter he wears insulated Carhartt overalls and Lucy Deckard brings him hot chocolate. No one would be lost on his watch.

A pinwheel spins in Jerry York's square of yard. His daughter won it at the Fun Frolic two years before. All the color has faded from it, but it still spins and makes a whispering noise you can't quite make out .

At the 7-Eleven, teenage girls with denim jackets and big hair share the pay phones with drug dealers. Cars with EASY DOES IT bumper stickers jam the parking lot at five-thirty and eight for the weekly Alcoholics Anonymous meetings. It's a good place to go if you're looking to play euchre or bum some coffee and a smoke.

Courtney stared at herself in the mirror and adjusted her neckline. "What do you think?"

I sat on the corner of my bed debating between jeans and parachute pants. "If you're going for heavy-metal princess, you're there," I told her.

"Nice," she said into her mirror. "And who are you supposed to be? Pat Benatar?"

I ignored her and decided on jeans, a denim jacket, and a muscle tee.

"Where are you going anyway?" she asked me.

"Just a party." I watched her as she arranged her hair. I felt like a lumbering giant next to her. "Really, have a good time tonight."

She cocked an eyebrow at me and grinned.

"You too, sis. Ugh, wait a sec. Let me fix this." She turned and straightened my collar, which was always twisted. "There. Better."

And I thought: I would miss this when she knew.

The party was at a house I'd seen before. It was a two-story bungalow near the highest point on the hill. A limestone wall with a steep staircase leading up to the porch. Sara met me there. She wore a russet gypsy skirt, a V-neck T-shirt, and black combat boots. She hugged me and I felt her breasts press against my jacket. Her hair smelled like apples.

"Hey," she said. "You look great."

"You too." *You feel great,* I thought.

Some kind of purple flower twined up the railing of the staircase to the porch, and there were more flowers than I thought I'd ever seen vying for moonlight in the front patch of yard. The house looked like one of those old Southern mansions, slightly decayed, but the plants made up for it.

Sara stopped me just as we were about to go up. She was suddenly as serious as when measuring biphenyls. Her fingernails were painted purple, like the flowers along the staircase. "I have to tell you something."

"Yes?" I asked, and held my exhale.

"This party?" Sara put one hand on my shoulder and looked me straight in the eye. "Lesbians are throwing this party."

I couldn't look away. "Oh, yeah?"

"Yeah." She nodded. "Are you okay with that?"

I suddenly felt like laughing but didn't. She stood there, I think, waiting for me to run screaming into the arms of a drunken frat guy.

"Sure," I said, as seriously as I could while smiling. "Thanks for the warning."

She exhaled for both of us and took my hand. "Come on."

If outside was fetid Southern fertility, inside was bohemian New York. Well, at least as I imagined it. Beaded doorways, beanbag chairs, and antique divans. Artichoke hearts, truffles, the obligatory mango. Fondue trays and red wine. In the background, k.d. lang crooned from her *Shadowland* album. The hostesses were two stout lesbians, Emmy and Tina, who acted mama to a pulsing horde of girls. We were all waiting for someone to make the first move, maybe, untrained in such gestures.

"Hey, look, Joan Baez brought Joan Jett," Emmy chuckled from her beanbag chair, waving to Sara. Sara rolled her eyes as we wandered though the house.

A collage of old Brownie cameras and lenses stared at us from the wall, all placed around a velvet Elvis painting, random mosaic tiles, and rhinestone eyeglass frames. Tina was a sculptor, Sara told me as I stared at the arrangement.

"I thought they just made statues," I said.

"It's called an installation." She handed me a glass of wine. "I think."

I sipped the wine, turned to her, and was startled by how close to me she was standing. "Is there anything you don't know?" I asked quickly.

Sara blushed and looked down. "God, do I sound like a huge know-it-all?"

"No, I didn't mean it like that," I said, then realized she was nervous. I changed the topic. "Do I really look like Joan Jett?"

She giggled. "No...your hair is too short."

"Okay, and who the hell is Joan Baez?"

Somewhere, my sister was giving her virginity to the boy who brought her the wrist corsage and gold-tipped champagne glasses. My father hurled along I-70, bending the speed limit and talking baseball on his CB radio. My mother was shooting pool and thinking tonight might be different. Verna watched Chinese tanks bear down on a single protester on the eleven o'clock news.

Sara and I sat on the back porch of the house on Pigeon Hill, counting stars and wondering if it was safe to touch each other. She told me that basil needed to be planted late in the season, and potatoes according to the moon cycles.

"From what you say about the groundwater, I'm surprised anything grows here," I told her.

"Yeah," she said, and turned to me. The small scar under her eye caught shadow, and she gave me the gentlest of smiles. "But there's always hope."

As Sara kissed me, Elias Grumman dreamed of wingless angels and Lucy Deckard turned off her Christmas lights.

The Accident

Mary Vermillion

All I wanted from Emery was a trip to Aldoburg Studios and a formal portrait for the living room. "We've been together two years," I said, "and we still don't have any good photos of us as a couple."

Stray curls from Emery's French braid clung to her neck. "Maybe you could paint us," she said. "Your portrait of my parents is gorgeous." She shifted her silverware on her plate and gazed at the remains of a chicken breast.

I squeezed some lemon into my iced tea and waited for her to continue.

"If the photographer figures things out, I could lose my job like those teachers in Callough." Emery had spent the summer obsessing over two teachers released by their superintendent. Both were gay. "That," Emery said, "was at a public school."

I made my usual response. "But it was an elementary school. And those teachers were new." Emery had taught P.E. at Sacred Heart High School for nine years. "And you're a winning coach," I said.

"You think that matters?" Emery began clearing the table. "You know my teams are like family. I can't believe you want to jeopardize that."

"We could go out of town to get our picture taken," I offered. "Lou could help us find a lesbian photographer."

"Lou's the answer for everything." She yanked the dishwasher open. "I bet she can help those teachers get their jobs back too."

Lou and I had traded *Charlie's Angels* cards in junior high and flirted throughout high school. Last month I visited her in Iowa City.

"We're not like Lou," Emery said. "We live in a small town. You've forgotten that."

But I hadn't. She reminded me every day.

{}

Biking on F86 usually soothed me. Cattle munched lazily, and clover sweetened the air. But I kept thinking about Lou. During my last visit she cut my hair at her salon, Making Waves. "Can I have my way with you?" she joked, wielding her clippers. When she finished, she and her partner ran their fingers over my buzz cut. It made me feel lighter, freer. So had the pride festival. I hadn't been to one in a while, so I laughed and joined Lou when she raised her fist and shouted, "Out is in!" Three or four drag queens blew us kisses, and she draped her arm around my shoulder. Emery always refused to hold my hand in public. She greeted my new haircut with raised eyebrows and a weak smile.

I leaned over my handlebars and pedaled faster. The sky darkened, and the cicadas grew louder. Around the curve was a white billowy thing. A little blond girl. Her nightgown whipped around her, and she waved her arms wildly. I skidded to a stop and knelt beside her. She was four, maybe five, with tears streaming down her cheeks. "My daddy's stuck. He's hurt bad."

She ran across the road and pointed down the embankment. It sloped gradually at first, then dropped into a culvert. At the bottom was a pickup with its wheels in the air. A man was pinned underneath from the waist down. A baseball cap lay a couple of feet from his head. "Daddy!" the girl screamed.

I couldn't move. My father had been killed in a car accident when I was nine.

The girl started wailing. "Daddy, Daddy, wake up!"

I gently touched her shoulder. "Listen to me," I said. "Your daddy will be okay." I prayed I was right. "I'm going to get help."

{}

I couldn't have found the accident again if it hadn't been for the police and the ambulance lights. The girl was perched on the hood of a patrol car. Her feet dangled above the ground, and her tininess sent a chill through me. How had she climbed that steep embankment? The cop standing next to her was pudgy like the teddy bear she hugged to her chest. She wasn't wearing a nightgown after all, but a large T-shirt over a swimsuit. Maybe her father was teaching her to swim. When I was about her age, my dad taught me to dog paddle. And he let me ride his favorite horse, Medallion Stallion. I nestled in front of him, proud and safe, while he handled the reins.

The girl sobbed. "I want Daddy."

The cop folded his arms across his paunch. "Like I said, sweetie, your daddy needs a doctor."

"I want Mommy."

"Mommy's waiting at the hospital. Pretty soon you can ride in my car, and we'll go see her."

"I want Daddy now," she said, but her voice was quiet. She looked exhausted.

I stepped forward. "Remember me?" I smiled at her, and she glanced up from her bear.

"You the one who called this in?" the cop asked.

I nodded.

"Guess you were in the right place at the right time."

{}

At the hospital, the girl huddled next to a woman who clutched a wad of Kleenex. I felt like an intruder, but I needed to know how the man was doing.

"I'm Gret MacDermott," I said. "I found your husband."

She gazed at me and smoothed a wisp of her blond hair. "Trish O'Brien," she whispered. Everything about her was thin: voice, hair, face, arms. "Keith is still unconscious. They're going to fly him to Omaha." She pulled her little girl closer. "He's never been in a hospital before except when Julie was born."

I'd spent a lot of time in the hospital the month after my mom's stroke. I drove her there five days a week—three for physical therapy, and two for speech and occupational. I also fixed her meals and helped her bathe until she regained some movement on the left side of her body.

"Mommy," Julie said, "I want to see Daddy."

"Soon, honey." Trish kissed the top of her daughter's head and stared right past me.

After my dad's funeral, I found my mom staring at her only photograph of my brother Joseph. He had died thirteen years before I was born when he was only six weeks old. In the photo, Joseph is tightly wrapped in his blankets; like my mother, bundled in her grief, he is unable to move.

{}

When I got home at one A.M., Emery was sleeping on the couch. I stood next to her, savoring the knowledge that she'd waited up for me even though I'd called her from the hospital and told her not to. A lamp glowed over her dark wavy hair, and a tennis magazine covered her chest, rising and falling with her breath. She was on her way to a tennis match when we first met. She needed to rent her top floor, and I needed a place of my own near my mother. It seemed simple at first. Mom would get through rehab and I'd get back to Des Moines—back to my life as a struggling artist, my part-time jobs and part-time girl-friends. But I never felt like Emery's tenant. We took turns making dinner for each other and went on long walks afterward. Then one afternoon I came home early and found Emery crying. "I don't know what I'll do when you leave," she said. I brushed away her tears with my fingertips and kissed her. She gasped, eyes open wide, but after a moment she kissed me back—her tongue tentative then eager, her hand trembling when it found my breast. She was delighted and awed by every touch, every curve, every rhythm. I wanted her always to believe that we—she and I together—were a miracle.

But I wasn't sure what she believed anymore—this beautiful woman sleeping on the couch. I lifted the magazine from her chest, and she opened her eyes. "Gret," she said, "are you okay?" She sat up. "How's the man you found?"

"He regained consciousness before they flew him to Omaha." I sat next to her on the couch. "But he's paralyzed from the waist down."

Emery put her arm around me, and I rested my head on her shoulder.

"He's a farmer. He has wife and a daughter who's only four." I began to cry.

"You saved his life," Emery whispered. "You saved their family."

I listened to her heartbeat and wondered if it was possible to save a family. "What if I were in the hospital?" I asked.

She stroked my hair. "That's not going to happen."

"But what if it did?"

"I'd visit you all the time and bring you whatever you wanted."

"What about the admission forms? Could I call you my partner?"

Emery stopped stroking my hair. She hadn't even told her parents about us.

{}

After work the next day I rode my bike to the O'Brien farm. I didn't expect anyone to be there. I just wanted to see their home. It was a white two-story shaded by huge oaks. A tire swing hung from a weeping willow, and across the gravel road a cornfield rolled toward a row of pine. It was the kind of thing I'd painted in junior high.

I propped my bike against the house. The front porch was cluttered with Julie's toys—a Big Wheel, a Fisher-Price house, a half-dressed Barbie. I peered through the screen door into the living room. On a table were two pies and a plate of cookies, probably from neighbors. When my dad died, our freezer was packed with casseroles. I heated portions of them, urging my mom to eat, but she'd lost her interest in food—and in me. She didn't even notice my tears when we had to sell Medallion Stallion and the farm.

I wondered what would happen to the O'Brien farm, and I studied a picture on an end table. Keith stood strong behind his wife and daughter. Would he be grateful that Julie had been a brave little girl, or would he resent his new and damaged life?

{}

"You're in the paper," Emery said without looking up from the mushrooms she was chopping. She wore the amethyst earrings I'd given her for her birthday. The fan on the other side of the kitchen blew her flowered skirt against her legs. "Some reporters called for you."

"Did they say anything about Keith O'Brien?"

She pulled a green pepper out of the fridge. "No. They want to interview you." Her face was expressionless.

"What's wrong?" I asked.

"One woman wants to interview you here. She was very nosy and wanted to know who I was."

"I helped save a man's life last night," I said, "and you're worried someone is going to think you're a dyke."

"You know I hate that word."

"Yeah." I grabbed the newspaper off the kitchen table.

"I have a right to privacy."

"I'll have the interview somewhere else. After all, this is your house." I waited for her to protest that it was *our* house, but she didn't. I stomped upstairs to my "studio."

It used to be my bedroom, so my easels stood between a futon and a dresser. Above the futon hung a painting of Emery serving a tennis ball, ready to unleash herself on a hapless opponent. It was my only painting of her that she let me hang. The rest were in the closet—gorgeous, sexy paintings tucked behind my out-of-season clothes.

I flopped down on the futon and looked at the paper. Keith O'Brien's accident was on the front page. When his pickup flipped, his daughter had been suspended upside down, hanging from her seat belt. She freed herself and found her father under the vehicle. She tried to climb the embankment to get help, but it was too steep, so she crawled through a drainpipe to the other side of the road where she hailed cyclist Margaret MacDermott. There was a quote from a cop: "It's tough for little kids to leave their parents. Julie had a lot of courage to leave her father and crawl through that drainpipe." I hadn't known about the pipe. It must have seemed like a never-ending tunnel.

{}

Three days after the accident, I finally checked on my mother. She was sitting in front of her TV, picking at some noodles.

"Did you make that?" I asked. She hadn't done much cooking since her stroke.

"Someone from church brought it over." She muted the TV.

"How are you feeling?"

"The same." She stared at a commercial for toilet bowl cleaner. On top of the TV was the photo of my brother Jeremy. "Could you run to Hy-Vee for me?" she asked.

"Why don't we go together?" Her doctor had suggested she get out more. "Or we could take a walk."

"Already took one," she said, "with Rosie from church."

"I don't know Rosie."

"That's because you don't go to church."

I'd set myself up for that one. "What do you need from the store?"

"I've got a list." She hefted a gigantic black purse onto her lap. Apparently she'd gotten a lot stronger.

"How come that Emery never comes over here with you? I thought you two were..." She trailed off, failing to find an appropriate word for what she imagined we were doing.

"We are," I said. "She's busy."

"Too busy if you ask me." My mother handed me the list. "I saw you in the paper—you and that little girl." She set her purse on the end table next to her unfinished noodles. "You rode quite a way to get help. It must feel good," she said, "to save someone's life."

{}

Keith O'Brien had been a heavyweight wrestler at Iowa State, but he looked small in his hospital bed, propped up with pillows and surrounded by flowers. What could I possibly say to him, someone who would never walk again? Why had I let his wife talk me into coming?

"I'm Gret MacDermott," I said.

He didn't answer.

I tried not to think about my mother's silence and stillness those days after her stroke, those weeks after my dad died. "Your little girl was very brave," I said. "You must be proud of her."

His eyes were bleary with painkillers—or tears maybe. He wouldn't be able to father any more children. He'd probably have to sell his farm.

"You wanted to see me?" I asked.

He moved his arms from underneath his covers and winced. "I wanted to thank you," he whispered. "Because of you, I got a chance to see Julie grow up. I got a future."

In the midst of immense loss, he was thinking about the future. I thought about my own, about Emery and my paintings in her closet. I imagined little Julie hanging upside down in her father's car, her arms and legs thrashing through the air as she struggled to free herself. I wondered how it would feel to stare down a long, dark tunnel, knowing you were leaving a wreck behind.

Upholstered Love
Sue Katz

"Tribadism!" I gasped. "It's been so long I almost forgot the name."

Shoshi choreographed our movements as only an active femme can do. We stretched out on her bed with our heads in opposite corners. Our legs were spread open and intertwined so that we could grind our crotches together. Mine was bony, hers like spongy cashmere. She held onto my thighs and I onto hers as we pulled ourselves rhythmically, clit against clit, wet slit against wet slit, the friction of genital full contact.

{}

It took us almost twenty years to arrive at this position. We met in 1972, in the revolutionary days. My girlfriend Lana was the drummer in an early commercial lesbian band. When they played in Provincetown, already developing into Cape Cod's queer resort, me and my best mate Muffer would join them, sometimes with Muffer's steady Arlene. The beaches were sizzling, as was the gay nightlife.

Shoshi was the waitress at the Tattle, where Lana's band was booked biweekly throughout the summer. Shoshi took good care of Muffer and me, made us feel like VIPs as we hung around, set after set. With her lanolin brown curls, her generous curves, her walnut tanned skin, and her hefty cleavage, it wasn't hard to be fond of Shoshi.

Shoshi let us stay at her rental on weekends when Lana and the band were gigging on the Cape. During the days, she would show us hidden dune beaches where we could take off our clothes and roll around on the heated silk sand. Sometimes we smoked dope and sometimes we dropped acid. Shoshi was into hallucinogenics, big-time, even when she knew she had to get to the bar for work that night. She claimed that grinding her teeth throughout her shift was a small price to pay.

Part of our mutual fascination was the difference in our worldviews. For Shoshi, the dark smoke of the bar and the blinding scorch of the sun had obviously obliterated any news of politics, even of the growing women's movement.

"How much you make an hour at the Tattle?" Muffer asked her one day as we were reclining at the edge of the sea.

"Depends on tips," she answered lazily.

"I mean besides tips."

"Nothing."

"Nothing?"

"Nothing. Just tips. But I don't do so bad."

"Thought about organizing the local waitresses?" I asked.

"Try not to think about much of anything in the summer." She pushed a joint my way. "Have a toke of this and chill."

One weekend, as we all hung out on the City Hall steps in Provincetown, I admitted to everyone that I wasn't sure I wanted to spend my whole summer following Lana's band, hearing the same repertoire over and over.

Muffer laughed. "Yeah, but you're too much of a jealous maniac to leave Lana alone with her groupies."

Lana and I looked at each other and we knew it was the truth. There was a big debate in the movement about monogamy at the time, giving all the sluts a good ideological justification for messing around.

Shoshi interrupted our dance of glances. "I have tonight off," she told me, "and I was going to go to the Baytide for a change. Want to come with me?" The Baytide was another local gay bar, but mostly for gay men.

I looked at Lana. "For me it's just work," she smiled. "Go with Shoshi. Do whatever you want."

Then came the dance of the nonverbal negotiation. I looked at Muffer with a questioning face. She in turn tilted her head at Arlene, her semi-comatose druggie girlfriend. Arlene shrugged, Muffer nodded, and I turned back to Lana with raised eyebrows, as if asking, "Last chance. Sure you don't mind?" and Lana smiled. The process concluded, I turned to Shoshi and said, "Great! Let's do it." Living life in collectives offered a certain sense of safety but cost a lot of time in polling everyone about everything.

In the end, Arlene got sick off some suspicious tranq, so Muffer stayed behind to hold Arlene's head over the toilet. Shoshi and I were off to the dark little club alone. We took the long way around, visiting the nighttime beach to smoke a massive joint and watch the waves, lit like neon by the low moon. At the Baytide we hardly knew anyone among the crowd of gay men, so we could drink our Cokes and dance our dances uninterrupted.

We were surprised that the club played ballads—that usually only happened in the lesbian bars—and when "A Song for You" came on the jukebox, Shoshi and I had our first slow dance. I scooped her up, my arms cradling her soft girth, and began the dyke double grind, our own groin-centered version of the fox-trot. Shoshi followed my lead with an appealing lightness and grace.

Shoshi weighed about one hundred eighty pounds at that point, and dancing with her was like dancing with a waterbed. She undulated in infinite softness against my bones. She padded out the space around me with sizzling, fleshy upholstery that I wanted to fold into my arms. I closed my eyes and sank into her perfect swaying. As the song ended I felt myself being firmly pushed up against a wall.

"Let's go fuck," she whispered.

"Fuck? Us?"

"Let's go finish off that vertical fantasy with a horizontal reality."

"I can't, Shoshi. You know I'm with Lana."

"You don't want me?"

"It's not that..."

"Then what's the problem?" She leaned against me, yearning and yielding. Her abundant soft breasts pressed against my rib cage. My pussy contracted in response. I felt gawky, awkward, but I was very much a faithful fool. Not only did Lana have flirtatious propensities, she had fans and followers galore. In our little world, she was a rock star. I wasn't going to give her the excuse that, just a few months later when she and Muffer would have clandestine sex, it turned out she didn't need anyway.

I pulled myself away from Shoshi, feeling like a cunt-tease. "I'm sorry. I can't. I think we need to go." We walked back in silence and I stopped at the door of the Tattle. As she headed for her apartment, I watched her layers of flesh swaying with each step. How sorry I was to give up my chance to bury my face in her plentitude.

Two weeks later we were back down the Cape, this time staying with other friends of Lana's. Shoshi's house was full of visitors, including her kid sister, and we made joint plans for Saturday morning. About ten of us headed for the giant white dunes of Truro. Our cooler was filled with provisions and my pocket was stuffed with acid dots. Those were still the days of pure Leary LSD dropped in little pink circles on a piece of blotter paper, which we cut up into individual squares and swallowed.

Shoshi led us for what felt like miles down the coast, away from the parking area. She was a master of ocean privacy. With no one else around, we disrobed and dropped the drugs. As the high started to come on, I became addicted to scaling the dunes for the thrill of sliding down on my naked belly. The fine sand provided a silken toboggan run for my drug-sensitive skin. Once I descended on my back, feet first, and nearly had an orgasm as the rivulets of sand split sensuously between my legs.

Shoshi led a pack of tripping primevals into the waves while the rest of us lazed on the shore, our backs propped against the tallest dune, watching the mesmerizing patterns only the combination of LSD and stunning landscape can produce.

I swung my head in a purposeful arc, the view passing as if in individual frames, to look at the woman next to me, Nina, Shoshi's sister. Apparently she was staying on the Cape for a few weeks because she had been advised to lay low. She was a shoplifter for hire—she stole to order. She was one of several girls who worked for a Robin Hood–like criminal in Providence, Rhode Island, who had just been busted.

I saw how stoned she was from the way she sank into the sand next to me.

"You okay?" I asked.

"The waves. The waves," she drooled.

"Nice," I said, noncommittally.

"The grandeur of the ocean makes you realize how tiny man really is."

"Man?"

"Yeah. You know, humankind."

"We're not men," I said. "You're like your sister. I've had this same argument with her."

"Argument?" she asked. "I didn't know this was an argument."

"Yeah, that's part of the argument, I guess." I was always amazed to find women who hadn't yet experienced that passionate click of feminism.

Nina and I lay back in silence. I felt my nipples cooking in the sun, but I was too ripped to get it together to reach for a shirt.

Our quiet was disturbed by a rushing noise from above, followed by a sickening clunk! I heard a moan close-by, and at some distance, I heard men's voices. I jumped up, looking toward the top of the dune. A group of teenagers or young men were rolling stones down at us. I yelled to the other prone women to move and then I saw Nina.

She was clutching the top of her skull with both hands, her head tucked tightly between bent knees. That clunk had been a rock meeting her skull. Blood began to seep out from between her fingers.

"Nina's hurt!" I called to everyone. The women along the dunes were scrambling away, crying in fear. Some were struggling into clothes in order to pursue our attackers. The bastards at top were yelling things. Muffer ran to call Shoshi and the others out of the water.

I knelt beside Nina. "Nina, talk to me. How do you feel?"

She was tensely balled up, holding her head as if it would crumble if she let go.

I knew some first aid. "Let me see your head, Nina. Here, relax your fingers. Let me check it. I know what to do." Under the influence of the acid, the blood seemed to flow in sparkling droplets, matting down her hair in a burst of glitter, coating her hands in red shimmers.

Shoshi arrived on the run. "Nina! My Nina!" She burst into tears on seeing the blood. "She's dying! She's killed!" Nina's body continued to tremble in fetal clutch.

"She's not dead or dying," I said calmly. "She's hurt and bleeding. Bring me a shirt or towel, Muffer."

I shook the sand out of the shirt while I continued to beg Nina to take away her hands and let me deal with the wound. Suddenly Shoshi pushed me aside and grabbed Nina's elbows, trying to drag her up into a standing position.

"What the hell are you doing, Shoshi?"

"I'll take her into the water to bathe her head with Mother Sea. We'll wash away all the bad vibes and she'll be fine. Come on, Nina. Come with me."

"Leave her alone!" I said. "You don't want that wound in water, or the bleeding will never stop. We have to apply pressure with this shirt."

"Pressure? It hurts her enough already. She's my sister. The waves will cleanse the cut."

I stopped to breathe, to figure out how to gain some control. Mayhem was beginning to take over. Shoshi's friends took her side and mine replied vociferously. A few were stumbling up the liquid sand hill to try to catch the assholes who had done it. Some of the women were cascading into a "bad trip" mode, verging on hysteria. I got a grip and realized that my personal responsibility was Nina. I concentrated on her.

Nina was rolled up in an impenetrable sphere and I was getting frightened at the amount of blood she was losing. As they all argued among themselves, I bent down to talk softly in her ear.

"I know first aid. The scalp bleeds a lot, so it's scary. We can stop the bleeding if you let me press on the cut with this cloth. Open your hands, Nina. Let me take care of things. You can trust me." I spoke with much greater assurance than I felt.

All the time I had my left arm out, restraining Shoshi, literally pushing her away. At last Muffer and Lana got it together to walk Shoshi down the beach. Within minutes I arrested the bleeding and Nina began to talk to us.

Everyone gathered around, calmer. We had to figure out how to get Nina back to the car and on to the hospital. We were still flying, hallucinating, tripping. Nina was too trembly to walk back so we took turns in pairs doing the crossed-hand sitting carry—something else I had learned in first aid. Even Arlene, Muffer's spacey girlfriend, took a turn. Like her sister, Nina was a big girl. It seemed like hours till we got back to the car. The effort sobered us up.

That night, sitting around Shoshi's living room, Nina resting on the couch in the corner with seven stitches in her scalp, Shoshi made a confession.

"I guess I finally understand about your women's liberation thing. Those guys—they just couldn't stand us all being women together, naked and happy. So they bombed us with rocks. Fuckin' violent maniacs."

Shoshi joined our working-class women's collective, but she didn't last long. She was thinking politically, seeing politically but she never really wanted to live politically. She fell in love with a pale autistic butch and went off to Brooklyn to play house. I think she wanted to put us behind her, guilty that she wasn't much of an activist. I hadn't heard a thing about Shoshi since then.

The Left started to disintegrate, so all the middle-class girls went to law school. I got really bummed out when Muffer's girlfriend Arlene totaled my Rambler while stoned on horse tranquilizer. She wouldn't take any responsibility. At least Muffer left her over that mess. I studied nursing before going to Nairobi for a long time, where I lived with a food distribution expert from Denmark. We moved to the Danish town of

Arhuus for a bunch of years, but when she ran off with a baker I came back to Boston.

{}

Muffer picked me up at the airport with her new girlfriend. She was kind enough to stop at Kmart on the way to her house so that I could stock up on my Jockey shorts. It was always the first thing I bought on visits to the States.

Back at their house, we sat down for a good gossip.

"So guess who called last week to wish me happy birthday?" Muffer said.

"Oh, shit," I cringed, "is this your way of pointing out that I forgot the big day?"

"No, I'm serious. Flash from the past. Guess."

"Your uncle?"

"Hey, that's not funny. They just tacked another fifteen years on to his sentence and transferred him to the penitentiary in fucking Florida."

"Sorry. So who called?"

"Arlene."

"Arlene?" I couldn't believe it. "She's still alive? You're still in touch?"

"Well, we weren't, but now we are."

"What happened? She ran out of downers and realized twenty years had passed?"

"Something like that. She's in California. Recovered, I think they say."

"From what?"

"It's a phrase. Clean and sober. She's done therapy and found herself and is into this twelve-step business. I guess they don't have it in Denmark."

"I've heard of it. So she found herself and then she found you. Just to say happy birthday?"

"More than that," Muffer said. "She also asked about you."

"Did you tell her to send a check to replace the Rambler?"

"As a matter of fact, that's just what she offered to do."

"Whoa! Let's start over. Arlene called you and established that she remembers birthdays and car accidents."

"She told me she feels she wronged you. That it's on her conscience. That she wants to unburden, make it up to you."

"Does the bitch have money? Is she working or something?" I couldn't picture Arlene holding a job. In fact, I could hardly picture her holding up her head.

"Somebody died, left her a bundle. She's living off the interest. Twenty grand a year."

I felt my usual angry response to hearing about unearned wealth, but I was curious what it might mean for me. "Go on. Go on."

"She asked me how to make it up to you, wrecking your car and all that. She said she thought she'd send you a grand."

"A thousand dollars? What did you say?"

"I said that would be nice."

"Does she know I'm in the States?"

"She knows you're coming, but not the timing. Thought we'd call and surprise her."

"Can I get more than a thousand?"

"We'll see."

Two days later, Muffer rang her up. "Arlene, guess who's sitting right next to me? Yeah, I told her what you said. Listen, I did some research like you asked." Muffer winked at me. "I'd say the car was worth at least fifteen hundred dollars. Here, you talk to her."

My principles went down the drain as I reached for the receiver. I had always said I wouldn't ever speak to her again. In Europe, people were scathing about the American recovery fad. Now all I could think about was getting my rightful slice.

"Hi, Arlene," I said with an attempt at dignity. "How are you doing?"

We chatted. I hinted at hard times: She was all upbeat. Finally I heard those magic words: "Would you permit me to make it up to you?"

I was nothing if not gracious. "Would I ever! Your timing is impeccable. It would help me settle in here."

"Where should I send the check?"

"You can send it here to Muffer," I told her. "I'll be here for a couple of weeks."

"You know that I love you. I always loved you," she said, and I heard that old whine but without all the chemical haze around it. "This has been sitting heavily on me a long time. Thanks for letting me make restitution."

I assented in vague mumbles. We exchanged addresses and I put down the phone.

Muffer and I looked at each other. She looked pretty satisfied with herself.

"Okay, what cut do you want?" I asked her.

"Ten percent?"

"Done. If it's for real."

"Oh, it's for real, all right. It's part of the recovery system—making it up to people you've tromped on. There's a lot of this compensation stuff going on."

"Okay, so you say. I get mine, you get yours."

That night we went out and met up with Lana for old time's sake. "Guess who's living in Boston?" Lana said to me.

"Christ! It's just one quiz after another. Just tell me."

"Shoshi. I saw her at a lesbian theater thing."

"How's she look?"

"She's about twice as big, her hair's gone white, and she's gorgeous as always."

I found Shoshi's number in the phone book. When I called,

her machine answered. "Hello, Shoshi," I told it, "I'm in Boston after a very long time. Can I see you?" I left her Muffer's number.

Shoshi called back two days later. During those forty-eight hours I found my stomach clenched, my breath short, my crotch alive, my hopes unreasonable. When her call finally came, our conversation was cautious at first and then she said, "This is silly. Why don't you come over and visit? It would be easier to talk."

She gave me directions and I borrowed a car from Muffer. After showering and dressing in basic butch black, I headed towards my unfinished business.

When she opened the door, I felt instantaneous comfort and familiarity. I reached down to hug her and smelled that "just-bathed" fragrance of soap and scented oil. It was almost a promise.

We went into her kitchen to make tea. One full wall was covered in photos of her life. A big section held shots of all of us in the old days. There we were in our leather jackets and combat boots, scowling together, looking mean. There we were naked on rafts on the Russian River during a trip to California. There we were stoned in front of an incomparable Provincetown sunset. There was a newspaper clipping of me and Muffer getting beat on by the cops at some demo. In almost all the photos, curling and discolored, Shoshi and I were next to each other, often with my arm around her, often with her big tits against my flat chest.

We stood side by side in her kitchen, silently looking at those images. As naturally as if there had not been a two-decade gap, I put my arm around her padded shoulders and she leaned slightly against me. The desire persisted.

She carried our teas into her living room and set mine down on a table next to a recliner. We filled in the past two decades, and while our journeys had little in common, our conclusions were similar. We were both happily single, working steady jobs and critical of the same social blemishes. Interesting as our discussion was, I was obsessing on how to maneuver myself out of the chair and next to her on the couch.

"Do you still smoke weed?" she asked. "I've got some nice material."

"I quit a few months ago due to advanced brain dysfunction. But for the sake of old times, I just might…"

Shoshi crossed the room to get her gear and by the time she returned, I was in the corner of the couch. She pulled out the same wooden pipe we had smoked together all that time ago in Provincetown. We passed it back and forth, grinning with excitement. I got down and crawled across her rug to look through her vinyls: Nina Simone, Carole King, Bonnie Raitt, Martha and the Vandellas. I chose Robert Flack and asked Shoshi to dance.

Now that Shoshi was approaching two hundred fifty pounds, the dancing had a different feel to it. Her breasts and her belly kept me at a distance. My right arm could only circle as far as her side. I concentrated on trying to establish that contact, from tit down to clit, which a leader needs to do her job. While I was busy with that, Shoshi was working on her own agenda. Somehow, by the end of the number, I found myself nearly naked.

I'm unsure how or when she did it, but my black silk shirt with the hidden buttons panel was completely open; my charcoal tweed slacks were unzipped, falling off my hips. When the song ended and I opened my eyes, I realized that we were grinding around in front of her picture window, which faced a major traffic intersection. As I shuffled over to close the curtains, my pants fell to my ankles and I dragged them along with me.

"Why not just go into the bedroom?" Shoshi asked me.

It was the invitation I'd been waiting for all evening. We lay on her bed and made love like the old days. It's not that

Shoshi and I had ever made love before, it's that we fell right into that early '70s style. Our lovemaking recalled the days when we were astonished by how natural, how comfortable, how hot and sticky sex between women could be. It was that brief period between pre-Stonewall, guilty, forbidden groping and post-HIV latex gloves, butt plugs, fisting, double dildos, and fetish scenes.

We rolled around, hugging and humping, her massive tits on my clit, my little ones on her ass. She was the fattest woman I had ever been with, an unique sensation of munificence, an affluence of erogenous flesh. Where my bony pelvic bone jutted, she had handfuls of lightly haired squishy meat. Her outer lips were like fully developed sexual organs, each a clutchable hunk of responsive tissue. She was a wonder to me, a lavish extravagance of sexiness to embrace.

"I haven't been in a relationship for a long time," I told her in one of our breathless breaks.

"Me neither."

"Why not?" I asked her. "I remember you as someone who always had a girlfriend."

"People learn. After three long-term relationships I noticed that even when I was with someone eight years or ten years, it took me longer to recover after the end than the time that was actually good. Just didn't seem worthwhile anymore. And once I got my mortgage and steady job, I no longer had the energy. I've got good friends."

"I'm the same way. I've got no limits when it comes to best friends. But I'm suspicious of lovers."

Shoshi rolled over and pulled the quilt up over us. "I was suspicious of you when I got that phone message the other day."

"Why?"

"My first reaction—don't get mad, okay—was to think: Is she going to call me a bourgeois sellout for having a mortgage and working in social services?"

"So I left you with a good impression? I'm glad you remember me as a laid-back nonjudgmental buddy." We both laughed.

"Maybe it has to do with my own ambivalence. Anyway, then I thought, *Shit, it's been twenty years...*"

"Nineteen."

"It's been twenty years, nineteen, whatever. You've probably changed too. I could never forget I got into feminism because of you."

"Because of that day at the Cape when your sister got hurt, right?"

"Right," Shoshi said. "Until then I didn't think it touched me. Then I saw there were no exceptions."

I rolled over on her; the quilt spilled onto the floor. "There is no escape," I whispered into her ear and then licked behind it, grabbing her gray curls in my teeth. I held her chubby wrist fast above her head, and with my other hand I grabbed one hunk of flesh after another, squeezing until she clutched her pillowy thighs around the leg I had thrust between them. I grasped the underside of her breasts and she shivered. I mashed her nipples into the fullness of her tits and she whimpered. Just as I was about to dive into the margin between her fleshy neck and her collarbone, she flipped me over and scooted away across the mattress.

She quickly lay down with her head opposite mine, scissoring our legs in the way that was once so popular.

"Tribadism!" I gasped. "It's been so long I almost forgot the name."

The Woodchipper Wife

Rebeca Antoine

Auggie woke as the cold light of morning hit her face through crooked blinds in a cheap motel. A flash of hard sun struck her eyelids. Bright red. Blood red. A faint hope rose in her that this day would not be like the others.

She felt Meg's breath hot on her back and reached behind her to pat Meg's thigh. Meg's arm rested stiffly on her hip; she lifted the arm gently, placing it flat on the warm space her body now slid away from. The room was colder than it had been the night before, and Auggie wondered if the motel had lost its heat again. This time she would not complain. The management, a stout, mustached man with pockmarked cheeks, seemed not to care. Only two of the twelve rooms were occupied, the other by an old man who played Billie Holiday records. Auggie saw him walk around the parking lot once a day, a full circle, then turn around and head inside.

She pulled the thin yellow blanket off of the other bed and wrapped it around her, the acrylic scratchy against her skin. Her bare feet felt every cigarette scar in the rough carpet as she made her way to the window. The blinds refused to close all the way and let in a slash of light that divided the room into uneven halves. By the time Auggie opened the blinds, the sun had ducked behind clouds, leaving the world covered in dismal gray. The same view she looked at every morning for the two weeks previous. Through the gentle sway of leafless trees, Auggie saw the drowsy flow of the Housatonic River. Each day, Meg suggested they should take a boat out but pretended that the weather worked against them, leaving the two relegated to this dreary room.

Auggie heard the squeak of the mattress as Meg rose from the bed but did not turn around. Goose bumps rose on her arms as Meg kissed the nape of her neck.

"Good morning," Meg whispered.

"Does the sun ever come out around here?" Auggie asked.

"You know what they say. Tomorrow."

"Tomorrow, then."

"I used to row this river every morning," Meg said, as though she had never told her this before, her arms clasped tightly around Auggie's chest. Meg still had rower's arms, strong and lean. The babies had made her thighs spread and her hips a little wide, but underneath still lived the power it took to traverse this river.

"How long will we stay here?" Meg asked.

"I paid through the end of the week." Auggie bent to the floor and picked up Meg's pack of cigarettes, half-empty, discarded carelessly during ravenous foreplay. Meg took the pack and put a cigarette in her mouth.

"Those things will kill you," Auggie said, lifting the corners of her mouth into a weak smile.

"So will a lot of things." Meg pulled the book of matches out of the pack and struck a match, the orange glow briefly lighting her face. "I thought we were leaving soon."

"The end of the week is soon."

Meg accepted this answer silently, kissed Auggie's cheek, and shuffled to the bathroom.

Two weeks they had stayed in this room with warped wood paneling, stained sheets, and four channels on the TV. And for two weeks, Auggie couldn't have imagined anyplace she would rather be. She found comfort in the bareness of the room, the solitude, Meg's soothing voice and soft skin. She forgot about the world outside of this stretch of dying riverfront, seemingly forever on the verge of being rebuilt. As she looked out into the gray morning, she wondered whose luck it was that she and Meg had found each other.

Meg was good enough to take Auggie in when she had just arrived in Boston with no friends and no other place to stay. Auggie's family money provided for her well, but she enjoyed the company of strangers. She had been on the road for more than a year solid, drifting back and forth across the country. It felt good to have a home again, someplace to unpack her bag, someone to come home to and wake up with. One morning, over coffee and eggs Florentine, Auggie asked Meg to get clean. Meg said yes right then and there, without hesitation. After weeks of cold sweats and diarrhea—the vestiges of addiction—Auggie offered to take Meg away from Boston for a while. Auggie hoped they'd make it to South Carolina at least, that they could travel together down the coast and feel the seasons change, maybe make it Florida and lie on a sun-drenched beach. But the three-hour drive to Connecticut was far enough for Meg to go.

The water rained down on the floor of the tub, thumping rhythmically. Auggie closed her eyes and listened as Meg's body interrupted the flow, her voice dancing around the drops of water still falling at her feet. The singing stopped, then the water.

"What's the matter, baby?" Meg's voice cooed from the corner of the room.

Auggie turned to see Meg, wet, walking toward her, leaving

a faint path of footprints on the rug. Meg raised her hand, warm from the shower's downpour, to Auggie's face and Auggie kissed her palm almost instinctively.

"Nothing's the matter, Mama," Auggie whispered. "Just hungry."

They ate breakfast at the diner downstairs, as they had each morning since they'd arrived at the Dew Drop Inn. The diner was a small place that never seemed clean, staffed by waitresses who never seemed sober. Between refills of coffee, the waitresses sat at the counter, shooting the women disparaging looks. Auggie ordered what had become her usual, two eggs, toast, and sausage, while Meg ordered hers, coffee, into which she added whiskey from her flask.

"Silver," Meg said. "Graduation present."

Auggie nodded and sipped her coffee.

"Don't be so quiet, baby. You're freaking me out." Meg lit a cigarette, her hands shaking. Her hands were always shaking.

"Sometimes I like to be quiet."

Meg took a sip from her flask.

"You really should eat something," Auggie said. "You haven't had anything since breakfast yesterday." Auggie started to raise her hand to summon one of the brooding waitresses, but Meg caught, then kissed, Auggie's palm.

"I don't need anything," Meg said, but Auggie thought the hunger must have been eating at her belly, ignored and filled by the burn of whiskey.

Auggie studied Meg's face for a moment, sallow and marked by deep bags under her eyes. Despite all this, Meg looked better than she had three weeks before, when Auggie held her body tightly against hers to counteract the chills and tremors. "It's okay, then," Auggie said, and pushed her scrambled eggs around her plate a bit before taking a bite.

"Where should we go from here?" Meg asked. "Do you want to go back to Boston?"

Rebeca Antoine

"We just left Boston."

"We don't have to go back now. But I've got to go back sometime."

Auggie knew Meg would have to go back. She had a past in Boston, an ex-husband, three kids—a suburban life she had given up to fuck women, do heroin, and dabble in some other things she wished she had done in her twenties. Now, Meg sat before Auggie as a thirty-six-year-old who didn't know what she wanted but for the moment believed that whatever it was included Auggie, a girl in her twenties with orange hair who called Meg "Mama."

"I've got to get my kids back," Meg continued. "Stay straight, get my kids back."

Auggie reached across the table and touched the skin of Meg's arm, soft and pale, now quivering almost imperceptibly. "You'll get your kids back." Auggie knew this was a long shot; in the months she had known Meg, she hadn't seen the children at all. Meg received photographs or drawings in the mail almost weekly, but her ex-husband had full custody and a new wife, which most likely trumped Meg's newfound sexual liberation and insolence toward societal mores.

"You'll like them. The youngest, Lena, after Lena Horne, she's almost five now." Meg looked out the window. "She's so smart. You'll like her."

"I'm sure I will." Auggie turned to see what Meg watched so intently through the grimy windowpane. Nothing. Just the passing of the sparse traffic on Route 34. Trucks and Saabs and SUVs, each on their way somewhere different, crossing paths in this particular moment.

"We should have gone somewhere with a pool." Meg sighed and drank down the dregs of her coffee.

"It's fucking November."

"A pool is still nice." Meg's eyes remained fixed on the windowpane.

122

"Look like rain today?" Auggie asked, already knowing the answer.

"Yeah. Looks like rain."

"You used to row in the rain, didn't you?"

"Yeah, I guess we did." Meg smiled and lifted the flask to her lips.

Auggie and Meg ventured farther from the Dew Drop Inn than they had since arriving there. Lake Zoar welled up just down the river, spilling over a dam into a meek stream. The beach was empty and quiet, save for a few pickup trucks parked outside the Lake Zoar Grill. Meg negotiated at the boat rental booth for a better price on a rowboat, and the proprietor put up a fight, even though it was obvious there would be few takers that day. Auggie and Meg strapped the boat to the roof of Meg's Volvo wagon, which, like Meg herself, was just beginning to show its age, just a few years past its prime.

"A few years ago," Meg began as she turned the key in the ignition, "a man from around here killed his wife, put her in a woodchipper, and dumped her in this lake."

"How did they find her?"

"They found pieces of her: teeth, bones, a finger. But mostly she just..." Meg raised her fist and opened it. "...disappeared."

"Downriver?"

"Maybe. Maybe to the bottom, sucked to God knows where."

Auggie pictured the woodchipper wife washing up on shore, her pulverized limbs indistinguishable from pebbles or driftwood. Washing up, then washing back out, no one the wiser.

A lighter popped out, and Meg held the orange tip up to her cigarette, cupping her hands like the lighter was a match about to give way to oncoming breeze. "I used to row this river every morning," Meg said.

"Oh, yeah?"

"You ever done this?"

"Not since I was a kid. Sleepaway camp." Auggie rolled down the window to let in some of the late-autumn air. Winter would come early this year; she could smell it. Auggie had a knack for knowing these things, when the seasons would change, when the first snow would fall, when the deer carcasses would start piling up on the shoulders of lonely country highways.

The car followed the winding road from the lake, back along the bank of the river, hugging closely to the rocky hillside. Meg pulled over to a clearing alongside the road, and the two of them carried the boat down a path to the muddy shoal. Auggie got into the boat first, Meg pushing it a bit farther out into the water before getting in. She took the oars in her hands and pushed and pulled the boat out to where the water was deep. Auggie felt paper-thin as the cold air moved right through her, chilling her hair and skin and bones. She pulled her jacket tight to her body and watched Meg row. When they reached the middle of the river, Meg put down the oars, letting the boat pitch and heave with the current.

"I used to live up there." Meg gestured toward the hills hulking over them. Rocky crags gave way to evergreens intermingled with spiny branches, all dark gray against the sky. "Eighteen years I lived up there. And when I went to college this is where crew rowed."

"So this is home to you."

"How long's it been since you've been home?"

"One year, ten months, and twelve days." Auggie recited these facts and tried not to think of the last words her mother had said to her: "This life you lead is beneath you." At the time, Auggie figured that at twenty-two she was old enough to choose a path that fit. "But it's not long enough, I guess." Auggie laughed gently, looking up at the bare branches of the quiet trees.

"Wouldn't you like one of these?" Meg pointed toward the small houses that lined the river, each with their own boat landing. Meg reached into her back pocket and produced the flask, holding it out to Auggie. "Graduation present," she muttered, barely audible.

Auggie took the flask and drank deeply from it, thinking the whiskey could warm her from the inside out. "I don't know that I could live here."

"I could do it." Meg rubbed her hands together. "The kids would love it. You'd be perfect out here."

"It's the middle of fucking nowhere," Auggie said.

"This is Connecticut, sweetie. There is no middle of fucking nowhere."

"Fine."

The momentary warmth of the liquor faded, and Auggie once again found herself chilled to the bone, wishing for gloves or a hat, or something besides Meg's old barn jacket, three sizes too large. Meg opened her hand in front of Auggie's face, presenting her with a joint.

"Light that up for me, baby." Meg smiled as Auggie took the joint from her hand, then picked up the oars again, pushing and pulling along the river's frigid skin.

Auggie almost posed the question but decided against it. Meg answered anyway. "I saved it for a special occasion."

"Special?"

"This is special. You and me. On my river. Me telling you that I love you."

"Is that you telling me?"

"Yes."

Auggie opened her mouth, then paused, finally saying, "Then I'll tell you too." She took the lighter from her pocket and lit the joint, inhaling and holding in the smoke before letting it out of her lungs. The smoke hung, suspended a moment, then faded. She leaned in and held the thin roll to Meg's lips.

"It's settled, then. I love you and you love me." Meg let the words out in small puffs.

"Sure, Mama." Auggie agreed that it was true enough. That she loved Meg as much as Meg could possibly love her, that maybe they could start a life together, if not on the banks of this river, then somewhere else.

"And we'll go back to Boston soon?" Meg asked.

"We'll go back to Boston."

Meg smiled broadly and let Auggie smoke the rest of the joint herself. Auggie felt her body sink into itself, pictured her flesh dissolving into the boat and leaking through the bottom, into the water that would soon be frozen over, solid enough to dance on. Children would play games on the frozen river, have snowball fights, overestimate its strength, and die in this river.

Auggie stood at the window in their room and watched the afternoon fade into darkness. She watched the old man walk his circle and go back inside.

Meg's breath felt hot on Auggie's skin as strong arms once again held her tight. Auggie held her body taut.

"What's the matter, baby?" Meg murmured, her lips against Auggie's ear.

"Nothing."

"You hungry again?"

"Maybe."

"I got something for you. Just a taste. Saved it for something special." Meg let go of Auggie and riffled through the suitcase, finally pulling out a small velvet pouch. "Just enough for you and me. One last time."

A pang of disappointment swelled in Auggie's chest. She tried to shove it down, push it away. "You know I don't do that."

Meg sat on the bed, a small plastic bag lying flat in her hand. Auggie turned back toward the window.

"Have you had that the whole time?" Auggie asked.

"It's just a little. You know how I was hurting."

"I know." Auggie turned to look at Meg again, and she was smiling. "Do you know that you'll die?"

"This is the last of it," Meg said. "I won't die on you."

Auggie watched Meg as she bent over the glass tabletop of the nightstand, thin white lines disappearing into her nose. Meg rolled over on the bed and patted the space next to her. "Take my hand, baby." Auggie climbed up next to Meg and took her hand, now cold from the lack of heat in the room. Meg opened her eyes, and Auggie saw the hungers collide—hunger for her children, for another high, for love.

"Meg?"

"Yeah."

"I'm hungry. I'll go out and pick us up some dinner."

Meg kissed Auggie's hand. "I love you, baby."

"And I love you." Auggie nestled her face in Meg's hair and kissed the cool, damp skin at the nape of her neck.

Auggie picked up Meg's keys from the dresser, feeling the weight of them in her palm. She heard the mattress squeak and turned to see Meg amble into the bathroom. Auggie closed her eyes and felt herself being sucked back into the circle, the cord of desperation that Meg had woven for herself. Nothing would change. Auggie folded two hundred-dollar bills and set the keys on top of them on the dresser. She headed out the door, down the fluorescent-lit stairs, and onto the road without looking back. She walked down the winding road, resisting the urge to stop a moment to catch her breath, fearing that any pause would make her change her course. She kept moving until she reached the dam that separated the lake from the river. Streetlights beamed down on her as she looked into the dark expanse of the water.

Auggie stood, out of breath, looking over the edge of the dam, feeling the loom of the surrounding hills, listening to the water rush beneath her in the darkness, imagining the fall, the impact, the cold water in her lungs. She imagined her body settling with the fragments of other women gone, disappeared, nestled in the muddy depths of the lake, only to rise up unannounced one day, on this shore or some other.

She heard the grumbling of a tractor-trailer behind her amid a steep row of pine trees; she turned around, stuck out her thumb, and took a few steps back to let the streetlight catch her full on. Truckers had always been good to her.

Open Space, Forever Shining

Siobhán Houston

"O Goddess...reveal your transparent presence within this
lotus heart as open space, forever shining."

—Lex Hixon, *Mother of the Universe: Visions of the
Goddess and Tantric Hymns of Enlightenment*

I rinsed soapsuds off the last stainless steel pot and balanced it artfully on the pile of drying dishes lined up on the
sideboard. Upstairs, I could hear the crowd growing, their
bare feet stomping in rhythm to the beat of the drum, the two-
headed *mridanga*. Silvery-sounding hand cymbals chimed as
guests and devotees danced and whirled on the walnut parquet
floor of the temple room directly above my head.

As I swept the red tile, gathering vegetable peels I'd strewn
in my haste, I conjured up the conversation I'd had a couple
days ago with Madhu, the temple president. I still burned hot

whenever I thought about it—his audacity in telling me when I should get married and to whom! We sat in his office, a room brightened with the intense afternoon sunlight so characteristic of Denver and decorated with hanging bleached wicker baskets of delicate ferns, adding a Victorian air. Madhu, a slender, pale, insipid man in his early thirties, spoke with such a pronounced Aussie accent that it was hard to understand him, although after three years my comprehension had improved markedly. At this point I hardly ever had to ask him to repeat words. His wife Devi brought in a pot of herb tea and a couple of mugs for us and glanced at me sympathetically. He stared into his mug as we talked, rarely meeting my eyes. I refused the offer of tea, not planning to be there long.

"Lata, I think it's time for you to get married," he began. "You've been at the temple several years now, and your guru agrees with me about this. I know it's sometimes difficult for us Western converts to accept the idea of arranged marriage, but it's a long tradition in India and for the most part it's worked out well."

The wicker chair I sat in creaked slightly as I shifted my weight, trying to somehow get comfortable. I knew Madhu had planned to bring this up with me, yet I felt put on the spot. Devi warned me about this a few days ago as we sat on the temple room floor, chatting and stringing delicate marigolds onto cotton twine with long, wicked-looking needles, making garlands to decorate the altar. Devi was a friend of mine, kind and sweet and way smarter than her husband. How on earth did she manage to stay married to such a dolt?

"With all due respect, Madhu, there's no one I'm interested in marrying."

He slammed his mug down on the desk, causing some of the tea to slop over the edge. He wasn't used to insubordinate women. "Still, there is someone who would very much like to marry *you*," he countered. "Kapila Das." Kapila was a short chubby guy with a great sense of humor and a scholar's inquiring mind. He seemed nice enough, an earnest, hardworking monk who would probably be a great husband for someone. Just not me.

"I'll think about it, Madhu. Really." Like hell I would. I rose from the chair and slipped through the door before he could continue describing his plans for me, almost bumping into Devi, who stood semi-hidden, listening at the doorway. She gave me a slightly guilty look as I hurried by.

Revisiting this incident now gave me the fiery energy I needed to quickly finish sweeping, my last task in a long day. After I finished, I tossed the broom into the corner, where it briefly teetered against the wall then fell to the floor. I didn't bother to pick it up. I was so tired. I'd been cooking the feast for hours, stirring huge pots of milky sweet rice with a wooden paddle so it wouldn't burn, frying the vegetable *pakoras* in wide woks full of the clarified butter prized by Indian cooks,

Just as I hung my damp apron on a peg and was about to head back to the ashram, Bhakti came by the kitchen, peeking around the corner of the doorway. She was festively decked out in a fancy turquoise silk sari bordered with lots of gold *jari*. Carved conch and red coral bracelets lay heavily on her wrists. The opalescent beads threaded into her pale braid in tandem with the dusky *kajal* eyeliner she'd applied made her look like a Scandinavian gypsy.

"Coming to the feast, Lata?"

"Oh, Bhakti, I don't know. I'm completely wiped out. All I want to do is to go back to my room and collapse." And something I had seen at last Sunday's feast was bothering me. My stomach tensed at the indistinct remembrance, but I couldn't pinpoint what had troubled me.

"Come upstairs for a few minutes. Sajjana brought her new baby and she wants you to see him. He's a complete darling," she pleaded.

"Okay, I'll come up for a minute. But then I'm going to get some rest,"

We hurried up the stairs from the basement kitchen and swung open the heavy wooden door, the sounds of chanting now intensifying. *Nag champa* incense wafted through the temple room, and it seemed as if hundreds of people stood crammed into the space, all chanting Sanskrit in staccato unison. An old Indian woman, her eyes closed, her arms raised in supplication, gyrated near me, silently mouthing "Radha, Radha," as if in trance. The woman was oblivious to the state of her sari, which had fallen off her shoulder and trailed on the floor.

The huge altar at the front of the room awed me as always. Statues of gods and goddesses resided on the gleaming black marble altar that ran the entire width of the room. There were Rama and Sita, Krishna and Radha, Hanuman and Ganesh, fashioned variously of brass and marble and wood and standing marvelously adorned in jeweled silk and fresh garlands of carnations, freesia, and roses.

I squeezed past the old *mataji* and stood at the back wall, chanting and clapping my hands as I looked around the room. No austerity here—Hinduism is a riotous, never-ending carnival of colors and aromas and flavors and sounds. This ecstatic style of worshiping had drawn me into the community initially. For the first two years I'd felt fortunate to live in a place saturated with such sensory opulence.

Lately, though, my enthusiasm for this sort of life was wavering. Forget my high-minded plan of being a Hindu nun for the rest of my life—that scheme was definitely a no-go at this point. Dragging myself out of bed in the desolate hours before dawn to shower and meditate had become excruciatingly difficult the past few months. I felt angry all the time, a free-floating sort of resentment that permeated everything. And I missed sex fiercely, but more than that I longed to be emotionally intimate with a lover again.

Now as I scanned the crowded temple room, Kapila merci-fully absent, my eyes rested on a clutch of young women, some straightedge girls with body piercings and wildly colored hair, dressed in sheer gauzy blouses, vintage dresses, and ripped fishnets. Suddenly I remembered why I hadn't wanted to come upstairs tonight. At the fringe of the straightedge group sat a young woman in her mid twenties, her legs bent beneath her, her knees poking out from ripped jeans, her short indigo-dark hair a fine fuzz covering her head. She gazed thoughtfully at the altar as her fingers thrummed against her thighs, matching the drum's rhythm. This same woman had showed up last week. I leaned against the temple wall momentarily, closing my eyes and feeling my stomach roil with tension. I needed to leave the room now, this second.

The delicate night air played over me as I emerged from the overheated temple. *I'll have to see Sajjana and the baby another time*, I thought. Crossing the street, I ran up the cement stairs of my house, tripping once over my sari's hem, narrowly miss-ing a fall by grabbing the iron handrail. I walked quickly to my room in the back, not bothering to greet my roommates who were chattering together in the living room.

I stripped and put on my nightgown, the comforting smell of freshly laundered sheets sheltering me as I lay on my futon, willing myself to sleep. I stared up at the ceiling, where water damage had made odd shapes that shifted weirdly as the vio-let moonlight stole through the room. Bits of hushed conver-sation slipped through the dark as Suni and Dhana talked of their upcoming marriages. *Prattling toads*, I thought hatefully, surprised at my own venom.

My anxiety-soaked mind didn't give me a break even at night. Recently during the rare times when I could sleep I'd had terrible dreams—vivid, epic nightmares that spun on seemingly forever. I might find myself in a filthy alley, sur-rounded by decaying garbage and the howls of wild animals.

Or living among an impoverished family struggling to find enough to eat, our torn and shredded clothing barely hiding our emaciated bodies. Once I dreamt I sat in a dreary college classroom, the steel clock with its stark black numerals above me ticking ominously, a stern professor lurking over my shoulder as I took an exam I was doomed to fail. Often I awoke feeling drugged, unable to figure out where I was, afraid and alone, my bedclothes sticky and tangled.

I knew it was time to leave this place. I'd felt it in my guts—my *kishkes,* as my grandmother would say—for a long time. But if I left the community, where would I go? Not back home. That was out of the question. I had no money—the slim savings I'd had when I joined was exhausted long ago. And I knew no one in Denver outside the temple.

Unable to sleep again tonight, I let my fingers slip in and out between my legs, the sensations soothing me as I called up images of sleek androgynous girls who longed for other women. The handsome young dark-haired woman from the feast stole into my room upon a cloud of passion and sank beneath my covers, joining me. In my imagination our bodies tumbled and flowed over each other, our tongues seeking out each other's sweetest places. Just before succumbing to my phantasms, I felt a surge of despair. It seemed I would never overcome my physical desires, no matter how much time I'd spend on my meditation cushion.

The next day at the main library downtown, I sat at a desk stacked with books. This place was my refuge and sanctuary. Fluorescent lamps strung from the library's cavernous ceilings reflected, halo-like, off the wooden desk's varnished top. I was reading a tome about the incorruptibles, Catholic saints whose bodies didn't decay after death. Photographs showed their corpses displayed in shrines and glass coffins, their remains darkened by decades of accumulated soot from candles and incense but miraculously well-preserved. Especially amazing was Saint Bernadette of Lourdes, who died at the age of thirty-five in 1879. Her body, now reposing in a chapel in France, had only discolored slightly more than a hundred years after her death. She looked eerily radiant, a holy Sleeping Beauty, as she lay in state in her full habit, eyes closed and a wooden rosary encircling her hands.

Enthralled by these stories, I didn't see the woman until she stood right in front of my table. Through the stack of books, I noticed a pair of legs clad in khaki cargo pants. My eyes slowly rose to take in the owner. It was the dark-haired woman from the feast, now wearing a beat-up tan leather jacket, the soft fuzz of her hair outlining the shape of her head.

"What are you planning to do with all these Catholic books? Flagellate yourself?" She grinned, her dusky brows raised above deep-set eyes, finding humor in her own joke. Her voice was a little deeper than I'd expected, and she was even better looking close-up. Unable to formulate a retort, I looked down at my hands, which were of their own accord straightening the books into neat piles and aligning the spines perfectly with the edge of the table.

She picked up a volume, quickly flipped through the pages, taking a bit longer with the table of contents, and set it down again. "Repression incarnate," she remarked in a teasing tone, smiling mischievously. "I saw you at the temple last night. You live there?"

"Yes."

"Really. For how long?"

"A little over three years. I joined when I was eighteen," I said, my face rouging slightly.

"Wow. Impressive." I wasn't sure if I was being taunted or complimented. "Were you raised Hindu?"

"No, Lutheran, actually. German mother, Jewish father." I flashed momentarily on the starkly decorated church I went to as a child, its severe wooden pews, the morose, balding pastor lecturing us from the podium, my mother pinching my leg hard to quiet my whisperings to my sister.

The woman sat down in the chair across from me, and our conversation continued, a bit stilted at first. Her name was Ginny, and she was a couple of years older than me, a grad student in anthropology at CU Boulder who worked in a café as a "barista," that last word pronounced mockingly. Sometimes Ginny would run her hands through her hair, or tap her fingers on the table, tattooing out a rhythm that seemed to echo in her head. She appeared at ease as we talked, her speech peppered with bantering remarks that seemed designed to dissipate my wariness. If I didn't know better, I'd have thought she was flirting with me.

"So," Ginny said, "do you ever go out to movies and concerts and things like that?" She rocked on the legs of her chair, artfully balancing for a few seconds each time she leaned backwards.

"No." I wished I were wearing anything but this worn cotton sari, pale gray with a maroon striped border. I felt awkward. "I know it sounds strange, but if you're trying to live a sacred life, those things are considered distractions."

"You know, I respect that, but no way could I live like that. If it works for you, though…"

But it's not working for me.

Ginny reached out her arms above her head in an exaggerated stretching motion, as if rising from sleep. "The life of a grad student, you know. Perpetually exhausted." Her T-shirt rode up slightly as she lifted her arms, showing a bit of her tanned torso. I looked at her midriff for a second—a completely unconscious movement—and felt my face pink with chagrin when she caught me staring. She raised her eyebrows a millimeter in surprise then glanced out the tall windows of the library that overlooked the art museum courtyard and its modernistic hulking and twisted red metal sculpture, a slight frown settling on her face. "Jesus, it's starting to snow again. Do you want a ride back to the temple? I've got to go to work." She stood abruptly and pushed the chair back under the table, shoving her hands into her back pockets as she faced me. Something in her stance seemed to challenge me.

"That would be great. Thanks. It gets cold waiting for the bus sometimes." I gathered my books, dumped them in the plastic reshelving bin, and accompanied Ginny to her vintage Toyota. I read the lavender sticker on her car's bumper: YOUR SILENCE WILL NOT PROTECT YOU. —AUDRE LORDE. *That's so true,* I thought.

I had never told anyone I was gay except for a few close friends and, of course, my high school girlfriend. But in remaining silent I'd abandoned my self. What made me *me* at my core felt withered and parched and scarcely alive. No wonder every day I descended lower into despondency, a massive slab weighing on my chest.

As Ginny and I drove toward the temple, I glanced at her, noticing how the planes of her face and her high cheekbones reflected the diffuse streetlight. Her dark straight brows were knitted as she navigated the glacial roads. I couldn't help imagining how Ginny's small breasts would fit snugly into my palms and how her skin would smell and taste as I placed featherweight kisses behind her ears, down her neck, in the hollows of her clavicle.

Sinking further into a daydream as the car sped along in the dark, I mused about my high school love, a tall, Rubenesque girl with deep-set eyes. I remembered burying my face in Liesl's silken breasts and the delicious friction that resulted when we rubbed our naked bodies together. The memories of the men I'd slept with before moving into the temple were hardly more than specters. Only the lovemaking I'd shared with a woman lodged in my daydreams like a bee encased in sweet, petrified resin.

Ginny pulled the car to a stop in front of the temple. Snapped out of my reverie, I teetered on a precarious edge for a minute, and then my words tumbled out: "Where do you work? I'd love to come by and see the café sometime."

"Sure, that'd be nice. It's called Penny Lane, on Pearl Street, a couple of blocks down from the Boulder Co-op." As she smiled, I noticed her front teeth were slightly crooked, giving her a rakish look.

"By the way, I'm planning to come by the temple again next Sunday for the love feast," she said, slightly drawling the word "love" and trying to suppress a smile at the trite double entendre. Our eyes locked for a long second, and then I grabbed my books with one arm and opened the car door with the other. As she drove away I strolled into the women's ashram, humming and smiling. Even Suni and Dhana and their damned eternal wedding chatter weren't going to get me down today.

Every Sunday for the next two months, except for once when she had to lead a study session, Ginny showed up at the feast. We'd sit together and eat and talk about everything and anything. Sometimes Madhu and other devotees cast stern questioning looks toward us, but I didn't care. I felt exhilarated when we were together.

Every chance I could, when I had a break from my temple duties, I'd sneak out and meet Ginny downtown, where she spent a lot of time researching her dissertation. I'd steal out of the ashram with a sari covering some street clothes, usually jeans and a shirt, my hair caught in a chaste braid, and catch the bus a few blocks from the temple. All the way down its Colfax route, that crazy patchwork avenue of pawnshops, upscale furniture stores and art galleries, bohemian coffee houses, pagan supply shops, and Salvadorian *panaderias* selling delicious pastries stuffed with thick cream, I'd restlessly look out the grimy bus window, counting the slow blocks until Broadway as the bus chugged through traffic. I always wore sunglasses so I could more easily avoid conversation with the lowlifes, prostitutes, drunks, and assorted ruffians who made up the majority of Route 15 patrons. Although I'd grown up in Los Angeles and was pretty streetwise, I felt nervous on the 15 and usually sat on the edge of an aisle seat as close to the front of the bus as possible, just in case yet another fracas broke out.

Once the bus pulled over at the busy Broadway intersection I'd bound off, quickly unwind my sari, stuff it in my backpack, and undo my long braid. It felt great to let my hair go free, wear normal clothes, and look like everyone else for a change. No puzzled stares, no smirks, no one coming up to me and asking for spiritual counsel or a copy of the *Bhagavad Gita*, and, most fantastic of all, no evangelicals wanting to engage in a belligerent discussion of imminent Armageddon.

Usually Ginny was already there, waiting for me, impatiently shifting her weight from leg to leg, wearing her ubiquitous sunglasses and backwards baseball cap, chewing on a toothpick. A smile would cross her face when she saw me, and then she'd remark dryly, "Always waiting for the femme. Story of my life." I'd hug her hard, enjoying her closeness and her scent, a mixture of coffee and soap and the sandalwood oil she daubed behind her ears.

Our arms around each other, we'd stroll over to the little Irish coffee house on Wazee across from the Tattered Cover and spend hours nursing mugs of French roast and nibbling almond biscotti (me) and chocolate chip scones (her) while we chatted. Sometimes we'd just read our respective books in silence for long stretches, our hands clasped across the rickety-legged wooden table. Often we'd wander over to the bookstore, mainly to browse, although sometimes Ginny would buy something she could use for her research on Chaco Canyon and the mysterious civilizations that had made this barren New Mexico valley their abode centuries ago. Then we'd park her Toyota strategically on a deserted side street behind a copse of trees and make out. *How had I gone so long without touching a woman?* I'd wonder in amazement.

I wasn't sure what the hell I was doing with Ginny, but I guess in any other context this would be called dating. One thing was certain: Since I'd been seeing her, my nightmares had for the most part abated and I felt I could survive the temple routine, at least for a while longer. Ultimately, though, "Things fall apart; the centre cannot hold," as Yeats declared. One afternoon as Ginny and I wound up another marathon session of lovemaking in her car, she started in on me.

"So, Lata, are we just going to keep screwing in the backseat, hiding from the devotees, or are we going to think about having a life together in plain view of the world? Something needs to change here. I can't handle this much longer."

I buttoned up the front of my shirt and combed my tangled hair with my fingers. "What do you want me to do?"

"Well, in a perfect world, I'd want you to move to Boulder so we could see each other more, go out at night, do things together, you know, have regular lives," Ginny massaged her temples hard, a sure sign she was stressed and a migraine was headed her way.

"That sounds like a great plan," I said. "But I don't think there are too many places in Boulder hiring Hindu priestesses. I've never been to college, I have no marketable skills, and my trust fund only has a few pennies left." I checked my hair in the rearview mirror, wetting my fingers with spit to make the frizzy front ends lie down.

"You can be really obnoxious, Lata," Ginny said. "And pessimistic. You're not alone. I'll help you. I have friends you can crash with for a while. You could go to school, get student loans, a part-time job. You'd be able to make it. You just need to decide when you're going to grow up. You're twenty-one, and let's face it, you're only in the temple because it gives you some sense of security." She took a deep breath and let it out in a great sigh as she pulled her T-shirt over her head and tucked it into her pants.

Shot through the heart and you're to blame. A fragment of a long-forgotten song lyric blew through my head, and I felt numb inside, chilled by the possible loss of this gender outlaw who made me chant litanies of ecstatic moans whenever she touched me and who could beguile my mind for hours. She was drawing a line and I knew it, and she knew I knew it.

"I have to go now. I'm cooking the evening offering," I said, locating my backpack, which was squashed under the front seat, and hoisting it over my shoulder. "But you're right, baby," I murmured into her neck as I hugged her goodbye. "I'll think about it and figure something out."

"I know you will. I'll call you soon," Ginny said, trying to catch my eye and gauge my mood as I got out of the car and ambled toward the bus stop. She peeled the car from the curb and gave me a brief wave as she headed back to Boulder and the café and her normal dyke life with her friends who were obviously so much more mature and together than I was.

As soon as I came in the ashram door later that afternoon from the bus, I rushed into the bathroom for a quick shower before heading to the temple kitchen. As I soaped up, I recalled where Ginny had stroked and kissed me. Faint red swellings rose up where she'd bitten my breasts. I cherished these hidden marks of our lovemaking; somehow it made our affair more real. When I finally came out of the bathroom, Suni and Dhana, obviously lying in wait, confronted me in the hallway.

"Tadit told us she was shopping downtown today and saw you walking around in *karmi* clothes and holding that girl's hand," Suni said heatedly.

"We told Madhu, and he wants to talk to you right now. He said to send you over as soon as you got back," Dhana chimed in.

"I knew something weird was going on. You didn't sit next to her every week at the feast just to preach to her," said Suni, her broad face reddening. "I can't believe this. We've been living with a lesbian all this time. It's disgusting. I'm surprised you didn't try to come on to us."

"Dream on, Suni," I muttered, willing myself to be civil. What had I expected? On some level I'd known I'd be found out eventually.

Suni and Dhana kept up their haranguing, their voices echoing through the hall, me still wrapped in a towel, my hair dripping down my back. Then their voices merged into a low humming somnolent sound like that of a swarm of honeybees gathering at a great distance. They were drones, these two, mindlessly serving their colony, their lives tracked along a narrow rut that traveled between hive and flower and the next flower then back again to the hive, a uniformity of purpose that tolerated no dissension.

I had to leave, now. And I had to do it for me, for my sanity and survival, not just to keep Ginny around. Whatever happened after I closed the ashram door behind me for the last time was uncertain. I was terrified. Those mystics I so loved to read would have urged me on with phrases like "Embrace the mystery! Walk into the fire!" and other clever axioms that sounded rousing and inspiring on paper. I felt, though, as if I were setting off for a journey through an English hedge maze, its dim cramped paths bordered by high, thorny bushes, the route full of frustrating dead ends. I might stroll for hours or days, entangled in the intricate network of walkways, unable to see more than a few feet ahead, the towering foliage blocking my view. I might never get to the center at all.

Pushing past my now silently staring roommates, I walked to my room and stowed into my backpack a few belongings, toiletries, underwear, a couple of books Ginny had bought me, and some letters from friends. Pulling on a bedraggled pair of jeans and a donated olive twill jacket, I neatly folded my saris and other devotional clothing in a mound on the floor, ready for the next new woman to wear. *May she wear these in good health and with many blessings. May we all be blessed and at peace in this crazy world,* I prayed as I slipped through the front door and into the alley, heading out to Colfax and the bus that would take me to Boulder.

Featherless Ducks

Anne Seale

It's a cold, gusty morning and I'm at the campground in Harmony Lake State Park, sitting on a picnic table with my feet on the bench, freezing my buns off.

A half dozen ducks are floating near the shore, their feathers fluffed against the wind. One suddenly breaks from the flock and paddles to the edge of the water, and the rest turn and follow. They waddle up and form a semicircle around me, staring intently and making clucking sounds in their throats.

"Okay," I say, "I *know* it's stupid to go camping in December, but my girlfriend threw me out of the house last night. Now go away and leave me alone."

They look at each other and then back at me. One quacks.

"What do you want? Food?" I ask. "I don't have any. No bread, no crackers, nothing. If I had some, I'd eat it myself. Now go on."

They continue to stare, shifting their weight from one webbed foot to the other.

"Git!" I yell.

They understand that one. They hurry away, their rear ends rocking indignantly. When they reach the water, they fluff up their feathers and glide in.

I wish I had feathers to fluff up. I'm wrapped in a sweat suit topped by a flimsy windbreaker, and I'm shivering like crazy. Most of the shivering is because of the cold, but some of it is a physical expression of my anger at Nita, the girlfriend who threw me out of the house last night. Well, okay, she didn't throw me out of the house; she only threw me out of the bedroom. This time, however, I didn't retreat to the sofa—I kept going. I grabbed our double sleeping bag from a garage shelf, tossed it in the capped bed of my GM pickup, and drove out here to the lake, my favorite place in the world.

It was dark when I arrived, but I knew the campground well and drove directly to my favorite site. It was available. All the sites were available—the place was deserted. I pulled in, crawled into the truck bed, and slid into the sleeping bag, trying to ignore the cold air leaking around the cap's louvered windows. Assuming a fetal position, I exhaled toward my toes, wishing I'd thought to bring an extra pair of socks. Even better, I should have purchased the more expensive bag that had guaranteed comfort to zero Fahrenheit.

"Why would I need that in Arizona?" I'd asked the salesman.

"Winters can get plenty cold here in the high desert," he told me.

"I know that," I said, "but I'd never go camping in the winter. And anyway, I got my love to keep me warm."

Who knew?

In junior high we learned how Native Americans used desert plants to satisfy their needs. From my perch on the picnic table, I survey the prickly bushes and sparsely leaved trees around the campground and wonder which one they had used to satisfy their need for caffeine.

I try to talk myself into driving to a warm, dry diner for coffee, but that would make me feel better and I'm not finished being pissed and miserable. The dark clouds hanging overhead oblige me by exuding icy drizzle. I hunch down in the windbreaker and pull the collar around my ears. To hell with women. Who needs them?

I watch the ducks bob idly in the wind-whipped water. They float a foot or two apart, but occasionally one paddles up against another and receives a soft, welcoming quack.

At other times, there is no welcoming quack. Instead there's an angry flap of wings and a jab of the bill. It reminds me of Nita last night when I swung her into my arms as she was coming out of the bathroom in her nightgown. I whispered in her ear, "How's about it, honey? In the mood?"

She broke free and shook her finger in my face. "You've got a lot of nerve, Melissa. I saw those sexy looks Judy was sending you at the party. What's going on between you two?"

"Nothing, I swear."

It had been a big mistake taking Nita to the office Christmas party, but the company had addressed the invitation to both of us and she got to it first. Most lesbians would be happy to work for such an accepting employer, but not me. I'd gotten into the habit of spending long erotic lunches in my secretary's apartment, so I didn't want Judy and Nita in the same room.

Yesterday afternoon, when we were hanging crepe paper strips from the office light fixtures, I'd asked Judy to please stay away from Nita and me that evening. I could have saved my breath. As soon as we got in the door, she brought us drinks and hors d'oeuvres and stayed to chat, casting suggestive glances at me whenever she thought Nita wasn't looking. I gave her all kinds of dirty looks, but she ignored them.

When Nita finally went to the ladies' room, I pulled Judy into a cubicle and told her she'd better leave us alone or start looking for a new job.

"You fire me, and I'll sue for harassment," she said.

"Harassment?" I whispered shrilly. "*I'm* the one being harassed. Isn't there another couple out there you can go break up?"

"There's no other couple I'm having sex with half of," she said.

I picked up a notepad and wrote "Ended sentence with a preposition."

What are you doing?" she asked.

"Keeping track of your errors for your next performance evaluation."

"*Performance*, Melissa?" she screeched. "*Your* perform-ance lately hasn't been exactly stellar. I've been faking it for weeks."

"Shhh!" I stuck my head out, but nobody was looking our way, thank goodness. Pulling it back in, I hissed, "You couldn't have been faking it. I'd know!"

Judy put her hand to her forehead and gave a loud moan followed by "Oh, boss, boss, *boss*!" Then she sashayed out of the cubicle.

I waited a few minutes so no one would put two and two together, then I went out and pushed through the crowd until I found Nita. "I don't feel to good. Let's go," I said, taking the drink from her hand and steering her to the door.

It was too early for bed when we got home, so I changed into sweats and watched TV for a couple of hours. I was so immersed in brooding thoughts—*Could Judy really have been faking it?*— that I didn't notice Nita hadn't spoken to me since we left the party. Therefore, when she shook her finger in my face, threw my pillow at me, and slammed the bedroom door, it came as a real surprise.

Two ducks leave the pack and head for a secluded cove. At least somebody's getting some. I wish I hadn't had it out with Judy. I adore Nita and intend to spend the rest of my life with her, but her libido isn't terribly strong. Judy's libido, on the other hand, is as robust as they come. Our weekday lunchtimes are extremely satisfying...to me, anyway. They're satisfying to Judy too; I'm sure of it. She just wanted to get back at me—that's why she said she was faking it. That *is* why, isn't it? I can't go another minute without knowing. I punch her number into my cell phone.

"Hello?" Judy says. Her voice sends my hormones charging.

"Judy, it's Melissa. I'm sorry for last night at the party. I'm not going to fire you, you know. You can put your prepositions anywhere you like. By the way, have you really been fak—"

She interrupts. "What's that clicking sound?"

"It's my teeth chattering."

"Where are you?"

"Out at Harmony Lake, at the campground. Nita and I had a misunderstanding."

"Oh, you poor thing," she says. "It's *cold* out."

"Believe me, I know. Can I come over?"

"No."

"No?" I heave a great sigh.

"They're fumigating today and all the tenants have to leave. I was on my way out when you called. But why don't I bring some coffee and sandwiches to the lake?"

Yes!

Forty-five minutes later she drives up and pulls into the space across from mine. She opens her red down parka and keeps me warm while I chug two hot coffees. Then we get in the back of my truck and eat the sandwiches, after which we crawl in the bag and warm it up with fiery kisses and friction. It isn't long before Judy moans and says, "Oh, boss, boss, *boss*!"

"Was that a genuine 'boss, boss, boss'?" I ask.

"Definitely," she gasps. Then she dives to the bottom of the bag and pulls down my sweatpants. Hearing a muffled *mew*

mew, I smile in anticipation of a tickly tongue game we've come to call "Catnip."

By the time I hear the crunch of tires on gravel, I'm majorly turned on and sweating profusely. Thinking it's a park ranger or something, I ignore it. But I can't ignore the slam of a car door.

I sit up and look out the window. "Holy shit!" I say. "It's Nita!" She's parked her BMW on the road and is walking toward my pickup.

From my nether regions comes a muffled "What?"

"Judy," I whisper into the bag, "stay exactly where you are and don't make a sound." I pull up my pants, slide out of the bag, and jump outside, latching the cap's door behind me. "Nita, baby," I say, pulling her over by the picnic table, "you found me!"

She blushes prettily. "I know how you love this place, Melissa, so I thought maybe you'd come here. Look at your poor face—it's bright red from the cold and all wet from the rain." She looks puzzled. "But how could it be wet? You were in the back of the truck."

"I just went in a minute ago. My fingers and toes were getting numb." I try to force a teeth-chatter, but it doesn't quite hack it.

It works for Nita, though. She gives me a big hug and cries, "Oh, honey! You might have frozen to death, and it would have been all my fault. I'm so sorry I accused you of having something going on with Judy. But it wouldn't be the first time you've strayed, you know." She sticks out her adorable lower lip.

I kiss it and say, "Sweetheart, didn't I promise you I would never do it again?"

"Yes, you did, but... Well, come on, let's go home. I'll follow you."

"No! I'll follow *you*." Who knows when Judy's head might pop up?

Before Nita gets in the driver's seat, she points to Judy's car across the way. "Whose Honda?" she asks.

"I have no idea," I tell her. "It was here when I arrived."

I consider getting "lost" on the way home so I can double back and leave Judy at her car, but I decide not to. Nita may be gullible, but she's not stupid.

As I pull into the garage, Nita hops out and pushes the button to close the double door. When it's finished grinding, she says, "I'll go make some hot chocolate, and then I'm going to take you to the bedroom and..." *wink, wink* "...really warm you up."

Whoop-de-doo! I'm going to get myself chilled more often.

Before going in the house, I walk to the back of the pickup and open the cap. Judy crawls out of the bag, and her hair looks terrible. I throw her a comb, my cell phone, and a twenty-dollar bill. "Wait half an hour and call a taxi," I whisper. "Have them pick you up at the corner."

"Why do I have to wait half an hour?"

"Nita's in the kitchen, and she might hear. By then I'll have her in the bedroom at the back of the house. Leave through the side door, but hang on to it. It slams."

"You're going to be very, very sorry for this, Melissa," Judy says.

"We'll talk about it Monday." I go in the house, locking the door behind me.

The make-up sex is fantastic. Nita is eager to please and much more responsive than usual. I'm lying on top of her with my hand between her legs when we hear a door slam. Her head flies up. "What was that?"

"The neighbors," I say.

"No, it was closer than the neighbors." She rolls out from under me and runs to the kitchen. In a few seconds, she returns and says, "Somebody in a red parka is walking away from our garage."

I grab my robe. "You stay here, baby. I'll go check."

By the time I get outside, Judy is way down the block, her rear end rocking like an indignant duck's. She must sense me watching, because she shoves her right hand in the air, middle finger extended.

"Who was it?" Nita asks when I return.

"Some guy knocking on doors, probably selling something," I tell her. Now, where were we?"

Nita lies down again, but she isn't as relaxed as before, and once or twice I catch her looking at me through narrowed eyes.

On Monday morning, when I try to start my pickup, the engine grinds but doesn't catch. Damn, Nita knows way more about engines than I do, but she's already left for work. On the second try, however, it starts. When I stop at the florist's to pick up a dozen white roses, Judy's favorite, I leave it running, just in case.

Judy isn't at her desk when I get to work, so I continue past and open the door to my office, heading for a closet where I keep a cobalt vase for such occasions. Judy loves the way the deep blue sets off the white of the petals; the gestalt is usually worth a couple of rounds of Catnip.

"Flowers? For me?" says a familiar voice. It's Nita, lounging in my desk chair as if she owns the place.

"Of course they're for you," I say. "I was going to bring…"

"Spare me the lies, Melissa. I just had a long talk with Judy."

"Judy?" I say like I can't place the name.

"I waited for her in the employee's lot this morning. And guess what, Melissa? She was wearing a bright red parka."

"No kidding? They're very popular this year." Then, since I trust Judy not to give away secrets, I ask, "So what did you two talk about?"

"*Mew, mew,*" Nita says nastily.

So much for trust! "Believe me, sweetheart, I have no idea what you're talking about. Where is Judy, anyway?"

"She told me to tell you she quit. She doesn't need all this grief, she said, and she almost smothered in your sleeping bag. And, oh yeah, her harassment suit is on." Nita swings out of my chair and slips into her cashmere coat, the one I gave her for Christmas.

"But, honey," I say.

"Don't bother coming home tonight. You can pick up your things on the weekend." She flounces out, her leather bag tucked tightly under her arm.

I spend the day composing an ad for a new secretary and trying to figure out Judy's filing system. I call her at home, but her answering machine tells me to leave a message unless I'm Melissa.

After work, my pickup won't start at all. The tow-truck driver turns out to be a butchy young thing in greasy coveralls. She jumps out and says, "How you doin' today?"

"Quite well, thank you." I admire her agility as she attaches a giant hook to the underside of my pickup.

I ask if I can ride along, and she says, "Why not?" A few blocks later when I undo my seat belt and edge toward the middle of the bench seat, she looks at me out of the corner of her eye and grins.

"Quack?" I say softly.

Penny for Your Thoughts

Rakelle Valencia

First, my dog had to like her, and he's not fond of many. He's a working dog, an Aussie cattle dog, a blue heeler—you know, he nips. Then, she wasn't to cause any disrespect to my horse. No flowers braided into his mane or teeny bits of apple cut up and doled out as prize offerings much in the way of a grandmother being cheap with her butterscotch drops. The big gelding is no child and doesn't take to condescension. He works for a living too.

Last, but not at all least, there was no way she'd ever ask to borrow my pickup truck. Not that the dented bucket of rust is in great shape now. Not like it once was, tricked out fancier than a silver parade saddle. But she'd know never to bargain on driving a cowboy's pickup. If she understood all of that, she might have me, a cussed bitch. More than she probably wanted, and less than she'd probably hoped for.

I wasn't going to settle for less, and I knew I'd probably

never find the entire deal. That made it safe. I wasn't one for commitment. I was all cowboy—ridin', ropin', dreamin', and never quite as faithful as a hound dog.

Then it struck me. I had found it, all of it, in one package of packed, feminine form. With *her,* I wanted to try the faithful part. Maybe I was in love. I was getting around to thinking on that, though not entirely there, when she nibbled my ear and whispered, "Penny for your thoughts."

My thinking had gone astray with words like *faithful* and *love.* I thought about some of those earlier, more promiscuous times when I'd been a randy cock of the walk. Earlier days. Okay, not much earlier.

And in a blip of mere seconds, I'd been thinking those old boots of mine slopped against the wall had patiently waited many a time, resting against many walls or under many beds. I wondered what got shoved under those beds, except for my jeans that I'd drop and kick out of habit, with a heavy clank from my prized belt buckle. My head got distracted remembering the different sounds that silver buckle made when it met wood or various types of rugs—throw rugs or plush wall-to-wall.

I was thinking about the menagerie of women I had visited, bodies of varying shapes and sizes sliding against my body. How I'd thrash and hump and pump until panting. And that led me to think about how I loved sex, and needed more and more and more, but still seemed to be missing something.

So I said to her, "I was thinkin' about you."

I rolled over in her arms, sucking at her lower lip until I could prop above her on an elbow and lazily fondle a breast. I do so love breasts, much to my parents' chagrin. Which made me think on how it left them wondering where they went wrong, until they gave up on me completely. But they'd wondered where they'd gone wrong before that, when I took up riding fast horses. Then I pondered on fast horses and fast women. Hey, it's not like I did any of it to damage my parents.

And actually it's the nipples. It didn't take my mind much to go there. Nipples are truly my thing, rolling and pinching them between my fingers, feeling the hardening of each fleshy nodule from my tongue's ministrations. It's the nipples. I could wrap my mouth around them all day, holding one between my front teeth to drag my tongue across the puckered tip, suckling like a wanton babe.

That brought my brain back into focus, and I tugged at the flowered cotton sheet to expose a plumped, pinked nipple. But then I had to wonder why sheets were always flowered. At least most of the women's beds I'd visited seemed to have some fluffy flower print. Maybe that was the type of women I had been visiting with. Made me think I ought to go on a mission to seek out other sheets—stripes, plaids, plains, starched whites, colors. Would the women be different?

My hunger engulfed a pert nipple, and I forgot about sheets as my hand gathered more of her rounded breast. I was latched on good, my mouth satisfied in its work, but my hands needed to wander. Some things, some people, just have to be kept busy all of the time.

Her moaning egged me on. It was like the rumbling of a purring cat until my weathered fingers found the oasis they were trekking to. I dipped in, going for the slippery wetness first, then trailing the fluid up her slit and over her clitoris, to play in slow circles. That moaning turned into short labored breaths interspersed with mutant vocal noises, soothing to my ears, but still my mind went elsewhere.

If I had a dick...if I had a dick right now, an engorged prick, I'd so sink it into her, filling her up and feeling her warm, wet sheath glove around my prod. I didn't need a dick to get her done, though. That's the thing about women: They don't absolutely have to have dick. I sank two fingers into her. She bucked, wanting more.

Beneath me, her body felt right. Her hot, sweating, writhing body—it belonged to me, was somehow part of me, and I wanted to give it the utmost pleasure. Go figure. I hadn't felt this way before, and flowered sheets be damned. I flicked her slippery clit with my thumb then pressured the shaft with tiny, quick circles, little, fast circles that I could get lost in, spiraling circles that continued on and on. A moan escaped my throat.

This wasn't just sex. It bordered on making love, or perhaps it was making love. I wasn't sure and would have to put some thought on it. Sex was one thing. I've had sex—good sex, randy sex, fun sex, exhilarating sex, sex I couldn't get enough of. This was different. It was all of that and more, or with a twist.

My mouth needed to be all over her, sucking at white, fleshy skin. Leaving reddened pockmarks, angry brands from fired irons, marking what I wanted to keep as mine. I worried her hide, nipped and bit, never getting enough, as if I were starved.

Climbing on low, I rode the undulating waves that her pelvis made to sink me farther into her, three fingers, four. She cried for more in small gasps, and I gave it all, all five fingers, palm, heel of my hand, and past my wrist. Wondering if it would ever be enough. Hoping I wouldn't lose my now buried forearm as a burning sensation crept its way to my shoulder.

Her legs flung wildly to pin my waist, encircling me in a vice-like grip as she clamped around my lost, pumping limb, screeching some sort of carnal plea then wailing in lament. Tears escaped her clenched eyes. The salty wetness rolled toward her conservatively pierced ears.

I thought she would surely cut my rangy arm off as I watched. Her face scrunched into contortions of creatures unknown. And I didn't care. I was thinking about her.

My dog jumped onto the bed and snorkeled my tight white ass with his cold, wet nose. The sheets had fallen away. Flowered petals descended in a flutter to expose bare limbs. I swatted the air in front of the stout cattle dog. The pup jumped down, circled in the discarded bed linen on the floor, and slept.

I flicked my tongue into the inviting hole of her smooth-skinned navel, grinding to the bottom with my wet prod's pointed tip. Her smooth fingers entangled my mop of short, brown hair and closed around the strands that tried to escape. My head was pulled away, and where my head went my body would likely follow. But rolling spasms entrapped my arm. I remained locked in opposing grips, my mind solely concentrated on her pleasure.

It took just a slight nod of my warmly engulfed, balled fist to produce surreal sounds from her gurgling throat. Waves rolled through her. With each twitch of orgasm, my sweat-soaked hair got yanked harder, exposing the straining cords of my neck.

I had only one hand free to do the rest of my bidding. I roamed over wide-open territory, hills, valleys, and mounds. Her full-figured flesh yielded to my prodding, except for those stiff, pert nipples that stood tall and held their ground.

Licking my starving lips, I pinched a nipple cruelly between my pointer and thumb. She bucked strong, almost expelling my arm from her slick innards.

Struggling through incoherent convulsions, holding through violent aftershocks, I rode with her to exhaustion, feeling the sodden crease between my own thighs tense to implosion.

In a still moment I whispered, "Shh...I was thinking about you."

House-Tree-Person Test

T. Stores

I. Construction

House

We're looking for a place to live, B.J. and me, together.

It's hard to find just the right house for both of us: office space for me, studio space for her, a yard or park for the dog, a landlord who will accept pets, enough light for her, enough square footage for me, no carpets, high ceilings, central to both our schools....

It's also less than a year that we've been dating. Too soon, all our friends say, to move in together. Forget the old joke about lesbians moving in on the second date; in our crowd there are rules about these things.

We sit in my apartment, a tattered commercial unit in an old building overlooking Boston Common, exhausted from our search, tired of bickering, discouraged with compromise.

"Maybe they're all right," B.J. says, staring out the tall windows into the trees.

"Maybe it's too soon," I say, wondering what's under the

'70s paneling on the walls and above the suspended acoustic tile ceiling.

We'll try again tomorrow. We want to build something that much.

Tree

To build a house in a tree, you must first find the right tree...*trees*.

When I was a girl, I climbed trees.

Pines were sweet and straight and tall. Hugging the rough bark, wrapped around the trunk, sitting on a branch no bigger than my wrist, swaying in even the smallest wind, I could sometimes see the ocean. I was part of the tree, and I saw faraway dreams. But pines are not the best for building. Each branch is offset from the other, like stair steps, which is good for climbing, but the lowest branch is too high, and who wants to shimmy up to one's home? When you nail into it, a pine will bleed.

A live oak is the best for construction. Its arms are a cradle, branches low to the ground and side by side. The live oak's trunk is solid and wide. It lives two hundred years, growing slowly over the nails, and eventually over the wooden construction. The tree house becomes part of the tree.

If you are very lucky, you will find a live oak and a pine together, the trunk of the sweet, sappy one between the solid, stretching limbs of the other. Both are evergreen.

When you build a house in the cradle of the oak, you can build around the pine...a house that will stand a hundred years and a house with a place to climb.

Person

I am tall. She has more curves.

I would like to make a place where I can see far, where I can still dream. B.J. wants us to build something solid, something that will last forever.

159

She is an incest survivor. I am another kind of survivor.

We decide together that we will build something together.

This is scary. Inside, I am afraid of heights. Inside, she is afraid of old dreams.

We decide to rehab this patchworked apartment overlooking the Common. The building is solid, nearly a hundred years old. In the '70s, when we were both girls, this construction was layered over with fake wood paneling, suspended under acoustic tile ceilings, shagged with burnt orange carpets, and lit fluorescent. But the ceilings are high, the windows tall, and the view distant beyond the trees.

We will build something together.

II. Deconstruction
House

I built my tree house from the parts of things torn apart.

My dad tore down the room he had added onto our house because the inspector Mom shouldn't have let in said it was unsafe. The roof could have come down on our heads. I took the extra-long two-by-fours (one of which Dad accidentally dropped on my brother's head…a "funny" family story for years) to use for the crossbeams to support the floor of my tree house.

I found two heavy doors in the Dumpster behind the university. The doors would be my floor.

That's really all you need for a tree house. Support and a floor. I imagined a frame of clear white fir, a tall peaked roof, sheer curtains at the windows, pictures on the walls, a chimney with smoke pouring forth.

All I really needed, though, I found in the rubble of something dissected.

Tree

A storm has blown over one of the huge elms in the Common. The roots are still mostly in the ground, and the branches are a maze, still intact. The dog is ecstatic for the sticks to chase. B.J. and I poke into knotholes, discuss what one needs to hibernate in these knotholes, sit on the trunk and dangle our feet while we discuss each next phase of our rehab...the deconstruction.

We throw broken twigs for the dog, escaping, for now, the plaster dust, the dangling wires, the rotted carpet rolled in the hall to be carted away. We have peeled away the layers and found these: plaster crown moldings, a hidden doorway, oak doors that slide into the wall, a huge fireplace, gold-leaf wall-paper, a brick wall in the kitchen, a marble bathroom. We have scavenged the burned-down theater next door for a filigreed floor-to-ceiling round mirror and a tattered poster of Sarah Bernhardt as Hamlet. We eat our lunches sitting on this fallen tree in the park, surrounded by branches of golden leaves, because the apartment is a mess.

One morning they have cut the tree into parts. The trunk lies in segments on the ground. Soon it will no longer be a tree. We count the rings, imagine the history of the tree, make up stories. We roll a huge section of trunk into the building and up the stairs to our apartment for a plant stand.

Back at work, we save all the wood we rip down to use again. "We're saving a lot of trees," we say.

Person

My body divided into parts like in the *Encyclopedia Americana* under "Human" as I collected scraps for my tree house.

Muscles one day. Huge, burning red sinews of raw liver like the cellophane picture you turn over the skeleton page. I had been dragging heavy doors out of the university Dumpster.

Hands. They swelled up and throbbed. I couldn't hold my pen in school the day after I used the rope to haul the wood up the tree.

Skin. Purple shins. Open sores and scrapes. You have to get all the bent, rusty nails out of scavenged wood before you can use it. Splinters lodged just under my surface.

I dragged my bruised and wounded parts into the top of the pine, wrapped my legs around the trunk and swayed, watching my brother and the other boys play war games below. They never saw me.

I wasn't there, and I was.

III. Reconstruction
House

We are almost too tired for the last part.

We argue over the paint colors, the light fixtures, the way we will redo the floor.

We compromise.

I saw both old wood and new and burn the trimmings in the fireplace. Our home is sweet with a forest smell: oak, pine, cedar, fir. B.J. brushes the walls and trim the colors of sky and growing things. We need no curtains on the tall windows because we are so high. All we see is treetops, leaves.

We separate the studio and the office with new drywall. I put her picture on my side; she puts my poem on hers.

From the Common, we look up and see our red brick building solid on the sidewalk and neat between empty lots. The balustrade on the roof is green with age, a fancy old crown. We pick out our windows, all three on both the fifth and six floors.

Home. We have built it together.

Tree

A tree house is never really finished. You have to build it again and again.

The tree grows. It bends and the house must bend as well. There are always additions to be made, repairs, redesigns.

Something new to be salvaged and hauled up by rope and muscle and hand.

There were lots of long days just lying there though. I was part of the leaves, part of the tree. I branched out, hid in the foliage, grew.

Person

"You have a great place," our friends tell us. "You," as if the living together has made us one person. We are not.

I sit in tall windows, uncurtained, high over the Common during her flashbacks. She curves into a girl under the quilts below the ornamental orange tree which sits on the tree trunk. I'm not exactly safe with the problems of her past, but her love is familiar and strong.

We make some things: a book, a painting, a home.

We take them apart: layers, trees, skin, paper, paint.

We create something new from the old pieces: house, tree, person.

Gravel

Judith Frank

Toweling off after a shower, Abby felt her ears pop and her heart begin its mad scramble. She closed her eyes and tried to pretend she was high on some nice drug, instead of percolating with chemotherapy drugs, anti-nausea drugs, thrush medicine, laxatives, and the steroids they gave her for the first three days after an infusion. Yesterday's treatment had been the final one. She opened the bathroom window to let in the raw spring air. It entered in uneven gusts, cooling her damp, flushed neck and face. The dog came in and applied himself to her wet ankles with an assiduous tongue. He was a little terrier mix named Tucker, and he had been decidedly unheroic when she'd come home from her surgery, tromping over her bandaged chest when she was lying down, shrieking in her ear at the slightest grumble of a truck in the distance. She nudged him away with her foot. She could hear the crunch of Claire's boots on the driveway, and the squeak of the wheelbarrow.

She wrapped her towel around her waist and turned toward the mirror, where there was a lot to take stock of these days.

Her big ridged bald head, not unhandsome. The thin fading scars that puckered her skin and slanted slightly upward toward the armpit: two handmade, inexpert seams sewing shut her chest. The bulge of flesh at the front of each armpit, at the top of each scar. The two small round scars where the drains had been. Her old radiation tattoos. She lay her palms on her chest, arms crossed, feeling the damp heat of her skin and the pleasant knobby surface of her ribs, a ship's hull. She gave her chest a virile grip; she flexed her pecs and felt them swell under her palms. As far as Abby was concerned, her breasts had been nothing but a huge can of worms ever since her first diagnosis twelve years before. Looking at her chest now, and enjoying the way its blankness broadened her shoulders, she marveled at how little she missed them. She knew it was improbable, but no matter how hard she tried to peer into the subterranean parts of herself to find a glimmer of grief, she always came up empty. On the contrary, she sought out the mirror. She secretly wished that her friends would ask to see her scars. She had strange and embarrassing fantasies about people accidentally walking in on her when she had her shirt off. She'd taken to wearing skintight undershirts with oxford shirts over them, unbuttoned. As the oxford whispered over the undershirt, it created a tease: Were there breasts under there, or weren't there? To Abby, this felt like a whole new and welcome way to be sexy.

Claire told their friends: From a gender perspective, Abby's having a ball. This seemed to their friends to be a pretty extreme case of looking on the bright side, but they were gamely supportive. Next, her doctors were going to go after Abby's estrogen, because her tumors were the kind that used it to grow on. Her ovaries were scheduled to be removed over the summer, and after that she would be put on a new class of drugs designed to mop up every last trace of estrogen produced by her body. She'd always known, she told her oncologist, only half-joking, that her femininity was killing her.

In the front yard, under a tempestuous sky, Claire was raking out the daylily bed, which had been mangled by the snowplow. This weekend she was getting the grounds of the house in order, raking and hauling plant debris into the woods, using a chainsaw to take down the trees that had broken or died under the weight of snow. A load of new gravel for the driveway was scheduled to be delivered that afternoon. She straightened and leaned on the rake for a moment, contemplating with a gloomy eye the grass the plow had gouged when it plunged through the reflecting stakes she'd put up to mark the boundaries of the driveway, and the big rhododendron whose entire middle had been devoured, in late winter, by hungry deer.

They lived in the woods, where the soil was rocky and acidic, and where the front of the house got sun for only a few hours a day. So last summer, Claire had planted around the front entrance plants that can thrive in shade: azalea, mountain laurel, euonymus. She had covered their beds with layers of mulch in hopes that they'd survive the winter, but their poor remaining branches looked withered and paralytic now, and she wasn't sure they'd pull through. It had been a long winter: It had snowed on Thanksgiving and never let up till late March. By January, the piles of snow the plows had pushed back from the driveway had come up to her shoulders. When she had taken the dog out at night, her boots had crackled on the icy driveway amid the absolute quiet of winter desolation, and looking up at the rows of icicles hanging from the gutters, and at the tall pines whose branches moaned and drooped under the weight of snow, Claire had felt like a lost girl in a demented fairy tale. Her girlfriend inside, shrunken by poisons.

Claire was thirty-four, ten years younger than Abby, and when she tried to imagine living without her, her mind went blank and dead. They had gone to the same college a decade apart and had met in a gym when Claire was wearing her college T-shirt and Abby came up to chat and flirt. She had been bisexual until she got involved with Abby. One day soon after they met they had gone on a hike in the hills surrounding their town, and Claire had confided that she found women more interesting and compelling than men but couldn't see herself giving up the exciting danger she associated with sex with men. Abby had given her a lazy and cocky smile.

In the past months, she had seen Abby through her surgery and through the frightening postsurgical infection that had landed her back in the hospital for a week and taken seven different antibiotics to get under control. She had seen her through periods of chemo when Abby lay on the couch, as wasted as an addict. She had leapt for the remote control to turn off the TV whenever George W. Bush appeared on the screen, because Abby's last cancer episode had occurred during the Gulf War, and they both believed that Bush presidencies cause cancer. She had filled the house with crackers, ginger ale, oatmeal, and macaroni and cheese, Abby's comfort foods. Yesterday she'd brought home ten dollars' worth of organic strawberries and washed and frozen them for smoothies.

Claire was a big girl, slender and strong. In a flannel shirt she looked like a farm boy, capable hands dangling at her side. In a little black dress she looked like Jackie O. She was stubborn and opinionated; Abby said that her opinions were sometimes wrong but always fiercely held. Claire was a lawyer, and her family was disappointed that she'd settled in Abby's small town to run a family law practice; they had always imagined her, Claire joked, as a senator in an Ann Taylor suit, commanding the floor. Still, Claire's mother was given to tousling Abby's hair and thanking her, on behalf of the whole family, for undertaking the difficult management of her daughter. Only Abby knew how goofy Claire was, and how much she sometimes craved being fought and overcome, or cradled like a child.

Now Abby went into the bedroom and lay down naked on the bed for a second and closed her eyes. Half an hour before she had taken Dexamethasone, which they gave her to stimulate her energy and appetite, so she was hoping to be roused any moment now. Last month, galvanized by the crazy energy of the steroids the morning after an infusion, it had suddenly struck her that she and Claire had been together for eight years, sharing a thirty-year mortgage, a bank account, several beloved animals, and a cancer diagnosis, but they had not yet merged their books on the living room shelves. "It's ludicrous!" she'd squawked at Claire, who was still in bed, and who'd groaned and turned over. That morning Abby had taken all the novels down off the shelves, put the duplicates in a box to sell at the used-book store, lined up the remaining books on the floor, re-alphabetized them, washed the shelves with water and Murphy's oil, and put the books back up. Only that night had the energy sapped out of her; she had thrown up dinner, and she spent the next few days in bed.

The dog went berserk and Abby heard the beep of a truck backing up. She heaved herself up and put on underwear and jeans and a sweatshirt and then went into the living room and peered out the window. The gravel truck had arrived and was backing down the long driveway into the turnaround in front of the house. She stood barefoot on the wood floor in a warm pool of sunlight, thinking vaguely that she should probably put on a hat in case the guy came inside. A few days earlier Claire had embarked on the gravel project, new gravel having apparently gone from being one of the many things they could spend their savings on to being an absolute necessity. In Abby's experience, when Claire reached this point, it was no use resisting. Her argument usually went: If they didn't take care of the problem now, it would cause an avalanche of other problems and ultimately seriously compromise the structural integrity and/or resale value of the house. So Claire had called quarries and found that what they needed was called trap rock. She had compared prices. She had described the driveway's dimensions to the guy at the quarry and, at his recommendation, had ordered a truckload.

"A truckload?" Abby had asked when Claire got off the phone, raising her eyebrows in feigned interest. She was sitting at the kitchen table eating pretzel sticks and reading *Entertainment Weekly* as dinner cooked.

"Yeah," Claire said. "That's apparently twenty-five tons of gravel."

Abby had looked up from her magazine. "Twenty-five tons!" she said. "That sounds like an awful lot." But she wasn't sure; she'd never done this before either, and it was Claire who was the authority about things around the house—Claire who, the daughter of an architect, had been raised to believe you could alter the environment you lived in.

It had sounded like a lot to Claire too, although she didn't say so aloud. "Think about it," she said, opening the oven, stooping to poke a fork in the baked potatoes. "Stone is really dense."

"True," Abby said. She hesitated to question Claire's judgment since Claire had carried the burden of every single decision and chore since Abby's illness. "But twenty-five tons? Isn't that the weight of, like, a Mack truck?"

Claire closed the oven and stood. "I really want a good cover," she insisted, intimating, to Abby's exasperated ear, that Abby would be satisfied with a half-assed job. "And you'd usually need a Bobcat to spread all of that, but he says he's going to do this thing called tailgate spreading, where he'll open the back of his truck just a tiny bit and let it sift out as he drives." Her hands were on her hips. If he did all the spreading, she added, it didn't matter how heavy the stone

169

was. And anyway, the gravel itself was surprisingly inexpensive; it was the delivery that comprised half the cost. She was revving herself up into certainty, with that driving, passionate, irrefutable rationality that always put Abby herself into a trance of conviction.

Now Abby stood at the living room window watching Claire talk to the gravel delivery guy at the truck window. Tucker was barking shrilly and insistently at the front door, and Abby yelled at him to shut up. She watched Claire gesticulate over the driveway; she was wearing sunglasses, and looked disheveled and flushed and beautiful from raking and the wind. The guy was nodding.

Claire stepped back, arms crossed, and the truck began to pull out. Abby heard its roar and the grind of gears, saw the back door rise a crack and then spring open. An enormous pile of gravel swept out onto the turnaround, raising a cloud of dust. Abby clapped her hands to her head. Claire shouted and ran toward the truck, and there was another consultation. A few minutes later, five huge piles, presumably five tons apiece, had been dumped onto the driveway, one of them blocking the garage, and Abby had run back into the bedroom to pull on some socks.

When Claire came in Abby rushed to hug her, laughing. "Oh, honey," she said, "that tailgate spreading didn't work so well, did it?"

Claire was stiff in her hug, and her eyes were huge. "What are we going to do with all this gravel?" she cried.

"It's fine," Abby said, soothing, laughing. "We'll spread it ourselves."

"He said we needed at least a truckload!"

"Yeah, well, at least it didn't cost too much." Abby was rummaging in the front closet for her work boots and gloves. She sat on the hall floor and started pulling them on.

"What are you doing?" Claire demanded.

Abby gazed up at her, her bald head huge and her lips pale. What Claire missed most of all, she thought as she looked at her, more than her breasts even, were her eyelashes. "Going out to shovel," Abby said.

"Are you kidding me?" Claire asked. "You can't go out there the day after chemo."

"Why not?" Abby asked, pulling on her Xena Warrior Princess baseball cap, one of a dozen or so hats she now owned, many of them brought over by friends, who had also showered her with large quantities of pot. "I'm all hopped up on steroids, remember?"

She walked past Claire and out the door into the blustery afternoon and trotted over to the garage for a shovel.

Last time, Abby had been radiant with terror and in love with everybody. She'd gone to a breast cancer support group and been dazzled by the courage of the women there. She'd dropped every thankless activity and relationship with relief, and when the radiation therapy ended, she learned how hard it can be to let go of illness and the thrilling permission it offers. She had spent the intervening twelve years trying to achieve what she considered the ideal distance from cancer: far enough away to let go of the fear but close enough to hold on to the electric joy of being alive.

This diagnosis, for some reason, had come without terror, even though it should have been scarier. Instead it came with a grim mix of incredulity and irritation. She balked at the idea of joining a support group, or contacting the local cancer resource center, or writing about it in her journal. It began to grate on her the way people flung around the word "chemo," as though they were on such intimate terms with it that they could use its nickname; she always called it "chemotherapy" herself, to set an example. She listened with a strained polite expression to the legions of acquaintances who reported that they knew someone who had undergone "chemo," and voilà! her hair had come back thicker, or darker, or curly.

It was breaking the news that was hardest for Abby. She begged her friends to spread the word so that she wouldn't have to do so over and over, but they were turning out to be preternaturally discreet when it came to cancer. She was reminded of trying to come out in college; in a community rampant with world-class gossips, she had been unable get the news circulating because everyone was suddenly, infuriatingly, respecting her privacy. She'd had to tell every one of her friends herself, making, she later said, lunch date after frigging lunch date. Now, she was learning to break her bad news gently and gradually, following up with assurances that the tumor was small and sedate and that her prognosis was still good. She made jokes so her loved ones could see she was still herself, and comforted people in advance so they wouldn't panic and fall apart. But they still did. She complained to her therapist that the house smelled sickening from flower arrangements and that her principal was insisting she take a medical leave over the spring semester. "And did you know," she added, "that the slogan for breast cancer in the American cancer establishment is 'Why Me?' It's even part of the hotline number. Can you believe that? Only Americans could expect to be so immune. It's disgusting. Why the hell *not* me?"

He said, "So you're saying it's not really that big a deal and that everybody's making it a bigger deal than it is."

Abby paused, and then laughed "Not to put too fine a point on it," she said.

A few weeks after her diagnosis she dreamed that she was being pushed onstage, a microphone forced into her hand, to deliver a stand-up comedy routine. After that, whenever Claire heard her delivering the news to people on the phone, and being witty and charming about it, she'd hold up a card she kept by the phone on which she'd written in big block letters: YOU DON'T HAVE TO DELIVER A STAND-UP COMEDY ROUTINE!

But there was another aspect of Abby's reaction to this new cancer, an aspect harder for her to articulate. Somehow, she sensed that having breast cancer the first time had made her a hero, but that having it again made her a loser. It was especially excruciating to tell those who understood best, her cancer buddies, the ones who'd survived breast cancer and Hodgkin's and melanoma, because every recurrence was a blow to them all and she knew she was demoralizing them. She also hated to be the one stigmatized with a recurrence. She could just imagine how she'd react if it happened to one of them. She'd step up to the plate like a man to help, but with a deep and guilty gratitude that it wasn't she who was sick again; and emotionally, part of her would begin to recede. She didn't want people to fly off the handle, but it frightened her that they might start acclimating themselves to the idea of her death.

Claire rushed out the door after her. Abby was emerging from the garage with a shovel in her hands, saying, "We'll need the wheelbarrow."

"Wait, just wait!"

Abby turned to look for where Claire had left the wheel-barrow, and Claire could see an angry mosquito bite on her scalp, in the exposed oval of skin above the clasp at the back of her baseball cap; it seemed to her a damning sign of Abby's obliviousness. "Stop," she barked.

Abby looked at her, leaned on the shovel's handle. "What? I just want to get started. It's okay." She was welled up with chivalry; she wanted to lunge in and hack away at this problem, to protect Claire from embarrassment and despair.

Claire saw the joyful resolve on her lover's face, and thought,

Baby, you have no clue. A rage whose cause she couldn't name was brewing in her. "We don't have a plan," she said.

Abby gestured expansively over the driveway, at the five enormous piles. The daffodils they'd planted at the edges of the woods were just starting to come up, and the bare branches of the trees were clicking and groaning in the wind. "How complicated could it be?" she asked. She had a tremendous urge to be planting the shovel into the big piles, shoving, heaving, scattering stones, sweating from physical activity rather than fever or nausea, taking her place among the striving people of the world.

Claire's face was cloudy, and Abby let her hand drop. Claire was slow to anger, but held onto it for a long time—the exact opposite of Abby, whose anger flared quickly but burned itself out just as fast. It wasn't a good combination for fighting. Abby usually passed through all the stages of a fight—outrage, hurt, seeing Claire's side, melting into empathy, apologizing, and getting ready to cook dinner—while Claire was just warming up.

"I just want to make a plan. You'll get started and then you'll get sick and it'll be totally up to me to finish it."

"That's exactly why I want to get started!" Abby exclaimed. "Can't you see that? In a few days I'm going to feel like shit, but right now I finally feel good enough to do something around the house."

"Can we at least make a plan for where to start?" Claire's tone was murderously patient.

"Why do we need a plan? We should start by the garage, so we can get a car out."

Claire looked at her bald girlfriend, who was rolling her eyes in a display of barely restrained forbearance. She couldn't believe that Abby kept trying to take charge; it galled her that she was leaping in and opining about how to deal with a crisis, when she'd spent the last three months so incapacitated she could barely read. An image was blooming in Claire's mind of the havoc Abby was going to wreak by randomly spraying gravel all over the place; she could see parts of the driveway ten inches thick, others barely covered, the wheelbarrow wallowing through a dense layer of sludge to drop the remaining three or four pebbles on the bare dirt nearest the street.

"We should start closest to the street," she said.

They haggled over this for a long time. Abby normally would have deferred to Claire, but now she found she just couldn't. It was stupid to start at the street; Claire was being unnecessarily complicated about this, insisting upon a degree of foresight Abby found paralyzing and ridiculous. Everything about Claire expressed stasis—the arms crossed resolutely across her chest, the unwashed hair plastered down on her forehead, the wraparound shades that hid her eyes and reflected Abby's face back to her as a big angry balloon. Claire was arguing that they should call their neighbors and ask to borrow one of their cars for a few days, and Abby was yapping, "Why? Why? Let's just get out one of our own cars. Why make it more of a big deal than it is?"

Finally, Claire stalked into the house to call their neighbors. Abby defiantly shoved her shovel into the heart of one of the piles by the garage, staggered backward with it, and heaved the gravel in the air. It fell and scattered with a splash. She did this three more times, and each time, the gravel slid down over the gash she'd made in the pile, erasing all traces of the shovel's mark. Claire emerged from the house a few minutes later, announcing that their neighbors could spare their minivan if she and Abby needed a car over the next few days.

So they trudged down the driveway to start shoveling at the street, Abby shaking her head, still thinking it was stupid not to start at the garage. Quickly, they devised a system: Abby filled the wheelbarrow, and Claire wobbled with it to the designated spot, dumped it, brought the empty wheelbarrow back, and then went back and raked out the spilled gravel. Once she began to work, Abby let her anger go and began to enjoy the metallic crunch of the shovel into the pile. She stepped on the edge of it with her boot and levered up a shovelful, shook and bounced it like a chef with a pizza in a pan. The sun was passing in and out of the clouds, and she quickly worked up a sweat; she took off her cap and peeled off her sweatshirt and wiped her head with it. She stood up, resting, breathing hard, and grinned at Claire, who was approaching with the empty wheelbarrow. "Not unlike working on a chain gang, is it?" she said. "I feel like we should be singing the blues."

Claire set the wheelbarrow down, put her hands on the small of her back, and arched into them with a groan. She straightened and looked dolefully over the driveway, which did indeed look like a penitentiary work site. "Oh, we'll be singing the blues all right," she said. That is, she thought, *she* would be. Abby would be lying queasily on the couch, watching *The Golden Girls*.

They had pondered the question of prostheses for a long time. For Abby it was more embarrassing to have people know she was wearing prostheses than it would be for them to see her flat-chested. A butch in falsies: What could be more mortifying? And yet she was an eighth-grade teacher, and the thought of her flattened chest being scrutinized by thirty nosy thirteen-year-olds wasn't that appealing either. It was a breakthrough when Abby came to realize that buying prostheses didn't mean she had to wear them all the time.

A few weeks before she was to begin chemotherapy, on a cloudy winter afternoon, she and Claire went to the local lingerie store that specialized in bras for breast cancer survivors. The bell on the door tinkled as they entered the store swathed in down coats, breathing steam. They headed toward the register, Abby's shoulders and elbows knocking underwear and bras off tiny hangers, their eyes scanning for the saleswoman with the most promising gender. There was a stocky salesperson wearing a black oxford shirt, but she was talking to a customer, and when they were approached it was by a woman in her sixties with dyed red hair, a brooch on her turtleneck sweater, and chains on her glasses. Her name was Marcia, and they gave each other sidelong looks as she led them to a back room marked off by a curtain. It was a comfortable space with fabric-covered benches in pastel colors, and another curtain creating yet another dressing room inside. Although she couldn't have put her finger on anything that was wrong with it, Claire had an uncomfortable sense that Abby was being incorporated into some notion they had about her shame. The two of them sat down on a bench, side by side. "Are you okay, Big Stuff?" Claire asked, when Marcia left the room for a moment.

Abby grinned. "Talk about a bull in a china shop," she said. She leaned over to kiss Claire, but quickly straightened when Marcia brushed aside the curtain and entered the tiny room again, smelling of perfume and asking which side Abby had had the surgery on.

"Both," they said. Claire's knee was jiggling anxiously, and Abby lay a hand on it to still it.

Marcia tsked. "And you're so young too."

It was a pleasant enough sympathy, practiced without being soulless. "Oh, that's okay," Abby said.

"What size bra did you wear, dear?" Marcia asked.

"I don't know," Abby said, taking off her coat. "I haven't worn one in a long time."

Marcia pulled out a tape measure and ran it around Abby's chest. Watching Abby lift her arms with cheerful obedience, Claire realized she was afraid that any minute Marcia was going to reassure Abby that even without breasts she could still look nice and feminine. And Abby shouldn't have to take that. She was such a good sport, the best-natured patient in the world under awful circumstances, and now she was going to have to deal with some straight lady's noxious assumptions about her gender. That possibility filled Claire with fury.

Marcia straightened and pronounced Abby a 36A. She slid open the door of a closet and started examining boxes; she took a few down and opened them up. There was a new technology that allowed prostheses to stick to the body instead of being sewn into the bra. Marcia held one form out with the back side up, and they each gave the sticky surface a tentative poke. Then, with an air of proprietary pride, Marcia slapped it hard onto her palm and turned it upside down to demonstrate how firmly it held.

Abby and Claire held out their hands, and she pressed a small, peach-colored silicone mound in each of their palms. They turned their hands upside down and looked at each other with impressed faces. Claire gently ran her hand over the soft surface of the fake breast.

"I want a smaller size than I actually was," Abby told Marcia. "I want the difference between wearing the prostheses and not wearing them to be very slight."

Marcia rummaged in the closet, reaching way in the back, and pulled out a box marked "Size 0." "That should do it," Claire said, laughing softly. She watched as Abby lay one of the small forms against her scars and pressed, then took a step back and assessed in the mirror. Her stomach bulged a little over the waist of her jeans, and her sandy hair was shaggy and unkempt; soon they would give her a buzz cut to prepare for it falling out. Looking at her, Claire realized she hadn't yet really been able to take stock of Abby's scars without her mind conjuring an image of the surgeon plunging a needle into Abby's scarlet, swollen, blistering, infected chest to siphon off orange fluid. She could see that Abby was finally healing well. But now, in a tiny room surrounded by mirrors, watching her lover focus on settling the peach-colored blobs in the right place, Claire was heavyhearted. Sure she could come to love this chest, as Abby was clearly coming to. It was just that she had passionately loved Abby the way she was. Claire pressed her hands between her knees. "Too much to the center," she said, and Abby peeled the left one off, grimacing. "Does it hurt?"

"No, it just pulls," Abby said. "Hey, what if I get a tattoo on one of the scars? I was thinking of a bow and arrow." She drew an imaginary arrow and narrowed her eyes, taking aim.

"No way!" Claire cried, stricken by the idea of more needles.

Abby had assumed that if they got these stick-on prostheses, she'd be spared having to wear a bra, something she hadn't done in decades. But that turned out not to be the case: Even though the prostheses were supposed to fit securely, Marcia told them it was recommended they be worn with bras. Abby grimaced with disappointment, and Claire placed a commiserating hand on her arm. "Well," Abby finally said, "I guess I can't have one of my boobs sliding down my chest in front of my homeroom class." Marcia persuaded her to buy two bras, since her insurance would cover them. "Okay," Abby said. "But listen up. They have to be extremely unfrilly. I can't emphasize that enough. If you have jog bras, that'd be ideal."

"I understand," Marcia said, and vanished into the store.

Claire put her hands on Abby's shoulders and squeezed. "How you holding up, champ?"

Abby lolled her head around like a prizefighter between rounds.

Marcia returned holding four bras on hangers. Claire and Abby took one look and said, "No."

"You didn't even look at them!" Marcia said reproachfully, and began holding them up one by one. "Not even this one?"

It was a very plain and pretty white bra, with a delicate V neckline. Claire stood and puffed up before it like a big threatened waterfowl. "No!" she squawked. "It's not her style."

After a long time, during which Claire wondered if they were being punished, Marcia returned with two unobjectionable jog bras. Abby tried them on and gave them the thumbs-up. As she got dressed, Claire stood, pink-cheeked and sweaty, their parkas stuffed under her arm. At the cash register, they were all super nice to one another, trying to compensate for any awkwardness that had occurred.

They left off shoveling for a lunch break, and after they'd eaten, Claire went into her study to make some calls, agreeing with Abby that they'd go back outside in half an hour. Abby took Tucker out to pee; he sniffed a pile of gravel, his tail wagging, and clambered up it. As she followed him around with a periodic command to "Go potty," Abby examined the driveway. If she flattened the side of the pile blocking the garage, it occurred to her, she might be able to get out the Subaru, their all-wheel-drive car. She could take one side over the flattened pile and the other along the edge of the woods. She took the dog back inside, came out, and began to dig.

Twenty minutes later, putting papers into her briefcase and getting ready to go back outside, Claire heard the grind of the garage door rising and the gun of the car's engine. She froze. What on earth was Abby doing?

Behind the wheel, Abby was inching back and forth into the tightest three-point turn she'd ever made. When she had the car facing forward, she shifted it into drive and aimed for the semi-flattened side of the pile blocking the way. She felt the car rise up the pile, tilt, and then sink into the gravel; the right-side tires rumbled over leaves and roots and stumps in the woods. Her heart was hammering. And then the wheels caught and she was over and easing the car gently around the other piles to the foot of the driveway. She got out and Claire watched from the window as Abby strode toward the house, looked over at the ruts the car had made, and smacked her hands together once in satisfaction. When she came in, calling "Hey, baby, guess what!" Claire came to the door and said coldly, "You could have damaged the car."

"But I didn't!" Abby sang, gloating.

"I was going to wait till we'd shoveled those piles a little flatter."

"I did!" She leaned smugly against the door frame, trying to disarm Claire. When Claire wheeled and walked away, she heaved a mighty sigh. "I don't get it," Abby said, following her into the house. "Why won't you let me take responsibility? Just because I can't *always* doesn't mean I *never* can."

"Because you start something and then the whole thing is dumped on me."

"You keep saying that! Aren't I an extremely responsible human being?"

"Normally you are, but you've been sick! I've been alone this whole winter." Claire sank into the living room couch, her shoulders crumpling.

"I've been here!" Abby exclaimed, sitting on the edge of the easy chair and thumping herself on the chest. Tucker took that as an invitation and jumped onto her lap.

"Not always," Claire protested. She was reining herself in, knowing that Abby would be humiliated if she could see the image of her that came to Claire's mind: a bald and wan invalid shuffling around the house, soaking in the bathtub, wafting into the kitchen to put the kettle on, while Claire was on the phone with the insurance company or the furnace people or the veterinarian, or trying to get someone to shovel off the roof .

"Oh, come on," Abby said, "even at my sickest I've been myself."

"How can you say that?" Claire burst out. "That night you

spiked a fever from your infection, you were delirious and dry-heaving and speaking in tongues. If I hadn't taken you to the ER, you would have died."

"Why do you keep saying that?" Abby had heard Claire make that claim to her friends on the phone, and she didn't know why it bothered her, but it did, a lot. She had never even been septic, although she knew she had come very close. "I was never even close to death."

"How do you know? You were unconscious the whole time!" Claire argued hotly. *God,* she thought, *it was so easy for Abby to say that.* She hardly remembered anything about her entire hospitalization, while the memory of it still electrified Claire with terror.

"I know that was hard," Abby said, leaning over and touching her knee. "But you know what? You can't keep me alive."

"I know that," Claire said, and Abby thought, *No, she doesn't, she thinks it's totally up to her.* "It's just," Claire said, her eyes filling with tears, "I'm worried it's always going to be like this. I want my girlfriend back."

Normally, Abby's empathy would have surged into life at the sight of Claire's tears, but now something stuck in her, like a stake in frozen ground. "I'm here! I've *been* here!" She was waving her arms in an extravagant gesture of trying to get Claire's attention, something she felt she'd been doing all day. The effort was exhausting her.

Claire was crying now. How could she explain the way the chemo had diminished Abby's life force? Abby couldn't see it when she was feeling better, but during those weeks it seemed as though her very spirit had vanished. "Not really," she said miserably. "I miss you. I miss your hair and your breasts and your eyelashes, and your swagger and your competence, and all those things I'm attracted to." She was thinking that if she just said it the right way, the most honest way, Abby would turn toward her with the warm and openhearted attentiveness she loved and help coax her desire back to life.

"What are you saying?" Abby demanded. "That you're not attracted to me anymore?"

Claire's heart sank.

Abby ran an agitated hand over her scalp, and set the dog down on the rug. She knew she was approaching dangerous territory, but she barreled on recklessly. "What are you saying? That I didn't do a good enough job of being the most cheerful and stoic patient in the world?" It was dawning upon Abby that she'd been performing a comedy routine for Claire too; the awareness came with a sickening sense of betrayal. "If you're not attracted to me because I've committed the terrible crime of *getting sick,* just tell me."

Claire put her fingers to her temples and pressed hard. It wasn't just yes or no, but she didn't know how to say that. The house was getting dark, and she realized she hadn't showered all day.

"Say it," Abby spat.

"What do you want me to say?"

"If you're not attracted to me anymore, just say so."

Claire looked at her. "I love you," she said. "But it's hard. You're really different."

Abby got very still—the great stillness before the brain registers pain. When she finally spoke, her voice was flat. "If you're not attracted to me, I want to break up. I'm not going to hang around hoping…" She trailed off, dazed and wounded to the core. Claire had taken such tender care of her. Abby was normally shy about asking for care, but she had felt she could ask Claire for anything, and that Claire would hold on to the image of her better, healthier self, keep it safe for her. And now it turned out Claire had lost her desire for her after all. Abby stared at the rug, unable to bring her eyes to her lover's face.

How could the bottom drop out so fast?

"Who's saying anything about breaking up?" Claire cried. "I'm just trying to tell you how I feel."

"Well, don't!" Abby struggled to her feet and staggered into the bedroom, where she collapsed onto the bed. When Claire came in a few minutes later, she found Abby in a deep, turbulent sleep, in her dirty jeans and sweatshirt, her arms thrust between her knees. She left the room and went outside and sat on the front stoop. It was getting late, and the wind was starting to bite. She wrapped her arms around her knees. She could smell damp earth and rotting wood and plant life, the organic stink of spring.

How, Abby wondered, do couples make it back from that point—from the shattering of the unspoken commitment—to see each other in the most generous light? Or was it more pertinent to ask how that commitment can *ever* last, fragile and miraculous as it is, in the first place?

Although neither of them could have said how, and although at a different moment under the influence of different and meaner stars they might not have, they did make it back. Over the next few weeks Claire shoveled and raked when she came home from work, and as soon as she was able Abby began to help. At night they sank groaning into bed, Abby's arms aching wonderfully, Claire curled behind her, her cheek pressed to Abby's naked back. Their neighbor came over as they worked, standing with his hands in his pockets, laughing at them and telling them about the time he accidentally ordered so much mulch it had supplied the entire street for two summers. Later, his son drove over on a rider mower with a wagon hitched to the back and hauled off a dozen wagonfuls of gravel for his parents' driveway. It grew warm outside. Abby's colleagues dropped by and caressed the newly grown fuzz on her head, and ate corn chips and salsa, and stayed too long. One evening Abby took Claire's hair in her fist and pulled her head back for a kiss, and Claire's eyes grew wide. The driveway remained thick and rippled for months; Abby and Claire's cars bounced over it when they came home. Then one day they noticed that it had begun to smooth out.

And when Abby's hair grew back, it was darker, and curly.

Drugstore Chocolates

Leslie K. Ward

"Do you love her?" you ask.

"Absolutely," she says.

You lean on your elbow, pulling against the steering wheel. She stands just inside the passenger door. The door alarm begins to sound; it startles you and you turn the key. The overhead light switches off. A harsh shadow cast across her chest disappears, and you look again at her face, lit softly by the amber streetlamp and waxing moon.

Never mind that you're parked in front of her girlfriend's house. Never mind that there's an honest man waiting for you at home in bed.

"You should really go," you say.

"I should," she says. But doesn't.

The fact is, you've been putting it out all night like a cat in heat, and none of this should come as a surprise.

Still, when she clambers back inside the car and kisses you full on the mouth—and oh, my god, is it painfully exquisite—you're shocked. You forget all about her girlfriend, your boyfriend, the nagging guilt you've felt ever since you stopped calling yourself a lesbian, and concentrate on nothing but her thick fingers gripping your jaw and the rough edges of the seat belt pushing into your neck.

The kissing stops. You pull away. The two of you sit stiffly for a minute more, until she says, "Drive down the road a ways," which you do, assuming for no good reason you're about to discuss what you've just done, which you don't.

This kiss you see coming. She paws at your breast. You bite her lower lip. Hard. In between you groan ragged things like "What are we doing?" and "Jesus, you've got to go." The song that's been playing for the last ten minutes, all drums and reverb, fades to an end. In the silence you untangle. She gets out. The alarm sounds; you leave the key in the ignition. She smiles, pushes the door until it latches, and leans against it with her hip holding it closed. In your mind you call out her name. She starts toward the house.

She is up the front steps before you finally drive away, turning left into the wrong lane, realizing your mistake as soon as the flashing lights crank up on top of a police car. Shit. You pull over. The cop is a woman, and she's family. Of course, you think. The irony of getting pulled over right now by a lesbian cop is not lost on you. Crazy universe. You remember a story you read recently about chaos, how a butterfly beating its wings in the Sudan could cause a power line in Anchorage to bounce for days. It's a comforting thought: that this mess you're dredging up might vibrate out into the cosmos, eventually dissipating like a pond ripple.

"License and registration," the officer says, as if she's told you a million times before. She shines her flashlight into your eyes. You wonder if she thinks you're straight. Or drunk. Or both.

You fight a sudden urge to tell her you don't usually act this way. That you aren't the kind of girl who who makes out with strangers in cars and drives like a maniac in the middle of the night. You fight the urge to tell her you hardly recognize your-self lately. That despite your long hair and lipstick and the musk-sour scent of men lingering on all of your clothes, you miss her. Well, not her, of course, but women like her. You miss the women who take up space, the ones who sit with their limbs spread wide, arms flung over the backs of chairs and around their girlfriends.

The officer tears off a ticket and hands it to you.

"Thanks," is what you tell her. "Thanks," and "I'll try to be more careful next time."

Coming home is not as difficult as you imagined. Your boyfriend has left the porch light on, and you open the door quietly so as not to wake him. Tiptoeing into the bedroom, you perch on his edge of the bed and wait to feel…something.

You expect that "something" to be guilt, but what washes over you is calm, tender, and infinitely more patient. It isn't love. If you had to name it, you'd call it compassion, but what strikes you most is how you feel closer to him than you have in months, and more like yourself than you have in years.

Leaning over, you plant a kiss on his forehead, still warm with sleep. He stirs, the feeling vanishes, and you're suddenly aware that if he wakes, he'll want sex, so you ease yourself off the bed and listen for the dry rumble to return to his throat.

Shuffling around to your nightstand, you strip off your clothes and crawl between the cotton sheets. You lie on your side facing away from him, pillows propped under your stom-ach, your back some inches from his, nothing out of the ordi-nary. Tonight will not be the first you stay awake hoarding thoughts of stolen kisses.

You're about to drift off when you hear his voice. "Honey?"

"Mmm?" You answer quietly in case he's talking in his sleep. Sometimes he'll drift back. You hope this is one of those times.

"Honey, is that you?"

"Of course it's me," you whisper.

"Did you have fun tonight?"

"It was all right, I guess."

"What did you do?"

"Nothing really. Go back to sleep, babe, we'll talk about it in the morning."

"Honey?" he asks again.

"Yes?" You know what's coming.

"Do you want to make love?"

Damn it. You hate the fact that he asks. The defeat hangs in his voice, damp, gray. You weigh the cost of giving in against the effort of an argument. "Not tonight, babe," you finally tell him. "I'm beat."

He sighs. Twice. The second one pisses you off, but you refuse to engage. You recall a time when making love with him was all you wanted to do. He was so exciting to you then, clean lines, hard edges. Of course, your mother had been thrilled, but that was never the point. You think back to the first Valentine's Day you spent together, naked the entire weekend, rarely farther than three steps from the bed. It had been decadent, half-eaten boxes of chocolates spilling onto the nightstand, half-swilled champagne bottles littering the floor, candles melted to waxy puddles on the windowsills. By Sunday night you had a huge case of cabin fever and a mess of a stomach, but when he put on his sport coat, some Nina Simone, and invited you to slow dance on the living room rug, the only thing you wanted to do was pull him under the covers and never, ever come out.

"Honey," he whispers. It's a whiny whisper. You ignore him. "Is everything okay? Why don't you want to make love anymore?"

Christ. "Babe, *not tonight* isn't the same as *not anymore.* Can we just drop it? I'm tired, and I don't want to argue with you about it. Not now. Not tonight. Please."

He's silent. "Fine," he says.

"I'm sorry," you tell him.

"Sure," he mutters. "Whatever. Good night."

You stare at the bedside table, at the stained oak frame that holds the journal entry you gave him as an anniversary gift. It was the first time you committed thoughts of love for him to paper. The light is too dim for you to make out the words. You've forgotten what they say. Mercifully, he starts to snore.

You lie awake, wanting like hell to relive tonight's kiss. It surfaces for a moment, bobbing in your mind like a fishing lure. Just as quickly it's swallowed by the memory of a conversation. You try to ignore it. It's hopeless.

"Do you miss being a lesbian?" he'd asked.

"Sometimes," you'd said, but when his face fell you wanted more than anything to take it back. "Nostalgically, I mean. I miss the community, belonging to something. There isn't a woman I want to be with more than I want to be with you, if that's what you're getting at."

"Oh, no, of course not. I didn't....I'm just curious, is all."

You took it as a good sign, later, that you cared enough about him to avoid the question.

The next day it hits you. You cheated. Nine p.m., at the twenty-four–hour grocery, in the cereal aisle, you set down a basket of frozen pizzas, dandruff shampoo, and diet cola. You leave it there, along with your appetite and the lazy hope that your relationship might never change, despite your indiscretion.

You've been savoring her kiss like chocolate, rolling its memory in your mouth for days. And you know even chocolate gets old when what you crave is more substantial.

You walk out of the store. The doors swoosh shut behind you. Your keys jingle in a familiar pitch as you pull them from your pocket. A few more seconds and you're inside the car. The base of your neck where she pulled at your hair, a detail you'd forgotten until now, flares hot enough to make you draw a breath.

You start the engine and turn on the CD player. Drums and reverb flood the speakers, the same song on unremitting repeat for the last twenty-four hours. What did she see in you that night? You lean in the way you were before the kiss and flip down the rearview mirror. You expect to be met with a sultry, come-hither stare, something worthy of Bettie Page or Marlene Dietrich. What you see is more like Shirley Temple on a bad-hair day. You flip up the mirror and try again, and then again, before realizing this little-girl-lost crap might have actually been the appeal.

Thankfully *Why you?* is only half the question. *Why her?* It's far too easy to blame this one on gender. You're smarter than that most of the time. You think about it, but mercifully the sensation of the kiss comes flooding back. Well, maybe it is that easy. And maybe gender be hanged.

You pull out of the parking lot, turn the corner, and head for the bar.

This little town isn't exactly known for its nightlife. There's one gay bar and you've just walked into it. Two pool tables, a dance floor, and a cocktail waitress who doubles as drag hostess Thursday nights. Tonight is Wednesday, which means karaoke, a handful of regulars, and lots of Guns N' Roses. You order a beer and pull up a stool at the counter.

It's early. The regulars are beginning to trickle in, though there's already a crowd. A lanky, wavy-haired boy sings Cher, licking his teeth and flicking back invisible tresses after each verse. Smoke from a clove cigarette mingles with the dry scent of tobacco. The girl holding the clove looks uncomfortable, forcing laughter, resting a rigid hand on her friend's forearm. University students? Probably not. Bachelorette party, that's your guess.

Leslie K. Ward

It's seems you're right, because here comes the bride, wearing a condom-covered T-shirt and a child's dress-up veil. Scattered among the prophylactics are strategically placed LifeSavers, placed on different regions of her body, each labeled with a dollar amount and a slogan. SUCK FOR A BUCK across her shoulders. I WANT MY TWO DOLLARS on her stomach. And MAKE ME AN OFFER I CAN'T REFUSE emblazoned across her chest.

You pull a wad of bills from your back pocket. The smallest is a ten. You wonder if the bride can make change. Whistling and catcalls force you to look again in her direction where a slick-haired baby butch is on her knees in front of the bride-to-be, tucking dollars into her bra strap and going to town on a LifeSaver just below her belly button.

This is why you are here. Sure, this and a quarter will buy you a phone call, but in an instant you realize your choice is not about which side of that LifeSaver you'd rather be on.

You pick up the porter, leave the butch with the bride, and make for the dance floor. It's quite busy for a Wednesday. Odd until you remember the full moon. No wonder. You've heard that twenty-eight days is the length of both the lunar and average menstrual cycle, and you're not a firm believer in coincidence. Or fate for that matter. Serendipity? Absolutely.

As fate would have it, *serendipity* is the word that appears in your head when you see her. The woman. Your kiss. *Oh, my god.* Your chest is tight. Your cunt tighter. She's standing across the room in jeans and a loose sweater, with strong cheekbones and spiked hair, one hand around a beer bottle, the other flicking ash from a cigarette, and damn it if she isn't looking right at you.

Is she with the girlfriend? You can't tell. A group has gathered on the dance floor, limiting your view to teasing glimpses. Every so often a channel forms and you catch her gaze like a current, broken and recharged. You walk over.

There's no girlfriend. Not that you can see anyway. You're within a few feet of her now and her eyes are amazing, honey at the centers, green around the edges. Her breasts push a curve beneath her sweater; her lips form a thin pout around a cigarette. She leans back against a shelf, rests her cigarette on an ashtray, and blows the smoke away from you. "Want to dance?" she asks.

"Damn straight," you answer. She reaches out her hand. Rough fingers curl tightly around your palm as she pulls you into the surging mass. The path you take through the crowd disappears almost immediately.

Up close she smells like vanilla, smoke, and something earthy: marijuana, dry pine. She leans into you, her cheek warm and smooth against your own. You think of all the places your bodies are touching, like imprints in the sun-warm sand. Around you, a hundred women are dancing. The pulse of the music takes you, and complete surrender feels like one deep breath away.

Commit the following thoughts to memory: the softness of her skin, the warmth of her hand on the small of your back, and supple curves that melt into yours, filling the spaces between.

Reunion

Karin Kallmaker

Everyone seems to have had too much to drink. The karaoke machine is turned up way too loud, and every other song is "I Will Survive." You're holding me close as we sway to our own particular rhythm.

"I'm sorry I had to be away so long." Your lips on my cheek are almost chaste, but through your crumpled dress shirt I feel the hungering swell of your breasts against mine.

"I'm glad your flight got back on time." Looking up from my drink to see you standing wearily in the doorway, still clad in the clothes from your last meeting, had been the highlight of the last six weeks. I'm trembling in your arms. It feels so good to have you home again. "You wouldn't want to miss Arlene's fortieth."

You kiss me on the lips, a brief press that makes my heart beat between my legs. "Arlene may be my best friend, but I'd rather be home with you right now."

I hold you tight against me, feeling like an empty well filling finally with welcome rain.

I'm tipsy. It's not the margaritas but the scent of your cologne teasing my nose that is intoxicating me. Everything about you stimulates the same pulse inside me.

I whisper in your ear, "I missed you so much, Ellen, so much. I need you. You know how. That way." My teeth briefly nibble your earlobe.

You run a thumbnail down my back. "You think I don't know? I want you too. They haven't cut the birthday cake yet, though."

"Outside, then. Right now." The ripple that flows through you shakes my confidence. I wanted to turn you on, and I have. Now I need you. and it's all I can do not to wrap my legs around you in front of everyone and beg you to be inside me.

You take a deep, ragged breath. "I'll take care of you when we get home, Beth. A quickie isn't going to do it for me. I want to spend all night, all morning, all weekend memorizing your body all over again."

"Sweet talker." I'm blushing and pleased. I move my hips into you and your fingers slip briefly inside my jeans to smooth the small of my back.

Your quiet laugh tickles my ear. "Eager, aren't you?"

"Underwear would just slow me down, whenever it is you want me to be naked for you."

"I want you naked now, honey." Your hand moves slightly lower as if to cup the curve of my ass. "Later."

I slowly shrug out of your grip and turn toward the patio door. The cool air hardens my nipples through the thin fabric of the spaghetti-strap tank top that has never failed to put a light in your eyes.

The backward glance I give you is explicit. With a slow rolling shrug one of the straps slides off my shoulder.

Your eyes are glittering as you gaze at my body. I see a thousand memories of a thousand nights with me swirling in your face.

Your shoulders tighten as your jaw slackens. Which night are you remembering? The airport parking lot when I dropped you off six long weeks ago? When we fucked madly in the backseat of the car? There were times while you were gone when I was so low that I got in the backseat and touched the spot where traces of our lovemaking are still visible.

I run my hand over my stomach, from right to left, and mouth at you as if I'm counting. I see another memory play on your face, the memory of the night you kept track of my orgasms with an indelible marker, crosshatching, five, ten, fifteen. Your inventiveness, your control of me left me drained of all energy but filled to capacity with love for you.

For a week the sight of the vivid black marks on my skin made me instantly wet. And you were there, again and again, climbing inside my body and head, exploding me from the inside out.

You have that same look in your eyes you had that night, like you can't believe I can be so needy, and that you are the reason I feel that way.

I want to be yours again. I've missed you. I've waited all these days, and two more hours seems like a punishment now.

With a last parting look at you, I cross the backyard to a shadowed gazebo. It's unoccupied, though Arlene tells stories of past trysts. I hear your footsteps behind me. You stumble when your eyes adjust and you see me on the bench, the tank top around my waist, legs spread and my hand inside my unbuttoned jeans, teasing my clit.

You quickly cross to kneel in front of me. "Don't make a sound."

You pull my hand free, then grasp my jeans roughly, yanking them down and pulling them off me. If someone walks in on us there will be no quick covering up. You're going to have me, right here.

Your fingers take over caressing my clit. I want to moan,

but I hold it back. I pushed you to get you outside with me, but you command me now.

"You are wet, aren't you? You missed me, didn't you?"

I nod. Your thumb flicks teasingly at my clit while your fingertips play at my wet opening.

"This is what you want, isn't it?" Your other hand finds a nipple and squeezes, hard.

I hiss as my body shakes in response.

You lower your head and my vision blurs. Your tongue is a tease on my slick outer lips. It moves sinuously through me but never quite brushes my clit. I move my hips, trying to get your tongue where I need it.

You raise your head after several minutes of tormenting me. I watch you lick your full, glistening lips.

"I don't have any lube, honey." Your fingers tweak my aching clit and my legs involuntarily snap together. You shove them apart. "No. Stay open for me. We'll do this the old-fashioned way."

Your hand cups my pussy, swollen with my wetness. I thrust against your palm, trying to say what I want with my body. Then your hand is gone again, and I feel bereft, near tears. I want to plead with you to take me. A tiny whimper escapes me.

"Don't worry, baby. I'm going to fuck you, after I enjoy the taste of you." I shudder helplessly as I watch you lick your wet fingertips. Your eyes close briefly as you smile softly. Then you're gazing at me in the moonlight, your mouth limed, your eyes filled with tenderness.

Quietly, "I love you."

Those three words arouse me like no other. For love you will do anything for me, to me, reaching into my heart, body, mind in any way that sets me on fire. I want to weep as you push two fingers inside me where you are so welcome, so wanted.

Your hoarse voice cuts into me. "I love that you need me this way. Get even more wet for me, and I will give you what you want."

I nod frantically as I shove myself onto your fingers. My mouth is abruptly dry as all the liquid in my body is summoned between my legs.

Two more fingers, hard, pushing me open. I've missed your fingers, your arms around me, the electric intensity of your voice when you are telling me what you will do to me.

"Are you wet enough?"

I grasp your forearm and pull it toward me. If I opened my mouth to say it I would scream.

"Trying to fuck yourself? No, baby. If you're going to get fucked, I'll take care of you, always."

I rest back on my hands so I can lift my hips as you thrust into me. Your thumb bumps my clit at the end of each surge, and I abruptly realize I'm going to come in a helpless flood. My moan is sharp.

"Not a sound," you remind me. You spread your fingers inside me, opening me up. My arms and legs are trembling now.

You wrap one strong arm around my hips, and your tongue taps one taut nipple. "Don't...make...a sound."

With a groan, you push your fist into me.

I am silently screaming, *Yours...I am yours.* Nights in our cold bed, days of missing your voice, I was lost until you walked in the door again. Until you smiled and caught me in your arms.

You reclaim all of me now, reaching up inside me, giving me what I crave, and taking what you need from my responsive, insatiable body.

Tenderness fades from your eyes. You read my expression, gauge my panting breath. You assess the eagerness of my hips rising to meet you. I balance on one hand and wind the other in your hair, my nails digging into your scalp. I want you to completely possess me. To believe again in what we have always had.

Your face stiffens from the pain of my nails. Your eyes narrow to slits. You twist your hand inside me. I gush and watch you grimace in satisfaction.

"That's right, baby. That's what you want. I love giving it to you."

Nice girls don't take their clothes off at a party. Nice girls don't beg to get fucked in someone else's backyard. I don't feel like a nice girl, not when I want you this bad. Tonight it will take all that you know about me to love away the pain of missing you.

"You like it this way and you're going to come for me."

I can hear the party, but all that's real is your fist slowly pulling out of me. I moan and try to follow it with my cunt, then I feel it again, pushing, taking. I choke back a gasp and move for you, taking it all and trying to show you how much I love it. Over the raucous singing I hear your fist making wet, luscious sounds against my tender, receptive flesh.

Your teeth pull sharply at my nipple while your fist plunges in then flips over on its way out of me. I thrust down, and you shove into me harder, knocking the breath out of me. I gush again.

"That's right. Please, baby, come for me. I want to feel it."

I nod helplessly, clenching my mouth shut though I've forgotten why. My passion, my adoration, my devotion is all suddenly too much to keep in and I pour onto your hand. You pull my head down to kiss me, wetly, harshly, while I jerk against you. I feel as if I'm never going to stop wanting this— your agile fist, your tongue in my mouth. It seems like magic, that you know how to make me feel this way.

You pull out of me when I finally stop coming. Your breathing is labored, and I hear your voice break as you say,

"I missed you so much. I don't ever want to be gone that long again."

"Darling," I murmur, and I wrap you close. Your tears on my hair are like diamonds.

In the distance I hear voices joined in the birthday song. We'll be missed soon. I don't care.

You stir in my arms finally. "Will that get you home?"

I feel delicious and wicked. Loved, owned. "Kiss me one more time. Then I think I'll be able to last." I smile to myself, thinking of the way I've left our bed turned down, the things you like ready to be used. I can wait now, and let anticipation of loving you build inside me.

You open your mouth to me and I am dizzied by the way you tremble as I kiss you.

A thousand memories of a thousand nights in your arms spill over me. Like every night with you, tonight has been and will be like no other.

We slip in through the patio door. The party has gone quiet. Cake? Candles? We stumble over each other on the way to Arlene's family room and are greeted by cheers and applause from our friends.

Arlene comes forward, reaching to embrace me but speaking to you. "Did you put this poor woman out of her misery?"

Mortified, I turn my blushing face into your shoulder and you hold me close and tight. With your customary aplomb, you answer, "I'm not saying a word, Arlene."

"Then why is Beth's face as red as a happy vulva?"

"Oh, jeez," I say into your shirt.

"I wouldn't know." You gently let go of me. "Be right back. I need to wash my hand. Hands. Oh, damn."

The screams of laughter turn my face even more red, but at least you are now blushing as well. You hurry off to the bathroom while I have to face our sniggling friends. Should I shrug like the sophisticate I'm not, and announce, "Ellen fisted me in the gazebo. More champagne, please"?

Or should I lamely try to lie with, "We were just kissing"? Nobody's going to believe me.

"It'd been six weeks," I finally manage. "That makes us practically newlyweds, so give us a break. Can we get some cake too?"

Arlene feels merciful, I think, because she accepts the distraction. I know you're back because I can feel the heat of you against my spine. You slip your arms around me from behind and pull me tight.

My eyes close, though I don't mean them to. I feel your kisses on the nape of my neck and I can't help the throaty moan that escapes me.

"Oh, you two, here." I open my eyes to see Arlene holding out a take-home container. "Have the cake later, when you need more energy. Now go home! Shoo! You're just depressing those of us who are single!"

You take my hand and I am falling into the heat of your eyes. The forgotten karaoke machine is playing "Always and Forever," and nothing could be more true.

Heron

Dawn Paul

Carlile saw the pond on Tuesday, framed for a moment in the dirty window of the train, like locking eyes with a beautiful stranger. Then gone. Back to the long gray blur of the route to the city. She had ridden the train five days a week for two years, minus two vacation weeks per year. The train never varied its route. Yet she had never noticed the small pond in the woods, never raised her eyes to the window at the exact moment the train passed by.

Through the rest of her ordinary day, she thought of the pond often. A gift. Several times she opened her lips to say, "I saw..." But she didn't mention the pond to anyone, not to the woman at the coffee shop, the people in the office, the teenager at the dry cleaners where she stopped on her way home. Not to Eva, at home, who was leaving her.

The next day was drizzly. Carlile forgot her hat, and the rain seeped through her hair and was cold on her scalp as she walked to the train. The train came and she sat in the same seat as the previous morning. She tucked her commuter ticket under the clip on the seat in front of her, as she did every morning. She unfolded her newspaper, as did the man in the seat beside her. As one body, the new passengers raised their papers in front of them. Carlile glanced at the headlines, at a photo on the front page of a ship listing heavily to one side but still afloat. *If I were a different sort of person,* she thought, *I would show this photo to Eva and say, "This is our relationship."* But she was not melodramatic.

She looked out the window and wondered if she had imagined the pond the morning before. She lowered her paper, refolded it, and tucked it back in her bag. She watched the landscape flash by, the back lots of tenements and factories. Then the pond, pale gray in the mist, ringed with wet black trees.

The pond was there the next day and the next, bright blue in the midst of chain-link fences, things grimy and abandoned. It was small. Carlile could have swum across it in twenty strokes. It was shallow, though she didn't know how she knew this. It was perfectly round, ringed with trees still green though it was autumn. A rock stood in the middle with a few dry rushes grown up around it. A bit of wild in the ravaged trackside landscape. She waited in anticipation for the sight of it, while the conductor quietly made her way down the aisle checking tickets. After the pond flashed by, Carlile stared out the window until the train jolted and huffed into the station. She had lost interest in the newspaper.

{}

On Friday morning, a tall gangly bird stood in the middle of the pond by the rock and the rushes. A heron. It seemed a reward for keeping watch through the week. Carlile awoke on Saturday morning thinking of the bird. She felt a moment's regret that she wouldn't ride the train that morning. Eva was already up, pulling on running pants and humming the same tune over and over. Carlile watched her brush her hair in front of the mirror, looked at her the way she would look at a stranger. Eva was lovely. Honey-gold hair, smooth skin, long graceful legs. Carlile watched her watch herself in the mirror. Her mouth twitched in a smile that was not for Carlile. Eva turned then, and smiled at Carlile, an automatic gesture less real than her smile for the mirror. Carlile opened her lips to say "Is there...? Are you...?" Instead she said, "I saw a heron yesterday."

Eva bent to tie her running shoe. "Really."

"From the train."

Eva stood, kissed her index finger, then leaned to place it on Carlile's cheek. "Gotta run."

{}

The heron was still there on Monday. It had long legs and a long neck. The feathers on top of its head swept back into a tousled crest. Its back was slate blue, its chest cream colored in the morning sun. Carlile saw it the next day and the next.

{}

It was early October. The leaves on the tops of the trees around the pond turned scarlet. Most mornings the heron stood still. But sometimes Carlile caught it in motion, a long leg reaching forward, the graceful neck curving as the heron bent to the water. Once it made a quick strike into the rushes with its heavy bill just as the train went by. On cold windy mornings it folded its neck, hunched into itself, and faced the wind. On cloudy mornings the pale feathers on its chest looked gray. In sunlight they shone white or gold, or even pale red, like blood in water. Carlile began to leave the house earlier in the morning to make sure she got a seat next to a window. She wondered how long the heron would stay.

Eva noticed that she left earlier, which surprised Carlile. For some time she had felt invisible at home. Eva asked if her workload had increased or if her boss had asked her to start earlier. Those two choices. That was how Eva asked questions. Carlile tried to remember the early days of their relationship, the days of wanting to know all of the life that came before they'd met. Had Eva always asked questions that way? *Was your childhood happy or sad? Goldfish or gerbils? Girl Scouts or 4-H Club?* Had Eva always narrowed her life to two choices?

Even when she was lost in thought or jotting a note, Carlile knew the exact moment the train passed the pond. It was as though her body counted the clacks and jolts from the depot to the body of water. She looked up and stared intently out the window. She saw details, as though time slowed those few seconds that the train flashed by the pond. She noticed how the tops of the rushes broke apart and spilled downy white seeds into the wind. She saw red and gold leaves blow across the surface of the water, the heron's feathers ruffle across its back as it turned to the wind.

{}

One morning, a woman in the seat beside her noticed Carlile looking out the window and followed her gaze. She looked back at Carlile, baffled, and Carlile had an uncomfortable moment of seeing herself in this woman's eyes: a young woman staring intently at nothing. Carlile looked down the aisle at the various heads, balding and coiffed, bent over their morning papers. She felt separate. A good or bad feeling? No, that was Eva's question. It was neither. It was simply separate, a lonely yet satisfying separateness. The train clattered to the station, into its berth, and its passengers poured out like termites from a log on fire. Carlile walked slowly among them.

{}

The trees around the pond turned deep gold and bronze. The morning sun was lower, and its light took on texture, like syrup. It had been a dry autumn. The pond was shallow and ringed with dry brown grasses. One morning a small flock of ducks was busy dabbling in water. They looked like travelers newly up and awake, preparing for their journey. The heron stood by the rushes. Once it raised its graceful head and looked directly at Carlile, as though conscious that she was watching from the train. Carlile was struck with gratitude.

{}

Carlile had fallen out of love before, felt it suddenly give way like a rotted staircase. When it happened, and it had happened several times, she knew that love hadn't existed in the first place. She had been mistaken, lulled, hopeful, hornswoggled.

So how does real love end? Had it evaporated, its passing unremarked by neither her nor Eva? They sat at the table one night, eating dinner: baked squash, rice, spicy ground beef. The open window let in clean October air. They were talking about ordinary things, and for a moment there was the old glow of love between them. Eva was laughing at something Carlile said; Carlile was pouring a second glass of wine. Then the phone rang. Eva gave an apologetic shrug and went to answer it. Carlile sat and finished her wine, and pleasure drained from the evening. She shut the window, turned off the lamp, and looked out at the squares of light in other people's houses. There was a half moon. She thought of the heron, sleeping with its head tucked underwing. She imagined touching the moon-bright feathers on its chest.

She stood up, restless despite the wine, and pulled on a wool sweater. In the next room, Eva was finishing her phone call. She raised her eyebrows, surprised, as Carlile gave a quick wave and stepped out the door. She wondered if Eva had assumed she would sit waiting, assumed they would spend the evening watching TV in bed then fall into sex before sleep— something that happened seldom now. She walked out the door feeling a bitter triumph.

{ }

It was a rainy morning when Carlile saw a couple sitting in the station. Their meager luggage was gathered around them. The woman sat slumped to one side, as though she'd had a stroke. She wore cheap tennis shoes with holes cut out for corns or bunions, something painful. The man sat with his huge hands hanging between his knees, the dirt of ages ground into the grain of his fingers. They were married, it was clear. They sat close but not touching. As Carlile passed, the woman lurched up then leaned against the man and whispered something in his hairy ear. He laughed loudly, wiping tears from his eyes. The woman looked on, pleased with herself. Carlile envied them, at least in the moment. They were the world to each other. She was no longer Eva's world, anyone's world. She started to cry as she walked out of the station. She was horrified; she seldom cried, let alone in a crowded train station. Once outside, she lifted her face to the rain to hide her tears. She dodged along the busy sidewalks hunched into her upturned collar. She thought of the heron, the way it drew up the tops of its great wings and sheltered its head between them. How it shook its feathers in the rain like a person shedding a heavy coat. She chuckled, pulled her umbrella out of her bag, and snapped it open. She shook the rain out of her hair and walked to her office.

{}

The heron was so often in Carlile's thoughts that she felt she should explain it to Eva. Not to do so seemed like keeping a secret from her. Lately they spoke about fewer and fewer things, just the daily practical stuff. Carlile couldn't remember the last time they'd talked about something that was not immediately necessary. One evening Eva was sitting still, something rare for her, cutting stray threads off a shirt cuff.

"Do you ever think about something all the time?" Carlile asked. Her voice sounded loud, almost shrill.

Eva didn't notice Carlile's tone. She held the shirt up to the light. "What sort of things?"

"That's what I'm asking—are there things you think about all the time?"

"No," Eva said. She continued snipping threads and cast a quick look at Carlile as though her task required her full attention.

So Carlile didn't tell her about the heron, how it shadowed her through the days, its breath light and warm on the side of her neck.

{}

One morning the heron wasn't there. Carlile raised herself from her seat, cupped her hands around her eyes, and pressed them against the window. No, it was gone. As she sat back, a little groan escaped her throat. The man seated next to her moved his thick woolen-clad arm away from her. The train clattered on.

She felt lost all day, as though she'd been living two lives over the past weeks. In one, she showered, ate, worked, shopped. She exchanged talk with Eva, waited for her in bed at night, and fell asleep before Eva lay down on her side of the bed.

In her other life she was in the stillness of the pond. With the heron. A wordless place. Acceptance in the bird's lidded dark eyes. In this other life she reached out her hand and ran her fingers through the soft pale feathers of the heron's breast, felt the warmth underneath. Now that world was gone. There was only the gray world of the everyday.

{}

The next morning the heron was again standing in its place in the rushes. Her heart leapt.

{}

She went to the library and found a shelf of bird guides. She chose one at random and leafed through it, looking for her heron. She felt furtive, the way she felt in middle school look-ing up words about sex in biology books and the dictionary. She found a picture of a heron looking blank faced but some-what sinister. The text beneath the photo described a typical heron: long legs and neck, dark bluish gray, etc. It was as dis-appointing as her secret research in middle school, the way the dry definitions never relayed the power of the words. The guide's description of plumage didn't begin to explain how the heron had come to fill her waking life.

{}

They visited Eva's sister, Lois. Lois had made coconut mac-aroons, Carlile's favorite, and built a fire in the woodstove. Eva and Carlile sat by the fire, and Lois brought out mugs of hot cocoa. They murmured "Thanks," but Lois brushed it aside, as was her way. She always seemed ashamed of her own kindness, as though tenderness were something one practiced in private. Her behavior was something learned young, Carlile thought. Eva had the same way.

Eva and Lois exchanged family news. Carlile watched two woodpeckers at a feeder outside the window. They were black and white, the male with a dab of red on the back of his head. They flew back and forth from the feeder to a cherry tree that still had hard dry berries. Carlile was mesmerized watching them. Lois noticed Carlile watching.

"See how the male always eats first? He's the dominant one, that's for sure."

Eva made a crack about Lois not letting him get away with it.

"Maybe the female lets him go first," Carlile said.

"No," Lois said. "He's the top bird. That's how it is in the animal world. No room for nice."

But we are the animal world, Carlile wanted to say. She was thinking of the heron, that its life wasn't that different from her own. She realized Lois and Eva were waiting for her answer. But she was thinking of the heron, its days spent in the pond, as she spent her days riding between home and the city. Eva gave Lois a triumphant look, as though Carlile had just proved a point they had discussed earlier. Lois shrugged and the two sisters went on with their conversation. Carlile continued her watch out the window.

{}

Carlile dreamed of the heron. She didn't remember the dreams clearly, and sometimes she couldn't distinguish them from her waking thoughts. But she remembered one dream in detail and knew it was a dream: She was attending a party in a mansion with large mirrored rooms and crystal chandeliers.

The rooms were crowded with people in silks and furs, talking and laughing. They all tried to get Carlile's attention as she elbowed her way through them. But she needed air. She slipped out a French door to a balcony. It was night, and on the lawn below, the heron stood by a torchlit swimming pool. She was sad to see it there, posing on the cold cement in the dark. But she was also overjoyed it had come for her. She called out to it and the sound woke her. Eva slept soundly beside her, her arm across her eyes.

{}

Carlile stepped inside the door and bent to remove her wet boots. Eva's jacket hung dripping by the door. Carlile was late. She stood in her stocking feet on the cold tiles and removed her coat carefully so it wouldn't drip on the floor. She stopped, one arm half in its sleeve. On the small hall table, in a glass, was a sprig of white flowers. Carlile breathed their sweetness, and the name floated up in her mind. Freesia. Her pleasure mixed with dismay that she had forgotten an important date. Their anniversary? No, it was an ordinary day, she was sure of it. That knowledge increased her pleasure in the sweet fragrance, the pure white petals and green stems. Eva had brought her flowers on an ordinary day.

She padded down the hall in her socks, holding a surprised smile on her face, wanting Eva to see it. Eva was sitting at her desk, her back to the door. She acknowledged Carlile with a wave but didn't turn around. She was working on her computer. Carlile stood in the doorway, moving from one foot to the other, unsure how long to wait. Eva turned slightly and looked at her. Her eyes were distracted, her mouth slightly annoyed. This wasn't the face of a woman who had brought flowers to her lover. Carlile turned away, bewildered. Later, Eva came out stretching her shoulders and rubbing her wrists.

It had been a long session at the keyboard. At their scanty supper, Carlile finally asked about the flowers. Eva gave a dismissive wave. Everyone in her office had received them to celebrate a new contract. Eva didn't like their cloying smell in her tiny workspace but hadn't wanted to throw them away. Carlile hoped Eva hadn't seen the foolish delight on her face when she stood in the doorway, when she had stood ready for them to begin all over again.

{}

The heron was stately and still. Carlile occasionally caught it in motion as the train rushed by. Always slow, dignified movements. One morning the conductor announced they would be traveling at half-speed due to a problem with the engine. The passengers muttered their irritation and flicked their newspapers. Carlile watched for the pond with great anticipation. She would have a long, luxurious look.

They chugged slowly along as the heron came into view, facing the train. Carlile stared and held her breath. It stretched out its wings. She was amazed at their breadth, like a huge cloak. It drew up one leg, lightly, then touched down and drew up the other, touched down and lifted again. It arched its neck, lifted its head, its wide wings still outstretched. The heron danced. The train made its way past the pond, and Carlile watched, transfixed, as the heron danced for her.

{}

Now Eva and Carlile seldom touched. It was awkward when they did, as though their hands had grown huge and heavy. When Eva touched Carlile, it was with an athlete's rough affection, an arm across the shoulders or a backhanded nudge. Carlile touched Eva by necessity, perhaps a shoulder with her fingertips to get Eva's attention. She placed her hand in the center of Eva's back as she moved past her in the narrow hall.

Carlile couldn't summon her body's memory of Eva's touch when they had been passionate about each other. She remembered calling Eva's name in the dark, remembered her breath coming deeper and deeper, the electric feel of Eva's lips on her neck. She remembered all this like someone remembering a childhood language spoken in a country far away.

One night Carlile reached out in the dark and ran her fingers down Eva's back. She heard Eva swallow, knew she was awake. She moved her hand to Eva's waist. When Eva didn't move away, Carlile reached around and cupped her breast. Eva rolled over onto her back. When Carlile traced her profile, dark against the faint light of the window, Eva pushed her hand away.

"Don't do that." Her voice was flat and irritated.

"What do you want me to do?"

Eva sat up and leaned over her. "I want you to quit asking me what to do." She said it loudly, as though they were in a noisy and crowded place. She said it as though she had said it many times, as though Carlile knew the entire history of that statement. But she didn't. All tenderness drained out of her. She pulled her hand back, waiting for Eva to get up and sleep somewhere else. But Eva rolled over and breathed deeply. Carlile couldn't tell if she was pretending or had fallen into the relieved sleep of one who has finally had her say.

{ }

From her distanced vantage point on the train, Carlile admired the supple strength of the heron. Its long neck, the soft pale feathers spilling down to the belly, its back and wings all shades of blue and even pink, like clouds at twilight. Its legs were straight and strong, and she imagined, as she looked out the train window, the tight bulges of its knees, like branches on an apple tree. Carlile's elbow rested on the sill of the train window, her head in her palm. She pushed her fingers through her hair, felt the springiness where it grew from her scalp. She imagined her hair as feathers, soft and resilient. To be covered in feathers. She looked at her hands: blunt yellow ends of bones pressed under chapped red skin. Her knuckles were full of tiny fissures and wrinkles, the backs covered with freckles, moles, and scars. Her fingernails were thick and rounded, like they were working their way into claws. She probed the sharp edge of a chipped tooth with her tongue. She imagined her narrow body under its heavy clothes, the sallow skin stretched over the joints, the slack muscles and bristly scatters of dark hair. But her wrists were slender, delicate. Lovely in their symmetry of small bones, each with its three veins running neatly alongside one another, electric as eels.

The woman sitting next to her wore an open-necked blouse and open-toed shoes with thin straps. So much skin exposed on such a raw day. She had fine-textured skin the color of coffee with cream. Her toenails were painted deep plum. Carlile looked again at her wrists. If she thought her body was as lovely as her wrists, would she show it to the world, the way this woman showed the soft skin of her throat, her perfect feet? What was it to reveal and be desired? She had taken it for granted once. Carlile pulled down the cuffs of her sleeves. What did Eva see when she looked at her now?

{}

Carlile was in a checkout line, leafing through a magazine, when she came upon a poem called "The Heron." Her heart jumped. At last, an expression of what she had been feeling these past weeks. She read very few poems and had the idea that all poems were love poems. But this one was about a heron killing and eating a frog, about the grim necessities of living. Where she had expected sweetness she found a mouthful of sand.

She knew enough of the grim necessities of living; everyone did. Surely that was not the stuff of poetry in a world full of backs bent to their tasks. She returned the magazine to its place and looked out at the wide parking lot. A single black-bottomed cloud dropped snowflakes so gently they seemed to materialize out of the air. The end of November. Winter was coming. She felt something well up in her chest, and just as quickly, she swallowed it down.

{}

In her waking dreams, Carlile began to talk to the heron. A silent commentary. The way the sun cast shadows of fence pickets along the sidewalk, like something alive and rippling. The music made by the tines of a rake clattering in the gutter. The late-autumn constellations that rose above the houses as she walked home from the train at night. She offered these glimpses of her world as small gifts to the heron. Then she began to tell the heron things about herself. Thoughts. Hopeful thoughts and what she loved. She could say these things, in these imagined conversations, without fear of ridicule or dismissal. She had a sense the heron could tell her things about herself that she didn't know, things shot through with sunlight, rimed with frost. The heron, in these waking dreams, knew her as more than she imagined herself to be. More than the Carlile whose mind drilled down the days one quarter hour at a time, making small choices, worrying petty worries. Was that not what she wanted from her beloved? To have her quirks and grace mined from her everyday dirt? Carlile listened hard, but the heron's voice was a breeze through a feather, a slender foot lightly breaking the surface of calm water.

{}

Carlile lay on her back in bed, sobbing, her face wet with tears, tears running down her temples and soaking her hair, filling her throat with thin salty mucous. She was crying like she had as a child, long and hard, past knowing why. Crying as a physical act, like swallowing or skipping, her thick, wet, suffocating sobs unconnected to emotion or injury. She woke in the dark, in silence, and touched her face. It was dry. She took a breath and her throat was clear. But before the surprise of all that, the heron's face flickered for a moment, and she was soothed and washed by the kindness in its look. She touched Eva's side of the bed and found it smooth and empty. The surprise of that was that she was not surprised.

{}

Carlile and Eva had met under a set of circumstances so star-crossed, by such ordered chance, it seemed they were meant to meet and fall in love forever.

They met at the airport. Carlile was arriving home, struggling with her carry-on luggage. A large shopping bag had ripped, and she was trying to hold it together while carrying a tote bag and small suitcase. A young woman moved through the crowd with an athlete's grace and came up to Carlile with a welcoming smile. It was like a dream.

"I'm Eva," was all she said, and she reached for Carlile's suitcase. The shopping bag slid out of Carlile's hand, and they scrambled to pick up its contents. Someone called Eva's name, and they stood and looked at each other.

A woman approached them. A woman who fit Carlile's description but didn't look like her. Carlile thought she saw a look of regret cross Eva's face. In the ensuing confusion and laughter, Eva ended up with several of Carlile's books from the ripped shopping bag. She tracked Carlile through a business card tucked in one of them. They met in the city so Eva could return the books. Neither Eva nor Carlile mentioned the possibility of mailing them. Carlile had delighted in Eva: her crooked front tooth, her loping walk, the pale down along her jawbone. The little notch in her left ear from a dog bite when she was five. And Eva, for some time, delighted in Carlile. A brief amount of time, considering the efforts on the part of fate to bring them together.

Now Carlile wondered if there are points in time when people are open to falling in love, like those moments when an overcast sky rips open to reveal the blue beyond. And whatsoever presents itself at that moment becomes the beloved.

{}

The sun dragged itself up later each morning into the short gray days of December. Carlile walked to the train depot in the half-light of early winter. The heron, curled against the early morning cold, was a dark question mark amid the pond's gunmetal. It drew in its neck, taking its great length into its body, yet its body gained no size. Rather, it seemed diminished, almost weightless on its thin sticks of legs, lost in the fragile shelter of its wings. Wind turned aside its feathers, and Carlile imagined its tender skin exposed to the raw chill. She wished she could reach out from the warmth of the crowded train and hold the heron against her body. But the heron was never so distant as on these early winter mornings. She allowed herself to wonder how much longer it could stay.

{}

Carlile tugged the collar of her bathrobe under her chin and stepped out the door to retrieve the Sunday paper. On Sundays she and Eva drank sweet milky tea and ate cinnamon-sugar toast in bed with the paper. These slow, sticky mornings were a carryover from Eva's childhood and the only one of their traditions as a couple that remained. Cold air stung Carlile's nostrils when she stepped outside. The geranium on the doorstep had collapsed into black slime. A white furze outlined the wrought iron railing. Carlile thought of the heron, the pond icing over. She walked into the bedroom with the paper.

"What's wrong?" Eva asked. She was sitting in bed with her knees drawn up, and she looked concerned. Her eyes sought out Carlile's. "What is it?"

Carlile felt like she might weep with the relief of being seen again by Eva. She fumbled for an answer, one Eva might understand.

"There was a hard frost last night. The geranium's dead."

"It's December. What do you expect?" She made an impatient gesture with her hand, wanting the paper. Carlile set it on the bed, and Eva pulled out her favorite sections. She read intently, brought her toast to her mouth without looking at it. Buttery crumbs fell, and she absently shook them off the paper onto the sheets.

"I'm going out," Carlile said.

"Out?" Eva looked up over the paper, a corner of toast halfway to her mouth. Carlile didn't answer. Eva shrugged and bent her head to the paper again. But not before Carlile saw the look of defeat on her face. It was Carlile leaving this time; it wasn't going to be all her fault, after all. Eva drew her fine golden brows into a look of fierce concentration that Carlile remembered loving. She turned her back to the bed, dressed, and grabbed her car keys. Eva glanced up as she left the room, and shrugged again.

Outside, a thin layer of frost lay over everything like a scattering of white stars. Carlile scraped frost off the windshield. A winter task, a winter day. Winter, and the heron would be gone. She had forgotten gloves but didn't want to go back inside for them. Eva might decide, after all, to demand answers. Carlile might tell her about the heron. Like all secrets, it would lose its power once told. Then she would have nothing.

She sat in the car and studied a map. There was the train track; there was a road. There, next to the train track, was a tiny circle of blue. She moved her finger from the blue dot to the road—where the road took a sharp left turn after a golf course.

She drove. It was still early, Sunday, and there was no traffic. Dead leaves along the curbstones were white with frost. A girl rode by on a bike, leaving a black line on the frosted asphalt. She had never considered going to the pond. It had appeared so suddenly that one morning that she wasn't certain it was real. There was a chance she was the only person on the train who saw it.

She found the road that roughly paralleled the train's route. At times she glimpsed the tracks running behind a warehouse or on a high berm above a drainage ditch. She found the golf course and parked the car on the side of the road just before the sharp bend. She crossed the road and slid down an embankment into a scraggly bit of woods littered with beer cans and broken glass.

There were no paths, but Carlile could see clearly through the stunted leafless saplings. Frost coated the crisp brown leaves underfoot. She walked past bushes with smoke-gray bark and hard red berries. She bent down and pushed low branches out of her way, trying to keep to a straight course.

The woods sloped upward, and she breathed heavily, the moist air from the bottom of her lungs fogging in the cold air. She couldn't remember the last time she'd walked in woods alone. The sky was white, as though the low clouds were filled with snow. Her foot broke through a patch of brittle ice to black frozen mud beneath. She felt like she had been walking a very long time. This was perhaps foolish, a mistake. The heron had come as a gift, seen from the train. In demanding more, she might lose even that.

Then she saw the pond through the trees, reflecting the pearl-white of the sky. She moved quickly, quietly, feeling light and graceful as she dodged heavy tangles of briars and fallen tree limbs. The heron stood in the middle of the pond in the rushes near the rock. The pond seemed larger than it looked from the train, and the heron seemed no closer. Carlile stood watching. She breathed and the heron breathed, its feathers ruffling gently along its sides. She remembered the dreams, the warmth under her hand.

For a long while she and the heron stood, without motion or sound.

"I'm here," she said. Her voice came out in a low raspy whisper, but the heron shied away from the sound. It opened its huge wings and flapped awkwardly, then stood and shook its feathers. It looked at her, then gathered into itself and drew its body downward. Its neck whipped back and it flexed its legs as it brought its great wings out and down. It strained for a moment, then lifted its wings and brought them down again. Carlile heard a sharp bright sound as the heron broke free from a thin layer of ice. It rose above the pale glow of the pond, its legs trailing behind. Each leg wore an anklet of ice.

The heron circled over the pond, neck and legs outstretched, like a dinosaur become bird. It tucked in its neck and flew over the trees, south.

Open water shone black where the heron had freed itself from the ice. It wasn't truly a pond, just a wide pool of stagnant water. Close up, Carlile noticed the dark scummy shoreline and two car tires mired in the mud. The cinder-block walls of a factory were visible through the trees.

It began to snow. She bent and picked up a feather, as long as her hand and violet blue.

An Hour or a Year
Jenie Pak

My lover believes in aliens. I don't. She believes in ghosts and demons, in heaven and hell, in mysterious psychic powers. She doesn't wear white in her hair. In Korean tradition, that's reserved only for a daughter whose mother has just died. She also doesn't sing or whistle, or clip her toenails at night.

"Lisa," I say, "just look at your nails. They're growing to the size of mushrooms!" Sometimes I replace "mushrooms" with "eyebrows," depending on my mood. "How do you expect me to deal with this?" I ask her.

I tell my mother that Lisa goes too far with her beliefs. My mother asks, "Who is Lisa?" *My lover, my girlfriend, my room-mate, my shower partner.*

"Oh, right," she says. "Are you still living with that les-bian?" I hear my father coughing in the background. He's always chewing on dried cuttlefish. Little pieces get caught in his throat ,and they wound him like shards of glass.

"In the year 2032 the world will sink into the ocean, and a new one will arise," Lisa tells me. "Did you know this apartment is haunted? A little child with a serious illness, maybe brain cancer, died while living here."

"Prove it to me," I say. "Have you actually seen the ghost? Did the mother ship land on our street one night when I was deep in sleep? Did aliens abduct you and inject you with their genes? If I hold up a spoon to your mouth, will it not be fogged over with your breath?"

Don't get me wrong. We talk about other things as well. *Take out the garbage, will you? But I always take out the garbage. If you loved me, you would take out the garbage.*

Lisa works at the Asian Women's Shelter. She bonds with women and kids every day. They share stories and shed tears. They hug, laugh, and swap jokes. I swap e-mails with techies all day. *Thanks for the latest chapters,* I type to authors. *The latest chapters are ready for review,* I write to reviewers. *Regards, best wishes, thank you very much, and have a nice day. :-)* I sit in a cubicle and daydream about changing my life. Having a new career doing meaningful work, where I know how to laugh, how to hug and cry! I imagine coming out to my father: "By the way, I'm a lesbian. I don't like guys. I like girls, get it? Do you want me to throw some more dried cuttlefish on the stove for you?"

I go to the beach by myself and stare at the water. There are fish in there, somewhere. And jellyfish and crabs and huge skirts of seaweed passing through them—blessing them all for a moment with a sudden, lingering kiss. Sometimes I dream of living underwater. I wake up one day and my lungs have transformed into gills. My arms grow spikes, and I have no choice but to live in the ocean since I pierce everything around me. *Goodbye,* I say to my girlfriend. *I'm sorry about your toenails.* She says, *Say hello to the mermaids for me.* My mother weeps, my father sheds a single, fishy tear. The techies e-mail their farewells. *Goodbye, Sandra. I guess this should be an interesting chapter. :-)*

Jenie Pak

My life is what it is, and I'm not sure I like it. Maybe if I start believing in leprechauns and angels, my fairy godmother will appear before me, in a cloud of some aromatherapeutic substance, and dress me up in wisdom and insight. Fairy godmother, please tell me what to do, how to live my life, whether I should go back to being a vegetarian or not.

What if a really sick child did once live in our apartment? What if she slept in the room I sleep in, ate her cereal in the kitchen, and stared out the same window I do each morning? Did she watch the kids across the street and wonder about their brains, those healthy, pulsing globs of peanut-butter thoughts she wanted to squish in her palms? I sit here at the table, look out the window, and imagine her looking past the row of houses, looking instead at the hills that lay like memories in the distance. How long would it take a bird to reach those hills? An hour or a year?

{ }

My mother was afraid I would die in the incubator. My two brothers born before me both died in there, like some meal waiting to be served. But they were spoiled somehow, left raw or overcooked, and my father returned to my mother's bedside a week later and said both times, "Yuh-boh, you are going to have to be strong. We have a ghost for a son. Let us make another."

Instead they got me, a big lesbo. While all of their friends' kids are getting married, I'm living in San Francisco with my "roommate," my "bestest friend." It's great how people can't bear to say the words: *lesbian, dyke, gay girl.* My mother asks, "Did something bad happen to you in college?" I want to tell her it's a blessing—this love for girls. It's like, before, there were hairy chests and eyes cutting through me like I was made of paper or vegetable, and now there's a street that only some have heard of, and now I know all the signs and gutters by heart.

"I met you because of a dream," Lisa says. "A week before I met you, I dreamt a piano fell out of the tenth floor of a building I was walking under. In the dream, the piano fell on me and crushed my organs. My bones had scattered down the block, and a woman came and gathered them all and made me whole again. Sure, I was just bones, a science-lab skeleton walking through downtown, but the next week, I saw you gnawing on a drumstick in the student center and all my bones sort of collapsed into the ground. I knew I had to introduce myself to get them in order again."

"That's sort of romantic," I say. "I can almost buy it." Then I add, "Hey, can't a person eat some fried chicken in peace these days?" I don't like what comes out of my mouth sometimes. The words make themselves up into these snappy, sarcastic faces and stick their tongues out. This is how I treat the people I love. Later I retreat to a private place, such as the toilet, and rearrange the words in my head. *That's romantic. Want some fried chicken?* Or, *I'm chicken, but you're romantic. Can I buy you some fried potatoes?*

At work, an author e-mails me and says, "I'm quitting. I won't be getting any more chapters to you. Forget the book. I'll return the advance. Tell your boss I'm quitting the world." This author frightens me; I send him a message back to try to find out more details. "Are you sure? Are you going on vacation? Did you win the lottery, or join a start-up and cash in on stock options?" When I get no response, I rock back and forth in my ergonomically constructed chair and fall over backward. I bang my head on the file cabinet and spill my coffee, ruining three signed contracts and the photo of Lisa and me posing in front of the paint pots at Yellowstone National Park. The sulphuric smell was really too much for us to bear, but in the photo you can't tell. We smiled, put our arms around each other, squeezed together toward the center of the frame. You should see the one we took right after that one. We're facing each other, each pinching the other's nose, down on the ground as if we're suffocating. When the author finally e-mails me back, two days later, the message reads: "I have decided not to quit the world. But I have still decided to quit the book. Microsoft is evil. I am not. Thank you for your concern."

{}

Lisa complains, "You're turning into a zombie. You're depressed. You don't even say mean things to me anymore. Sandra, where are you? Do you hear me? Where are you?"

"Stop shouting," I say. "Maybe I've been snatched up by your friends from Saturn and I'm waiting for the opportunity to impregnate you with little Saturn babies. They'll have eyes of licorice and their tongues will grow as long as waterslides. They'll rip through your belly and crawl out, one by one, and pull your hair out while you dream of planting turnips."

My conversations with my mother aren't any better. "Why don't you meet a nice boy?" my mom begs. "You're a young lady now—wear some dresses and grow your hair out."

"The mother is talking to herself," I reply. "She is making jokes and enjoying herself, and the daughter is silently crying inside."

My father used to sing operas—slow, sad ones with just enough dramatic high notes mixed in. "Do you want to learn them?" he'd ask every now and then, and I always shook my head, mouthing the words silently. It's not that I was timid or believed I couldn't reach those high notes as well as the low ones. I just couldn't imagine being so serious, so heartbroken—especially over someone else's story. Plus, I secretly believed my father didn't know all the words, suspected he mixed in random Korean words with the Italian. I also learned what the songs were saying, why they had to be sung. The heroine poisoning herself over a lover's betrayal, the sick artist on his deathbed watching the leaves falling off the maple tree, one by one.

"Your father can hardly speak," my mother says. "We barely talk anymore. He keeps a spiral memo pad around his neck with some string."

"What's wrong with him?" I ask. "What do the doctors say?"

"They can't figure it out. Something about the vocal chords being misshapen...they need to take more x-rays."

I tell Lisa about my father. "He used to sing beautifully," I say. "Even if he didn't know all the words, somehow he made it all right." I lean my head on her shoulder, wait for her to put her arm around me.

"The body is a mysterious thing," Lisa tells me. "It has its own plans for us, and your father is meant to be silent for now."

I remember my father shouting for most of my childhood. He was an extreme man, either throwing furniture across the room and threatening to burn down the house, or sitting by the window writing his poems in a steno pad he'd had for years. I remember his eyes, all his pain shooting through them in a moment of fury. I remember his body, hunched over his desk in the half-light, scribbling and erasing his lines.

Last summer, Lisa and I took a road trip. Lisa wanted to see the world, and since we couldn't afford that, we settled for the States. I wanted to see if we could make it out alive—the two of us in her blue Buick, highway stretch after highway stretch, like swimmers in the ocean reaching for land. Sometimes it was just us on the road, especially at night. It was like the body of the world was sleeping and we were two rebellious cells, refusing to belong to anything but ourselves. We talked about a hundred different things. We talked about our dreams, our parents, where we wanted to be in five years. Lisa said she wanted to build a straw-bale house and grow all her own vegetables and herbs. She also wanted to form a band and write songs that interwove social consciousness with her beliefs in the supernatural, the afterlife, the intangible.

"Oh, great," I said. "You can name it *The Ghostly Homos.*" I tried to think of where I wanted to be in five years but couldn't come up with anything. I didn't care where I lived or what material I lived in. I didn't know where I wanted to work or what I wanted to do when I wasn't working. Except the beach—I wanted to be close to the water every chance I got. I wanted to watch the waves coming for me then change their minds at the last possible second.

"Last night I dreamt we had an earthquake," Lisa told me. "And we sat crouched under the doorway and watched our plates and bowls fly by. The bookshelf tumbled over, and you said to me, 'This is not an earthquake. This is your imagination.' You stood up to pick up the books, and I grabbed you by the waist, and you said, 'Darling, this ain't no dance.'"

{}

We are watching a Korean miniseries in the dark. The boy has just lost his arm in a mill accident, and his younger sister is blaming herself. They weep together in the hospital room, the boy saying he has forgiven her. Our bodies are close but not touching. The blue light from the television set makes us colors, characters of our own.

"That's a stupid dream," I say. Just last night I saw Lisa dancing with a woman at the club. At least I thought I did. It was for ten seconds, or thirty, or for a minute. I saw her put her hands around the woman's waist and slide her thigh between hers. I was mad, a little drunk, and started dancing with the woman closest to me. She had a crew cut, and I ran my hands through her hair and saw all the jagged edges of my life appear before me like some sort of holograph. "Lisa!" I shouted, but she didn't hear me. She was gone, and the woman

I was dancing with picked me up and took me to the bathroom. She had sharp teeth and a sharper smile. "Lisa," I murmured into the cold floor. I saw her face then—how it had looked when we had first danced together, radiant with sweat and nerves, excitement and tenderness.

{ }

"Your father can speak a little again," my mother tells me. She is giddy with pleasure, and though we're speaking on the phone, I can see her smiling big, showing off her large front teeth. I have inherited those teeth; people have commented on it. "My, what large teeth you have," they say. "All the better to chew lettuce with," I reply. Sometimes I substitute "chew lettuce" with "chip wood." Then, of course, I remark on their unusually large ears—"Did your mom perform at a circus?"— or comment on their nose hair—"Sharper Image sells some really great clippers for that." I hear my father cough in the background then attempt to say my name over and over like an inconsistent mantra.

"How is Lisa?" my mother asks. "Why don't you two come and visit us?"

"Lisa is busy right now with work," I say. "Thank you for asking."

Lisa is gone. She's moved to Seattle to crash at a friend's and work on her singing career. "You should have believed in me," she said. "I will love the girl who bathed me in milk and honey (I actually filled a whole bathtub with gallons of milk and jars of honey, scrubbed her down with oatmeal, and rinsed her off with champagne), the girl who wanted to tell me so many things I would wake in the middle of the night and she would still be whispering, half-asleep. But now she asks me to guess, and I can't."

Believe the girl loved you. Believe you wanted so many things. You should have loved the girl who believed.

Jenie Pak

I take to climbing hills and standing at the top, pretending the world is my kingdom and this the eighth day of creation, and if I will it, all the computers will shut off and so will all the printers and television sets and espresso machines brewing their delicate, sinful foam. My father's voice will be smooth as lanolin, the hills I stare at each morning will burn a bright orange, and runaway kids will reach into their pockets and find a thousand bucks. Lisa will wake up to angels grooming their pink wings upon her shoulders and knees, and I will be next to her, and I will believe it, I will believe all of it.

The Glue

Christy M. Ikner

"I hate your fucking mother!"

For Becca's sake, I didn't want to cause a scene, especially given everything that had already gone wrong this morning, but I was coming unglued—which wasn't acceptable. That's not what I do: I'm "the Glue." I hold things together no matter what.

It was my Glue-appeal that first attracted her to me.

It was my Glue-effect that held her to me while her crazy ex threatened and accused.

It was my Glue-magnitude that had brought us all together as a family.

And I knew it was my Glue-attitude that would keep us together.

But this day, our magic-filled wedding day, was proving to be the solvent stronger than my epoxy—the Goo-Off that would cause this carefully orchestrated arrangement of people, schedules, menus, and preachers to come undone, sending everyone whirling in a million directions. It would be like one of those movie scenes where something blows up and the charred hero flies through the air, toward the camera, so viewers can see the exhaustion and pain reflected on his face. That would be me: a seared hero.

My beautiful Rebecca looked at me over her shoulder. She sat very still, though I saw her impatience grow as she waited for her cousin to finish putting up her hair. *Look at her,* I thought. *A vision of beauty, impatient though she is, enduring a zoo of combs, bobby pins, and hair spray, all at my request.* There she was, my gorgeous wife-to-be, offering me a rare portrait of her sitting still. She was usually going in three different directions at once, and the only time I got to look at her, really look at her, was when she was sleeping. But there she was, radiating, glowing in the mirror.

I slumped on the floor beside her chair. Three women at once—Becca, her cousin, and my sister—all screamed at me just as I reached the floor.

"Baby, you're already dressed," Becca said. "You'll wrinkle your clothes. Stand up. Now tell me what's wrong."

I stood and smoothed out the crinkles in my linen pants. "We're within minutes of the ceremony and your mother had the nerve to ask me *again* if I was sure I didn't want to wear a dress. How many times do I have to answer that question?"

"Just let it go, baby," Becca said. "We're almost there."

She was right. We were almost there... But over the past two days I'd had my doubts.

{}

We live in a small town with one hotel. Six months before our ceremony we made sure we reserved rooms for my drunkard uncles as well as Becca's mother and three fathers. Yes, she has three fathers. This factoid alone kept me from worrying about her mother and her harsh opinions of our "homosexual relationship." Her mother had married young, had a baby, had an affair, divorced the bio dad, insisted he leave town while also giving up his parental rights, remarried, and required the stepfather to adopt Becca. In addition, the stepfather had a brood of four daughters and two sons by three different wives, one of whom he'd married twice. Marriage number two didn't last—shocker! So Becca's mother married again, making this one work for the past eighteen years. She was determined that Becca consider husband number three her final father, completing her dad collection.

This was the explanation given to the hotel clerk when we insisted the rooms be separated as follows: Mom and Dad, drunk uncle, Dad, drunk uncle, Dad. Who could know that two days before the ceremony the pool cleaner's meth lab would blow up the supply room, shutting down the one and only hotel in town?

"Hello, everyone. Welcome to our home."

Since our living room, den, and every bedroom were now filled with five odd men and one overbearing mother, it was fortunate Becca and I had made a pact not to have sex the week before our wedding—just to keep it hot. Now, sleeping in the laundry room with our cat and dog on a pile of Wal-Mart blankets, the promise of no sex was assured. Actually, we tried once because there was just something about the smell of fabric softener that made us horny, but we kept banging against the washer, prompting Becca's mother to knock on the door and tell us that if we were doing laundry she needed to add her personals to the wash because that long trip had made her bladder weak. Problem solved. It's just about impossible to have sex with the idea of your mother-in-law's pee-soaked size-24 panties scorched into your brain.

"I'm the Glue, baby," I told Becca. "Just stick with me and we'll get through this. Tomorrow is the rehearsal dinner. We'll make it."

Becca smiled. Together we were a force to reckon with. A horny force, but a force nonetheless.

The ceremony rehearsal couldn't have been more perfect—that is, once the lesbian Episcopalian priest threw dad number two out of the church for threatening to punch dad number three in the mouth if he didn't let him walk Becca down the aisle. His reasoning? He was the tallest of the dads. From the church we paraded to the restaurant for dinner. On our dime, my uncles just about drank us out of our honeymoon money. Granted, they did insist on making up the tab by taking us out for a bachelorette party at the local strip club.

You know the saying, "If it sounds too good to be true, it probably is"? Within forty-five minutes we were all kicked out of the club by the lesbian Episcopalian priest—moonlighting as a bouncer—because one uncle wouldn't stop yelling, "I hate these skinny bitches! I like a woman twice my size!" and the other one just had to touch a booby.

"I'm your Glue, baby. I'm your Glue."

I woke early the next morning to an extraordinary gift: I watched my princess sleep. Her dark hair flowed across her face, and her perfect lips allowed a cute little snore to flow through. To think this amazing dainty-at-heart woman lying with her head between our washer and dryer would in a few short hours be my wife was nearly incomprehensible.

And then the phone rang.

"Honey, wake up. Wake up, baby." I gently shook Becca.

"What time is it?"

"Time to get up. We have a problem."

Becca sat up quickly, banging her head on the ironing board. "What's wrong?"

"Jim the caterer just called."

"And?"

"He's refusing to serve the roast beef."

"What?"

"He said he had a dream that mad cow disease had made his wife go crazy and he doesn't want to jinx our wedding or make either of us sick from infected roast beef." I sat back waiting for her tears. Instead she smiled.

"You're fucking with me, aren't you?"

"Honey, I'm—"

"I know you're just trying to get a rise out of me." She was giggling.

"Baby, I'm telling you the truth. Jim wants to serve chicken instead."

"I don't want chicken," Becca frowned. "If I wanted chicken I'd have KFC cater the fucking reception, complete with mashed potatoes and sweet tea. This isn't a fucking hoe-down."

Becca says "fuck" a lot, but it's just so beautiful coming from her feminine mouth.

I knew it was time for the Glue to step in and take control. "Honey, I agree with you that we wanted a fancier affair, but nobody will remember what meat we served. All they'll remember is your ravishing face and amazing dress and the glow you'll cast over the entire service and celebration." The Glue was good.

Becca was a little teary. "Oh, baby, I guess you're right. The rest of the service will be perfect."

I kissed her, lost in the moment, until a loud, insistent knocking startled us out of our reverie.

"Good morning!" It was Becca's mother's shrill, sing-songy voice. "Did you put my privates in the dryer?"

"Um, not yet," Becca said.

"Well, what am I supposed to do?" her mother nearly screeched. "I've already showered, my robe is flapping in the wind, and now I'm air-drying. Besides, I heard you can get chapped if you don't wear underwear. That's all I need...to be caught on camera scratching my hoo-ha at my only daughter's commitment thingy."

"It's a wedding, Mom."
My eyes were burning again.

We spent the rest of the morning playing musical showers with the dads and uncles.

Since it was our wedding day, Becca and I assumed we'd get to shower before anyone else. But somehow I was worked in between a dad and an uncle, and Becca had to fight her way in between the other two dads, which left them standing in the hall staring at each other with dad number one wanting to flip a coin for the privilege of walking their daughter down the aisle. Sounds innocent enough, but it's no pretty picture to watch two hairy men in boxers argue over who would flip and who would call.

"I'll flip."

"I'll flip, you call."

"You call, I'll flip."

"It's my quarter."

"It's probably stolen."

"No, I worked for it, unlike you and your unemployment quarters."

"Disability is not unemployment!"

"So now laziness is a disability?"

"Well, you sorry sack of shit…"

I'm not sure how the argument ended because right then the doorbell rang. I made my way through the kitchen to the foyer, where I heard loud sobbing through the thick mahogany front door. I stopped in my tracks, took a breath, and said to myself, *I am the Glue…I am the Glue.* I could've said that a thousand times and it wouldn't have prepared me for the sight of our Delta Burke look-alike florist, Mattie, standing on my front porch, crying and holding a box filled with brown, wilted flowers.

"Hello, Mattie," I said calmly, pretending I didn't see the

"flowers" that couldn't possibly be the crisp, white gladiolas we'd ordered for our ceremony. "What can I help you with?"

She fell to pieces. "Oh, God...oh, God...my cooler went on the blink last night and everything is ruined, just ruined." She fell through the front door with her box of dead flowers. "I've got to sit down. I'm gonna be sick...just sick. I told J.D. that blower was going out. It's been making a *tink tink tink* sound, and he told me to shut up and that I didn't know anything about refrigeration." Pointing to the "flowers" she continued, "Now just look at who was right."

I am the Glue...I am the Glue...I am the Glue.

Just then my poor unsuspecting angel came in, drying her hair with a towel and wearing her white, comfy robe. "Hi, Mattie," she said. "Are you here to drop off the boutonnieres?"

Mattie burst into tears. "Oh, God...oh, God..." She held up a little brown ball atop a thick green stem. "They never stood a chance! Oh, God!"

I, the Glue, looked at Becca. "Honey, we have a situation."

"Okay, *now* you're fucking with me, right? Please say you're fucking with me."

I had no answer for her, so the Glue went into action to keep things together. Mattie was still sobbing. "Mattie...Mattie, stop crying. Here's what I need you to do. Are there any flowers of any kind left in your shop?"

"I have some green plants," she told me. "And the cooler that's holding the wreaths for Sammy White's funeral this afternoon is still working."

"Perfect," said the Glue.

Becca and I returned to our houseguests and began the process of making our way to the church. We carefully went over the schedule with the dads and uncles; their only job was to show up by eleven o'clock with their pants on.

I'd written a love poem for Becca, and before we arrived at the church I planned to stop by the park where I'd asked her to marry me, read her the poem, and hold her close to me. I'd brought along some champagne to toast our future and thank our pasts for bringing us together. I was carefully placing my love treasures in the trunk of the car when my good mood was violently interrupted.

"I don't want to put my dress in the trunk—it'll crinkle." It was Becca's mother. "Will you hang it on that little hook thingy in the backseat for me?"

"Oh, I thought you were going to come with the dads," I said.

"I'm not waiting on those old farts. They don't know how precious a wedding day is. I want to be there with Becca to help her get ready."

The Glue's romantic moment was ruined. *It's okay. I'm the Glue...I'm the Glue. I'm on my way to the church to marry the love of my life. I'm the Glue.*

Becca came to the car carrying her dress.

"Where's the other dress?" her mother asked.

"What do you mean?" Becca said. "I'm the only one wearing a dress."

"My outfit is hanging in the garment bag," I said.

"Your *outfit*? My stars! Are you wearing a tuxedo?" She looked like she'd just eaten something nasty.

"No, I'm just not wearing a dress."

"How 'bout we get going?" Becca—oh, thank God for Becca—piped in.

For several miles I silently stared out the car window, focusing on the deep blue sky. That afternoon, the weather couldn't have been more perfect. It would've been a glorious day for an outdoor wedding. Becca had initially wanted an outdoor affair, but the Glue was afraid it might rain. The event had to be perfect for my fiancée, and I couldn't risk wind, rain, hail, tornadoes, flocks of birds, locusts, or any other acts of God ruining our day.

I tried not to think about the champagne rolling around in the trunk getting warm or the love letter burning a hole in my pocket. I told myself Becca and I would have time for romance later that night. The Glue would adjust and keep things together. But just then the Glue was reminded that her future mother-in-law was in tow.

"If you don't both wear dresses, does that mean one is the man and one is the woman? And if you both wore pants, would you both be the man? But if you were both the man, would you be gay or straight? Oh, I'm so silly. Of course you'd still be gay, because you'd be two men getting married. Oh ,well, as long as you're both happy."

"Look, we're here…finally, we're here," I said. "Honey, I'll help you carry your wedding gown to the dressing room, and then I'll go check on the caterers and see how things are moving along." I helped Becca from the car and carried her dress to the changing room. I changed into my outfit and went to get status reports on the many elements that were to come together to make this day perfect.

The Glue was feeling good until she entered the reception hall and saw Leona, the wedding planner, puking into a wastebasket. It was one of those slow-motion moments where you're not sure what to do. Here was this prim and proper woman wearing a two-piece eggplant ladies' suit and dangling silver jewelry—whom I was paying five hundred dollars to keep things moving in a timely fashion at the event of my life—with her frosted head in a trash can. *What do I do? What…do…I…do?* I looked searchingly at Jim the caterer, who shrugged. "Probably mad cow disease," he said smugly. "Lucky for you, I'm serving chicken."

Before I could utter the self-sabotaging words "What else could possibly go wrong?" the cake was delivered. It looked perfect and grandiose in its huge pink box. And indeed it was perfect—a perfect representation of Babe Ruth in full swing, hitting a home run. The attention to detail was superb; in fact, I could almost hear the crowd cheering—which would have been fucking great if I'd been at a fucking baseball stadium! The Glue was in the fucking reception hall of the biggest disaster of all time, and the Glue was coming undone. Completely fucking undone!

I turned to find Becca to tell her we needed to call everything off. We could go on our honeymoon and forget the entire ceremony and reception. *It's not legal anyway. Let's just run while we still have our dignity intact.* I was rehearsing my speech on my way back to the dressing room when Becca's mother came out of nowhere.

"I'm starving. Are the caterers set up yet?"

"You could say that," I mumbled.

"Honey, are you sure you don't want to wear a nice dress? You'd look so beautiful in taffeta or lace. I brought an extra dress because I wasn't sure what I wanted to wear. You could borrow my peach dress if you want."

Yes, the Glue would look striking in a size-24 peach taffeta gown. Absolutely. Bring that shit on. We'll do this affair up right. My bride would be honored to say her vows to a fucking piece of fruit!

I smiled weakly and dodged her defensive line, finally making my way to the dressing room and my beloved.

"I hate your fucking mother!"

For Becca's sake, I didn't want to cause a scene, especially given everything that had already gone wrong this morning, but the Glue was dissolving. I slumped on the floor beside her chair. Three women at once—Becca, her cousin, and my sister—all screamed at me just as I reached the floor.

"Baby, you're already dressed," Becca said. "You'll wrinkle your clothes. Stand up. Now tell me what's wrong."

I stood and smoothed out the crinkles in my linen pants. "We're within minutes of the ceremony and your mother had the nerve to ask me *again* if I was sure I didn't want to wear a dress. How many times do I have to answer that question?"

"Just let it go, baby. We're almost there."

She was right. We were almost there. It was twenty minutes before the ceremony. Twenty minutes before I—in front of two hundred people—devoted my life to someone who was my reason for breathing.

Becca stood before me wrapped in sensual white lace. As I gazed at her I realized the important thing was our love for each other. The flowers, the reception, the food—none of that mattered. Our ceremony—our vows and promises—that's what the real glue was. That's what would bind us forever.

Becca and I were married surrounded by green jungle plants and funereal wreaths. We didn't figure Sammy White would mind. Besides, we returned them to the funeral home in time for his family to pay their respects. We ate chicken like we were at a summer picnic and smeared Babe Ruth cake in each other's faces for the photographer. We laughed at the thought of the Little League players who were celebrating their championship with a three-tiered wedding cake topped with figurines of two women kissing.

My wife in her wedding dress and I in my pants danced and danced and danced, knowing our day couldn't have been more perfect. As for me, I changed my name. I'm no longer "the Glue." These days I simply go by "Lucky."

Pining After Grace

Amy Hassinger

I come to this café with Grace to try to salvage what's left of our friendship. We used to come here in the evenings and sit until closing, eating Belgian waffles and trying out ideas on each other like earrings. We couldn't contain our voices then; we didn't have to try. But now we sit here and say little. Grace listens for the ring of the bell above the door, hoping for Toby. She is beautiful, like everyone who comes to this café. Her cheekbones are chiseled like cut glass; her eyes shine with passionate intelligence. She has faith in the worthiness of her life. I've always hoped her faith would rub off on me.

"How was it?" asks Grace, speaking out of the corner of her mouth as she lights a cigarette.

"Fine," I say. "I guess."

"Did they like you?"

"They were courteous. How can you tell?"

"Yeah, you can't, I suppose. What's the job, exactly?"

"Filing, collecting data, company research. Good pay."

"Mmm," says Grace, looking toward the door. She doesn't

believe in good pay. Grace believes in justice, sacrifice. She will run an after-school program in Harlem for homeless children when she graduates. She will arrive early and leave late, waiting until the last child is safely tucked into his shelter cot.

The bell rings and Toby walks through the door, smiling at the woman behind the counter. He stops when he sees Grace and grasps his heart as if he's been shot. Grace laughs. The café quiets—people turn from their conversations. Toby is tall, broad-shouldered, with deep brown skin. He wears his hair in tiny braids that stick up from his scalp. He staggers to our table and drops to his knees, kissing Grace's hand. Her honey hand. A man at the next table applauds, and Grace rolls her eyes, blushing.

Behind Toby, a wiry man stands on his toes, bouncing faintly. "Judy!" he shouts.

"Hi, Jeremiah," I say into my coffee cup.

"I was just talking about you. Are you coming to the march on Friday?"

"What march?"

Toby turns the chair next to Grace backward and straddles it. "What march?" he repeats, disbelieving.

"Don't you know about the Audubon building, Judy?" Grace asks me, concern across her brow.

I shrug.

"They're going to tear it down and build a new biotech center," Toby says.

"The university is," says Jeremiah, sitting in the chair next to me. "It's their property and they want to tear it down."

"So?" I say.

"Jude!" exclaims Toby. "The Audubon Ballroom is where they shot Malcolm. Where he gave his last speech. Where truth and justice died."

"It's a historical landmark," says Jeremiah.

"The university wants to tear down a historical landmark

and replace it with a laboratory dedicated to genetic warfare," says Toby.

"And making money," Grace adds.

"They want to erase history! It's fascism. Not to mention another stab in the backs of black Americans," Toby seethes.

Jeremiah rests his arm on the back of my chair.

"You must have seen the flyers, Judy. They're all over campus." Grace is disappointed in me.

I shrug again.

"Anyway," says Jeremiah, "there's a march on Friday. Toby organized it."

Toby's hand is on Grace's knee. "Me and Grace," he says, leaning into her. She whispers to him. His hand massages her thigh while her lips gently articulate words.

"I hope you'll come," Jeremiah says.

I met Jeremiah a few months ago. Grace set us up. The four of us—Grace, Toby, Jeremiah, and I—had dinner together at The Symposium. We ate stuffed grape leaves and drank sangria; we discussed corruption, police brutality, foreign policy. Jeremiah, I learned, was editor in chief at the *Spectator*; next year he'd be writing for *The Village Voice*. He seemed anxious for me to like him; he kept glancing at me as he spoke, gauging my reaction. He wasn't bad looking, and I could tell he was kind, but Grace's undisguised hopes for us turned me off.

She spoke eagerly as we walked home, selling Jeremiah. "He's so sweet, Judy. I can tell he really likes you," she said, squeezing my hand.

"Mm," I grunted. Jeremiah threw a glance at us over his shoulder. He and Toby were walking up ahead.

"What do you think?" Grace whispered.

"I think he's a megalomaniac," I said loudly. "Did you hear what he said about the *Spectator*?" I mocked him, " 'My hours there are brutal, but I do it to keep the paper afloat.' As if he's the only reason it runs!"

"Shh—Judy. He's just trying to impress you." Grace was disappointed. I snorted, insulted. She'd hoped I would accept Jeremiah as a stand-in for her.

But he was persistent and I was bored. The next weekend I went with him to see a friend's quartet play at Augie's. I drank vodka tonics and watched the bass player's fingers fondle the strings. Jeremiah made painful attempts at jokes, and I laughed to be polite. When he rested his hand on mine, I didn't move away.

Toby slaps his hands on the table, startling me. "Guess what—I'm in!" he shouts to the whole café.

"Sweetie, that's excellent!" Grace kisses him on the mouth.

"They liked my style. Look out, Greenwich Village." He holds a hand up for Jeremiah to slap.

"What did you get, Toby?" I ask.

"A one-way ticket to success. NYU accepted me. I'm going to be studying how to nail the asses of all the corporate bastards I can find."

"Just don't sell out, Toby," teases Jeremiah, leaning backward in his chair. "I hear paying back those loans can be pretty rough."

"Who's selling out?" Toby sips from Grace's coffee mug.

"How was that interview today?" Jeremiah asks. He adjusts his glasses and looks at me expectantly. He adjusted them the same way last week in my bed before he touched my breasts, studying them as if they were embalmed.

"Fine." I tell him.

"What interview?" Toby asks.

"Judy spoke with someone at Merrill Lynch," says Grace brightly. "Financial research."

"Oh," says Toby. "That's cool. Dinner's on you for the next three years." He laughs and turns his wide smile to Grace, who approves.

I stand and twist into my coat. "I'm gonna head back. I have shitloads of reading."

"Are you sure?" says Grace, looking at me with a forced frown. I smile sarcastically. I'm tired of her concern.

Jeremiah stands with me. "Judy, can I walk you home? Or, I mean, not that you couldn't get home safely yourself, I just thought—"

I look at Grace—she's whispering again in Toby's ear.

"Sure," I submit.

I've never made friends easily. It requires a self-assuredness I lack. With Grace, though, it was different. I felt from the beginning as though fate were playing a part, as though we were destined to be close and it was simply a matter of executing the roles already written for us. We met the first semester of our freshman year, and for me it was like falling in love.

My roommate at the time hardly spoke to me; if she did, it was only to ask me if I knew what time lunch was being served, or where the registrar's office was. In the evenings she shouted choppy syllables of Mandarin into the phone, and on the weekends she went home to Queens. Women lined the hallway of my dorm floor nightly, leaning against the closed doors of their bedrooms, identical receivers propped against their ears. Cigarette smoke and nail polish fumes collected in the halls. Most nights I buried myself in my bed.

I developed a habit of getting stoned and visiting the cathedral in the afternoons. I'm not a religious person; I grew up with a fiercely atheistic mother who believed organized religion was no different than organized crime—worse, even, because it dealt in lies and false hope—but something about that church fascinated me. The sanctuary was filled with a vast silence; the air seemed to vibrate with it. I would walk the halls, stopping to pass my fingers through a skein of smoke unwinding above a candle flame, imagining I was touching a prayer. I watched the Holocaust memorial—an emaciated man in bronze standing limp, echoing Christ—as if waiting for it to speak. Once, I listened to the music of a solo violin whirl into the cavernous vaults. I sat for hours afterward in that hard wooden pew, gripping the edge of my seat, feeling that if I let go I might rise like the melody, spinning slowly toward the distant arches. Part of me wished I could.

One afternoon, I saw Grace there. She was with a tour group, standing in front of the National AIDS Memorial. I recognized her; she lived on my floor. I had seen her before curled on a sofa in the lounge, a textbook in her lap. I watched her lift her black hair off her neck with a lazy hand, watched it fall heavily back when she dropped it. She had a book bag slung across her chest, and I admired the way she stood: firmly on two feet, not leaning. I mixed in with the tour group and followed them to the next spectacle: the bronze Keith Haring altar, finished in white gold leaf. I half-listened to the tour guide explain how Haring had finished it just before his death, and how it weighed six hundred pounds, but my attention was on Grace. I glanced at her every few minutes until her eyes met mine. I thought she knew me too. She seemed to look at me with a deep recognition, the same kind I felt when I looked at her.

I approached her as she stood before the altar. "You're on my floor, right? The seventh? Reid?" I asked, pretending I wasn't sure.

She looked at me with surprise. "I guess."

"You cutting out on class too?"

"No. I'm done for the day. My art history teacher was talking about this place and I wanted to see it."

I felt her awe at the cathedral's beauty, and ridiculously, I was proud, as if I were showing off my living room. "I come here all the time," I said.

"It's amazing."

"They have concerts here too. All kinds of things."

I finished the tour with her. When it was over, we left the building together. "Hey," I said. "I thought I'd grab a coffee at the café on the corner. Have you been there before?"

"No." She smiled, amused. She could tell I was flirting with her. "They've got great hamantaschen."

I learned that afternoon that Grace was from Washington, D.C., and was pre-med but already questioning. "Everyone is so worried about their grades. I think they truly believe the world revolves around whether they get the top score on their biology quiz. After every class, it's 'What did you get? What did you get?' They don't even care to learn from their mistakes. It's just, 'How can I raise my grade?' It makes me ill."

"Sounds terrible," I said.

"The thing is, my family will probably disown me if I don't become a doctor. My father's a doctor, and both of my sisters. It's the typical Japanese-American overachiever thing. One of those unwritten rules." She sipped her coffee. "Do you have any of those?"

"In my family? No, we've got all our rules set down in our family handbook, *Guidelines for a Moral and Productive Life*. I could have our office send you a copy."

Grace looked at me sideways. Tiny dimples dented her cheeks. She asked me about myself, and I told her I was from a town in Connecticut where kids drove Audis and Jaguars to school and sipped from hip flasks between classes. I said I wasn't sure what I was majoring in—maybe political science, maybe English, maybe women's studies. Maybe philosophy.

"You're well-rounded," she teased.

"I'm a woman of many interests," I said, lying expansively. The truth was I didn't want to major in anything. I was taking a philosophy class I couldn't bear; I spent the hour staring out the window at the barred college gates, wondering if I should transfer to someplace upstate, where they had lawns. Some days I walked out midway through the lecture, looking pointedly at my watch as if I were late for a dental appointment. But even from the start I couldn't tell that to Grace. I wanted to be my best around her. And when I talked about philosophy with her, I could almost convince myself I did want to study it. Kant's theory of the sublime *was* fascinating when she was around. She had a way of picking up an idea and looking at it from all sides, as if it were a fossil, or a polished stone. I brought my nascent ideas to her like beachcombings and let her hold them, turning and turning them in the light of her mind.

Before Toby, we were inseparable. We trekked down to the Met together on Friday afternoons, and she told me what she had learned that week in art history. I went with her to get her belly button pierced. She held my hand all night when my grandmother died. I taught her how to smoke a joint, and we'd get stoned and go into the quad to stargaze. We never actually saw any stars—the city lights made the sky too pink—but we'd pretend we could see them, reciting the names of constellations just to feel the words on our tongues: Orion, Cassiopeia, Andromeda, Pegasus. We'd lie under our tiny patch of pink sky and talk. She'd fume about the latest piece of news that upset her: the civil war in Liberia, or the treatment of women in Afghanistan. I'd try to make her laugh. I'd tell her about the arrogant prick of the week: a guy in my Native-American lit class who spoke of the symbolism of menstruation as if he were an authority, or the smooth-skinned beat wannabe who ate alone in our dining hall with a book of poetry, raising his moony eyes to each big-breasted woman who walked by. When she laughed she looked at me as if I were the only person who could make her smile. I thought I could feel the pull of understanding between us, like the current of an underground river.

But once Grace met Toby she became serious. She switched to a double major in anthropology and multicultural studies. She joined Community Impact. She spent less time with me. I began sleeping with men indiscriminately and drinking wine to make me giddy, to make the nights blur by like the view from the window of a moving train. I would call Grace after not hearing from her for a few days, and when she said she was busy and couldn't talk I hung up obediently, pretending I understood, pretending I wasn't destroyed by her indifference, even though without her I felt as if I were being sucked into the anarchic anonymity of the city, spinning loose and off-kilter into the future.

Jeremiah and I step outside. The wind rushes at us like a zealous canvasser. Leaflets and newspapers scatter across the sidewalks, plaster themselves against telephone poles and garbage cans. The cathedral looms over Amsterdam Avenue, framed by scaffolding and blue plastic tarps. Our Lady of Perpetual Construction.

"It's warm," I say, inhaling the night air.

"There's a cold front coming in this weekend. We could get snow." Jeremiah stands close to me, wanting to hold my hand.

Across the street from us, the Peace Fountain guards the entrance to the cathedral grounds like a Scylla. It's a bronze sculpture, the inscription of which notes that it "celebrates the triumph of good over evil." The archangel Michael, sword in hand, has just beheaded Satan, whose head hangs from the claw of a great crab. Michael, winged, is half perched on the face of a contented-looking sun. The sun sits atop the crab, which in turn is set on a gigantic double helix—a symbol for the creation of life, no doubt. I've never understood the giraffes. There are nine of them, scattered about. Michael caresses the neck of one while another balances his hooves against Michael's wing and another kisses the sun. They are my favorite aspects of the statue. Who knows what giraffes have to do with conquering evil? Yet there they are, frolicking, stretching, living.

I think of my room on 114th Street with its single window facing an air shaft, the stench of piss wafting up from below. Instead of heading up Amsterdam, toward home, I cross the street and climb the stairs to the fountain.

"Where are you going?" Jeremiah calls after me, following. A low concrete wall circles the fountain. I sit, the statue blocking my view of the street, and pull a joint from the inside pocket of my coat.

"Judy?" Jeremiah says from the other side of the statue.

"I'm right here," I say.

Jeremiah's head appears. The floodlights illuminate his curly hair, making his ringlets shine like little halos in the night. He steps toward me, stopping to finger one of Satan's horns.

"Wow," he says. "Baffling." He stands back and looks up toward the arc of Michael's wings. "I never knew this was here."

"There's a whole garden," I say, gesturing over my shoulder. Behind me the grounds open into lawns, shrubs, plots of soil planted with dormant seeds waiting for warmth. We can't see where it ends from here. "Judy, this is amazing! How long have you known about this place?"

"Oh, I don't know, a few years." He sits next to me. I pull on the joint and hold the thick smoke in my lungs. Jeremiah looks awkward. I offer him a drag. He shakes his head.

"Ruins your memory," he says.

"Bullshit," I tell him. He fidgets with his zipper. I feel the pot spreading its fingers through my brain.

"So, you think you'll take this job?" he asks, for something to say. "If they offer it to you?"

"They won't."

"Don't be so hard on yourself. Why wouldn't they give it to you? You're more than qualified." He likes to compliment me, and though I know he means well, it rings false. He knows nothing about my qualifications.

"I didn't go."

"What?"

"I didn't go to the interview. I didn't feel like it."

"Oh," he says. This puzzles him, I can see. I like to puzzle him. He's very innocent, really, which makes me devilish. "Did you decide you didn't like the work or something?" he asks. "I can understand that—it doesn't sound all that exciting."

"No," I say. "I just didn't feel like going."

I pull on the joint. Jeremiah kicks the heel of his sneaker against the wall. The sound beats like a pulse in my head.

"I've heard there's a peacock that wanders around free here," I say, to see what he'll do. He looks at me warily. "It howls really loudly, like a wounded beast or something."

"Right, Judy," he says.

I shrug. "One of the old ladies who works at the cathedral told me. I don't know why she would lie." I'm telling the truth. I've seen pictures of it; they sell them in the gift shop. It's strange, I know. What does a peacock have to do with the cathedral, with religion? It's as incongruous as the giraffes. But I have no doubt it's here. I haven't seen it yet, but I look for it whenever I come.

Jeremiah snorts skeptically and continues to kick the wall. I know I'm being cruel—he wants to believe me and I'm daring him not to—but I can't help myself. I've been angry with him since I met him. I can't help feeling as though he's here on assignment, as though Grace has sent him here to watch out for me: the rejected friend, in need of company, in need of consolation.

"Judy," Jeremiah says, his voice trembling slightly. He's playing with his zipper, zipping and unzipping it in an insistent rhythm. "Any idea where you'll be living after graduation? I mean, you're thinking of staying in the city, I know, but any idea where?"

"Not really, Jeremiah. Not a clue."

"Where's Grace going to be living?"

"She and Toby are looking for a place."

"Yes, right." He hesitates. "Are you still pissed at Grace?"

"I'm not pissed at her, Jeremiah," I say, percussing the *p*. "There's nothing to be pissed about."

"Okay. You just seem mad about something."

"I'm not. All right? I'm not mad. I'm stoned." He clears his throat, looks down at his zipper again.

"Judy, well, the reason I bring it up is that I've been thinking about something," he says briskly, hoping to change the mood, to lighten the doom in the air. "You know, I've got a place lined up for next year. On the lower east side."

"Mmhmm," I say.

"It's within walking distance of the *Voice*, which will save me money because I won't have to take the subway every day, but even so, you know, it's expensive to live alone. I'm hoping to find someone to share the rent with." He hesitates, gauges my expression. "And I thought, well, if you weren't committed elsewhere yet, that maybe you'd think about it. About living with me."

"What?"

"I know we haven't known each other very long." He laughs softly. "And I don't want you to think I'm proposing marriage or something. I just thought it might be convenient for the two of us."

"Convenient?"

"Are you shocked?"

"Well, yeah," I say. "I'm surprised, yeah."

He nods with that serious consideration that makes me want to shake him. "I know it's kind of soon. I just—I guess I just feel comfortable around you. I didn't really have anyone else to ask. I thought it might be fun."

Living with him—for a moment I consider it: the unending nights of political musings and tentative embraces. The frequent visits from Grace and Toby, Toby's jokes about Grace's foresight in setting us up. The self-satisfied set to her face at seeing a task accomplished, a wrong righted, an old friend coupled.

"I don't think so, Jeremiah," I say. "I don't want to live with you."

"Okay," he says, looking toward the garden. He's avoiding my eyes; I can tell he's hurt. "That's fine. I know it's kind of soon." The noise of the traffic wells up around us, devouring the silence we create.

He turns back to me a moment later; his eyes rest sadly on my lips. "If you don't mind my asking, what are you going to do?"

"What do you mean?"

"Next year. I mean, you've got to do something, right?"

"I'll find something."

He nods again, zips and unzips his zipper. "I really don't want to be presumptuous," he says, "but I've just been wondering—well, it just seems like you're unhappy. And I guess I'm wondering what would make you happy."

"Who is? Happy."

"Well," he laughs self-consciously, "I am. I'm happy enough. And so's Toby. And Grace."

"Fuck Toby and Grace."

He sighs. "Okay," he says. "It's none of my business."

"Is that what Grace told you?" I say, accusing him. "That I'm unhappy?" I can see all three of them, Grace, Toby, and Jeremiah, discussing me over coffee, as if I were the next march, the next protest, the next injustice to conquer. I see Grace's cold concern wrinkling her forehead as she sips her coffee and rests her hand on Toby's.

"No," he says. "I could figure it out on my own. It's kind of hard to miss, to be honest. I think Grace is worried about you too."

"Well, you can tell her to stop her fucking worrying. I don't need a live-in therapist, Jeremiah. What does Grace think, anyway—that I won't be able to live alone? What does she think I've been doing for the past year?" The words are slipping from my lips. I hear my voice shake with emotion, and I'm embarrassed. The threat of tears pricks my eyes; I grit my teeth to stop them from coming.

Jeremiah is silent, looking at his shoes.

"She's the one who has something to learn about being alone," I say. "When does she ever spend a minute without Toby?"

He shakes his head sadly. "Judy," he says softly, "you can't wait around for her forever. You can't spend your life pining after Grace."

I'm stunned. I sit silently, meeting Jeremiah's gaze. His eyes are soft—with sympathy, perhaps, though it could be condescension. I have nothing to say.

Impulsively, I let my torso fall backward into the forsythia bush that grows up against the concrete wall. The budding branches prick my neck and scalp. I slide my weight backward and crash through the branches onto the muddy ground below.

"Judy! Are you okay?" Jeremiah calls from above. I giggle quietly, amused at myself. I'm crumpled in the broken branches of a forsythia bush; the leg of my jeans is snagged. I've ripped the shoulder of my army jacket. My hair hangs from branch to branch as if I've spread it there to dry.

"Judy!" Jeremiah calls again, his voice tight with worry. *He must think I've gone over the edge. Literally,* I think, and giggle again. I hear a soft thud as he jumps to the ground. He pulls back branches, looking for me. I hunch down, closer to the mud, and see an opening in the brush. I shake my leg loose and crawl, mud oozing between my fingers, mud cooling my knees and dirtying my jeans. Jeremiah rustles nearer and I'm suddenly filled with adrenaline. This is a hunt, and I am the hunted. I scramble for the opening like a mouse for its hole.

Reaching it, I stumble as I stand and almost fall into Jeremiah. "Judy—" he begins, his arm extended, but I'm running. Away from the Peace Fountain, away from the damaged forsythia, away from Jeremiah. I'm running toward the towering cathedral.

Mud slurps at the heels of my boots, slowing my steps. Jeremiah is behind me, his footsteps quickening. I slog along until I reach the paved driveway, where I can run faster. I keep my eyes focused on the massive stones of the cathedral wall and the iron scaffolding that confines them. My feet slap against the pavement; my heart accelerates wildly, like a subway car rattling against the tracks. Jeremiah reaches the driveway behind me and stops, out of breath. "Judy, come on!" he yells, but I've reached the scaffolding. I begin to climb.

I hoist myself up to the second, the third, then the fourth rungs, feeling the iron wobble beneath me. The wind whips through my hair and chills my cheeks. It drowns out Jeremiah's pleadings from below. A passing bus sends a tremor through the scaffolding. I grip the metal tighter. My hands are slippery with sweat. Carefully, I turn my body until I'm facing away from the cathedral. I sit on an iron bar and tuck my feet under the one below me. I can see the tops of buildings from here. Antennas and soot-caked stovepipes pose like strange birds on the tarred roofs. Below the rooftops, the streets flow with light. A constant stream of cars rushes to one destination only to change course and rush on again to the next. To my left, the cathedral grounds end at a cliff bordered by a chain-link fence. The black mouth of Morningside Park yawns below, spotted by a few streetlights that burn dimly.

Jeremiah, of course, is right. I've been waiting for Grace to return to me, for her to cast off Toby, like she did me, and acknowledge me as the truer love. I've been waiting for her to become the person I used to know: the Grace who was less self-assured, less self-righteous, more willing to laugh and to defy what was expected of her. But she is not coming back. She no longer exists; I'm not sure she ever did. I wonder if our friendship was nothing more than an elaborate illusion I crafted, a delicate sculpture of glances and laughter and words, of insubstantial air.

The wind dies down. The traffic noise has lapsed momentarily, and I hear the faint tinkle of a bell as the door to the café opens and Grace and Toby step out. He holds the door for her, and she steps under his arm, pulling her jacket more tightly around her. She lifts her hair from the collar of her jacket. A lock of it blows across her eyes and she tucks it behind her ear. I look away, embarrassed by her beauty. Jeremiah has noticed Grace and Toby too, and I'm afraid he'll call out to them, that they'll rush over, that I'll become an emergency, an obligation.

Then, I hear it.

A howl rings through the garden. I look down, toward the Peace Fountain, to where the sound is coming from. There, perched on the back of one of the giraffes, is the peacock. Illuminated by the floodlights, it casts a turquoise glow over the whole statue—over Michael's wings, his sword, the smiling face of the sun. Its tail fans out rakishly; the blue-green feathers shine like sunlight on a gasoline slick. Its head is thrown back, its throat open, and it wails a sustained lament.

Suddenly the peacock stops and looks around as if he expects applause, then he begins once again, this time at a higher pitch, as if responding to his own earlier cry. His voice rises over the rush of traffic on Amsterdam and cuts through the smoky darkness, suffusing the night like a fragrance. Grace and Toby have both stopped to listen. Grace stands apart from Toby, and when he speaks to her she doesn't respond immediately but waits until the peacock finishes his song and begins to preen. As he does his turquoise light shifts over the surface of the statue, animating it for an instant, making it seem as if Michael has bent his head to whisper in the ear of a giraffe.

Done preening, the peacock hops off the statue—from the

giraffe to the sun, to the back of the crab, and onto the ground—waddles aloofly past Jeremiah, and disappears into the garden.

A rush of joy fills me. I feel vindicated somehow, not only because I've found the peacock and shown Jeremiah that it exists but because Grace has seen it and heard it too. I feel as if I've proved something to her, though I couldn't say what. I want to cry out in triumph. "Hey! Hey, Jeremiah!" I shout. He looks up at me, his face slack with wonder. "See!"

I turn toward Grace, hoping to catch her eye, but she and Toby are already rounding the corner of Amsterdam and 114th, walking hand in hand.

Dublin Buy & Sell

Maggie Kinsella

The golden days of September sunshine mute into the heavy gray of October. The rain falls in sheets, washing the streets of Dublin, turning them into quicksilver. The sky hangs low, blurring into the stone buildings, and Frances is still alone.

{}

"It's been nearly two years." Nora swings a leg over the arm of the chair and studies her friend. "You can't pine forever. She left you. She's a fool. Now get over it."

Frances wraps her hands around her coffee mug and pretends to be fascinated with the curls of steam. Nora's bluntness shreds the air and causes the knife to twist once more. Nora means well—she's held Frances together often enough when the weave of her life threatened to tear beneath her, but her forthright concern is too rough an affection right now.

Radclyffe the cat mews plaintively. Frances lifts her onto

her lap, grateful for the distraction. "I should feed her. She's probably hungry."

"Don't go changing the subject on me." Nora leaves the chair in a fluid motion and drops to the floor at Frances's feet. She rests her elbows on Frances's knees, then pushes her friend's hair back with gentle fingers so she can see her face. "I know you're still hurting. But it's been two years. That's long enough. You need to move on. Get a life, get fit, get a lover."

"I'm not sure I know how." Frances pets the cat. Anything rather than look at Nora.

"You could start by coming down to the club with me and Flick tonight."

"No!" The answer comes swift and sharp. Not there. That was where she'd met Aisling five years ago. And where, gossip has it, Aisling goes with her new lover. "I don't want to be in the way—"

"Bullshit. And you know it. It's never been like that. Admit it, Frances. You're running scared."

She swallows hard and covers Nora's large freckled hand with her own. "Fine, I'll admit it. But please, not tonight. Let me get used to the idea."

"Next week then. No arguments—unless you have a date."

Frances summons a weak smile. Satisfied, Nora heads into the gray afternoon.

The evening looms long. Darkness falls by seven, and Frances sits at the window with Radclyffe on her knee. Below her third-floor flat, traffic streams through the rain in a constant river of motion. Nora's right, she knows. It's been too long since Aisling walked out, leaving her for a slender young woman with cropped hair and a stud in her tongue. A girl with street smarts and panache, outgoing and confident. Everything Frances is not.

She hasn't been on a date since then, hasn't kissed another woman, hasn't curled around another body in her bed. "Get a life, get fit, get a lover," Nora said. Getting fit is probably the easiest. She picks up Nora's discarded *Buy & Sell* paper, turning to find the secondhand fitness equipment. A treadmill to echo the monotony of her life.

The personals at the back catch her eye. Men seeking women. Women seeking men. So many of them. A partner to complete your life. Frances would like to scoff at their desperation but can't. At least they're trying. Men seeking men. Women seeking women. She hesitates. *Get a life*. The paper trembles in her fingers, and she thinks there's no life for her in the pages of the *Buy & Sell*.

The small advert is halfway down the second of the two columns:

Bi-curious unattached country woman, 31, seeks female, 30–40, for first-time experience. Genuine. Reply to box 5374.

Genuine. Are there really any people like that left in the world? Frances buries her face in Radclyffe's fur, but the cat squirms away. Bi-curious. Either you're attracted to women or you're not. Frances tries to sift through the shades of gray. She's heard the stories, of course. Now that it's trendy to be a lesbian, more women are trying it; for them it's nothing more than another sexual conquest, one that brands them as risqué and open-minded. They're experimenting with bisexuality as casually as they would a new recipe for chicken.

But the woman on the other side of the ad intrigues her, and Frances tries to imagines what she's like. She's shy, she decides. Maybe she's been married to a farmer; perhaps she has a daughter. Hair as brown as the turf bogs, curling around strong tanned shoulders. Soft-spoken, wearing jeans and a sweatshirt.

Acting on an impulse that would have scared her half to death if she'd stopped to think about it, Frances leaves a voice message.

{}

The clouds are low on the Irish Sea, and Frances takes a walk along Dún Laoghaire Pier, obediently following Nora's second instruction: *Get fit.* The sea curls to shore, and she tastes salt on her hair when the wind whips a strand of it into her mouth. The ferries leave for England across the slaty sea, and Frances is still alone.

{}

"Is that Frances?" The voice on the other end of the phone is mellow with the rounded vowels of the Midlands.

Frances grips the receiver tightly. "Yes," she answers, and waits.

"I'm Margo. You answered my ad."

"Oh," she says, and curses herself for her stupidity. But it's been three weeks since she left the message. Three weeks of walks around Dublin in the quest for fitness. Three weeks of being dragged, silently protesting, into the bars with Nora and Flick in search of a life. Three more weeks without a date.

"I liked your message," Margo says. "Can we meet?"

What were you doing for the past three weeks? Frances wants to ask but knows it's a lame question. Anyone confident enough to place an ad in the *Buy & Sell* has probably been exploring the dozens of women who replied. Margo's probably just being polite.

"I live in Offaly," Margo says. "I'm sure you don't want to drive all the way out here. Why don't I come to Dublin?"

"Sure," says Frances, and the curl of insecurity starts. On

the phone she can barely say two words to this woman. What will they talk about in person?

"Can you suggest somewhere?" Margo asks.

Frances's mind is blank, and she scratches through her memory. "There's a bookstore with a coffee shop attached in Dún Laoghaire. The Turned-Down Page. It's on—"

"I know it," interrupts Margo. "I often go there when I'm in Dublin. I know it's short notice, but how about tomorrow?"

Frances's palm is clammy. She's making a date. Her first date in two years. "Saturday's fine. I'm not doing anything." In a confiding burst she rushes on, "I've led a quiet life since my lover walked out on me two years ago. I miss her still."

There's a moment's silence, and she wonders if she's said too much. Margo will think she's still moping, not exactly a prime candidate for a relationship. But then Margo's ad didn't say anything about a relationship.

"It's hard, isn't it?" Margo offers quietly. "Missing someone, missing them so much your teeth ache from clenching them together to stop the tears."

"Yes," says Frances, and the compassion in Margo's voice is nearly her undoing. "Yes, it is."

"Tomorrow then. Five o'clock?"

"That will be lovely," says Frances, and she realizes with a rush of warmth that she's already looking forward to it. "How will I know you?"

"You'll see my book title," says Margo. "Bye now." A click as she hangs up.

Frances stares at the receiver. She's made a step. A small step.

{}

"You answered an advert?" Nora's shriek hits the high Georgian ceilings of Frances's flat. "A bi-curious ad? Jesus, Mary, and Joseph! Fran, what on earth were you thinking?

Are you cracked altogether? You've never been a recruiter."

"She sounds nice," Frances offers. "Sincere. Her ad said she was genuine."

"They all say that," scoffs Nora. "They fuck you, then, curiosity assuaged, they leave you for a football player with a thick dick that doesn't have to be strapped on."

"You told me to get a life and a date."

"I did. But I was thinking more of *one of us*. Not a straight woman who'll use you and cast you aside." Her tone softens. "I don't want you to get hurt again." She points to Radclyffe, who's shredding the couch with needle-sharp talons. "Learn to defend yourself. Grow claws."

"Maybe I won't need to," says Frances.

{}

Frances walks into the Turned-Down Page, attempting to appear confident. Her heart skitters like a rabbit, and even knowing she's looking good is a shallow boost at best. She's tamed her light brown hair, slicked it back so it will stay tidy; she's wearing jeans and a baggy shirt. Nothing too threatening, nothing too dykey. Ordinary clothes—ones that conceal her still unfit thirty-four-year-old body.

Margo hadn't said where she would be, but the coffee shop seems a good place to start. It's as busy as ever. Frances hovers at the door and studies the patrons. She eliminates the couples sitting close together and the mothers with children. She spots a woman sitting alone in a corner, idly stirring a coffee, but she looks too young. Frances scouts the place for the woman of her imaginings—she of the curly turf-brown hair and weather-beaten skin. There's no one in the coffee shop like that.

She moves into the store, where shoppers are browsing. The scattered armchairs are filled with people curling up to read. There's a woman, thirtyish, with blond hair styled just so. Frances surreptitiously tries to see what she's reading, but she knocks into the chair and the woman glares at her. After realizing the book is a biography of some rock star, Frances smiles an apology and moves on.

Her eyes have passed over the woman in the corner twice before she really sees her. She's curiously still, an open book facedown on her knees. She sits precisely—knees together, both feet flat on the floor. Frances sees huge eyes set in a small face, and a petite body hidden under a large sweatshirt. Dark hair hangs straight to the woman's shoulders, and there's the glint of a small stud in her nose. Her demeanor is quiet, and Frances thinks of the tranquil pools you sometimes find hidden in the rocks on the seashore.

This has to be Margo, Frances thinks, but even so, she doesn't want to approach directly to see what the book is. She angles in obliquely, trying to peer at the title without being too obvious. The woman turns her head and their eyes meet. They're slate-blue, clear, direct. *Genuine.* The woman raises the book so that the cover is plainly visible. With a small jolt of recognition, Frances sees the title: *The Well of Loneliness* by Radclyffe Hall.

"Hello." The woman stands, carefully marks her page, and offers Frances her hand. "I'm Margo. You must be Frances." Her fingertips flutter against Frances's palm. Margo barely tops five feet, and she smiles up into Frances's face. Small lines adorn the corners of her eyes, placed there by laughter or the sun.

Frances realizes she hasn't released her hand and she drops it, but there's no awkwardness. "My cat is named Radclyffe," she says. As an introduction, it's a clumsy one, but somehow she thinks Margo won't mind.

"A grand name for a cat," says Margo. She smiles and her eyes crinkle up. Definitely laughter lines.

"Shall we have coffee?" asks Frances.

Margo nods.

{}

"I like her." Frances juts her chin defiantly at Nora. "And she seems to like me. I'm seeing her again this weekend."

Nora pours some cabernet, carelessly splashing it into the tumblers so that some of it spills onto the table. "And what about in bed?"

Frances folds her arms defensively. "There's more to a relationship than sex."

"So you're not lovers. Have you kissed her?"

Silence stretches and Nora sighs. "I'll take that as a no."

Frances sips her wine. How can she explain to Nora how it feels? She knows she's hanging on a fine silver thread, but she can't stop. Being with Margo is an adventure. She's feeling her way slowly, but she already cares for this woman and she treasures their small touches. Four dates they've had now, and they hug goodbye and give each other a kiss on the cheek. Sometimes she holds Margo's hand, rejoicing that her new friend allows that in public. She wants to kiss Margo properly, but she's fearful of rejection.

"I think it'll work," she says to Nora, and the words, spoken aloud, are her reassurance too.

{}

October rolls on in a haze of mist. Frances walks along Grafton Street among the tinkers and tourists. She pauses to listen to a busker's love song, and she thinks about no longer being alone.

{}

The fifth date: Margo is coming to Dublin and they're having dinner at a fancy restaurant. Frances chose it with care;

266

she's going to try to kiss Margo tonight and she doesn't want garlic breath to spoil the moment. No Italian or Indian, nothing spicy. A seafood restaurant in the city. She has asked for a table by the window. It's more expensive than the pub restaurants she frequents, but she wants it to be memorable.

Frances has wine chilling, and she's bought some farmhouse cheese to go with it. She even splurged on fresh flowers. She tries to see her flat through Margo's eyes, then stands at the bedroom door visualizing Margo wrapped in the butter-yellow sheets on her bed. The picture comes easily.

The doorbell rings, and she greets Margo at the door with a glass of chardonnay, taking her hand and leading her into the apartment.

"This is gorgeous, Frances!" Margo enthuses, and she demands to see the rest of it.

Frances shows her the small kitchen, the hastily cleaned bathroom, even the spare room that she closed the door on without tidying. Margo walks into Frances's bedroom and turns, taking in the floor-to-ceiling bookcases, the sunshine sheets, the love chest at the end of the bed. She studies the book titles then the photos by the bed.

"Is this Aisling?" She touches the frame carefully.

Frances nods and waits for the shaft of pain, but there's none. She watches Margo study the photo intently, with a care that goes beyond passing interest.

Frances moves closer. "That was taken in Galway," she offers. "About three years ago." Her former lover's features stare up from the frame, laughing for the camera as she boarded the Aran Islands ferry. But now it's Margo's breath on her neck she's feeling. Margo is standing close, so close that if Frances turns her head, their lips will touch and they'll be kissing. So close to the moment. Margo's breath hitches slightly, and Frances can hear her shallow breathing, suddenly fast and uneven.

Frances starts to turn her head. *Now,* she thinks. *Now. Just do it.*

"Fran! Where are you? I know you're here! The door was open!" It's Nora, clumping through the flat, hunting Frances down, her feet echoing on the polished wooden boards.

Her broad face appears in the doorway, and Margo moves away, puts some distance between them. Frances's lips tingle from the almost-kiss.

"There you are! And you must be Margo."

Margo nods, smiles in greeting, and seems to take Nora's blatant inspection with equanimity.

"What do you want?" asks Frances. The disappointment of missed opportunity is intense and it's hard for her to be polite to Nora.

Nora stares pointedly at her. "Sorry if I interrupted something, although if I did, it's about time. I was passing by and thought you might offer me a glass of wine." She grins suddenly. "And I wanted to meet Margo."

Trapped, Frances goes to pour a glass for Nora. When she returns, Nora and Margo are chatting away like old friends. Talking about her, she realizes. She waits, letting the chatter wash over her, then checks her watch. "We have to go, Margo. The reservation is at eight."

Margo rises, and they leave Nora to finish her wine in the flat. Frances turns as they start down the staircase. Nora smiles and gives her the thumbs up.

They're only five minutes late for their reservation. The waiter consults the book, then weaves the couple to a table at the back of the room. There is an excellent view of a large rubber plant and the back of a child's head at the next table.

"There must be some mistake," says Frances, politely. "I requested a table by the window."

"I'm sorry, madam." The waiter is scrupulously polite, but he won't meet her eye. "This is the only table we have available."

She can see an empty table for two, prominent in the center of the wide window, with the myriad glitter and life of O'Connell Street parading outside. On it there's a sign marked RESERVED.

"Maybe that table there?" she says. "Seeing as we're here and those guests have yet to arrive."

"I'm sorry, madam. That table is reserved for one of our regular guests." His emphasis on "regular" stops just short of being insulting.

Frances swallows and opens her mouth to protest further, but Margo squeezes her hand.

"This is grand," she says. "It's cozy and private."

The waiter brings menus, and silence falls while Margo and Frances study them. The prices are higher than Frances expected, but she wants to give them an evening to remember. Maybe the night that will start their relationship properly. With a kiss. Her fingers touch her own lips, remembering what nearly happened at her flat.

Opposite her, Margo flicks through the menu. A small line creases between her eyes.

"They've got a good selection," says Frances. "Why not have the lobster tails?"

Margo smiles. "I was thinking more of the pasta primavera."

It's the cheapest item on the menu, and Frances misunderstands. "This is my treat," she says firmly. "Have what you want."

"It's not that." Margo flicks the pages again, studying the options. "I'd really like the pasta."

The waiter returns to take their order, and Frances chooses mussels and lobster tails. Margo orders melon and the pasta.

"Is it freshly prepared?" she asks the waiter, who nods. "Please, can you ensure the sauce hasn't come into contact with shellfish?"

Suddenly mortified, Frances realizes Margo must be allergic to fish. In despair, she forgoes the mid-priced bottle of wine she'd decided on and picks one of the most expensive ones. The waiter nods as if he hadn't expected anything less. She escapes to the ladies' room, and on the way back she sees notices the RESERVED sign has disappeared from the table by the window.

After the wine is poured, Frances says, "I'm sorry. I didn't know you were allergic to seafood."

Margo places a hand over Frances's. "Hey, don't worry. I didn't tell you since you sounded so excited about this place. The pasta sounds grand and this wine is heavenly."

Frances turns her palm, and their fingers entwine, meshing together naturally. "We could have gone somewhere else. That's what… That's what it's all about—give and take." The word she was going to say sits thickly on her tongue. It's too early to talk about love. But she knows she's at the top of a gradual slide. Yet she still doesn't know what Margo's agenda is. Doesn't know what Margo wants from her. The future is suddenly hazy, as if seen through smoke, and the golden, comfortable pictures she's daring to dream may dissipate as quickly.

She wants to ask. She's never pinned Margo down and asked her questions, specific questions, Frances-and-Margo-type questions. She's been content to let things unwind at their own pace, but now the urge to know where she stands is fierce. Her grip tightens on Margo's fingers.

"Margo, you never told me why you placed your ad," she begins.

The waiter arrives with their first course, and the question is lost in the placing down of plates, arranging of cutlery, and the "Is everything to your satisfaction, madam?" questions.

The mussels are delicious—small and firm and oh, so sweet. Frances finishes them and polishes her bowl with the thick, crusty bread. Her lobster is equally good, covered in a creamy sauce. She watches Margo eat her pasta, delicately but with obvious enjoyment. The conversation comes freely. So easy to talk to Margo, such a flow, opinions in common and differences acknowledged and accepted. They linger long over dessert, over coffee and liqueurs, ignoring the disapproving stare of the waiter. She thinks about leaning forward, taking Margo's lips over the half-filled coffee cups, kissing her senseless over the Benedictine glasses. But the waiter's blank stare dissuades her.

The table by the window remains empty all night, but Frances no longer cares, and they're the last customers to leave.

Outside, the city is busy; the pubs throw noise and light onto the pavement, and the streets are crowded with raucous people. They can walk the couple of miles to Frances's flat or find a taxi. The night is clear and mild, and they elect to walk at least part of the way, passing out of the city toward Rathmines.

Margo takes her hand. "I've never told you," she said, "about that ad. You must be wondering."

"I am," Frances says, and waits. Her feet keep pace with Margo's shorter stride, and she watches them: one, two, one, two...

"I've had boyfriends," says Margo. "But I was never really comfortable with them, never felt that connection with someone special. Sex was all right, but it never worked well for me. Not like it did for my friends. And I got to wondering..." She trails off, jams her free hand into her jacket pocket.

Frances is silent. An emphatic silence—she's heard tales like this all too often. It's one that reverberates around her friends, around her acquaintances, around her past lovers.

"I know my ad said I wanted a first-time experience," says Margo. "But I don't want that anymore."

Frances's heart sinks, her hopes dashed.

Margo's pace slows, halts. "I want you," she says. "I want it all, but only with you." Tugging gently on Frances's hand, she pulls her into a darkened shop doorway. Her hands run up Frances's arms, up around her neck, and she traces her lips with a careful finger.

The kiss, when it comes, is a slow, gentle merging of breath, of lips, of soft, entangling tongues. The trust and desire builds, expanding from Frances's heart. The kiss escalates, and her whole body is caught in a spiral of wanting. Her hips push slowly into Margo's in an instinctive seeking for more, for the connection. A liquid rush courses through Frances's body and her heartbeat accelerates. Want and need, twin emotions long dormant, rise up, and finally she pushes Aisling into the past, where she belongs.

When they break apart, their breath mingles moistly between them. Turning, Frances wraps her arm around Margo's waist, and with one accord their feet turn for home.

{}

The long November nights creep in, car headlights pierce the sheets of rain, and the trees are bare on St. Stephen's Green. The firelight flickers in the cozy flat in Rathmines, Radclyffe chases the dancing shadows, and Frances is no longer alone.

Attempts at Rescue

Sandra L. Beck

Louise woke up from a stroke-induced coma on September 21, 1983, one week before she died—her eyelids snapping open with a force characteristic of sudden realization. Louise's wooden cuckoo clock had just completed its ninth chime, and a steady rain tapped against the window.

Had Phil Banks, who sat a few feet away from her bed reading *The Boston Globe,* been watching her, he would have seen her brown eyes focusing, sharpening, zooming in, not just to her physical surroundings—that is, the plastic Ayer Assisted Living Center furniture, the paintings on the wall, both of them copies (Van Gogh's sunflowers, Monet's water lilies)—but also inward to the landscape of her coma that was, at the moment of her awakening, still a competing reality. He would have heard her lips opening and closing once, twice, three times, making whispery sounds like puffs on a cigar.

But a wind had picked up outside, and the branches of a lilac scratched against the windowpane.

"Key West," Louise said, "is it still underwater?"

Phil peeked over the top of the obituary section. "Louise, you've come back to us!"

"Hurricane Diana."

"What are you saying?" Phil let the newspaper fall to the floor and dragged his chair by its tubular metal arms closer to the bed. He took Louise's hand and patted it as one would a dog's head.

Louise's eyelids fluttered, opened wide, drooped shut, and fluttered one last time before closing again. She whispered, "Bayley's down there." Then her head lowered to the pillow, reclaiming the warm hollow it had occupied for the past two weeks.

"It's all right, Louise, the water's receded. Nobody died," he said.

Since yesterday, Phil had been going through a stack of postcards from Bayley, Louise's granddaughter, looking for a telephone number or an address where she could be reached. There were four cards from Florida, two from California, and one from Louisiana. He studied the photograph Bayley had enclosed in the one letter she'd sent. In it she stood between two elephants, one a baby. Looking from Bayley's face to Louise's, he saw the resemblance: the determined jawline, the fine thin hair.

Puh, puh, puh, puh. Louise's lips pouched together to form what appeared to be a kiss.

Phil enclosed Louise's wrist within the circle of his thumb and forefinger, comparing the childlike size of hers to his own, feeling her pulse. *How close we are to being dust,* he thought.

A crackling sound at the window made him look up. A spray of leaves and twigs whirled past. At ninety-two beats per minute, Louise's pulse was rapid and feathery, like the heartbeat of the baby robin he'd rescued from a neighbor's cat when he was ten, its blue-veined chest quaking in the palm of his hand just moments before it died. He tucked Louise's hand under the covers, tiptoed out the door, and shut it noiselessly behind him.

At the front desk, Jax, the receptionist, was smacking her gum and singing into the telephone, "Ring my be-e-ell, ring my bell, I know, dingalingaling..."

"Jax!" he said, still tiptoeing.

"Yes, sir." She hung up the receiver and with both hands swatted Goldfish crackers from the front of her dress. "Excuse me, sir." Jax smiled. "Mr. Banks?"

"Yes?"

"I just want to say that you sure are handsome with all that fine-lookin' white hair. Whole lotta men your age would kill for half a what you got."

Phil patted down the sides and back of his head, feeling for any out-of-place hairs. Ever since reading an article in *GQ* on hair-loss prevention, he had spent fifteen minutes massaging olive oil into his scalp every morning before washing his hair with a plant-based freesia-scented shampoo and then fifteen minutes brushing it.

"Please make sure to come get me if Mrs. Erlandson's granddaughter calls." He hoped he had left the message at the right number. A woman with a muffled, sleepy-sounding voice had answered. She'd said, "Who?" when he'd asked for Bayley.

Jax covered her mouth with both hands. "Is Mrs. Erlandson passed?"

"No, she just woke up."

{}

At the end of August 1982, Bayley's two friends, James and Christopher, whom she'd met in Provincetown that summer, were driving up the Cape to drop her off in an area of Scituate known as Egypt Beach, on their way to Boston to visit

Christopher's mother. Where Route 3 splits off into Route 3A was the direction they should have taken to get to her grandmother's house but didn't, a mistake no one noticed until they got to Quincy, twenty miles out of their way.

James, steering the car one-handed, the other supporting both a cup of coffee and a cigarette wedged between his second and third fingers, said, "You're the one who used to live there."

"I never learned the way," Bayley said. "I don't have a license."

Christopher, seated in the backseat, leaned forward, propped one elbow on James's seat, one on Bayley's. "You mean you can't drive?"

She had heard this tone before: *You don't like chocolate? You didn't go to your prom?* Bayley shrugged. "My grandmother always drove me everywhere."

"We'll show you how, won't we?" Christopher said. He brushed aside James's wavy auburn hair and kissed him on the neck.

"Yessiree," said James. He squeezed Bayley's thigh. "With three people driving we'll make Key West in three days."

An hour later, when James's red Buick convertible chugged up the driveway and a two-toned green Cadillac with fins became visible over the hood of their car, Bayley let out an "Oh, shit. She's here."

"Wow!" James said. "1958, isn't it?"

"We'll wait down the street," Christopher said. "Put some Metamucil or something in her coffee, then when she goes to the bathroom you can get the jewels."

Bayley checked the car clock. "She's usually at the St. Clairs' playing cards in the afternoon."

"Chickening out?" James narrowed his eyes and took a deep drag on his cigarette.

Bayley laughed. "Cut the Mafia routine, James."

A movement in the living room window caught her eye. She saw the curtains sway and then her grandmother's face, stark, pale, and floating, apparition-like, amid late-afternoon shadows. Struggling to get out of the car with two plastic grocery bags filled with clothes and other belongings, she kissed James goodbye and said, "If I stay for a couple of nights, she'll give me money too."

As soon as Bayley got inside, her grandmother said, "Who were those people? They look like they need haircuts, at least if they're men. Are they men?"

"Oh, Nana, of course they're men."

At five-thirty, while roast beef sizzled in the oven, Bayley sat on the floor in front of her grandmother's bulky uphol-stered chair. "Nana," she said, "will you stroke my hair?"

Bayley heard the crinkling sound of the crossword puzzle book being stuffed into the drawer, which also housed family photographs, a thesaurus, brownie recipes, a supply of butter-scotch LifeSavers, her grandmother's ledger-size checkbook, and two eighteen-carat–gold sections of a broken chain-link watch. "I can get at least six hundred for them," she'd told Chris and James in the car. "And there's a gold ring she never wears with a huge amber stone surrounded by six little dia-monds. A fifty-thousand-year-old insect is trapped inside it."

"I'm moving to an assisted-living apartment complex."

"A nursing home?" Bayley welcomed the familiar movement of her grandmother's fingers circling her scalp, its hypnotic numbing effect, but she couldn't remember ever being able to relax. Slowing down her heart and breathing into a kind of paral-ysis used by certain species of animals to fool predators into thinking they're dead was the closest she'd come.

"Yes, but the building I'll be living in—at least while I can still get around—people have their own apartments there. Mr. St. Clair said he'd sell the house and auction off all the furniture and rugs for me. If your mother were still alive, I wouldn't have to, but that's how it is when you get old."

Louise's fingers stopped moving. Bayley sensed she was thinking about the accident. Bayley turned her head from side to side, nudging them back into motion. She was six years old when her parents had flown to St. Thomas on vacation. They were to stay at Bluebeard's Castle—Bayley had asked her mother if a man with a blue beard lived there—as guests of her father's boss, Bill Prouty, owner of Prouty Real Estate. Had it not been for engine trouble in Mr. Prouty's Cessna 172, Bayley would have grown up in St. Thomas. Mr. Prouty had hired her father to head up the Island Sales division. At the time, certain wealthy people, like the Rockefellers or the DuPonts, her father explained, had begun to take a keen interest in buying islands—especially those that could only be reached by private boat. There'd been a funeral and a stone marker planted in the family plot in Mt. Auburn Cemetery, but the bodies were never found after the crash.

"You know, Bayley, even after all these years, I still can't catch my breath." Louise sighed. "It was so sudden. If your grandfather hadn't seen to my interests before he died, I don't know what I would have done with you."

Bayley and her grandmother looked at each other in the same helpless manner that reminded Bayley of the time she'd been swept off her feet by an undertow. She'd acquiesced to its crushing force, water invading every orifice, claiming her. A lifeguard intervened, yanked her out twenty feet from shore. He carried her up the beach to where Louise sat huddled beneath an umbrella, a shell pressed to her ear.

"Just the same," her grandmother said. "Maybe it's for the best. I mean about Mr. St. Clair selling the house, of course. I don't like to bother the neighbors because there are always strings attached. Once they've shoveled your walk or mowed your lawn, they think they own you."

"Like how?"

"Oh, they invite you for lunch, want you to drop by for

cocktails, play cards, and with you moving to Florida...You promise to come visit me?" her grandmother said.

"Yes, Nana," Bayley said, thinking she should wait until she got to New York to pawn the watch pieces and the amber-and-diamond ring.

"How old are you now, Bayley?"

"Nineteen." She turned her head to catch a glimpse of her grandmother's face. Somebody in the Boston pawnshops might recognize her. "Why?"

"You have one more year to go before some part of you throws in the towel. When you turn twenty, there'll be one molecule in your kneecap or maybe in your liver or earlobe that'll suddenly plop down and say, *That's it, twenty years, I'm done*. Louise took a deep breath. "And when you get to be my age, four fifths of the molecules that were jumping around, all excited as you please to be alive when you were born, are lying around too, watching the last fifth knock themselves out before the big finale."

Tears amassed behind Bayley's eyes. She felt pressure building there, her face a swollen mask. She wanted to take refuge in other goodbyes they'd spoken—the kiss-on-the-cheek immortality of them—to stave off what seemed to be the finality of this one.

{}

The Weather Channel began broadcasting in 1982, and that same year, after she'd moved to the Ayer Assisted Living Center, Louise Erlandson, at age eighty-three, pledged the final year of her life to it, turning on the television every day of the week when she sat down at eight A.M. in her upholstered chair—one of two pieces of furniture she'd been allowed to bring with her, the other being a side table—and shutting it off fourteen hours later when she went to bed.

Hurricanes were her favorite weather event—"nature's tantrum," as she referred to them that first late summer–early fall season. She'd say to anyone who came to her door—the newspaper boy, the young plaid-suited Seventh-day Adventists, the A&P delivery man—"How about that Debby off the coast of Aruba? Isn't she the spitfire!" or "Have you seen Alberto on the news? He's just a terror—one minute on the rampage at ninety miles per hour, and the next lying down like a lamb."

Phil hadn't had much to do with Louise, not since the time he'd brought her some onions from the senior center's community garden. She had recently moved to the center and accepted them with a cascade of cheerful finishing-school "thank yous" and "aren't you thoughtfuls." That night she'd tossed the onions up onto his balcony. He couldn't forget the sound of them—the four thuds on his wooden balcony. He'd been assembling a Vermont autumn foliage puzzle—the first of two white steeples was in place—when he'd heard it. He'd gone to the balcony door, jerked open the blinds, and seen his four prize-winning Red Barons lying there, bruised.

A month after the onion incident, Phil, who lived a floor above Louise, and who also fulfilled the role of manager, heard crashing noises coming from her apartment. Phil listened to the noises for several minutes, trying to identify what they might be before going downstairs. When he heard something that sounded like a hammer clanking against metal, he decided it was time to investigate. He knocked twice when he got to Louise's apartment, but he didn't get an answer.

"Louise?" he called. "Louise? It's Phil." He was yelling now through the door. Still no response. "It's the Onion Man," he whispered. He heard creaking sounds in the hallway to his left and right, and turning, he caught the silhouettes of Alice Chamber's sail-shaped nose and Nora Blackburn's bumpy one poking out of their doors. "I'm just checking to see if she's all right," he announced in a loud I'm-not-guilty tone of voice and unlocked Louise's door with his master key.

The first thing he saw was Louise seated on the edge of the couch. She wore a pair of rubbers and a raincoat.

"It's just terrible, Phil. I didn't know what to do. I tried to fix it, but I think I made things worse."

When Phil stepped in his corduroy slippers sank into the rug with a squishy oozing sound. Tracking a hissing noise coming from the kitchen, he encountered a film of brownish water covering the linoleum. The two cabinet doors beneath the sink had been flung back, their metal handles having dented the wood veneer of the cabinet doors on either side of them. Leaking bottles of cleaning fluids, frothy Brillo pads, flannel pink-flowered rags, and a whisk broom were stacked in a bluish soggy heap. Behind him, the Weather Channel broadcasted live footage of a flooded town: tin rowboats loaded with Red Cross personnel in yellow rain slickers, a dog standing on the roof of a car, and a person, chest-deep in water, propelling himself out the front door of his house, a statue of the Virgin Mary in his arms.

Phil sighed. From a jagged crack in the drainpipe issued a steady spray of water that had, Phil expected, ruined the electric range and the wall behind it. Patches of paint had flaked off. Previous layers showed through: eggshell-blue, pale lavender, canary-yellow.

"Why, Louise, I believe you have indeed accomplished that—made things worse." Phil knelt, reached under the sink, and turned one of two oval knobs to the left. The flooding ceased. "But there—voilà! It's all over now."

"So what else do you grow in your garden plot?" Louise asked, turning down the TV volume, "besides onions?"

Phil laughed. "Shallots, garlic, and leeks. Good for keeping the cholesterol at bay. Where's your mop? Gotta get this floor dried before the linoleum curls."

"Good for keeping people at bay too. In that closet." Louise pointed to a door on the other side of the stove.

"I believe you'd say the same if I grew carrots or cabbage." He took out a mop and a plastic bucket.

Louise stared at him, ventured a hint of a smile. "Maybe so," she said, "but I've got my reasons. After my husband left me for another woman, I took up rose gardening. Friends told me it'd take my mind off things. I went and bought all the different roses, hybrids—whatever newfangled species the American Rose Society was trying to inbreed—but they all succumbed to the beetles, every last one. No matter how much I took care of them—and believe you me, I was out there every day, May to September, getting pricked by those damned thorns."

"Brown thumb, Louise. It happens."

Louise continued. "So I said to the roses, 'Okay, I'm finished with you. Hear that?'"

The Weather Channel had switched from flood coverage to a forecast for New Orleans.

"Sunny and seventy. Getting warm," Louise said, unbuttoning her raincoat.

Phil began mopping the floor. "I bet you never kissed a one of 'em, though. My sister-in-law, Polly—she's dead now—kissed whatever she was trying to grow. 'Think how hard it is starting out in unfamiliar surroundings,' she told me. 'A kiss on a regular basis can make a difference of several inches, an extra sweetness or a fuller bloom.'"

"I don't believe kissing is the answer to everything, Mr. Banks."

{}

In Key Largo, Christopher, James, and Bayley stopped to eat at a place called Eve's Ribs. The boys weren't speaking to Bayley because she hadn't helped with the driving. Three days earlier, before getting on the New Jersey turnpike, they'd stopped in a town called Linden where James had given her driving lessons. For a couple of hours she drove up and down residential streets, keeping to twenty-five miles an hour.

Once on the turnpike ramp, with James urging her, "Okay, now speed up to fifty," she had started to duck down, as though dodging bullets. "This is murder!" she screamed when a wave of insect bodies splattered across the windshield. Bayley veered over into the breakdown lane and stopped the car. Her face flushed and perspiration dampened into a V shape on the front of her pale blue T-shirt. Bayley sat for a few moments before getting out of the driver's seat and moving to the back, where she stayed for the remainder of the trip.

Now, sitting at the opposite end of the picnic table from Bayley, James and Christopher, huddled over their daiquiris, engaged in a duel with alligator-shaped swizzle sticks. From time to time they looked her way and whispered something. A young woman dressed in a turquoise tank top that complemented a reddish tan approached Bayley's end of the table. Blue-black hair flowed over each breast, reaching to her waist.

"Hi, I'm Patrice. What can I get for you?"

Bayley noticed Patrice's arms, the muscles smooth and long—like a swimmer's, she thought. "I'd like the roast chicken with coleslaw and fries, please."

Patrice wrote something on a pad of paper. "Those guys with you?"

Bayley glanced at Chris and James and was annoyed to see them both looking at her. James stuck his tongue out.

"No, and I'd like an iced tea with a slice of lemon."

Patrice's face brightened. "Right-oh." She snapped off the page with Bayley's order. "The food'll be a few minutes. We don't get much call for chicken here. Mostly it's ribs, ribs, ribs, like your boyfriend over there ordered."

"He's not my boyfriend," Bayley said in a loud voice. When James had hooked up with Christopher at the end of the summer, she'd told him, "There's no way I'm staying with you. I don't share." She might have been willing to, had she been attracted to Christopher. He had a bulky cement-column body and a lazy left eye. When she'd first met him, his right eye looked into hers as though keeping her occupied while his left wandered, gaining backdoor access to sensitive areas. Bayley glanced at Christopher now, his smirking "Biggie Rat" gangster smile, his lewd lazy eye. She wondered what about him James was so turned on by.

Patrice approached the table and set down Bayley's iced tea. "I'll show you the elephants while you're waiting, if you like."

"Elephants?"

"Yep. The owners run a small circus." She pointed toward a door next to the kitchen. "We can go out that way."

Following a few yards behind, Bayley took in Patrice's languorous gait—catlike in the way she glided over the flagstone steps leading up a small hill to the corral. Fifty feet away from it, a swarm of black flies surrounded Bayley. The sun was high and bright overhead. The combined smells of mud, elephant waste, and wet hay nauseated her. Breathless and dizzy, for a moment she wanted to run back inside but didn't, intrigued by Patrice's bold manner and challenged by the fact that she'd gotten Bayley to admit that James was not her boyfriend.

Patrice turned on the faucet, picked up the hose, and aimed it at the two waiting pachyderms, one a baby. "It took me two weeks to get where I didn't gag when I came up here."

Clots of mud and hay sailed off their skin. The elephants nosed their trunks toward the stream, taking sips with two fingerlike appendages. "It's one way they relax. Me too." Patrice shifted the spray at Bayley.

"O-o-oh!" A tickling sensation eddied across her arms and face. She shivered, excited by Patrice's smile—the stunning white-tooth flash of it—as much as by the cool shower. "I can see why," she said.

"This is Rose and her daughter, Delilah. And you know my name. What's yours?"

"Bayley."

Both elephants—Rose first, and then Delilah, imitating her mother—extended their trunks toward Bayley. They opened and closed their trunks several times then inserted them into their mouths.

"What're they doing?"

"Smelling—their way of getting to know you. Where are you from?"

"New York," Bayley said, thinking of the week she'd just spent there trying to pawn the watch pieces and amber ring. She'd gone back to James's apartment every night with a different excuse as to why she hadn't been able to: *The assholes only offered three hundred a piece.* *They said I had to show a driver's license.* *There's a police check for goods worth more than five hundred dollars.* But none had been the real excuse—the fact that she couldn't part with them. "How about you?"

Delilah took a few steps closer, stretching her trunk through the fence toward Bayley's pants.

"Ohio originally. You got a carrot in your pocket?" Patrice grinned.

Both said "Sounds like a Mae West line" at the same time, shot each other a look, and laughed.

The night Bayley, James, and Christopher stopped in Emporia, Virginia, Bayley had overheard their conversation in the shower: Christopher suggested to James that they steal the amber ring from her. She decided to keep it and the watch pieces with her at all times—in the pillowcase at night and in her pocket during the day. She touched them now, reassured.

"Have you worked here long?" Bayley asked Patrice.

"A couple of months. I'm trying to save enough money to continue traveling."

Rose, making scratchy sounds that reminded Bayley of television static, lifted her trunk and stroked her daughter's head, smoothing here, prodding there.

"She's comforting her," Bayley said.

"Sweet, isn't it?" Patrice said.

{}

One Sunday morning, two weeks after he had finished with the painting and repairs in Louise's kitchen and hired a cleaner to remove the water from her rug, Phil opened his front door and found a potted ficus tree sitting on his welcome mat. Its ten or eleven leaves, their tips shriveled to crisp brown, clung to branches that had been pruned to form a lollipop shape. He stood in his doorway for a few moments, as though waiting for someone. When one of the leaves fluttered to the floor—the casualty of an unexpected gust of cool breeze—he picked up the tree and rushed inside.

A rose-colored gift card fell out when he set the tree on top of his television set. Phil read it aloud:

IF YOU THINK THIS PLANT WOULD IMPROVE WITH A KISS, THEN
PLEASE, BY ALL MEANS.
—LOUISE

Phil bought professional gardeners' brands of plant food bulbs that imitate sunlight, and he embarked upon a feeding, watering, and kissing—every leaf—regimen for the next month. He modified an old lampshade—removed the spokes, cut a slit down the side, and fit it around the base of the tree to prevent Maxine, his aged Siamese, from using the potted plant as a litter box.

By the end of the month—it was early December—the ficus had sprouted twenty new leaves and several branches had grown a quarter of an inch. At first—his sister-in-law Polly's heartfelt gardening advice notwithstanding—Phil had felt silly kissing the leaves. It wasn't until he added the image of Louise's face to the equation that the prospect of the tree's recovery took on proper meaning. Phil even brought the tree downstairs to show Jax.

"What do you think about afternoon tea?" he asked her.

"Are you asking me on a date, Mr. Banks?"

"No, I mean with Louise."

"I've been wondering when you were going to get around to it. Ever since you took that plant into your care, Mrs. Erlandson looks awful happy. A few days ago, she gave the A&P deliveryman a tip! Imagine that!"

A smile flickered across his face—on and off and then on again, like lights during a storm, the power source unsure. Phil smoothed his hair with both hands.

{}

While Bayley negotiated with James and Christopher ("What do you want in exchange for letting her come with us?"), Patrice removed seventy-five dollars from the till at Eve's Ribs. Then she told Mickey, the cook, that she was taking a break. She went up to the corral to say goodbye to Rose and Delilah and then to the room she rented from the owners. She stuffed her tent, sleeping bag, and clothing into a green lawn-and-leaf garbage bag. "It's how much salary they owed me anyway," she told James and Christopher after they agreed to give her a ride if she filled the gas tank and bought them dinner.

The drive from Eve's Ribs to Key West took them three hours. By nightfall—after wandering the streets, taking a ride on the Conch Train, and going to the pier to watch the sunset—they'd found out about the abandoned two-story house on Angela Street. Twenty-two people occupied it. There was electricity, running water, and a working telephone line. Bikers resided on the first floor; on the second floor lived hippies.

The first floor was strewn with leather saddlebags, chrome motorcycle parts, beer cans, army surplus bedrolls; the second with candles, gondola-shaped wooden incense burners, wine bottles, and an assortment of buckets and pans that collected rain when the roof leaked. In the first-floor hallway stood a camouflage-colored pup tent owned by a biker named Fudge, an ex-marine in charge of screening new tenants and collecting money for the food kitty. Nobody knew who had been the first person to break into the house or whether the owners were ever coming back.

"Really? It's free?" James had asked the young guy they met by the pier at sunset that first evening in Key West. He was wearing an eye patch and a black bandanna.

"Just say the innkeeper sent you."

"The innkeeper?"

"That's the password. Fudge won't let you in if you don't say it. The bikers are really picky, but the only thing you have to do is contribute toward the food. Some people work at the fish plant and they score free fish. Others share their food stamps. Here." He removed a stub of a pencil and stick of gum from his pants pocket. He popped the gum into his mouth, scratched the address into a layer of sugar that adhered to the inside of the wrapper, and handed it to James. "Go four blocks down Duval, then right two blocks on Angela."

"I can't believe it," James said. "There's got to be a catch."

A gentle breeze stirred. The dark silhouettes of palm trees stood out against a deepening magenta sky.

"Wasn't the sunset incredible?" Patrice took Bayley's hand. They passed James and Chris, who were busy looking for Ernest Hemingway's house. She took a deep breath. "Mmm...night-blooming jasmine...smells so good."

Even though she and Patrice had gotten to know each other quite well in the car (James had spent a lot of time watching them in the rearview mirror—"Hey, save some for later," he'd said, timing one of their longer kisses), Bayley longed for her grandmother's touch.

"What if they don't let us stay?" Bayley asked Patrice.

"Don't worry, there's always the beach, and I've got a tent!"

Bayley held tighter to Patrice's hand.

The first thing they saw on Angela Street was a row of Harley Davidson motorcycles, "hogs," all painted different colors—orange, aqua, yellow, lavender, white—lined up on the street in front of the house. Bayley was amazed by the orderliness—a foot to a foot and a half of space between each, every front wheel cocked to the right at precisely the same angle. All the chrome parts—wheel spokes, handlebars, seat trim, engine—displayed an eye-piercing gleam under the street lamps that were just coming on.

James repeated the password, and the four of them were ushered upstairs to the second floor.

"Welcome." A young woman dressed in a brown and rust-orange sarong approached them. "I am Naomi." She dipped a little, as though she were going to faint, but then revived suddenly. "Please make yourselves at home. There's plenty of space for everyone."

The room measured about twelve by sixteen feet, Bayley guessed. Two windows showcased a sky determinedly holding onto the final rays of sunset—violet with yellow-gray streaks. A Chinese lantern covered a single lightbulb that dangled from the ceiling in the center of the room. Sheets, blankets, and two green tarps hung from clotheslines that crisscrossed the room, partitioning it into eight sections. Sighs and moans came from behind one of the tarp sections. Patrice nudged Bayley. They exchanged glances and told Naomi in unison, "We've got a tent."

{}

The day of the afternoon tea, Phil awoke at six A.M., heated up an apricot Danish and a cup of coffee, and read the chapter "Getting the Table Ready" in Margaret Lynne Dare's latest book, *Festive Settings*. At eight, when he heard the Weather Channel go on in Louise's apartment, he mopped his kitchen floor, vacuumed the living room rug, scoured the toilet, and finally, at eleven-thirty, set out Louise's favorite tea and desserts on the coffee table in the living room. The phone rang at one-fifteen. It was Jax.

"Everything will be just fine, Mr. Banks," she said.

"I don't know. The heart at my age is a dangerous thing. A good piece of pecan pie is about all the excitement it can stand."

At two o'clock, Phil knocked on Louise's door.

"Where's my tree?" she said. "I thought you said it was ready to go home."

"It is. But I wanted to show you where I keep it—the lighting and the temperature and the—"

"I can't leave my house just now... There's a tornado watch." Louise pursed her lips.

"How about I put on my television?"

"Deal." Louise wrapped her raincoat tighter around her body and followed Phil up the stairs.

Once inside, Phil made a beeline for the living room, switched on the TV to the Weather Channel, and gave the ficus branches a plumping. He offered to take her coat.

"No, thank you," Louise said. "I don't want you getting any funny ideas about why I agreed to come up to your place."

"The ficus is in here," Phil called to her.

"Oh, you sly devil you," Louise said when she surveyed the table arrayed with a box of Lipton black tea, a bowl of sugar cubes, a pitcher of cream, Stuckey's pecan log rolls, and slices of Sara Lee coffee cake.

An advertisement for a program called *The World's Most Venomous Snakes* came on.

"My husband was one of those—most men are," Louise said. "Maybe not you, of course. You brought my tree back to life. Bayley gave me the thing. It was dying on her too."

"Just needed love," Phil said.

"Oh, come now."

"I've won three blue ribbons this year alone."

"Ribbons for what? Onions?"

"Eggplant too, and best kisser—"

"That a new strain of squash?" Louise grinned.

"At the county fair," Phil said, staring at her mouth. Her lips seemed fuller, a deeper red.

Phil's staring didn't go unnoticed. "Beach-rose. Don't you remember? The same color as the walls in my kitchen?" Louise moved a few steps closer to him.

"How could I forget?" he said. Louise's face appeared flushed, her brown eyes suddenly a comfortable place to stroll into, sit down, and relax.

She planted her hands on her hips. "How much for a turn?"

"Louise, has anyone ever told you...?"

"Not since I was..."

Phil put his arms around Louise the way one might a china doll or some other very fragile thing and pressed his mouth to hers. The Weather Channel had switched back to the tornado watch. The announcer spoke faster and faster. "It's moving north...northeast...yes, it's aimed straight for us, breaking all kinds of records!"

"Finally," she said, her face a few inches from Phil's, "we're going to get some relief from this low-pressure system that's been hanging around here lately."

{}

Six months later, Patrice was tending bar three days a week during happy hour at Sloppy Joe's. Bayley, having discovered she had a knack for getting more than just a likeness, that she could capture a glimpse of a person's soul, charged five dollars apiece for fifteen-minute eight-by-ten-inch pastel portraits. She had paid a ten-dollar license fee to set out two folding beach chairs on the sidewalk in Mallory Square. When she worked, she averaged thirty dollars a day—enough to afford champagne brunches for her and Patrice at The Blue Parrot and still have a few dollars left over for the food kitty. The twenty-two housemates had expanded to twenty-seven—five new hippie residents—and the line for the bathroom was longer than ever because most everyone, including James and Christopher, had jobs cleaning fish at the plant. Bayley and Patrice had begun taking baths together.

One evening, a half-hour before the usual household dinner of fish, rice, and salad or fish, rice, and okra, there was a knock on the bathroom door.

"Bayley?" It was Fudge.

Bayley and Patrice looked at each other. The bikers never came up to the second floor and the hippies never trespassed downstairs, except to go in and out the front door.

"Yes?"

"Somebody called for you a little while ago. Phil, I think his name was. Couldn't hear him very well—storm season, lots of static. "He said your grandmother's in a coma."

Ever since Bayley had first met Fudge, she'd thought his voice sounded like someone talking underwater—garbled baritone. He once told her he'd gone to a conservatory in Chicago to study opera. Bayley couldn't imagine him in any other role than "hog owner." (Fudge's was the yellow one.) But now his voice seemed shored up tight, closer to tenor. Bayley made a little choking sound. "Thanks, Fudge." She glanced at Patrice.

Patrice held out her hands as though ready to catch something.

"You're welcome. It's okay if you need to take more time in there," he said.

Bayley and Patrice heard him say, "Back off," followed by a commotion of shuffling feet and mumbling people. After a few seconds, all was quiet.

Bayley took her grandmother's ring and gold watch pieces out of her pants pocket, held them in the palm of her hand. She had continued to carry them with her wherever she went. She sat on the edge of the tub and stared at the insect—crooked proboscis, stick legs crumpled, body twisted as though death, like life, had proved a struggle. Her heart began to flutter—a hot-dry sensation, a moth beating its wings against light, a rustling of brittle leaves on pavement.

"You know the story of *Dorian Gray*?" she asked Patrice.

"The portrait that ages instead of its subject?" Patrice said.

"And his soul is in stasis, trapped in some kind of limbo." Between thumb and forefinger, Bayley held up the ring for Patrice to see. The diamonds cast exquisite rays of light into the murky brown-yellow mass. "My soul is stuck in there like that insect. I'm paralyzed. I scream, but no sound comes out. The diamonds tease me, illuminate the dark place from which there is no escape."

Patrice sat beside her and turned on the hot water faucet. "That's a bit dramatic. Come on. Let's take a bath. You'll feel better."

"When he destroyed the portrait, he got his soul back." The ring slipped from her hand, landing with a clatter on the floor. They both looked down. The amber had broken loose from its setting, cracked open. One of the two grape-size halves still encased the insect, but Bayley noticed a peculiar smell, a burst of some ancient elixir—frankincense, nutmeg, cinnamon—she couldn't be sure. Droplets of moisture beaded on her face. Steam swirled up from the rushing water, swathing her in a fine blinding mist. "I can't breathe." Suddenly she felt Patrice's fingers stroking, gentle warm streams cascading across her skull; her body didn't offer its usual resistance. In her veins she felt a stirring of new life.

{}

Phil was there when Louise died. She had spent the last week of her life slipping in and out of consciousness. He stayed with her from eight in the morning until dusk and then returned to his apartment to sleep. On the day of her passing, he brought with him a five-by-eight manila envelope that had arrived for Louise in the morning. There was no return address, but its cancellation mark read, "Key West, Florida." Phil sat in the chair beside Louise's bed, placed the envelope on the nightstand, and touched her shoulder.

"Good morning, Louise," he said.

She mumbled something he didn't understand.

"What?" He leaned over, his face close to hers.

"Open it," she said, her voice a whisper.

Phil slid his forefinger under the flap, pulled out a lump of tissue paper that had been taped shut. He unwrapped it and arranged its contents: two halves of an amber stone, a gold ring setting with six diamonds, and what appeared to be two sections of a gold chain-link bracelet, on the bed next to her pillow. "Broken," he said.

Louise picked up the piece of amber that contained the insect, turning it this way and that. "I'm happy just to get it back," she said.

"What do you mean?"

"We have this insect to thank for our lives. If it hadn't emerged from the primordial soup, taken the next step in evolution, we wouldn't be here. If Bayley has achieved the same—found love— she won't need to steal anymore." Louise sighed.

Suddenly her face seemed to let go of all expression; the lines circumscribing her mouth and eyes softened. Her skin took on a pearl-like translucence—tiny points of light sparkling through mist.

"Stay with me," she said, squeezing his hand.

They held each other's gaze until darkness intervened, sparing each the pain of having to be the first to look away.

Contributors

Rebeca Antoine, a Connecticut native, received a BA in English from Yale University and lives in New Orleans, where she's an MFA candidate in the Creative Writing Workshop at the University of New Orleans.

Born in Boston, Sandra L. Beck has spent time in San Francisco, New York City, London, Paris, Pakistan, Indonesia, Thailand, and South America. From 2001–2003 she served as an assistant editor for *Willow Springs* magazine, and in June 2003 she earned an MFA in fiction. She lives in Seattle, Washington, where she works as a figurative artist and writer.

Cheyenne Blue combines her two passions in life by writing travel guides and erotica. Her stories have appeared in *Best Women's Erotica, Mammoth Best New Erotica, Best Lesbian Erotica, Best Lesbian Love Stories 2003,* and on various Web sites, and her travel guides have been jammed into many glove boxes. You can see more of her work at www.cheyenneblue.com.

Stefanie K. Dunning is an assistant professor of English at Miami University of Ohio. Her work has appeared in *Melus, Black*

Contributors

Renaissance/Renaissance Noire, Stanford University's *Black Arts Quarterly,* and on www.exittheapple.com. She was one of the original eleven cofounders of *Red Clay* magazine.

Judith Frank teaches English at Amherst College and is the author of *Crybaby Butch* (Firebrand Books, 2004). "Gravel" is for Elizabeth Garland.

Carol Guess is the author of several books. She teaches at Western Washington University and lives in Seattle.

Amy Hassinger, a graduate of the Iowa Writers' Workshop, has published a novel, *Nina: Adolescence.* Her work has appeared in *Best Lesbian Love Stories 2004, Natural Bridge,* and *Blithe House Quarterly,* among other places. She has also written a history textbook, *Finding Katahdin* (University of Maine Press). She lives in Illinois and is at work on her second novel.

Siobhán Houston is a queer femme, mother, doctoral candidate, and priestess whose work has appeared in *Best Lesbian Love Stories 2003* and *Mentsh: On Being Jewish and Queer* (both from Alyson Books), *Weird Sisters,* and *We'Moon 2004* as well as numerous journals of spirituality and religion. A Harvard Divinity School alumna, she lives in Colorado with her butch/gender outlaw spouse, Rae.

Christy M. Ikner writes for monthly GLBT publications, including *Out & About Nashville, She* magazine, and *WOW Women Out West.* She lives in Nashville with her partner Jenn, their son Garrett, Garrett's cat Oliver, and Oliver's dog Liza.

Karin Kallmaker is best known for having published more than a dozen lesbian romance novels, from *In Every Port* to *All the Wrong Places.* In addition, she has published a half-dozen science fiction, fantasy, and supernatural lesbian novels under the pen name Laura Adams. Karin and her partner will celebrate their twenty-eighth anniversary in 2005 and are Mom and Moogie to two children.

Sue Katz has lived, worked, and published on three continents. A wordsmith and rebel, she is now writing and editing in Boston and is an activist in the National Writers Union. She recently completed her first novel, *Above the Belt,* about the impact of the 1982 Israeli invasion of Lebanon on an Israeli martial arts institute run by a woman. You can reach her at writer@suekatz.com.

Maggie Kinsella lives in Ireland and sells Wexford strawberries by the side of the Sligo road. She has plenty of writing time. Her short stories have merited honorable mentions in various literary competitions, but the strawberries are easier to sell.

Leslie Anne Leasure received her MFA in fiction writing at Indiana University. Her fiction has been published in *Blithe House Quarterly.* She is currently finishing her novel, *Leaving Maggie MacAllistar,* and a collection of Pigeon Hill stories. She lives in Massachusetts.

Claire McNab is the author of three mystery series (Detective Inspector Carol Ashton, Undercover Agent Denise Cleever, and Kylie Kendall). She lives in Los Angeles and is madly in love with her editor at Alyson Books. (Claire, that's what you get when you leave it up to your editor to write your bio for you.)

Judith Nichols was born in Columbia, Missouri, and attended Earlham College and Pennsylvania State University. She teaches at Vassar College.

Contributors

Jenie Pak received her MFA in poetry from Cornell University and has writing published in *Alligator Juniper*, *The Asian Pacific American Journal*, *Blithe House Quarterly*, *Dangerous Families*, *Five Fingers Review*, *Love Shook My Heart 2*, *Many Mountains Moving*, *The Oakland Reviews*, and *Watchword Press*. She lives in Seoul, Korea.

Dawn Paul writes fiction, poetry, and plays. Her work has appeared in *A Woman's Touch: New Lesbian Love Stories* and *Steady as She Goes: Women's Stories of the Sea*. Her play *The Nest* was a winner in the 2002 New Voices annual 10-minute play competition. Dawn is the editor-publisher of Corvid Press and the senior poetry editor for *The Ensign Literary Review*, an online and print journal. She lives in Beverly, Massachusetts.

Anne Seale is the author of the comic mystery novel *Packing Mrs. Phipps* and its forthcoming sequel, *Finding Ms. Wright*. She has performed on many gay stages, including the Lesbian National Conference, where she sang tunes from her tape Sex for Breakfast. Her stories have appeared in many anthologies and journals, including *Dykes With Baggage*, *Set in Stone*, *Wilma Loves Betty*, and *Harrington Lesbian Fiction Quarterly*.

T. Stores is the author of three novels, *Getting to the Point* and *SideTracks* (Naiad Press), and most recently, *Virge*. Her stories, poems, and essays have appeared in *Out*, *Sinister Wisdom*, *Blithe House Quarterly*, and other places. A professor at University of Hartford, she lives in southern Vermont with her partner and one-year-old twins

Rakelle Valencia has written short stories for *Best Lesbian Erotica 2004* and *2005*, *Ride 'em Cowboy*, *On Our Backs*, and *Ultimate Lesbian Erotica 2005*. With Sacchi Green, the dynamic duo is contracted by Suspect Thoughts Press to produce *Rode Hard, Put Away Wet: Lesbian Cowboy Erotica* (2005).

Mary Vermillion, a lifelong resident of Iowa, is the author of the mystery novel *Death by Discount*. An associate professor of English at Mount Mercy College in Cedar Rapids, she has published fiction, nonfiction, and literary criticism in anthologies and journals.

Leslie K. Ward lives in Anchorage, Alaska. Her short fiction has appeared in *Pillow Talk II*, *Bedroom Eyes: Stories of Lesbians in the Boudoir*, and *Best Lesbian Love Stories 2004*. Leslie is an MFA candidate at the University of Alaska Anchorage. She is also a dancer, dance instructor, fledgling second mom to a kick-ass ten-year-old, and head over heels in love.

Yvonne Zipter is the author of the nonfiction books *Ransacking the Closet* and *Diamonds Are a Dyke's Best Friend*, the nationally syndicated column "Inside Out," and the critically acclaimed poetry collection *The Patience of Metal*. She was a finalist for the May Swenson Poetry Award, a semi-finalist for the Pablo Neruda Poetry Award, and tied for third in Chicago Public Radio's "Why I Should Be Poet Laureate of Illinois" contest. Her poems and humorous essays have appeared in numerous periodicals and anthologies, and she is a recipient of the Sprague-Todes Literary Award. Her story "Günther's Wife" won first place for flash fiction in the Literary Potpourri Two-Year Anniversary Celebration Contest. A Midwesterner nearly her whole life, she has lived in Chicago for more than twenty years.

Credits

Rebeca Antoine's "The Woodchipper Wife" first appeared on Blithe House Quarterly: A Site for Short Gay Fiction (www.blithe.com), Fall 2003.

Sandra L. Beck's "Attempts at Rescue" first appeared on Blithe House Quarterly: A Site for Short Gay Fiction (www.blithe.com), Spring 2004.

Stephanie K. Dunning's "The Unripened Heart" first appeared on Blithe House Quarterly: A Site for Short Gay Fiction (www.blithe.com), Spring 2004.

Judith Nichols's "Lesbians in Poughkeepsie" first appeared on Blithe House Quarterly: A Site for Short Gay Fiction (www.blithe.com), Winter 2004.

Jenie Pak's "An Hour or a Year" first appeared on Blithe House Quarterly: A Site for Short Gay Fiction (www.blithe.com), Spring 2001.

Dawn Paul's "Heron" first appeared on Blithe House Quarterly: A Site for Short Gay Fiction (www.blithe.com), Spring 2004.

T. Stores's "House-Tree-Person Test" first appeared on Blithe House Quarterly: A Site for Short Gay Fiction (www.blithe.com), Winter 2004

Yvonne Zipter's "Third Date" first appeared on Blithe House Quarterly: A Site for Short Gay Fiction (www.blithe.com), Summer 2004.